PRAISE FOR

"The balance of sobering themes an[...] [...]s touching tale of female friendship and personal growth."

—*Publishers Weekly*

"For fans of women's fiction with a little romance thrown in . . ."

—*Library Journal*

"Talley packs her latest southern romantic drama with a satisfying plot and appealing characters . . . The prose is powerful in its understatedness, adding to the appeal of this alluring story."

—*Publishers Weekly*

"Relevant and moving . . . Talley does an excellent job of making her flawed characters vastly more gray than black and white . . . which creates a story of unrequited loves, redeemed."

—*Library Journal*

"Talley masters making the reader feel hopeful in this second-chance romance . . . You have to read this slow-burning, heart-twisting story yourself."

—*USA Today*

"This author blends the past and present effortlessly, while incorporating heartbreaking emotions guaranteed to make you ugly cry. Highly recommended."

—*Harlequin Junkie*

"Liz Talley has written a love story between a mother and daughter that captured me completely. By turns tender and astringent, sexy and funny, heart wrenching and uplifting, *Room to Breathe* is an escapist and winning story that will carry you away with an imperfect pair of protagonists who just might remind you of someone you know. A delight."

—Barbara O'Neal, author of *When We Believed in Mermaids*

"There is no pleasure more fulfilling than not being able to turn off the light until you've read one more page, one more chapter, one more large hunk of an addictive novel. Liz Talley delivers. Her dialogue is crisp and smart, her characters are vivid and real, her stories are unputdownable. I discovered her with the book *The Sweetest September* when, in the very first pages, I was asking myself, How's she going to get out of this one? And of course I was sleep deprived finding out. Her latest, *Come Home to Me*, which I was privileged to read in advance, is another triumph, a story of a woman's hard-won victory over a past trauma, of love, of forgiveness, of becoming whole. Laughter and tears spring from the pages—this book should be in every beach bag this summer."

—Robyn Carr, *New York Times* bestselling author

"Liz Talley's characters stay with the reader long after the last page is turned. Complex, emotional stories written in a warm, intelligent voice, her books will warm readers' hearts."

—Kristan Higgins, *New York Times* bestselling author

"Every book by Liz Talley promises heart, heat, and hope, plus a gloriously happy ever after—and she delivers."

—Mariah Stewart, *New York Times* and *USA Today* bestselling author

"Count on Liz Talley's smart, authentic storytelling to wrap you in southern comfort while she tugs at your heart."

—Jamie Beck, author of *If You Must Know*

Deconstructed

Bayou Bridge

Waters Run Deep

Under the Autumn Sky

The Road to Bayou Bridge

Oak Stand

Vegas Two-Step

The Way to Texas

A Little Texas

A Taste of Texas

A Touch of Scarlet

Novellas and Anthologies

The Nerd Who Loved Me

"Hotter in Atlanta" (a short story)

Cowboys for Christmas with Kim Law and Terri Osburn

A Wrong Bed Christmas with Kimberly Van Meter

Deconstructed

a novel

Liz Talley

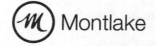 Montlake

Published by Montlake, Seattle

www.apub.com

Amazon, the Amazon logo, and Montlake are trademarks of Amazon.com, Inc., or its affiliates.

ISBN-13: 9781542032834
ISBN-10: 1542032830

Cover design by Caroline Teagle Johnson

Printed in the United States of America

To my great-grandmother Grace Killough Swindell, who was brave in a time when women were supposed to sit down and shut up. She left her philandering husband, bore out the Great Depression with her two daughters, and worked her way to becoming the head seamstress at Foley's Department store in Houston. She knew how to tear away, keep the good parts, and make something new again.

CHAPTER ONE

CRICKET

My mama always says, "Sugar, life changes before you can blink your eyes."

The woman isn't wrong.

Marguerite loves rattling off southern wisdom the same way Sally Field's character did in *Forrest Gump*. I'm forever saying "My mama always says" the same way Forrest does in the movie, much to the dismay of my thirteen-year-old daughter.

But this year, blinkin' or no blinkin', I found out the choco-lates in *my* box were actually dog turds. Oh sure, everyone's year had been going badly with dirty politics nailing us left and right like a bully with a dodgeball. But adding insult to injury this spring was finding out the man I loved was screwing my daughter's tennis coach.

That I obtained this knowledge on the first truly warm afternoon was even more insulting. That morning, I had put on my grandmother's watch and found a half-priced shirt I didn't really like but had bought on sale wedged between two forgotten sweaters. I tugged on the floral abomination just so I could say I'd worn it. And then I dropped my daughter, Julia Kate, at school and headed for Printemps, the antique shop my grandmother had started with one of her friends because they had wanted to try their hand at importing sturdy English tables and filigreed French chairs in order to be career women. Their pastime had turned into a Shreveport treasure, boasting antiques that made merchants all over the South pea green with envy. I had inherited the business from my grandmother, who'd bought out her friend and then skipped over my mother because my mama didn't want the "dusty dinosaur," anyway.

But me?

I adored Printemps.

I had just finished my chicken salad sandwich and was tackling the last few issues in my new office space, which was formerly a broom closet. I had moved the store location at the beginning of the year from a rambling, leaky building in Highland to a safer and better-traveled location off Line Avenue. My husband, Scott, and I had bought the house for a song right after we'd married, thinking one day we might restore it and live there, but as time went by, we never had the gumption to oversee the costly rehab. Then the zoning shifted to commercial, and the house was there when I needed it. The old Doric home had been gutted in order to provide an expansive space to display the pieces, but storage was a huge issue.

I stood in the closet surveying shelves, trying to figure out how I could fit my filing cabinet so I could reach it from my desk without throwing out my back.

"You figure out a solution yet?" my new assistant, Ruby, asked as she passed by carrying a duster.

"I will once I take out these shelves. The desk only fits at this angle, which means my calendar will have to go right here." I swiped my hand Vanna-style across the chipped paint where a century of broom handles had left their mark. I probably should have painted before moving in, but it was temporary. My plan was to eventually renovate the sad upstairs, put in an elevator, and create more retail space and perhaps a venue for supper clubs and baby showers. I could create a new office upstairs at that time.

Sliding the coffee creamer and extra paper towels into a box, I squinted one eye and then the other, envisioning how I could make the space workable . . . and cute. Let us not *ever* forget cute as a qualification for everything in life.

Ruby reversed her course and reemerged framed in the doorway. "What about moving your office to the kitchen? That filing cabinet isn't fitting in here." She said it like an apology. The way she always said things. As if she weren't certain she should have an opinion.

Ruby wasn't wrong about the filing cabinet, but I needed some privacy to figure the books, order crap, and, okay, play on Facebook.

"I can't work next to the refrigerator. It would be dangerous . . . to my behind." I gave her a smile, and she gave me a weird look before skedaddling off.

I stifled my sigh.

Ruby had started as my assistant when we moved the inventory to this new space. Carolyn, my former shop assistant, had decided to retire to stay home with her grandbabies, so I'd started looking for a new person to hawk Tiffany lamps and Asian ginger jars with me. Ruby came in to inquire about a position an hour after Carolyn delivered that bomb. Younger than me by a good decade, pretty in a way some might find unconventional, and seemingly eager to start as soon as I needed, Ruby seemed like an answered prayer. But still I wondered if she was the right fit. Hard to know because she held herself back like she didn't trust me.

She probably didn't. I knew very little of her background, but her work ethic kept reminding me that I didn't have to be friends with an employee. Still, it would just be nice if we could have a conversation that didn't feel so forced.

Ruby emerged again, carrying the white taffeta 1950s Givenchy cocktail dress I'd found at, of all things, a yard sale. Unfortunately, I had missed the moth holes that dotted the hem, along with the stain under

3

the right arm. Before I realized that saving it was futile, I had thought I could dye the dress and wear it to my cousin's black-tie Savannah wedding in late summer. Just as well, since I would have had to contract three stomach viruses and live on a diet of lettuce for five months to fit into it, and no dress is worth a life without Girl Scout cookies.

But as much as it pained me, the dress wasn't salvageable. I had put it in the "not salable but maybe it has another use" bin I kept in the kitchen/storage area.

I waited for Ruby to say something as I scooped up the notepad I'd dropped onto the shelf. I needed to make a list. New stapler, crates, and a smaller office chair. I scrawled the last few items before looking up. "You need something, Ruby?"

She thrust the dress out. "You put this in the nonsalables?"

"I did."

"Do you mind if I take it? I could give you something for it."

"Why? It's got moth damage and a big stain."

"Um, I'm doing a little project," she said, uncertainty shadowing her words, making me feel like the big bad wolf. Which was weird because most people thought I was a kitten. I *was* benign, mostly. From a young age, my mama had taught me to stand up straight, be gracious, make others comfortable, give charitably, and always be a lady. A smile was your best accessory, after all. So as much as I smiled at Ruby, I found myself up against a locked box with the younger woman. She wouldn't let herself relax around me, and it made me wonder about her life. Who had hurt her? What had made her so reserved and wary?

"Sure. Take it." I smiled again.

"Thanks." She disappeared like a fart in a breeze.

"Hmm," I said, adding "thumbtacks" to my list, wondering why she wouldn't tell me about the little project. What kind required a vintage haute couture dress of little value?

"Oh my God, I adore this fabric," a voice said.

What the . . .

4

I blinked and looked around. It sounded like someone was in the office with me, but I was totally alone.

"It's super pretty," someone else said.

Glancing around, I noted a vent centered on the scarred wall. Directly on the other side of the wall was the showroom that featured some of the vintage quilts and silk drapes imported from France. Minutes ago, I had noticed Julie Van Ness and her eternal sidekick, Bo Dixie Ferris, walk into Printemps. Both women were friends of mine, but not friend friends. More like the kind of friends with whom I might dangle a glass of wine at a party and talk about how amazingly the soccer coach filled out his Umbro shorts. Julie didn't work beyond doing Junior League stuff, and Bo Dixie wrote a gossip column for the local society page.

Yeah, page.

There was only one page in the shrinking *Shreveport Daily* dedicated to those who attended fundraisers and threw *darling* wedding showers. Probably because only a handful of people cared . . . and they were the ones throwing the parties.

I shouldn't eavesdrop. Such a low thing, eavesdropping. But I was no angel, and those two were infamous for having the skinny on anyone and everyone within a hundred-mile radius. What would it hurt? Plus, I couldn't help that the vent allowed me to overhear their conversation. Total happenstance.

"Nancy Parrington found a vintage dress here and wore it to the Dallas Symphony Derby. Everyone raved. I think something like that would be perfect to wear to cotillion this year. Or my cousin's engagement party this fall. Or maybe something to take to San Francisco for Shaun's conference," Julie said.

I gave a fist pump. The display of luscious dresses, jaunty hats, and even vintage shoes had been a hunch and a secret project of mine. Period dramas on streaming television services had given modern women a peek at how gorgeous dresses once were, making them more desirable, and I had spent half a year finding the designer gems I had in my collection. Nancy had fallen in love with a soft-yellow Balenciaga and declared she'd send more people to Printemps to "upcycle." I murmured a silent thank-you to my mother's best friend.

"You already have your cotillion dress. Besides, Nancy's old."

I made a face. Bo Dixie should stick to bad write-ups of Mardi Gras balls . . . not fashion. Nancy's sense of style was timeless and flawless.

"True. But maybe I want something unique for the California trip. What about this?"

"Ugh, you'd look like someone off *The Crown*. It's stuffy," Bo Dixie said. And who listened to Bo Dixie, anyway? She dressed like she was in high school. "All I'm saying is don't settle. You need something fabulous because *you-know-who* will be in San Francisco." The last part Bo Dixie sang in a gleeful voice.

"Shush, Bo," Julie whisper-shouted.

"Oh, come on, no one's in here."

I sat back, feeling a little guilty but very curious about *you-know-who* in San Francisco. Didn't sound like it had anything to do with Julie's husband. Maybe it was an opportunity. Julie had been making noise about being an influencer. She, unlike Bo Dixie, had a head for business and a nose for style.

"Can I help you ladies find anything?" Ruby asked, her tone sounding like she'd rather help them find the door.

"No, thanks. We know what we like," Julie said.

Silence for a few seconds.

"Okay, then. Enjoy looking around. If you have any questions . . ." Ruby didn't finish the thought. Her voice wasn't unkind, just . . . something. Like she knew these two were mean girls.

"What in the hell is Cricket thinking letting someone with a nose ring and tats work here? Her grandmother would roll over in her grave," Bo Dixie said.

I had just written "hanging file folders" on my list, but hearing my name made me pause.

Julie laughed. "Cricket's grandmother housed women of ill repute in her house on Piermont. I don't think she would disapprove. Now, her mother . . . that's another story. She'd fire that one on the spot."

"And her daddy wouldn't disapprove, either. You know he went plumb crazy and ran off with a stripper."

I glared at the wall as if I could see Bo Dixie. That woman better thank her stars I wasn't Clark Kent, or she'd be toast.

Gossip was the king of sports in Shreveport, and my daddy had been the talk of the town twenty-five years ago. Of course, now he lived in Florida with that very stripper and, if I were totally honest, was much happier than he'd ever been running the family-owned insurance company. I got along with Crystalle and her silly Pomeranian just fine now, but my father's midlife crisis had hurt me for a long time. Lotsa therapy there.

"Poor Cricket," Bo Dixie said. "And now the same thing's happening to her."

I froze.

Wait . . . *what?*

"You know Scott has to be cheating. He's like a dog on a scent around Steph. It's almost sad," Bo Dixie continued.

Scott? Wait . . . my *Scott?*

"True. And I heard from Ron Meyer that Steph gives professional-level blow jobs. I bet Cricket has never hit her knees," Julie said.

A Mack truck slammed into me.

Blink. Of. An. Eye.

I stumbled backward, smacking my elbow on the doorframe. Nerve-tingling pain shot up my arm. I slapped a hand over my mouth to keep from screaming. Or stop the vomit rising in my throat. My other hand clutched the material over my heart.

My husband was . . . getting blown?

By a Steph? Who was *Steph*?

Wait, I knew a ton of Stephanies, but they were all milquetoast women who would never mess with my husband. Or at least I didn't think they would. But who really knew the people they talked to at bake sales or committee meetings? Someone could pray out of the same mouth she . . . she . . .

I couldn't even think it.

"Ohmygod, this dress is perfect," Julie said, as if the words she'd uttered about my husband were no big deal. Of course, she didn't know I was standing on the other side of the wall trying to hold together the heart shredded by the bomb she'd tossed.

"I *love* that dress!" Bo Dixie squealed. "It looks just like something they wear on *Mad Men*. If you don't want it, maybe I could—"

"You don't wear a size six."

"No shit. I wear a size two. But it can be altered," Bo Dixie laughed.

I backed out of the closet, Julie's and Bo Dixie's voices fading as I zombie-walked to the kitchen, mind blown, stomach lurching, heart beating in my ears.

Scott *wasn't* cheating.

The very idea was . . . preposterous. He wasn't that kind of guy. I would know if Scott were up to something like doing someone on the side. Just like I knew when he snuck a cigar at the country club or ate the last of the fudge. The man was as subtle as an elephant sneaking into a room.

No. Scott wouldn't cheat on me. We had just taken a romantic getaway to the Caribbean over the Christmas holidays, frolicking on the beach and having pretty decent piña coladas and sex. Oh, and not to mention, he and I had just taught a healthy-marriage class at our church last year. A man who taught other men how to be the husband God wanted didn't go off and have an affair, for Christ's sake. And he'd just been named the University Club's Man of the Year. I had helped him write his acceptance speech. They were wrong. Just mistaking his friendly nature and lame flirting ability with something more nefarious.

But what if . . .

I slid inside the ancient kitchen, my breath coming faster and faster. Like I might hyperventilate. Thankfully, the kitchen was empty . . . and contained paper bags.

Don't freak out. Take a deep breath. This is all a mistake.

But how could I know for certain? If Julie and Bo Dixie suspected Scott was screwing around, other people might, too.

I pulled out my cell phone, wondering who I should call. Who among my friends might know something more than idle gossip?

Maybe Cyndi? She spent a lot of time on various charitable committees and always knew who bed-hopped around town. Her husband had cheated on her, so she'd totally rat out Scott.

I dialed her number while mentally composing what I'd say to her.

Hey, Cyndi, have you heard anything I should know about Scott and a certain someone?

Or get right down to business?

What's up, Cyn? Is Scott banging someone on the side?

Not crass enough? Maybe I should scrap "banging" and go straight for "fucking." I never used the f-word, even in private . . . but finding out one's husband could be cheating called for strong language.

I didn't have to decide whether to use the f-word or not because the call went to voice mail. Rather than leave a message, I clicked the END button. No need to act hastily. Once it was known I suspected Scott of cheating, I couldn't take the accusation back. Most of my friends were married, and one casual word to their husbands would put the ball in Scott's court. Men stuck together that way. They would think they'd done Scott a solid by giving him a heads-up about my suspicions.

I needed to think hard before I did anything I'd regret . . . better to keep my mouth shut and eyes open until I could sift fact from fiction.

Maybe I should confront him and see how he reacted.

9

Or pretend I didn't hear what Julie and Bo Dixie had said. Avoidance. Safety. I was good at pretending . . .

"Hey." Ruby opened the door, the tempered look on her face fading when she saw me plastered against the wall. "What's wrong?"

"Nothing," I said too high pitched, like I'd been caught watching porn or eating a doughnut while on Weight Watchers. Note: I was always on Weight Watchers.

She studied me as I starfished the wall. "Your friend just bought the vintage Halston."

"She's not my friend." I swallowed the acid searing the back of my throat and pushed off the wall, trying to look casual. "But Julie will look good in that dress, which may bring us more business."

Ruby moved into the kitchen, tossing glances my way as she walked to the fridge. Like I was a ticking time bomb. Heck, maybe I was. "Are you sure you're okay?"

"Yeah. Fine."

Ruby looked worried, her small face furrowing, her brown eyes shifting over to the cold coffee in the urn and then back to me. She knew something was wrong.

And it was.

Or maybe not.

"You know, I don't think that chicken salad agreed with me," I lied, pressing my hand against my stomach.

At the same time, Ruby said, "Okay, I'm going to shift that display of plates to the corner hutch thing—"

"That's a Louis XV sideboard. The plates are Théodore Haviland Limoges." I straightened and tried to pretend I was okay.

"Yeah. That's what I was going to say. Maybe you better go home? Jade is coming in later, and she can finish moving the boxes out of the closet—um, your office." Ruby opened the fridge and pulled out a bottled water. Then she turned. "Can you drive yourself?"

"Yeah. Just feeling yucky." Understatement of the year, that. I averted my eyes so she couldn't see how freaked out I was.

'Cause I was.

I'd loved Scott ever since that night he'd walked up to my door wearing a paisley bow tie and a shit-eating grin, ready to take me to the debutante ball. He was five years older and so sophisticated. He made me laugh, taught me to sip good scotch, and relieved me of my virginity when I snuck him into my bedroom. He was my guy—father to my daughter, pea to my carrot, Michael to my Jackson 5.

So this couldn't be happening. I was *not* that pitiful woman who happily went about life signing up to chair the Renaissance Fair committee, sipping margaritas while some bimbo shtupped my husband on the side. That faceless woman was pathetic, duped by kind words and flowers, oblivious to the rot in her marriage.

That woman was not Catherine Ann Crosby.

I was better than that.

Or I thought I was.

"Okay, then." Ruby moved toward the open doorway that would take her back to the front desk, where she could survey the store. Any other day I would be worried about no customers. At present I was relieved.

My toes inched toward the back door. "Oh hey, I got a lead on an estate sale in Marshall that includes vintage clothing and some cast iron." There. Talking about regular stuff made the panic subside. Sort of.

"Oh, well, that's . . . nice." She looked confused.

I tried to smile but couldn't manage it. "Julia Kate has a tennis tournament in Lafayette, but Scott said he'd take her."

And then it struck me.

Stephanie.

Olivia's trim, perky tennis coach was named Stephanie. Could that be the Steph dropping to her knees? No way. Tennis Pro Steph was really nice to me.

I shook myself, focusing on Ruby, who was staring at me in expectation. "So I thought maybe we'd let Jade work the store and you can go with me to scout some inventory. If you want." I managed not to choke when I thought about why Scott might have been volunteering to take our daughter on overnight tournaments.

Would a hot young tennis coach be banging a balding middle-aged man? I just couldn't see it. Why would that cute, much younger woman want Scott?

"You want *me* to go with you?" Ruby sounded surprised.

Carolyn and I had spent many a Saturday morning scouring estate sales and random garage sales in older areas of the city. I had thought bringing Ruby along would allow me to know her better, maybe get her interested in the challenge of a good find. The younger woman had seemed to enjoy learning about our inventory, and I envisioned us armed with Starbucks and the will to find treasure among old vacuum cleaners and baby furniture. "If you'd like. I do a lot of ordering from England and France, but many customers like traditional southern pieces, too. Never know what you might find in Aunt Ethel's attic."

Ruby bit her lip. "Um, well, I thought I would . . . I mean, I sort of need the hours because—"

"You'll be on the clock. Of course."

Relief flashed in her eyes. "Great. Yeah, that would be good, then. Meet you here? Or . . ."

"Here is fine." Nodding again, I played the role of bobblehead, wanting desperately to get the hell out of there, away from everyone.

I needed to think. To process. To snoop.

Reaching beneath the chipped kitchen cabinet where we stored our personal things, I grabbed my purse before saluting Ruby with a half smile, trying to pretend I was the woman I'd been fifteen minutes before. Before I'd been stupid enough to eavesdrop through a closet vent. Before Julie and Bo Dixie had cut the rope to my anchor, setting me adrift, pushing me toward hysteria. Or cold numbness.

Which of those was worse—to feel or not to feel?

But wait, I couldn't do either yet. Not over unfounded gossip. In fact, Julie and Bo Dixie might have known I could hear them. Those two little schemers could have winked at each other and dreamed up my husband receiving fellatio from some heartless skank named Steph. They'd probably stifled their laughter, tickled Phi Mu pink to play such a horrible joke on me. In my mind I pictured them—thin, pretty women with their shoulders shaking in silent mirth, a gleam in their mean eyes.

Gotcha, Cricket.

Ruby jarred me from my ruminations by attempting a smile of her own, shadows of concern flickering in her brown eyes. I turned away so I wouldn't cry.

"Hope you feel better soon," Ruby said, her voice soft like the worn hoodie she slunk into work wearing each morning.

"Thanks. Later," I replied, slipping out the back door, blinking against the outside world as I walked to the minivan Scott had bought me when Julia Kate was six years old. Back then I thought I was pregnant with baby number two. Another baby never came, but I still drove the van because it made car pool easier . . . even if it made me feel as sexy as my aunt Clarice's girdle. Maybe I should drive the Spider more. Put the top down. Let the wind blow through my hair.

That's probably why my husband was cheating on me. I chose comfort over sexiness every time. But who wanted to wax her hoo-ha and wear a thong? Truly?

I refocused because I had work to do. Scott would be at the bank until five o'clock. Then he'd toddle over to the club to oversee Julia Kate's lesson . . . or get a blow job. Whichever.

I had at least three hours.

If Scott were cheating, there'd be signs. Maybe nothing too overt, but the man wasn't the most detailed of people. He dropped deposit slips on the floorboard of his truck all the time, and he'd been known to leave his sand wedge on random holes at the club. Locking himself out of the house was at least a yearly occurrence. Careless wasn't his middle name, but it was at least a first cousin.

Time to figure out what the hell was going on before I tied myself up in knots. Everyone knew I hated complications.

Especially when they happened in the blink of an eye.

Damn it.

CHAPTER TWO

Ruby

Something was wrong with Cricket.

That morning she'd arrived with a smile and muffins from Sue Anne's Bakery, determination on her face, an ugly shirt assaulting my eyes. But that was how Cricket always arrived, with the exception of exchanging muffins for doughnuts and the ugly shirt for one that wasn't as garish but still didn't flatter her. What I couldn't do with a wardrobe if I had her curves . . . and money.

Me? I was what my gran called *pioneer tough*, with a whip-thin physique and hair that frizzed at the slightest hint of humidity. Sinewy, strong, and designed to withstand hot Louisiana summers. I might as well be a walking advertisement for a pickup truck.

I snorted as I thought about how I wasn't made to be soft. Well, what of it? Tough wasn't bad, and I didn't mind being like rawhide most days.

Looking down at the check Julie Van—I squinted at the signature—Ness had written, I had a sneaking suspicion it was one of those pieces of fluff that had my boss looking like she'd eaten a beetle. But I didn't blame Cricket. As soon as those two had waltzed inside, I had wanted to slink away and plaster myself against a wall, too. Julie and

Bo Peep were the sort that made me feel substandard and twitchy. Both wore trim workout clothes that hugged their thin bodies, carried purses that had little gold letters that could have cost twenty bucks at Target or a thousand from some fancy store like Saks or Neiman's, and carried themselves with the protection that privilege gave a person.

I shouldn't judge someone based on the little symbol near the bottom of their yoga pants or the fact they drove a white sporty SUV that cost triple what I make in a year, but I knew they were judging me . . . because I heard them.

And for the record, I liked my tats and adored my diamond-stud nose ring, so they could go eat a bag of . . . worms.

Yeah, I was trying really hard to clean up my bad language.

The little bell rang over the door, and I glanced up to find the guy I had been thinking about more than I should lately.

Ty Walker.

The man was slick as greased owl . . . poop, and he seemed to know it. He wielded his charm like a Ginsu knife, cutting through every defense I threw up. His golden-streaked brown locks, baby blues, and very nice body had pinged on my radar the first time I'd laid eyes on him a few weeks ago, when he'd come in to arrange delivery of several pieces he'd bought one day when I'd had class. He was that guy—the one all the girls used to watch on the lifeguard stand with his mirrored sunglasses, bronzed shoulders, and flashing white teeth. The one you fantasized about but never had the balls—ahem, I mean guts—to talk to.

"Good afternoon," I called out.

His smile flashed as he tucked his Ray-Bans into his shirt. A guy like him always wore Ray-Bans. Tom Cruise effect.

"Hey, I was hoping you'd be here."

"I'm always here. Well, when I don't have class." I tried not to fidget. I didn't want him to know how nervous he made me. Because he did.

He glided toward me, smooth and confident, propping a forearm on the glass countertop and leaning in. Expensive cologne wafted. Not overdone but noticeable. "I forgot that you're still a college girl."

"I'm twenty-eight years old. That's *not* a girl."

"I'll say," he teased, raking his gaze down my torso.

My immediate response was to look around for my hoodie. I had gotten hot earlier and had shed it when polishing the new silver service that we were going to put on the front table. Underneath, I wore a tight Lycra shirt that showed the skin between the hem and my favorite jeans. "You flirt too much."

He gave me a gator smile. "Only 'cause I'm good at it."

I snorted and tried to find my coolness. This guy melted me even if his words were a little too cocky, bordering on douchey. "I'm assuming you're here to pick up the carpet Cricket ordered. It's in the back."

"That's *one* of the reasons."

Pleasure flooded me because I totally got that message.

Ty Walker wasn't my normal kind of guy. Hell, I hadn't had any kind of guy in a while. When I first started classes at Bossier Parish Community College, one of my classmates, a benign dude who loved to wear dorky T-shirts, had asked me out for coffee. It had sounded like a very grown-up kind of date. I went, and after he bought me a latte and showed me pictures of his pit bull, he inquired if I wanted to go to his car and have sex. He'd asked in the same way he might ask me if I wanted a pumpkin cheesecake muffin from the pastry case. I answered, "Not really," and I hadn't been on a date since. Actually, I was sort of tired of my own company, and once or twice, I had wondered what it would have been like having sex outside Starbucks in a car with Cedric. Probably anticlimax-ic with a side of dog hair on my new sweater.

So I was primed for this grown-up frat boy to talk me out of my thong. "Oh yeah?"

"Yeah," he said, his voice softening in that intimate way that had something in my belly warming.

For a few seconds we stared at each other. Like a Hallmark movie or something.

Finally, he said, "I wondered if you'd like to go out sometime? I have these tickets for—"

Please let him say *Zombie Matrix* . . . or the opening of *Shield of Death* . . . or . . .

"—Gritz and Glitz in three weeks and would love for you to come with me."

I blinked. Gritz and Glitz? What the hell was that? And *weeks* from now? "Umm . . ."

Ty leaned back. "I have to fly out to LA and will be there for a week, so maybe we can hit dinner or something next week. But I'm going to need a date for the gala, and I could think of no one I would rather go with than a foxy college student who works at an antique store and makes me a little crazy with how pretty her mouth is."

He lowered his gaze to my lips, which of course made me nervously lick at them. "I'm not sure—"

"Of me?"

Bingo.

"No, what I'm trying to say is . . ." I trailed off because I couldn't figure out how to say I wanted to go out with him but not to that particular torturous event.

He grinned even bigger. "Oh, I see. You like to play hard to get, but that's cool. It's kinda sexy."

Squealing brakes.

"I'm not playing hard to get. I'm just not rolling over for you to scratch my belly, Mr. Walker. Besides, I don't do galas . . . or brunches . . . or monograms."

His smile disappeared, and he looked like a dog who'd gotten into the trash. "I'm sorry. That was stupid. I know you're not playing games. I'm just so into you and—"

The irritation inside me subsided as I waited for him to finish.

"I'm so screwing this up. I know a girl like you doesn't need me to drop dumbass pickup lines." He shook his head, giving me a wry smile.

Goodness, he was a snack and a half. And owning his mistake. Not to mention he'd admitted to being into me. I lifted a shoulder. "Okay, so you screwed up. Now you know."

"Yeah." He sucked in a big breath. "Can we just ignore that really bad attempt at flirting? I mean, I totally tempted the fates when I bragged on my game."

That made me smile. "Fine. Let's erase the conversation."

"Whew," he said, swiping fake perspiration from his brow. "Now about that carpet."

"Right. It's in the storeroom wrapped and ready to roll. How would you like to pay?"

He held up a sexy finger. Okay, it wasn't sexy. Not really. "Just so you know, I am already learning, because I started to say something inappropriate under the guise of flirting and didn't. See? I learned my lesson."

"And show remarkable self-control. I admire a guy who has lots of control." Okay, I hadn't meant it that way, but he liked it. His eyes lit up, and those lips curled just perfectly at the corners.

Ty pulled out his wallet. Expensive leather. Or so I assumed. I took his platinum card and processed it, stapled the receipts, and handed both over.

"Okay, Mr. Walker, follow me," I said, slipping from behind the register and walking toward the back room. He may have murmured something under his breath. Probably an innuendo. That made me smile a little.

Ten minutes later, he and I had managed to get the heavier-than-it-looked carpet loaded into Ty's father's truck and strapped down. For really heavy purchases, Cricket had a guy who came on Fridays. But like I said, I was pretty strong.

"There," he said, shoving the tailgate into place. "I hope this works in my living room because I do *not* want to have to load this again. Way heavier than it looks."

"It seems versatile. Like you can use it for something formal or casual. I don't know your look, but . . ." I trailed off because although I worked at an upscale antique store, I knew nothing about expensive furniture. I had grown up in a house where the furniture was hand-me-down or bought on credit from the local furniture outlet. Our couch had been a floral velvet with a wagon wheel. Oh, and then a camouflage one my uncle had financed at the Bass Pro Shops. We'd used a remnant of carpet under the dining room set that had been given to my granny by a friend who'd moved to Idaho.

Yeah, I had grown up on the Balthazar compound north of Mooringsport, which was right outside Shreveport. My family had lived there since my great-grandfather, who'd left Natchitoches after a knife fight, settled in the area because there had been a lot of trees and not as many law-abiding tattletales. The Balthazar family settled into businesses that skirted the law but still allowed them to show up on the family pew each Sunday. My grandfather owned a tree service, and his brother had a junkyard and garage that repaired transmissions. We weren't exactly like the families represented in reality series about people in the South, but we weren't far off. Most of my uncles and cousins had done some time. A little distribution here. Some bad checks there. And a B and E or two. Too many aggravated assaults and resisting arrests to name. We were known for being trouble, and ever since Ed Earl had landed me in a women's correctional facility a little over two years ago, I had removed myself from the family. The only person I ever talked to was Gran, and that was on the phone over coffee every morning.

"You could always come over and give me your opinion," Ty said, sliding those mirrored sunglasses into place, hiding the baby blues. But the effect wasn't dampened. I loved the way he looked in sunglasses, that longish hair curling at the ends and brushing the gold metal.

"I wasn't asking," I said hastily.

"I know. I was offering. And I want you to come with me to the gala. Think about it."

Me at a gala was like a hooker in a nunnery. I would be out of place among women like Julie Van Ness and Bo Dixie Whatever Her Name Was. Besides, I had nothing to wear. I wasn't even sure what someone wore to a gala, but I was fairly certain it was something sparkly and designer. I could barely afford my cell phone bill. Tuition was reasonable, but living on my own meant I was responsible for all the bills. None of my former friends were where I was in life, thanks to the vacation Ed Earl had given me. Many were married or had gotten the hell out of Louisiana. The ones who had stayed weren't too different from my Balthazar family. I didn't need their influence or them telling everyone in north Caddo Parish my business.

Ty looked at me expectantly.

"I don't do galas. How about meeting at a bar or going to Chili's or something?"

Ty laughed like that was funny. Like going to Chili's was a joke. But I liked Chili's.

"You're so adorable," he said, and for a minute I thought he might be gay because I had never had a guy call me adorable. But I knew he wasn't gay, and maybe guys who drove expensive trucks and dressed in polo shirts often used the word *adorable*. I wouldn't know.

"Seriously," he continued, reaching out a hand and brushing my forearm. "I want you to come with me."

"Take one of the girls who likes that crap. I don't want to wear a fancy dress and be ignored by people who I don't want to talk to anyway. I'm sure you got women lining up to go with you to eat grits."

He squinted his eyes in confusion behind the glasses. I could tell because it made his nose wrinkle. "We don't eat grits."

I had been joking. Obviously he wasn't good at recognizing dry humor. That and the presumptuous statement about me intentionally

21

playing hard to get were marks against him. Still, the whole package might be worth taking a chance. But I didn't want to put on heels and a gown to do it. "I'll think about it."

"Great." His resulting smile looked as content as a cat in sunshine.

I didn't know whether to be pleased or alarmed. Instead I decided to do what I did best—duck out. "I have to get back. Catch you later."

Then I trotted up the two freshly painted steps to the front porch with the lush ferns. The bell tinkled as I entered the old house that smelled of lemon oil, age, and leather books. Cricket had set a bowl of gardenia blooms in a silver pitcher next to the cash register, and that scent filled my nose as I skirted the counter and sank onto the counter-height leather chair. My phone showed a few texts, mostly from my class group chat. I had been taking business classes at a local community college with the hopes of getting an associate's degree and a better job. I loved working at Printemps. Well, *loved* might have been too strong of a word. Printemps was a good job for what it was. Cricket paid me decently, and the work wasn't hard. The alternatives had been a sandwich-delivery place or a housekeeping gig at a hotel—and they had wanted to do a background check. I much preferred to sit behind the counter, studying for my econ quiz and enjoying the air-conditioning.

Glancing over, my eye caught the white dress I had snagged from Cricket's Bin of Requirement. She hadn't gotten the joke, but I assumed she wasn't a Potterhead the way I was. I reached out and stroked the material. The stiff taffeta provided nice structure to work with, and though it had originally been white, the patina of age had gilded it a creamy color that seemed more pleasant to me. I don't know why I asked her if I could have it, since the stain under the arm looked rusty and the irregular holes suggested some moths had thrown a rager. Still, my fingers itched to turn it into something that honored its history.

I had only pulled out the sewing machine Gran had bought me with her egg money a few times since moving in, including to make curtains for my sterile duplex. But something about that dress called to me. Cricket said it was a Givenchy. I had heard the name. Maybe a perfume or something.

As I lifted the dress, it made a soft swish. Like a sigh. The pleats were wide, making billowing panels, and it looked as if it were missing a belt. The bodice buttoned up the front to a collarless neckline. The sleeves weren't exactly capped, more of a sloping end to the bodice. The stain glared at me. I wrinkled my nose and allowed my mind to trip back to what else was in the bin. If I could find a more defined skirt, I could piece the bodice to something in black. Or a deep blue. A wide belt with tiny rhinestones would dress it up. I could create something gala worthy.

Wait.

Was I really considering going to the ball, Cinderella-style, piecing together something old in a trunk thinking that it would be good enough to hobnob with Shreveport's nobility? And really, how noble were they? No Fortune 500 companies here. Just a few timber guys, a bunch of oil-and-gas people, and old family money. The city was like the stepchild of Dallas society. So why was I worried that I wouldn't be good enough?

'Cause your mama was a barmaid, and your daddy ran off west to join up with a motorcycle gang. And you've been in prison, chickee.

There *was* that.

I laughed at myself and carefully folded the dress and set it on the back credenza where Cricket kept the Rolodex of suppliers and VIP customers. She was old school that way. In fact, that was the very best way to describe her—like someone out of the fifties.

The phone rang.

I answered. "Printemps. Can I help you?"

"Hey, uh—"

"Ruby," I filled in.

"Yeah, Ruby," Scott Crosby said, without a trace of chagrin in his voice. "Sorry about that. I'm bad with names."

"It's okay."

"Is Cricket there?"

"She went home early. I think her chicken-salad sandwich didn't agree with her." Why had I offered up that information? But then again, Scott was her husband. It was okay to share such things.

"Oh. Well, I tried calling her cell phone, but it went to voice mail."

I didn't know what he wanted me to say. "Um, well, I'm pretty sure she was heading home. Maybe she put it on DND because she was lying down or something."

A girlish giggle sounded in the background. I glanced at the clock. Two fifty-three p.m. School wasn't out yet. Maybe this was about Julia Kate? But for some reason, I didn't think so. Because Scott grew quiet, and I could envision him shushing whoever it was.

"What's DND?" Scott asked.

"Do not disturb," I clarified.

As much as I liked Cricket, I didn't have the same feelings for her husband. Of course, I'd only met him two or three times, but he'd always been dismissive. Cricket may carry expensive purses and slide on jewelry that cost a small fortune, but she was always considerate and treated everyone as if they were her friends. Happy puppy-dog eyes and quick smiles were her trademark, and though I still felt uncomfortable around her, she went out of her way to include me. Like inviting me to go to estate sales with her. Like we were friends.

We weren't. But it was nice that she had asked me.

Her husband was the type I had never cared for—a little smirky, too comfortable in his surroundings, like he owned the world. He had a little of Ty's charming swagger, but it was kind of icky on a late-forties guy who had thinning hair and sunspots and wore jeans that would look more appropriate on someone twenty years his junior.

"Maybe so," Scott said, another feminine noise sounding before he huffed, "Shh!" at whoever was making it. But there had been giggling and then that shushing, and suddenly I felt a knowing tingle at the nape of my neck.

"Well, if she comes back or calls, tell her I'll be late tonight. I'm taking Julia Kate to lessons, and then she wants to eat at the club with some of her friends," he said.

"I'll do that, but maybe you should text Cricket." I wanted to add on "weirdo," because who asked a person he barely knew to give a message to someone who wasn't there?

"Oh. Yeah, of course. Sorry about that. I've been distracted, and I hate when she doesn't answer the phone. You have a good day, Rosie."

I blinked several times at those last words, and I was just about to mutter "You too" when I heard the click.

Setting the receiver back into its cradle, I tried to stop my mind from going where it shouldn't. To the sounds in the background, to the woo-woo feeling that I'd had too many times, to Cricket's face when she'd left earlier claiming bad chicken salad. Something was going on, and because my granny had said I was as sharp as a hedgehog cactus, I was certain that a certain skeevy husband was doing my sweet boss ten kinds of wrong.

I had that same feeling the night before my daddy joined the biker gang. Like things were about to change and not for the better.

Great.

CHAPTER THREE

CRICKET

I stared at the box in the bottom of the closet for a good ten seconds. Nothing about it seemed weird. Just a plain shipping box like something I received almost every day from Amazon. But Scott had hidden it in the back under the Peter Millar chukkas he'd bought on sale but never wore. He and I were the same in that regard. We loved a good bargain even when it sat in our closet untouched.

Glancing at my wrist, I noted the time.

Five fifty-five p.m.

Scott had texted that they were eating at the club and would be late. Still, Julia Kate had school the next morning, so they would be back soon. Poor Julia Kate. I had been thinking only of myself for the past few hours, but how would our daughter deal with the knowledge her father had cheated? That our family would be no more. The image of her tear-streaked face flashed before me. Maybe I should stop what I was doing. Maybe I should forget about what I had heard and just go along to get along.

Or maybe I should find out the truth before I decided anything.

I ran a finger along the cut tape of the box, wondering what Scott had been hiding.

When I had left the store that afternoon, I had driven aimlessly for a good thirty minutes before stopping at the liquor store that carried my favorite wine and nabbing two bottles. I saw the treasurer of the Caddo Magnet PTA buying vodka, chatted with her like my whole world wasn't imploding, grabbed a bottle of Grey Goose just in case, and then drove home only to find my mother pulling weeds in my front flower bed. It was nearly cocktail hour when I pulled into our drive, which was why it startled me to see my mother bent over, fanny wagging as she jerked stringy growth from my pine-strawed beds. My mother adored a martini or a stout whiskey each afternoon. .

I didn't bother pulling the van into the garage. Instead I stopped on the flagstone drive with the thyme crisscrossing it and lowered the window. "What are you doing, Mother?"

She tilted the brim of her big floppy hat with a gloved hand and glanced toward me. "Pulling up this nut grass. Your beds look unseemly. The way you keep your house is a reflection of who you are."

My mother found fault with almost everything I did, wore, or said. Let's not even get into my hairstyle. I had become mostly impervious to her passive-aggressive digs. After all, ignoring my mother was the only sport in which I had ever excelled. Gold medal worthy. "Well, I appreciate the free labor."

Her downturned mouth reminded me of the grumpy jack-o'-lantern Julia Kate and I had carved the previous fall for the annual Shine on Line. Not that my mother was round or orange. No, quite the opposite. My mother was country club thin with creamy skin she slathered with Pond's cold cream every night of her life. She lived to seek and destroy age spots, and Dr. Feliz Miranda, plastic surgeon to south Shreveport, had been receiving holiday cards from my mother for well over thirty years.

My mother rose and arched her back. With a wince, she removed her gloves and eyed the small clumps of weeds dotting my walkway.

"Get Scott to put those in the trash. Not the compost heap. They'll spring back up next year like a bad penny if you don't."

Of all the people in the world who could be at my house an hour or so after I'd found out Scott might be having an affair—and with an attractive, fit former tennis star at that—my mother was the absolute worst. I would welcome a terrorist over her. Come to think on it, my mother *was* a terrorist. She knew exactly how to get me to do what she wanted, utilizing a network of intimidation, propaganda, and guilt. I loved her. I did. But she was a piece of work, as most would say.

"Okay, Mother." I shut my van door, opened the vintage Louis Vuitton bag I carried, and used the key fob to lock the vehicle. "Would you care for a cup of coffee? Or tea?"

"You know I require a vodka martini," my mother said, folding her gardening gloves and placing them in the Chanel tote she always carried with her in lieu of a purse. Inside the expensive canvas, the woman had everything from Xanax to an extra pair of underwear. Marguerite Sutton Quinney was never unprepared.

Juggling the brown bag from the liquor store, I punched in the code for the front door. "I got liquor right here."

Pippa, our energetic Italian greyhound, skidded into the foyer with a low growl. Upon recognizing me, she ran elegant little circles, her tail whipping in a frenzy as she gave me the greeting she thought I deserved. Of course, Pippa nearly knocked my mother down. Maybe if the woman ate a few carbs, she would be more stalwart against my affectionate canine.

"Really, Catherine, you should keep this animal in a crate. Dogs are not to have free rein of a house. Louie and Martine are always kenneled."

I rolled my eyes and bent to receive the balm of true love from the only creature who loved me no matter what. Louie and Martine were ridiculous teacup poodles who my mother kept on pillows next to her velvet settee, where she plotted her Machiavellian takeover of my life.

Being an only child wasn't for the faint of heart. My friends used to be jealous. They hadn't thought about what all that single-minded attention did to an awkward girl. My father had vamoosed with Crystalle, leaving me the sole target of Marguerite. Only my grandmother had been able to take my mother down a peg. She'd taught me some of her tricks (ignore her and do what you want), but not enough to give me much peace.

"Pippa is fine as she is," I said, looking down at the adorable, slim face. Pippa's chocolate-brown eyes radiated such love that my heart may have knitted together a centimeter or so.

I turned, entered the kitchen, and set the bag on the granite, withdrawing the vodka. Maybe I needed a martini or twelve myself. Mother glided behind me, secretly petting my dog. I knew this because I caught her kissing and doting on Pippa when she thought I wasn't looking. My mother said a lot of things—the kinds of things she thought she should say because she seemed to enjoy being self-righteous, but she also didn't always *do* what she said. She kept Snickers in the drawer under the oven beneath the cookie sheets, she watched *The Bachelor* (even though publicly she called it trash), and she let her dogs sleep with her (although she told everyone she would never allow a dog to sleep on her expensive sheets). Also, if Marguerite knew that Scott had cheated on me, she would fillet him with the skill of a bayou fisherman.

"Don't skimp on the vodka," Mother said as she settled on the couch in the hearth room, turning on the urn table lamp and lifting a copy of *Architectural Digest* into her lap. She sent me that subscription every year on my birthday . . . for herself.

I shoved the wine into the fridge to chill and grabbed the cocktail shaker. Usually, Scott made the drinks, but even a novice like me could pour vodka and vermouth and add olives. I grabbed proper martini glasses because my mother would expect as much, and I wished for the umpteenth time in an hour that I had not tried to make a utility closet my office. Because then I wouldn't know about my husband. Then I wouldn't be wishing my mother would leave so I could poke through Scott's office to see if I could figure out who he might be doing. Or maybe I should be looking elsewhere. He had a fireproof safe where he kept important documents. And a gun safe. Where else might he—

"Any day now, Catherine. I'm parched."

I poured the martini in the glasses and made my way to the hearth room, tossing Pippa a biscuit and letting her outside en route.

"Here you go," I said, wagging the drink in front of my mother.

She took it, sipped, lifted an eyebrow that could mean anything from *Acceptable* to *Pour it in the toilet*, and sighed. "We need to talk about the gala in a few weeks. Your father is supposed to be bringing his trollop to the event. He said Scott invited him to sit at your table, and I find that unacceptable."

This was news to me. I had talked to Dad last week, and he hadn't said anything about it. Scott liked my dad, but he'd never invited him to visit. We always went to Florida, mostly because the golfing was better, and it generated no talk about my father's midlife crisis over drinks at the club. "I didn't know."

"How do you not know?"

I shrugged. "I haven't really had the chance to speak to Scott much. He had a tennis tournament at the club this past weekend."

I nearly choked over those words. For years, he'd asked me to take up tennis. To do something together as a couple. I had always hedged. Running an antique store took up a lot of my time, as did mothering my daughter. Sitting on PTA committees, helping to chair the silent auction for the St. Jude golf tournament, and teaching confirmation at church kept me running in circles. My intentions had been good. I figured that once Julia Kate started driving, I could do more with Scott. Maybe I had done this to us. Maybe my lack of knowing anything about the bank and his hobbies had sent him into the arms of another woman.

"Junie Minter told me that Scott has been drumming up business for Donner Walker. You know anything about that? Maybe that's why he wants your father to come to the gala. Your father and his trashy wife have obviously made a lot of money with that storage business of theirs."

That was an understatement. My father may not have been smart about where he dipped his stick and had lost quite a dime in the divorce settlement, but he wasn't dumb. He'd invested in storage facilities and a string of car washes in Florida, making back what he'd been forced to give my mother by her sharky lawyer several times over. I knew Scott had been having drinks and dinner with Donner Walker, an investment guy who'd moved to Shreveport a few years back. The man was the older brother of Scott's best friend from college who had died in a tragic car accident, but I didn't know Scott had been helping him with clients. Scott was always careful about crossing boundaries as a banker, taking pride in being ethical, but then again, he had promised to cleave to me until death do us part. Did cleaving mean being faithful? I wasn't sure.

"I don't know, Mother. I can ask him when he gets home."

My mother shook her head, and her hair didn't move an inch. "No. Just do not allow Bernard to sit at the bank's tables. Make sure he's in the back. Behind a fern."

To say there was no love lost between my mother and father was obvious. My mother loathed my dad, but she still missed him. I heard the longing in her voice. Once when she'd had too much bourbon on Christmas Eve, she'd cried over him. I had never seen her cry before, and it had been somewhat horrifying and frankly a relief. Because I had always wondered if she missed him . . . or if she'd even loved him. Always hard to know with my mother. "I'll talk to Melissa Peete, who's in charge of corporate sponsorships. And you know Daddy. He proba-bly won't come anyway. He hates coming to Shreveport."

I could make no promises. If Scott insisted, I would relent. The bank had two tables. I would ask that my mother be seated far from my father and Crystalle if they did, indeed, show.

My mother flinched before taking another sip. "Better he stay away."

An hour later, I waved as my mother drove away, hoping she'd be okay to drive. The martini hadn't been strong, and she lived two streets over in a huge colonial house with a pool that had been featured in *NWLA Columns* last year. The title had been "Backyard Oasis," and my mother had bought and mailed copies to all our cousins in Baton Rouge.

As soon as I closed the front door, I scrambled to the office.

It didn't take me long to confirm what I already knew. I paid the house bills, but the bank paid for Scott's cell phone. A quick call to May, Scott's assistant at Caddo Bank and Loan, got me his account number. The next call to AT&T landed me a chatty rep who helped me into the iCloud. And since Scott frequently used the same password, SCOTTGOLF1, so I could log on to our household accounts, I easily accessed his texts for the past month. The dumb butt had been sexting one Stephanie Brooks. The same Stephanie Brooks I wrote a monthly check to at the country-club tennis center for Julia Kate's lessons. No mistaking things like "I've been dreaming of your lips" and "What are you wearing?" as convo about Julia Kate's tennis stroke.

What I had thought was an inordinate interest in sharing his passion for tennis with his thirteen-year-old daughter was actually Scott sharing himself with the bouncy Stephanie.

Or maybe he wasn't sleeping with her yet—those texts could be simple flirting. I just couldn't reconcile Scott with a guy who slept with his daughter's tennis coach. It seemed so far-fetched.

But Scott was at the very least entertaining the idea of jumping the net to a younger, hotter option.

My first inclination was to drive down to the club, pull out a racket, and beat the ever-lovin' crap out of that little bitch. All those times she'd chirped hello and talked about how much Julia Kate had improved her backhand, smiling into my eyes, suggesting I consider taking lessons, too. The woman had to have balls of steel under her tennis skirt, though how she hid them under something that short was beyond me.

My second inclination was to call the dirtiest divorce attorney in Shreveport and make Scott wish he'd never been born.

My third inclination actually happened. I dropped to my knees on the new carpet I had put in last January and shattered like a snow globe tossed onto cold marble. The slivers of my self-worth glittered and throbbed. I was doomed to never be whole again. I cried until my head hurt, curled into a ball, Pippa sitting beside me looking helpless and reluctant to make eye contact. But she stayed, sinking onto her haunches with a sigh that mirrored the desolation inside me.

And at that moment, I didn't regret giving in when Julia Kate had begged for a puppy. As much as I bellyached about feeding, bathing, and cleaning up after her, Pippa beside me, a stalwart friend seemingly sympathetic to my sobbing, was better than having a hamster . . . which is the pet I had countered Julia Kate with. And speaking of Julia . . . my poor baby girl. Her daddy was a lowlife. We'd both been duped by him.

After a good thirty minutes of ugly self-pity, I struggled to my feet and walked to the bedroom I shared with Scott. What else was he hiding? I knew he was texting inappropriate things, but what more did I not know about the man I slept beside?

That's how I had found the box under his unused chukkas in his closet.

Sucking in a breath, I unfolded the flaps and looked at the package inside. It took me a minute to comprehend the fuzzy ears and the bushy tail. What? A Halloween costume? What in the world . . .

And then I saw a tube of something and lifted it.

Anal numbing gel.

I squinted at the label before darting my gaze back at that bushy foxtail. The end of the tail was a rubbery triangle thing. My eyes widened as I realized what I was looking at.

A butt plug.

I threw the tube of lube onto the tail, shoved the whole shebang into the box, and folded the flaps, all the while making little *eep* noises because . . . ugh.

And then I remembered last year when Scott had asked me to look online at some sex toys. He'd been thinking we needed to up our game and experiment in the bedroom. He'd mentioned some ring things and a butt plug. Or was that anal beads? No matter. I had nipped that idea before it could bloom into something that kept me from sitting for a week. It was fine for some, but a no-go for me.

I backed out of the closet, wondering what this find meant. Had he bought that months ago hoping I would change my mind, or was he experimenting with the tennis pro? The seal on the tube of lube had been broken, and one of the foxy ears was bent. The image of Stephanie's foxtail swishing beneath her tennis skirt flashed in my mind, and I bit my knuckles as tears gathered on my lashes.

Oh God.

Not only was Scott cheating on me, but he was playing weird sex games with things that seemed, well, very uncomfortable.

A sob emerged as I caught my expression in the bathroom mirror.

Stupid woman.

Hysteria began to burble up inside me. I pressed my hands against my eyes and panted like a wounded animal. Not a fox. No. But some other wounded creature. Another sob tore loose before I muttered, "No . . . no . . . *no.*"

And as I said those words, something inside me stilled. Deep down under all the hurt and shock was an ice-riddled part of my heart that whispered, "Keep your head, Cricket."

I dropped my hands, lifted my chin, stared at myself in the mirror.

With resolve.

With the first flickering of anger.

This calculating coolness came from my mother. My mother always did the correct thing. She lived by unwritten rules. Heck, she even embraced the written ones, which is why she fussed when I went over the speed limit. But she also knew how to control her emotions and evaluate a situation with a levelheadedness that made her a force to be reckoned with. She was a pain in my ass, but she'd modeled composure her entire life. Now I needed to draw on what my formidable mother had taught me.

Scott would be home in an hour or so.

He didn't need to know that I knew anything about him, Stephanie, and his potential foxy frolicking. I wasn't exactly certain that he'd gotten totally physical with the woman, but all signs pointed in that direction. I also wasn't sure how to confront him. Or *if* I should confront him. Or if I should just go ahead and smother him in his sleep. But one thing was certain—things were about to change.

And not for the better.

Damn it.

CHAPTER FOUR

CRICKET

Five days later

"Do you have a car phone charger by chance?" Ruby asked as she rooted around on the floorboard of the 1977 Spider Veloce that had belonged to my grandmother. Sue Ellen Sutton had bought the convertible right after I was born, the day she'd moved her home for battered women—some of whom, yes, were ladies of the night—to a bigger house closer to downtown. As a philanthropist and one of Shreveport's five feminists, my grandmother Sue saw the swaggy car as a symbol of what a woman of the 1970s could be—independent, modern . . . and windblown.

She'd driven it every day to Printemps.

I, on the other hand, rarely drove the car because it was a stick shift and made me feel conspicuous with all the bright red and zippiness. Besides, my van had air-conditioning and lumbar support so . . .

Yeah, boring.

And that was probably my whole problem. Which is why I had pulled it out of the garage earlier when I learned that Julia Kate was going to spend the night with a friend to celebrate the beginning of spring break and my husband was going to the club to meet with a client. I figured that was code for "chasing some skirt." And now that I knew what skirt he was chasing, I could see for myself if my suspicions were true.

So I was parked several houses down from the tennis pro's cute little cottage.

With Ruby.

"I think the charger's in the bag. I put some protein bars in there, too," I said, lifting the binoculars I'd found in my husband's duck-blind bag from my lap and training them on the craftsman-style house with the brass mailbox. Thing was, I'd never used binoculars before, and I'd twisted the knobs seven ways to Sunday with no clear result. I couldn't see anything and cursed the fact that the tennis pro I was spying on had a tall privacy fence that blocked the view into her backyard and detached garage. I couldn't tell if Scott's truck was sitting in the hidden driveway or not. Would Scott be so stupid as to have parked in the driveway of a woman he was secretly screwing? Maybe so, because I hadn't seen his truck anywhere on the street.

I had studied him for the past four days, and nothing in his demeanor suggested he was sliding the sausage to someone else. I had scanned the internet (erasing my browser history, of course) for ways to tell if your significant other was cheating. Scott hadn't suddenly started grooming himself differently or buying me gifts. Our intimacy had waned long ago, so it wasn't like he'd recently stopped being into me. He wasn't spending more money or changing his routine. Well, other than being into Julia Kate's tennis lessons.

I knew I was resisting the obvious, but I couldn't help that I didn't want my world to fall apart. Not over a few texts and some idle speculation. But that afternoon, everything had changed, forcing me outside of my comfort zone and landing me on a snooping expedition.

"Why'd you bring protein bars?" Ruby asked, lifting her head from the recesses of the floorboard, holding up the monogrammed bag.

"Well, I didn't know how long we'd be on this stakeout."

I could feel Ruby studying me, trying to figure out how she'd ended up sitting there with me when she should be studying for the midterm in her business class. I didn't want her to feel like she had to do extra things just because I was her employer, but I was glad she was beside me. Should I say that? Would that insult her? I didn't know what to do.

Finally, she sighed, took the binoculars out of my hand, and turned them around. "You'll have a better chance of seeing if you try this way."

Oh. Yeah.

But in my defense, both ends looked the same.

I put the correct end of the binoculars to my eyes, but even then I couldn't see anything but blurry darkness.

"If I had known you wanted to go on a stakeout, I would have worn black," Ruby said, glancing down at her tight khaki leggings and violet blouse that could have cost $500 or $5. Ruby wore it with some cool vintage jewelry and a pair of high-tops. She had a particular style I liked—breezy, young, but also comfortable.

"It was last minute. And besides, we're in the car."

Ruby's nose wrinkled. "Yeah, about that. The van would have been a better choice."

"What's wrong with this car?"

"Don't you watch movies? Stakeout cars are supposed to be nondescript." Ruby ripped open a granola bar and took a bite.

"Yeah," I acknowledged, thinking I probably should have brought the minivan. Dime a dozen in this town. "But this car is . . . perfect."

"If we were Thelma and Louise," Ruby said, with a somewhat chocolaty lift of her lips.

Suddenly I saw us as that duo, except maybe switched. Ruby seemed more like the confident Louise, knowing how to use a gun, making all the right moves, and I was the duped, trampled-upon Thelma. I didn't want to be Thelma, though. I wanted to be proactive.

"Well, at least I wore all black," I said, sweeping a hand over my black yoga pants and matching hoodie. It was early spring and no longer cool, but I had dressed for stealth. I wiped the sweat from my forehead.

"Which would work better if you covered your hair," she said, looking pointedly at my recently lightened hair, which I'd pulled back into a ponytail.

So I wasn't good at spying on my husband. Sue me.

For the past few days I'd pretended everything was fine . . . even when Ruby and I had gone to the estate sale Saturday morning. My preconceived bonding hadn't really happened, though we had found two pairs of the most splendid burgundy velvet curtains and a valuable chandelier that just needed some minor repair. Ruby had been stoic but interested at each stop, and I had been quieter than normal as my mind nattered away at what Scott might be doing to the tennis pro in Lafayette while I poked through worn sheets and bad paintings. I managed to fake my way to Monday morning, dragging my somewhat depressed self to work because I had no good reason to stay in bed and bemoan the black hole in my soul. I had vowed to tell no one until I could prove Scott was sleeping with this twit. I had so many questions. Had he really gotten physical with her? Was it just about sex? Did he love her? Was he planning on leaving me?

At the end of the day, Ruby had walked in with a caramel macchiato and glanced at the yellow roses sitting majestically on my desk.

"You got me a macchiato," I'd said.

Ruby looked down at the drink and then up at the bags under my eyes. "I figured you needed it."

"Why?"

Ruby looked real hard at me. "I ate the chicken salad, too."

I took three swallows of my sugary drink and said, "I think Scott is cheating on me."

Ruby's eyes turned to glittering topaz gemstones. "Then we need to take that sonofabitch down."

Something about the way she came so quickly to my defense, like we were a team, made things a little better. I'm not sure why. I didn't know Ruby well, but her proclamation checked a box for me. She made me want to do something about Scott.

So here we sat in my grandmother's convertible.

Ruby kicked her Converse shoes up on the dash, drawing my attention from the blurry binoculars to her, framed against the darkened street where Stephanie lived. My assistant sipped wine from a foam cup. I had sort of bribed her to come with me with booze.

"Tell me again why we're doing this?" she said.

"I want to—" I paused, trying to think why I had insisted we sit five houses down from Stephanie Brooks's house at nine p.m. I didn't finish the thought because I wasn't exactly sure. All weekend I had fantasized about catching Scott with his pants around his ankles. Visions of me storming into Steph Brooks's bedroom, melodramatically slapping Scott, and telling him he'd hear from my lawyer had danced like sugarplums in my head. Then he'd trip over said pants around his ankles, chasing after me, begging for forgiveness.

But now that seemed ridiculous.

But still, I wanted to see the evidence for myself.

How did I relay that to Ruby?

"If you see him with her, it will make it real?" Ruby asked, her voice as soft as the night gathered around us.

I blinked away sudden tears. Thank goodness she understood that I needed to see his infidelity with my own eyes. Even if I sort of knew the truth.

Scott *was* probably cheating on me.

And despite my constant proclamations about how strong our marriage was, the fat truth was that Scott and I weren't in love. Oh, we loved each other in the way you love a person who makes a life with you, who shoulders the hard stuff with you, who shares the shampoo, the dishes, and the kid with you. But I was no longer "in love" with Scott.

And he wasn't "in love" with me.

I mean, obviously.

"You're right. Something inside me needs to see him with her. I don't know why," I said finally.

"What if you don't see him tonight?"

"I don't know. I haven't figured out what to do yet," I said. Truthfully, I hadn't absorbed what all this would mean for me. For our daughter. For the safe life we'd made. Felt like too much to take in.

"Cricket, if he's cheating on you, you have to have a plan. You have to—"

"But it's not that simple. I have Julia Kate to think about it. We're a fam—"

"You can't let him get away with this. I mean, you're not going to overlook him screwing around, are you?" Ruby didn't look so much like the quiet creature who slunk around the antique sideboards. She looked bold, bristling with outrage, and interesting. I liked this Ruby. And note to self: be careful giving Ruby wine; she gets feisty.

"No, but . . ." I didn't want to say what I had been thinking because Ruby couldn't understand. She wasn't married, didn't have a daughter, a mortgage, a life like mine. "My life is complicated."

More bristling from Ruby. "Everyone's life is complicated. You can't run from this."

"I'm not. It's not like I'm going to pretend this away. I just don't know what I'm actually going to do yet."

Okay, so I had thought about *D-I-V-O-R-C-E* and even sung it in Tammy Wynette's voice in my head. I had even imagined moving out of the brick house on the golf course and finding something cute and less like the big house I'd never wanted in the first place. Julia Kate and I could be happy in a cute three-bedroom in South Highlands. Eventually my daughter would be okay with no club swimming pool and no cruising the streets in a golf cart. Maybe. But even so, the idea of breaking apart our safe little world hurt too much to think about.

And it would get messy. Julia Kate would be devastated. People would look at me with pity. And since Scott and I held investments in both our names and he owned half the building Printemps was in, our split wouldn't be simple. At all.

"It's already done, you know," Ruby said.

"What?"

"Change. It's happened. You can't stick your head in the sand."

I wasn't. Not really. "I'm not."

"Instead of doing this, you should hire a professional." Ruby sounded so certain. How did she know these sorts of things? She was so young. And nothing like the woman who stayed out of my way at the store, glancing at me as if she expected me to snap at any minute.

No, this woman had teeth. And confidence.

"Why would I pay someone to catch him when I can do that myself?" I asked.

"You need proof that's admissible in court. Pictures."

"I don't want to go to court. I want to confront him myself. I want him to know I know."

"No, you don't." Ruby delivered this with an adamant pointer finger.

"Who *are* you? Where have you been hiding the real Ruby all this time?"

She gave me a smile. "Yeah, so I guess I'm cautious around people I don't know, especially women like you."

"Women like me?"

She made a flat line with her mouth. "Women who have money and security. Women who wear expensive clothes and talk about things like cotillion and debutantes."

"I'm not like that."

The corners of her mouth lifted. "I know. I mean, you talk about that stuff, but I know you're not shallow. And earlier when I saw you crying—"

"You saw me?" I hadn't meant to cry, but Scott had sent me flowers. He never sent me flowers, and because I had read that stupid "Thirty Signs He's Cheating On You" article, I knew that sending me flowers wasn't a sweet gesture. It was guilt and another nail in the coffin of our marriage.

"Yeah, and seeing you cry over that asshole pissed me off. That's why I came with you. Because you need help." She twisted her dark hair around her finger and narrowed her eyes. "But the first thing you have to be is smart about how you handle this."

Irritation blindsided me. "How am I not being smart? I've sat on this for days. Do you know how hard it is to lie beside a man you know is screwing another woman and not say anything?" My words escalated as I spoke.

Ruby's eyes flashed sympathy. "I get it, Cricket."

"No, you don't," I said, sadness edging in on my anger. But I didn't want to be sad. I liked the edginess the deep anger brought me, along with a burning determination that made me want to do something proactive, something that said I wasn't going to sit back and accept being cheated on. My mother's inherited coolness dissipated as emotion washed over me. "I'm not sticking my head in the sand or taking any shit from Scott."

Ruby's eyes widened when I opened the car door. "Wait, where are you going?"

I slammed the car door. "I'm going"—I leaned over and grabbed the bag that held the professional digital camera Scott had bought for our trip to Alaska last summer—"to get proof, admissible or not."

"Cricket, wait," Ruby said, but it was too late. I strode down the sidewalk, slipping quickly along the oleander bushes lining the next drive, hoping no looky-loo out to walk his fluffball would see me. A dog barked in the backyard next to Stephanie's house. I muttered "Crap" under my breath and jumped in a bush. A sharp branch raked my cheek.

"Shit," I breathed, slapping a hand to the scrape.

What was I doing? I wasn't even sure Scott was at Stephanie's. He had left the house an hour before, saying he needed to have drinks with a client and talk about some potential deal. He could be actually doing that, and not the horizontal mambo with the tennis coach.

A piece of shrubbery tangled in my ponytail. I pushed it away, slipping my hood over my head like I should have done when I exited the car. Sweat rolled down my back as I realized I was actually hiding in the neighbors' bushes—trespassing at that—so I could catch my husband cheating. Who had I become? Better yet, what had Scott made me?

I poked my head out and looked around at the sleepy neighborhood turning in for the night, porch lights glowing against the inky sky as cicadas sang a lullaby. The street looked pure Americana, with its manicured lawns and 1920s cottages, like it couldn't be part of something so tawdry as adultery. Inside me determination awakened, wrapping itself around sheer bravado.

Who was I?

A woman who frickin' deserved the truth. And there was only one way to get that—see if Scott's truck was parked in the carport.

So I moved quickly, skirting the brick-lined flower bed of Stephanie's next-door neighbor before peeling off and darting toward the latched fence.

Just as I lifted the latch, I heard a door open in the distance.

"Whew," I breathed, ducking into Stephanie's backyard, pulling the latch closed. My heart thumped in my ears as my camera pack bumped against the wooden slats.

"Oh crap," I whispered, groping for the camera to stop the thunking.

I pressed myself to the rough wood, squeezing my eyes shut, praying I didn't get caught trespassing. I heard a whistle and then a door slam. If my powers of deduction were correct, it had come from the house behind Stephanie's. My sigh caught against the fence just as a set of teeth sank into my ankle.

"Ahh." I kicked, shaking the small furball latched on to my ankle with the tenacity of a seed tick. One strong jerk and the dog flew off. The pooch yelped, scrabbled to its feet, and came back for more. High-pitched barks erupted as the five-pound Yorkie launched itself at me again.

"Get!" I hissed, swatting a hand at the beast.

The thing obviously wasn't open to reason. It kept bouncing at me, yipping, growling, and baring tiny teeth. If I hadn't been so panicked, I might have stopped to admire the defense the dog was mounting. I might even think it was cute.

But its teeth were razors, and the barking was way . . . too . . . much.

"Shhh!" I waved a hand in front of it, getting another nip in the process. I moved the dog aside with a sweep of my leg, shaking my wounded hand. "Son of a—"

But as Fluffy scrabbled back at me, I noted the carport held only one car—a cute little Lexus RX 350. No truck.

Dang it.

All this for nothing.

Fluffy jumped, teeth bared, and I caught the small dog under its belly, lifting it right before the Yorkie ripped my left leg off. Immediately the little dog started crying horrible little "I'm hurt and dying" yelps that would have broken my heart if my hand and ankle weren't throbbing.

The back door banged open. "Sunny?"

Oh, holy hell. Stephanie.

"Sunny? Baby boy, are you hurt?"

I heard shuffling and backed into the shadows, still holding the dog I hadn't found the least bit sunny out in front of me. The thing wriggled and yelped even more. When my back touched the side of the house, I set the pup down. Sunny shot like a bullet toward his owner, still yelping as if I'd bitten him instead of the other way around.

"Aww, what's wrong, Sunny? Is that mean ol' tomcat after you again? Come to Mama, baby."

I closed my eyes and prayed the woman didn't come out to look for the mean ol' tom. *Please don't come out. Please. Please. Please.*

I shouldn't have done this. I should have stayed in the car with Ruby, complacent, content to suspect. What had this little venture gotten me? Nothing. Except some dog bites I'd have to explain and a scratch from the oleander bush. Scott wasn't even here.

The yelping of the dog subsided, only to be replaced by high-pitched barks. Sunny didn't give up.

"What is it, boy?" Stephanie asked.

Another shuffling sound on the stoop made me cringe. She was going to come out here and look around. Stupid woman. Didn't she watch horror flicks? You don't go outside in the dark to investigate unless you have a—

"What is it?" a deeper voice asked.

I slapped a hand over my mouth so I didn't scream.

It was Scott.

"I don't know. Probably the cat that's been getting into the trash cans." Stephanie sounded like she was closer. Maybe she'd inched down the steps. Trying to take small breaths, I mimicked a statue frozen against the beige siding of the house.

"Come inside, baby. I have to leave in a few minutes," Scott said, using a voice I hadn't heard in ten years. It was his flirty "I'll do naughty things to you" voice. "I found the cherry lube."

My mouth opened and closed several times. Cherry lube? Really?

"But maybe I should check . . . ," Stephanie trailed off.

Then I heard a giggle. "Oh, my bad little fox. Move your hand lower. Oh yeah, that's nice."

My hands fisted. Screw Fluffy the psycho dog. The only rabid animal out here was me. The urge to attack rose inside me. I'd scratch and bite and . . . beat them with the water hose stretched out across the backyard. I'd tear them limb from limb and . . .

I sucked in a calm, measured breath. Logic had to prevail. I had a tool of reason looped around my neck. Cameras didn't lie. If I could get the camera out and turned on correctly, I could sneak around the corner and get a shot of Scott and Steph, who if the slurping sounds were any indication, were making out on the back porch. I carefully pulled the strap over my head, my other hand cradling the case so it didn't bump up against the house. I could hear the dog still growling low in his throat, but the two lovers seemed too caught up in each other to detect my presence.

I managed to unzip the case inch by painful inch, praying the sound couldn't be overheard. Easing the camera out, I searched for the small ON switch. Would turning it on make a glow? I couldn't remember how to work the stupid flash, but I probably needed to engage it because of the cloying darkness. Crud, I should have planned to use the camera on my iPhone. *That* I could work, and it was usually in my . . .

Oh, crap on a cracker, I'd forgotten to turn my iPhone in my hoodie pocket to vibrate. What if it rang? Or did that little ding thing when someone commented on a Facebook post.

I shoved the camera back into the bag, pulled my phone from my pocket, and found that the phone was already turned to silent.

Whew. That could have been disastrous.

I pushed the home button and noticed a text message on the screen. It was from Scott.

Still at Superior. Running a bit late. Will be home by 10:00. Save me some cheesecake.

That son of a biscuit.

I couldn't believe the nerve of the man. No doubt he'd pictured me at home watching reruns of *Downton Abbey*. He'd envisioned me picking up my chirping phone and smiling, grateful I had such a thoughtful husband who worked so hard. He'd likely thought I would text something back like, See you soon. Drive safely.

Good little wifey.

I shot daggers at the message, pressing the little camera icon on the home page.

Screw him.

He was about to find out just what kind of wife I was when I caught him cheating.

Launching myself from the wall, I took two huge leaps, avoiding an uneven patch of ground. I rounded the corner with my phone held in front of me, wondering if I should yell *Busted* as I made my appearance. I didn't even care if that turd dog got a piece of me. I was getting this picture. I held the phone tight, my finger in position as I leaped, clicking the little round button as my feet hit the ground. The flash blinded me.

I took a step backward, blinking madly, before squinting against the porch light. I zeroed in on the spot where Scott and Stephanie stood.

Except they weren't standing there.

The frickin' back door was closed, with no rabid, fluffy dog in sight.

"Crap," I whispered, dropping the hand holding the phone against my thigh. I had missed the golden opportunity of catching Scott playing octopus with Stephanie. How had I missed the sound of the door closing?

Planning the bank Christmas party? No problem. Hosting a shower for a hundred guests? Got it. Wrangling a class of kindergartners on a field trip? I'm your gal.

But pressing a little button and getting a pic? Epic fail.

As I stared at the empty spot, a horn sounded.

Ruby.

Moving like a hound out of hell (or a feisty Yorkie with an attitude problem) was on my heels, I lurched toward the gate, unlatched it, and sprinted toward the red convertible idling curbside. The camera thunked against my stomach with each step, mocking my attempt at gathering evidence.

God, I sucked.

Or maybe I didn't and that was the problem. Stephanie probably sucked better, and that's why my husband was shacked up with her in her cute little wrong-side-of-the-road cottage role-playing a woodland creature with a freaking butt-plug tail. If I had done more work on my knees, I'd probably be cleaning up the last of Sunday's cheesecake with Scott while watching TV. Instead I ran like a madwoman, sliding à la Bo Duke across the hood of the Spider, before diving into the classic car.

Ruby hit the gas, making the tires squeal a little.

"Are you crazy?" Ruby said, heading down the dark avenue toward the side street. "And that little slide across the hood was dope, by the way."

I waved my hand, trying to catch my breath. "I . . . uh . . . I've been going to step class at the YMCA."

"Impressive," Ruby said, shifting gears and hooking a turn onto the next street. Swinging back to the left, she headed toward Line Avenue on the street parallel to Stephanie's. There, halfway down, sat Scott's Toyota Tundra with the flashy jacked-up wheels and brush guard. The man had no doubt cut through the two dark properties sitting behind Stephanie's house. Neither had a fence, which made it easy to mosey on over to Stephanie's. How horny did a man have to be to sneak through another person's side yard to get a piece?

"There's his truck," I commented as we rolled past.

"So it is." Ruby looked at the truck like she wanted to take a bat to the headlamps. That warmed my heart a little. Or the piece of my heart still hanging around.

She looked over at me. "So?"

"I didn't get the picture, but I nearly got eaten by a Yorkie."

Ruby cast a puzzled glance my way as she pulled out onto Line Avenue.

"Stephanie has a dog." I plopped my foot on the dash and rolled up my yoga-pant leg. No blood, but I'd have a nice bruise just the size of a Yorkie's mouth. I pushed my hood off and grabbed the hem of the hoodie, ripping it over my head. My tank top was soaked in sweat, and several chunks of hair had fallen from my ponytail to cling to my sweaty neck.

"I hope you punted that thing to Albuquerque."

"It was kinda cute . . . if not absolutely vicious," I said, wincing as I probed the bite on my hand.

"I wish you hadn't taken off before I could finish what I was saying."

"Well, I had to do something more than sit on my hands," I said, pulling out a compact mirror from my purse and dabbing at the deeper scratch on my cheek I'd gotten in the bushes. "Do you know how hard it was to do nothing . . . for days?"

"But you don't need to confront him this way. You don't need to show him that kind of crazy."

Okay, so maybe dressing in black, staking out the other woman's house, and trying to get a picture of Scott with her was a few bricks shy of a load, but being proactive made me feel . . . not so much a victim.

Until Julie Van Ness had uttered those horrible words, I'd lived in a bubble of my own design, and by all accounts, it was a very nice bubble filled with good fabrics framing the windows, gas lanterns hanging beside the right address, and a family that looked mighty nice on the Christmas cards I ordered at the local stationery store each year. I had been floating high in that shiny bubble—even higher since I had reopened a new and improved Printemps.

I had felt valued. Loved. Somewhat successful.

But now I was nothing but a husk of the woman I'd been. I'd been robbed of my security, sidelined as a woman, relegated to a leftover . . . and why?

I had no clue.

Sure, at forty-two I fought crow's-feet and cellulite. After giving birth to my daughter, I'd gone from a size 8 to a size 10. Okay, sometimes a size 12 in brands that ran small. But I worked out and tried to avoid french fries. I used so much freaking cream with retinol, it was a wonder my face could curve into a smile. And I got regular pedicures, showered daily, and never farted in front of Scott.

But maybe this wasn't about me. Maybe it was because I wouldn't try the anal beads, whatever the hell those were. A woman had to draw a line sometimes, and shoving things up my bottom was one I wasn't interested in crossing.

"Maybe Stephanie likes anal beads," I muttered.

Ruby hit a pothole. "What the—"

And that's when I felt the car tilt drunkenly with the telltale thump of a flat tire.

"You gotta warn me when you're gonna say things like that," Ruby said, pulling my limping car to the side of the road near a cluster of houses on a dark street.

"Sorry," I said, pulling my phone out of the hoodie I'd dumped on the floorboard. "Just came out."

"Anal beads?" Ruby asked, putting the car in park and turning to me.

"Never mind. Forget I said that," I said, wishing I'd filtered myself with the sex-toy talk. "And I have Triple A."

I clicked the home button on my phone, and my sweaty, pale face emerged on the screen . . . instead of the picture of Scott violating Stephanie on her porch step. Like an idiot, I'd hit the turnaround button and taken a selfie. My eyes were narrow, mouth pressed into a line, determination etched into every feature . . . even though my neck looked suspiciously turkey-like. Perfect selfie of a very pissed, hurt woman. Proof of disaster right in my hot little hand.

Ruby shook her head. "Anal beads . . . good Lord."

CHAPTER FIVE

RUBY

Griffin Moon, my first cousin and a somewhat upstanding member of the Balthazar clan, wasn't the kind of man who made people feel comfortable. I knew this, but I also knew that if I called him, he would come tow Cricket's car and that he would have a gun. Hey, we live in one of the more dangerous cities in Louisiana. And Triple A was probably going to call him anyway. Might as well skip a step.

Griff climbed out of the tow truck looking a bit dangerous himself . . . and miles away from the men who peppered Cricket's land of golf courses and stucco mansions. Griff practiced spitting and scratching himself regularly. Probably simultaneously, too.

Cricket's eyes widened as my cousin approached wearing tight jeans and an equally tight T-shirt. A wicked curved tattoo inched up his neck. Scruffy boots clomped onto the cracked pavement as he eyed the wounded car.

"Nice wheels," he said, by way of greeting.

"Not mine," I said, sliding off the back of the car, where I'd parked my butt while waiting for my cousin, the owner of Blue Moon Towing, to play white knight.

Cricket eyed Griff like she wished she'd insisted on Triple A instead of letting me call in a favor.

"You don't have a spare? How does that happen?" he asked, dark eyes flickering toward Cricket, who immediately frowned.

"Well, that's why we called you," she said, looking annoyed.

I wasn't sure if Cricket was annoyed because Griff was being somewhat condescending, because she actually didn't have a spare, or because she finally had proof of a cheating husband. Probably all three.

"Come on, Griff," I chided, knowing that he sometimes reveled in sitting on his high horse, not that I'd had the occasion to experience this over the past few years. He was almost a decade older than I was, and was known for getting all patriarchal on his younger cousins, especially me, since I was the only female in the wild bunch. Obviously, he also didn't mind extending reprimands toward bouncy, older blondes.

He gave me a flat look. "Y'all wantin' me to tow it, right?"

"Oh, you mean that's what the truck with the hook is for?" Cricket said like a real live smart-ass and not the Cricket who would have normally apologized for not having a spare. Whatever had happened to my boss in the last twenty-four hours was halfway encouraging but mostly unnerving. If she thought I had shown my true colors, she needed to look in the mirror at her own plumage.

Or maybe I needed to look harder at her, too. Women like Cricket seemed so together, so untouched by life's problems. I had thought patterning my life after hers would elevate me and give me more opportunities. But here she sat, as broken as her fancy convertible.

Griff's eyes glittered with annoyance, and he stopped looking friendly . . . which is to say he looked almost the same as he normally did. He'd never been a merry fellow.

Cricket seemed to realize Griff didn't have much of a sense of humor. If anything, my boss could read a room. "I'm kidding. Thank you for coming, Mr.—"

"Moon. But everyone calls me Griff."

"Again, thank you for leaving the comfort of your home, Mr. Moon," she said a little too sweetly.

"Eh, it's not really that comfortable." This time he actually looked at Cricket, perhaps even checking her out, which I found interesting because Griff was a no-nonsense guy, and though Cricket wasn't necessarily frivolous, she was so not his type. But then again, she *was* wearing a thin and somewhat damp tank top and tight yoga pants. And her boobs were about two sizes bigger than mine and pretty dang up there for a woman in her early forties. Griff wasn't the kind who would make a pass at a woman stranded on the side of the road, but he wasn't blind, either.

I made a face at my cousin while he blatantly ignored us and walked around the car, muttering things I probably wouldn't understand and would never need to know about towing cars. I had never cared much for cars, like my boy cousins did. Instead I was content to sketch and help my gran sew projects for the church bazaar.

Cricket watched Griff with equal interest, like she was trying to figure him out. My cousin wasn't unattractive. Quite the opposite—he had girls all over him when he went out to play. It was that big, strong-jawed, bicep thing he had going for him. That, and he rescued cats. Which was weird for someone like him, but girls seemed down for him, if the way he cycled through them was any indication.

Griff came around to the front, stopping beside us. He crossed his steely arms. "I want to reiterate that it's dangerous not to have a spare. Still, in this case it wouldn't matter because the rim is damaged. What did you hit?"

Cricket narrowed her eyes. After her rough night, I worried that she might freak out on my cousin. She seemed to be teetering on the edge of sanity. She *had* snuck into someone's backyard, dressed like a ninja, to get proof of her husband's infidelity.

"I'm the one who was driving, and it was a huge pothole. I didn't see it," I said. Normally, I would have, but Cricket had made that anal-beads comment, and that had fried me. I had never expected to hear those two words coming from her mouth in a million years.

Griff gave me his stern-daddy look just as Cricket held up a hand. "It's fine, Ruby. Let's just let your very judgmental cousin get on back to his not-so-comfortable house, and we'll call Triple A."

"They would just call me back out here. Look, I'll get the car on the roll back. You have someplace you want me to tow it?" Griff studied Cricket, his eyes intense.

Cricket blinked a few times and then sort of deflated. It took me a few seconds to realize why. How was she going to explain this to Scott when he thought she was home eating a late dinner and waiting up for him? I shouldered my way in front of her, looking up at my cousin. "We could just take it to the yard, maybe?"

Griff shrugged.

"What's the yard?" Cricket asked.

"Griff has a locked yard to keep vehicles overnight. It will be safe there." I shot her a purposeful look, one that tried to relay that this would buy her some time. Once Griff took the car, we could figure out how to get her home before Scott found out she wasn't there. Or at least come up with a story to cover for the fact she was tooling around Shreveport late at night in a convertible.

"That's fine. I can also recommend a place where you can get a tire for this model. Won't cost you an arm and a leg like"—his eyes flickered over to Cricket—"other places south of town."

I rolled my eyes and inhaled the cooling Louisiana air, hoping Cricket wouldn't notice the dig at her side of town.

She did.

"That's okay. I can find my own garage. On my own side of town."

He glanced away, but I saw the irritation. "Might take a while to get a setup for a car like this. You can call me tomorrow and let me know what garage is going to charge you double to fix it, and I'll get my guys to take it there."

"Perfect, and perhaps you could give us a ride to a place where we might call an Uber safely?" Cricket managed a smile that was as tight as a bowstring.

Griff made a face. "I'm not a taxi, blondie."

Coming to the rescue, I zeroed a stern gaze on my older cousin. "I know Gran would appreciate you making sure me and *my boss* have a safe location to get an Uber."

Griff may have blanched . . . if a guy with tan skin and scruff on his jaw could grow pale. I knew he wouldn't want me tattling to Gran. And I would if I had to, because he was being a total ass.

"Fine." He turned, walked back to his tow truck, grabbed a pair of gloves, and started flipping some switches. The hydraulic lift began dropping the hook-and-chain thing he'd use to tow Cricket's not-so-nondescript spy car.

"Thanks!" I hollered, turning back to Cricket. "Grab your stuff . . . Austin Powers."

Cricket snorted and then opened the car door to start gathering the empty cup, the crumpled protein-bar package, and the tools of snoopery she'd employed, tossing everything into a monogrammed bag. She moved to the curb and sank down on her haunches, no longer perturbed but more resigned to how effed up our night had gotten.

I grabbed my backpack, realizing that tonight would be a long one because I still had an assignment due before class the next day and needed to study for a quiz. Across the street, a man wearing a faded T-shirt poked his head out his front door. I waved, giving a what-can-you-do shrug. He held up a hand before disappearing inside, closing the scarred door.

Neighborhood watch.

A few kids hung out in a nearby park, and I could hear catcalling, whooping, and the sound of the basketball bouncing on the court. A few cars rolled down Line Avenue, one slowing to investigate the wounded car but zipping off when they realized a tow truck was on the scene.

Griffin moved gracefully for such a hulk, and within a few minutes, the car moved toward his tow truck, a magnet to a pole, pulled steadily onto the platform he'd lowered. I moved to sit beside Cricket, who sat biting her lower lip, deep in thought.

"You know, his moon is all wrong," Cricket finally said.

"What?"

"On the side of his truck. That's a crescent moon, and everyone knows that a blue moon is a full moon. Of course, if he used a full moon, it would look like a circle and not as effective marketing-wise. Still, it's sort of misleading."

I looked at the writing on the side of my cousin's cab under the crescent moon. BLUE MOON TOWING. "I don't know if anyone really knows or cares. I mean, maybe it's ironic."

"Is it?" Cricket asked, looking lost in the space she occupied. I realized this could be a delayed-shock sort of thing. She had just caught her husband with another woman.

Really, this whole misadventure from start to finish had been a mistake, and I had gone along with it because for one thing, she was my boss and I owed her some kind of loyalty. But it was mostly because I felt bad for her. I knew how she felt—used up, tossed aside like a stiff tissue found in the bottom of a forgotten purse. My uncle Ed Earl had done that to me—tricking me into participating in his meth distribution without my knowing. I mean, now I feel stupid for not having seen that his *"Do me a favor when you go into town"* was a way to send his product to his "guys." Yeah, I got busted for being a mule and didn't know the packages of wild game I was taking to donate for "Hunters for the Hungry" were feeding their drug habits. Since it was a third strike and my lawyer was an idiot, I did time for it. The betrayal cut deep, which was why I wasn't talking to my family. Except for Gran. And now Griff, I guess.

But that's how I had gotten myself roped into Cricket's escapade. Because earlier when I'd seen Cricket staring at the yellow roses with such a tragic expression and then saw the fat teardrops drip from her chin, I'd felt moved to do something.

First I had gotten her a sugary coffee drink from Starbucks when I went out to check the PO box, thinking that was at least something, but then she'd up and admitted to me that she thought Scott was cheating. At that moment, white-hot anger seared my soul. And all I could think about was how nice people like Cricket always ended up dealing with jerkoffs like Scott. Yeah, life was unfair, but sometimes that inequity just got to me. So I asked her what she needed me to do, and she had asked if she could pick me up for an assignation that night.

Sure, I was a little suspicious about what that might be, but I hadn't imagined she'd planned surveillance on the girlfriend's house.

Thankfully, she'd brought wine. Good booze was expensive, so I shut up, sipped the more-than-ten-dollar bottle of wine, and rational-ized that it was harmless.

Of course, I hadn't expected her to bolt and trespass. Such irrational behavior. But then again, Cricket couldn't be logical about her husband doing the nasty with another woman. Time to get a little tough with her. After all, Cricket needed to hire an investigator, talk to an attorney, and make a plan. Harebrained schemes like breaking into someone's backyard and snapping pictures were how a person ended up in jail. Then Scott really would have all the cards.

And now my big mouth had landed me back on Griff's radar and with less time to study for my microeconomics quiz. All because I couldn't help myself from wanting to right wrongs, fight injustices, and make bad guys pay. This was coded into my genetics. After all, my great-grandfather had killed the guy in that knife fight only after walking by and seeing the dude beating the crap out of his wife. Not his circus. Not his monkeys. And yet he waded into the fray like the ringmaster.

Cricket's phone dinged, and she pulled it out of her bag. I slid a glance down, doing some spying of my own.

Where are you?

"Damn it," Cricket groaned under her breath. She looked up at the stars winking against the black velvet above us and exhaled. "Scott beat me home."

"So? Just tell him you went out."

"To where?"

"The store or something. Or you can say I called you and needed something. Um, that I left the store unlocked."

"No, I'm not throwing you under the bus."

I snorted. "Who cares? Cover your own ass. I know how to take care of mine."

She looked at me for a few seconds before she typed, Went to Ruby's house to help her with some stuff for the shop. Got a flat tire on the Spider. Getting towed now.

That made sense. Maybe.

"Better to stick as close to the truth as possible," she said.

Her phone vibrated. Ruby? The gal that works for you?

She typed Yes.

Okay. I was worried.

"Fuck you," Cricket said.

Griffin glanced over his shoulder, cocking an eyebrow.

Cricket's cheeks pinked even in the dimness. "Oh. I said that out loud."

That made me laugh. Griff narrowed his eyes at us sitting there like two birds on a wire, studying her phone. "She's had a bad night."

"I sense that," my cousin called back, going back to work.

Still staring at her phone, Cricket said, "I don't care that I said it out loud. I wish I could punch Scott. Or knee him in the cods. Or both." Another ping. We both looked at her phone.

Where's Julia Kate?

Cricket narrowed her eyes as her fingers flew over the phone keyboard. **At the Brauds'. Be home in half an hour.**

I looked up as the sound of the lift stopped. Cricket's car now sat piggyback on the tow truck.

Another ping.

Going to bed. Long day. Tired.

"I bet. Screwing someone half your age has to be hard for a forty-something sleazeball with a mild case of ED." Cricket clicked her phone off and tossed it back in the bag.

"He has ED?" That would be justice, at least.

"Maybe it's only with me," Cricket said, sounding sad.

I didn't know what to say. Sex was something I rarely discussed with anyone. Truthfully, though many might look at me and my past and assume I'd had much experience in that department, I hadn't. My first love had been Dakota Roberts, and we'd taken that plunge together when I was sixteen, sweetly erasing my virgin status. After he'd broken up with me, I went out with a few other guys, and their awkward and not-so-attentive lovemaking had traumatized me enough to keep me from jumping into something physical without at least having some investment beforehand. I was the wrong person to have a conversation about sex with. For real. "I'm sure that's not true."

Cricket's face reflected absolute misery. "Somehow this hurts more than I thought. I'm not a frigid prude or anything, but the older I get, the less I want him touching me, taking up my time. God, some of this is my fault. I just got used to doing this or that for seven point five minutes before he returned the favor for less than three. He hasn't even asked for sex for, like, months. Not since we got back from the Cayman Islands. Honestly, I've just felt *relieved.*"

What to say to that? I glanced over at Griffin, hoping he couldn't hear this vulnerable admission, and then did my best to make my boss feel better about her sex life, or rather lack of one. "Well, you've been married for a while. Everyone settles into knowing what their partner likes, and, um, when you get older, you lose some of that initial passion. I think."

"He wanted to experiment with sex toys, and I shot him down without even considering it. I didn't want to do freaky stuff."

Griff may have had an ear cocked in our direction, because he darted a glance our way before catching himself and going right back to unhooking chains.

"Yeah," I breathed. I *really* didn't know what to say to that.

"And when I was, like, 'No way,' he said he was joking. But maybe turning him down drove him to Stephanie. Maybe this is my fault. Maybe I should have tried the anal beads or the other things he showed me on that website."

"I would have turned that down, too, Cricket. I wouldn't do anything I wasn't comfortable with. None of this is your fault. Not wanting to push the boundaries of, uh, what you do in the bedroom is not justification for cheating."

She looked up at me with tears sheening her eyes. "You would have said no, too?"

"Yeah, that would have been a hard pass."

A sigh of relief escaped her as she looked over at Griff, who had turned toward us.

"Okay, Mrs. Crosby," Griffin said, walking over and readjusting the cap on his head. "Got you loaded. You gals ready? Or do you need more time to . . ."

His words faded as if he wasn't sure how to proceed.

Cricket's eyes widened, and I felt protective of her. I hoped like hell Griff hadn't heard our conversation, but the slight softening of his expression and the solicitous query made me suspect he had. Griff wasn't a bad guy. He'd probably maim Scott if I asked him to.

I looked at Cricket. "Ready?"

She pushed off the curb. "Sure. Thank you, Mr. Moon."

Griff didn't say anything more. Just watched as we gracelessly climbed into the cab of his truck. The cab smelled like coffee and—I squinted at the green-tree freshener dangling from the rearview mirror—pine. A stack of bills bundled with a rubber band sat on the dash, and another ball cap with the Blue Moon logo sat beside it. The cab was clean, like I knew it would be. Griff had always been disciplined. That's why he ran a successful business.

He swung into his seat and shut the door, giving us automatic intimacy.

"We good?" Griffin asked.

Cricket's phone trilled.

She sighed when she looked at the screen. Punching the ANSWER button, she tiredly said, "What? I said I'd be home."

Because we were in close quarters, I heard Scott say, "Did you pick up my dry cleaning?"

I felt her answer before she said it. "No."

"I told you I need a white button-down for tomorrow. There are none in my closet. You said you would get them."

"I forgot," Cricket said.

"Damn it, Crick. When you say you're going to do something, you should do it. Now I'm screwed. What's been going on with you? You never forget stuff like this. I'm sure you saw that *I* didn't forget the anniversary of our first date. You got the flowers, right?"

"Sorry about the shirts. Wear the blue one. I'll pick the dry cleaning up tomorrow." Cricket pressed the END button before her husband could respond. She lowered the phone and screwed her eyes closed. "Sorry about that."

Thick discomfort pressed on all of us. No one liked to be plunged into someone's jacked-up life uninvited. And yet here I sat, ass deep in my boss's personal business.

Griffin pulled away from the curb while simultaneously turning on the radio. Van Halen roared from the speakers, instructing us to "Jump."

Too damned late.

"I hate him. I really hate him." Cricket's words scattered like buck-shot, powerful and angry.

Griff leaned forward to look across me at my boss, who had pressed her hands into her eyes. "You want me to kill him for you?"

Cricket dropped her hands and looked over at Griff. "You do that sort of thing?"

Griff grinned. I had only seen him do that maybe four times in my life.

"He doesn't kill people," I clarified just in case Cricket thought my cousin was serious.

"I know," Cricket said with a slight smile. "Besides, I don't want Scott to die until I make him pay."

Griffin pulled through a Family Dollar parking lot, looping around and pointing his tow truck north. "That's the spirit, sunshine."

CHAPTER SIX

CRICKET

A week later

I smiled at Ling Stewart as I handed a slice of pizza to a kid who had the biggest set of braces I had ever seen. Or maybe it was merely that he was small. Junior high kids were odd. Some of the girls looked like twenty-two-year-old bombshells, but the boys in the same class often resembled babies with their round faces. Or perhaps puberty hadn't yet hit, based on how this kid looked.

"Something wrong, Cricket?" Ling asked, passing the same boy a bottled water, side-eyeing me with concern. I guess I hadn't really said much since we'd started passing out rewards to all the honor students. Sometimes I wished we could give the pizza to the kids who didn't do so hot on the nine weeks' report cards. Some of them had bigger fish to fry . . . and didn't have a mama who would write the paper for them.

"I'm fine," I replied.

"You seem tired."

"No. I'm fine." I wondered if my undereye cream had failed me. *Damn it.* The Facebook advertisement had promised me I would look ten years younger and never again have unsightly smudges beneath my baby blues. I had ordered the product one of the foggy evenings when I had been sitting on the couch nursing my third glass of chardonnay. I also now owned the world's softest hoodie, some deodorant that you could use everywhere on your body, and a 3D puzzle of the Tower of London. Seemed grief and wine made me trigger happy. Scott made a smart-aleck comment about the Amazon boxes on the porch and how I must be on my period when I bit his head off for saying something about my shopping spree.

As if the man would even know when my period was.

"Hmm." Ling lifted a thin shoulder before shooting a quelling look toward her son, who was messing around with his friends, being a little irreverent for an academic scholar.

Yeah, so I had been wearing nothing but my pajamas for a week. My initial anger and determination had fizzled into something crushing that I had no control over. Luckily, Ruby and Jade—as valuable as their names—were capable of running the store through the week. Ruby seemed to understand that I needed space, though every time I spoke with her, I could sense she wanted to say more, wanted to tell me to snap out of it. Still, she'd given me breathing room on this whole cheating debacle. But that morning I had scraped myself off the couch, showered, and put on a bra so I could come to the middle school and hand out pizza to honor students. This was their reward for doing everything right. And *my* reward for doing everything right was a divorce staring me in the face.

Yippee.

"Cricket?" Ling queried when I went radio silent for too long.

"Seriously. I'm fine." Ling and I had never been super close friends, but we drifted toward each other at every PTA event. Her son had started preschool with Julia Kate, and they'd tracked at the same magnet schools, sometimes in the same class, other times not. But we liked each other and had done mama wine events or charity shopping gigs together.

She knew me well enough to know that I was upset. So I needed a fib. "I'm just dealing with my mother. You know how Marguerite is."

"She's a piece of work."

See? Everyone knew that about my mama.

"Yeah. She's on me about what I'm wearing to Gritz and Glitz and about sending Julia Kate to Camp Winnetonka for six weeks this summer. I'm just not willing to have my child gone for so long."

"I understand," Ling said, swiping a towel over the table. "Darren wanted Mitchell to go to chess camp and programming camp back-to-back. That child can't handle being away from home for three weeks. Of course, Mitch would kill me for saying so to a friend's mom. But he gets super homesick. And Gritz and Glitz? I'm so not going this year. I can't stand toddling around in high heels chatting with people I don't like. You're a better woman than I am."

Yeah, not so much. I didn't like sipping bad liquor and talking about who slept with whom, either, especially since I knew I was now one of the *poor clueless women*. But Scott went to every charity and social event he could, hobnobbing with potential customers and drumming up business for Caddo Bank, and I had always been his partner, dressing tastefully, smiling charmingly, and doing my best to win him clients. I said the right things, sucked up to people who could make our 401(k) bigger, and played the stupid game. Scott and I were a team. Emphasis on *were*.

Because our dynamic duo had been split the moment I heard "cherry lube" come out of his mouth. No doubt about that.

Now I just had to figure out how to finish it. And that concept was so overwhelming that I shut down every time I thought about attorneys, divorce, and Julia Kate in therapy blaming her parents for her drug addiction or failed relationships.

I knew my life was changing, but I couldn't embrace it.

I wanted a do-over. On exactly what, I wasn't sure. But I didn't want to be where I was now.

"I'm on the silent-auction planning committee, so I sort of have to go." I conceded this with a beleaguered sigh. So she would know that's what was bugging me. And not the fact that my whole world was upside-down.

"Guess you do." Ling wrinkled her nose before casting another glance toward her only child.

"So, Ling, I need some advice. My grandmother gave me a classic car—a Spider Veloce—and I took it out last week to run the engine. Short story is I hit one of our infamous potholes and now I need a new tire. And a rim thingy. So do you know who works on older foreign cars?"

Ling stared out into the distance, her dark eyes unblinking. Like a prophet about to lay something down. "Take it to Roscoe's Garage over on Seventieth. They're the best. Tell them that Ling Stewart sent you."

Ling's husband owned the local BMW dealership, and the woman prided herself on knowing who to use for anything having to do with vehicles. In fact, Ling knew people who did all sorts of things—monograms, upholstery, and the best Botox for the cheapest price. The woman was a font of information times ten, which meant she would also know who might help me with my other problem.

"Cool. Oh, and, um, so while I'm getting recommendations, I have a friend—no one you know—who's looking for a private investigator for some things that happened with her elderly parents. She wants someone discreet but someone who is very good at his or her job. Any clue? I mean, she asked me, and I really have no idea about that sort of thing."

"A private investigator?"

Hearing Ling say that out loud sounded so tawdry. "Well, yeah, I guess. She doesn't know if there's something going on and doesn't want to make waves in the extended family . . . at least not until she's sure whatever's happening is criminal."

Ling handed bottles to the two kids who ran up, hands out. A chorus of thank-yous erupted before she turned to me. I folded the empty pizza box closed and set it under the table, hoping that she didn't see through my lie. My scenario sounded legit. But maybe Ling knew about Scott. I hoped she didn't. It would be disappointing if she did and hadn't told me.

"I can ask Darren. He might know. Sometimes they have to repo cars and use private eyes." Ling tilted her head and eyeballed me.

I tried not to squirm. "That would be awesome."

She pulled her phone from the back pocket of her skinny jeans. "Let me text him. He's probably playing online games in his office, anyway."

"Thanks." I started breaking down the pizza boxes, noting a few feral-looking boys lurking nearby. We were supposed to give them only two pieces, but we always had leftovers, and thirteen-year-old boys tended to be wolfish when it came to pizza. "Should I—"

"Open that gate? Um, no. If you give one an extra slice, you will have to give them all an extra slice. Plus, I told Mrs. Overstreet we'd put the leftovers in the teachers' lounge. You know how teachers are about leftovers."

I managed a hollow laugh. "Well, she better get there before Coach Fred."

Ling flashed a grin because the portly gym coach was well known for wiping out treats before the other teachers were even aware there were goodies in the lounge. But then again, all is fair in love, war, and food in the teachers' lounge.

I shot an apologetic look at the lingering boys and started stacking the boxes. They vamoosed away from the parents, scattering like wild birds to clump beneath the oak trees on the grounds. No junior high kids wanted to be around their parents. Case in point, Julia Kate stood chatting with her friends, sneakily pulling her phone out and checking God only knows what. My daughter flipped her hair over one shoulder and glanced in my direction. I gave her a half smile, and she quickly looked away.

"Okay, so Darren said there's a guy who used to work for the sheriff's department but now works repo and private investigations. He's good. I'll send you his contact information."

"Thanks. This will really help her. She's pretty distraught."

Ling clicked on her phone, and I heard the resulting ping. "Okay, I'm taking this ice chest back to the gym. Why don't you take those to the teachers' lounge, and then we can come back and help clean up."

Thirty minutes later I climbed into the warmth of my van's interior. The day had been a bit breezy, and my well-loved Town & Country felt like a piece of home. Julia Kate was riding car pool with one of her soccer teammates so I could run up to Printemps if I wanted to check on things.

But I didn't.

I just wanted to sit here in this unknown neighborhood outside of the school, soaking in the sun and pretending everything in my world was okay. What would be wrong with that?

Except eventually I would need a bathroom, some sustenance, and to pay my quarterly taxes, which were due. So living in my van wasn't going to work out, after all.

And it was beyond time to shake the blues away and roll up my sleeves.

I made myself pull out my phone and open Safari. I needed an attorney, and I needed one who didn't know Scott, which would be harder than most would think. Everyone knew Scott because he made sure they did. He schmoozed his way into charity boards, political fundraisers, and business deals. We rarely went to dinner or the movies without someone stopping to chat with my husband. So I needed a woman. A sharky, nail-his-balls-to-the-wall female attorney.

Asking that of Ling would be too obvious, so this would be up to me.

I typed in FEMALE ATTORNEY SHREVEPORT.

A bunch of male names popped up. Of course they did. And these were all guys that I knew. No, thank you.

So I clicked the first female name that I saw. Jacqueline Morsett.

After looking at her website and her pedigree (impressive) and reading reviews on several sites, I dialed the number.

"Morsett and Vickery. This is Samantha. Can I help you?"

I could hardly get the words out.

I want a divorce.

"Hello?" Samantha asked again.

"Um, yes. Hi. I'm calling to maybe set up an appointment with Ms. Morsett."

"Sure. Are you already a client?"

"No. Um, I'm new. I'm actually looking for an attorney, and I wanted someone who was, well, a woman." Was I supposed to admit that I wanted a female to handle my case? Was that reverse sexism? Did I care?

"Divorce?" Samantha asked.

"Yeah."

"I get it. Jackie was the attorney for mine. That's how I ended up working for her. And it's okay to want a woman. I could kind of hear that in your voice." Samantha sounded warm. Friendly. Like divorce was no big deal.

"Oh, okay."

"Jackie loves to talk face-to-face with potential clients. She's super personal like that, but unfortunately, she's out for a deposition. So what I'll do is get your name and your number, and once I talk to her, we'll set up a time for you to chat. She likes to meet clients before she takes them on."

If I gave my name and number, it would be real. An attorney was going to call me. I was going to meet with her. Wheels would creakily move forward. Fear seized me, but I shook it off like a bad chill. I couldn't hide from this. Scott had been cheating on me, and I wasn't in love with him enough to save the marriage, no matter how painful divorce would be. "Um, okay. My name is . . . Catherine Crosby. Catherine with a C."

"Okay, Catherine. Give me your number and a good time to call, and Jackie will be in touch. May take her a day or two. Is that okay?"

"Sure."

One minute later, I hung up. Then, since I had already pulled the trigger on a divorce attorney, I clicked on the phone number Ling had given me, my heart beating in my ears.

I was doing it.

Seizing my own life by the horns and steering it where it needed to go . . . even if it was really smelly and quite a struggle.

The phone rang and was answered. "Patrick Vitt."

No *Can I help you?* or delivering his title. Just a straightforward kind of guy.

"Hi, my name is Catherine Crosby, and I'm interested in hiring you for some work."

Five minutes later, I had a link for a form I would fill out detailing what I needed from my new PI guy. As soon as I filled out the form, signed an agreement for services, and sent a deposit, Pat Vitt, former investigator with the Caddo Sheriff's Department and former head of Lucky Diamond Casino security, would start getting the goods on Scott.

Rubbing my fingers against my eyes, I released a heavy but determined sigh. I'd pressed the launch button and my course was set. This missile would hit my marriage and blow my sanity to smithereens. But after the dust settled, I would find a new place for myself. A place where I could grow and hopefully thrive.

This was my wish.

That I would not just let life happen to me but instead direct my life toward something better.

Looking into the mirror, I saw the resolution and sadness in my eyes. I flipped the sun visor up, started the van, and drove home.

Twenty minutes later, I pulled a stick of butter out of the fridge to bring it to room temperature so I could make a pound cake for my neighbor who'd had a bunion removed. Nothing made a person forget she'd lost half her foot like cake, right?

The back door opened, startling me, and in walked Scott. I glanced at the clock. Home at four thirty?

"Hey, sweetheart," Scott said, dumping all his junk onto the counter. Keys clanked, papers wafted, mail spilled. I tried not to frown. "You finally got dressed. Good girl."

I rolled my eyes even though he couldn't see them.

"So how was your day?" he asked.

Fabulous. I hired a divorce attorney and a private investigator to remove your testicles from your person and place them in the palm of my hand. "Oh, it was fine. I went to West Highland Middle School to pass out pizza to the honor-roll kids."

Scott went to the pantry and pulled out pita chips. Funny how annoying all that crunching was when you were falling out of love with someone. I was pretty sure that's what I was doing. I'd cried my tears, and now I was in the process of letting go, distancing myself so I could protect myself. Hey, I had taken psychology in college.

He stood over me as I measured out flour, crunching and dropping crumbs on the floor. "Always at that school, aren't you? They should give you an award or something."

I rolled down the top of the flour bag and placed it in the storage container, sealing it against pestilence and any ill will that might befall it in my pantry. "Yeah. Sure. I'd have to arm wrestle all the other helicopter moms to get it. So what are you doing home early?"

He did some more of the annoying smacking thing, the bag crinkling each time he fished out a chip. "I had a meeting in Natchitoches that finished early. Since I gotta take JK to tennis clinic after soccer, I thought I would come home and have an early dinner with my girl."

I blinked.

His girl?

"Well, that's a nice thought, but I wasn't planning on cooking tonight," I said.

He crackled the bag some more. So irritating. "Thought we'd grab a quick bite at El Verde before I had to go. Just catch up. Spend some time together." He wrapped an arm around my waist and pulled me to him, dropping a kiss onto my neck.

My first inclination was to lean into him. This was muscle memory craving the intimacy that I always longed for. That sweetness that had once risen between us, the feel of his skin, his lips on my pulse point, the comfort of his body against mine. But then as soon as my neurons fired that way, my brain overrode the impulse. I used my hip to send a message. "I can't. I have to bake this cake for Janice. She had a bunion removed today."

"Seriously? Your husband wants to take you out on the town and you're more interested in baking Janice a cake. Have you seen her ass lately? You can skip the cake."

Yeah, falling out of love was like cleaning a window you didn't know was dirty. Suddenly things were so clear.

"Don't be mean. And an early dinner at El Verde is hardly 'out on the town.'"

Scott popped me on my own expanding bottom. "Look, I'll grab a shower, you put the cake in, and we'll go to dinner when it's out of the oven. Or we can stay in and have sex on the kitchen floor. Your choice."

I whipped my head around and stared at him. He arched a brow like he knew the answer. Hey, I loved the chips and guac at El Verde. I opened the oven and shoved the Bundt pan inside. "Dinner out sounds fine."

"Ha, I already knew the answer." Scott snorted good-naturedly and moved away from me, and for a teeny, tiny moment I felt a flash of guilt for pushing him away. This was why he'd taken up with the tennis slut. Even though I knew women weren't supposed to call other women sluts because there was no shame in liking sex. But there *was* shame in liking sex with another woman's husband. So . . .

"The cake will take forty-five minutes. That okay?"

"Sure. I have some calls to make," Scott said, emerging from the pantry, crumbs dotting his sports coat. His hair had thinned on top, and the lines around his eyes were prominent, but he still looked like a well-aged Hollywood type with his flashing grin, tanned expanse of jaw, and way of carrying himself. Still handsome. Still so familiar. My heart hurt when I thought about what he'd done. How he'd ended us.

Scott was so different from the man who kept crowding my thoughts more than I wanted to admit. And I don't know why I kept thinking about Griffin Moon. It was weird, really. Because on first sight, Ruby's cousin had irritated the crap out of me with his whole judgy blue-collar thing. But then when we were sitting in the cab of the truck, Ruby in the middle of us like a referee, and me on the other side, still grappling with what I had discovered, Griffin had looked over at me. At that moment, I believed that if I had pushed hard enough, he would have driven his surprisingly tidy wrecker to my address and whipped my cheating husband's butt.

The image of the rough-around-the-edges tow truck guy pounding my preppy banker husband appealed to me more than it should. Griffin had tangled hair, scruff on his chin, and tats. He wasn't my type on a good day. And definitely not on the night I had been slapped with proof that Scott was an adulterer. Yeah, my "type" had been dumping cherry lube in forbidden places on another woman, so what did I really know about men?

Men. H'uh. What are they good for?

Absolutely nothin'. Uh-huh, uh-huh.

I bopped my head to the unsung song with the wrong lyrics as I thought about another man when I still had the problem of the current one. Still, something about the way Griffin Moon had regarded me had stuck with me. Maybe it was because I imagined he'd peeled away my facade . . . that somehow he could see the shattered woman under the bravado. It wasn't a "like recognized like" sort of thing. No, that man hadn't seemed vulnerable at all. But he'd probably seen his fair share of beaten-down people . . . and perhaps he assumed I was one.

And that stuck in my craw.

Because I didn't want to be that woman.

I'd had my moments of scrabbling around on the ground looking for the pieces of myself over the past week, but I was done. Paper people are consumed by fire, dissipating into ash before scattering into the wind, never to be whole again. But others, those made of steel, used the fire to forge an edge. The heat hardened them, creating razor determination, melding them into something stronger.

My anger would create steel. So there was no need for anyone to cast sympathetic glances my way.

My phone chirruped, and I glanced down at a text.

Ruby.

How are you?

I set the timer and picked up my phone.

I'm good.

Little dots appeared.

Good.

I smiled at my phone, feeling gratified with where I was—I was beginning to accept and pivot. Then I glanced at the doorway where Scott had disappeared, picked up the phone, and clicked on the link Patrick Vitt, PI, had sent me. I had forty-five minutes until I had to go fake my date with my husband. Might as well fill out the agreement to engage Vitt's services. It was time to catch the cheaterpants on camera.

Side-eyeing the cake that was starting to rise in the oven, I smiled again. Maybe I would bake Scott a cake on the day we divorced . . .

Nah. He wasn't worth a Bundt.

CHAPTER SEVEN

RUBY

I stared hard at the door of my cousin's private investigation office before I knocked. For the past few years I had walled out my family, pretending I was an orphan or maybe someone who'd been knocked in the head and had forgotten who she was.

Because I had *wanted* to forget who I was.

The Balthazars had a reputation, even if some of them, like Griff, had managed to escape the shit stain of our birth. This particular cousin, Josh "Juke" Jefferson, had done okay for himself; well, for a while, anyway. That was because he'd married up to a woman who toed the line and made sure he did, too. He'd gone to the police academy as if to thumb his nose at the criminals in his family and had lived a good, upstanding life down south until his wife had gotten cancer and had the gall to die. That had been three years ago, and Juke had drowned his sorrows for months, eventually crashing his cruiser and getting dismissed from the force. Without a job or purpose for living, he'd headed home and hung out a shingle in north Shreveport, vowing to catch secretaries who stole petty cash and deadbeat dads who didn't pay child support. So far he'd managed to complete a few dozen cases and drink his liver into early retirement. My gran had relayed the fact that Juke had been told by his doctor to quit the hooch or die.

I hoped he'd chosen the former, but I was fairly certain meeting his maker didn't scare Juke.

So even though I'd promised I was done with being a Balthazar, here I stood, prepared to bring another back into my life. All thanks to Cricket.

Thing was, my boss needed to get her shit together, and if that meant asking another one of my cousins for help, then I would do it. Because running a business wasn't as fun as it seemed. And I had been captaining the ship that was Printemps for far too long. Okay, it was only a little over a week, give or take a few hours, but I didn't like haggling with old birds who saw imaginary scratches on their console tables, and I hated dealing with jerks in France who delayed shipments for a third time.

Stupid Gaston.

His name wasn't Gaston, but the jerkface acted like that fictional blowhard, so that's what I called him. Admittedly, I also had an issue with pronouncing his real name.

I turned the knob on the battle-scarred door and tried not to glance yet again at the sign for the bar below Juke's office. The Bullpen had only been open for six months, but it seemed to be doing a steady business. And I couldn't stop darting glances at it. Just in case another piece of my past popped out to toss a bag into the dumpster or something. I was certain that the place was successful because half the crowd came to see Dak's dimples. The other half came to talk about his time as an all-American catcher for the LSU Tigers. That he'd played with the Yankees wasn't nearly as interesting as reliving his home run in Omaha the year the Tigers won the championship. This was Louisiana. LSU reigned supreme.

The doorknob to Juke's office was sticky, and the dank air that wafted out as I entered North Star Investigations made me wrinkle my nose. I had to focus on the task at hand—getting Cricket someone who could prove Scott was a dirtbag. Surely Juke could manage snapping a few incriminating pictures. Tangible proof of adultery. Then Cricket would be golden for nailing his cheating ass.

Therefore, I could not be distracted by the guy I had once loved who was probably downstairs slinging beers.

Focus.

"Hello?" I called out. There was no one at the desk occupying the middle of the office. If it was a desk. Stacks of scattered papers, a bulky computer, and a collection of coffee mugs pointed in that direction, but I couldn't actually see the desktop. In the wastebasket next to the scarred wooden leg, I could glimpse what I assumed were empty whiskey bottles.

Not a good sign.

"Juke?" I called, eyeing the only other door, which was closed.

A resulting crash and several colorful curse words came from within. After a few seconds of thumping, a toilet flushed. Five seconds later, my cousin Juke stumbled out, looking like something that slept in an alley.

I could see he didn't recognize me, but why would he? The last time I'd seen him had been at Loralee's funeral, and he had looked totally out of it. And since I had been fresh out of Long Pines Women's Correctional with shorter hair and eyes that had seen too much, I didn't expect him to clue in that I was his baby cousin.

He narrowed glassy eyes at me. "Help ya?"

"Maybe."

Juke shuffled over to a creaky rolling desk chair and sort of fell into it. He huffed as he sat, deflated like a week-old Mylar balloon. He motioned toward one of the two wooden chairs, likely swiped from my pawpaw's shed, and said, "Okay, whatcha got?"

"Well, first. I'm Ruby."

"Yeah. So?" He tented his hands across his expanding waistline. Juke was in his forties. I think. And he totally didn't know who I was.

Which could work to my advantage. I could keep the distance between me and my family. But Griff's towing business was pretty much next door. Might as well be up front.

"I'm your cousin," I clarified, sitting gingerly on the chair. "Leta and Bobby's daughter."

Juke made a squinty face. "Ruby? I thought you were, like, twelve years old."

"Um, no. Let me refresh your memory. You were at my trial. Ed Earl. The meth. Me getting time for distribution."

His vision cleared. "Oh. Yeah. You totally got hosed, but you had a shit lawyer. Eunice should have sprung for Morris Gatlin. You wouldn't have served time. So what you doin' here? I could have sworn Eunice told Mama you'd changed your name and turned your back on the fam."

Eunice was my grandmother, and she was fairly close to Juke's mother, my great-aunt Jean. Juke's mama wasn't the sharpest tool in the shed, but she made a mean buttermilk pie and knew how to get any stain out of any fabric. She liked to knit and had taught me how to make scarves when I was ten years old. Between Jean and my gran, I had learned tatting, embroidery, and how to sew pleats, hems, and zippers into the dresses I made. "I did. Change my name, that is. And I *have* been avoiding the family, everyone except Gran. Betrayal makes the heart grow brittle."

"Eh," Juke said, nodding as if he understood. "So . . . ?"

"My boss needs an investigator."

"So why isn't *she* here instead?"

Good question.

I cleared my throat. "Because she's too busy crying buckets and pretending her husband isn't boinking her daughter's tennis coach."

"Man, it's always the tennis coach." Juke said it like it was a fact.

"Is it?" I asked.

He shrugged. "Or the babysitter, administrative assistant, or maybe a nurse. You know, someone like that."

I wasn't sure what he was getting at, but I didn't really want to analyze. I needed to get Cricket off her couch and back in the shop. I had cobbled together a list of potential lawyers, and noticeably absent was my former court-appointed attorney who basically did very little to help me and actually said my name wrong at the hearing. Even the judge had looked disappointed in him. But Cricket had money, so she didn't have to bend over and catch hold of her ankles on this divorce. Slimy Scott wouldn't even know what hit him, and I took a bit too much pleasure in the visualization of his smug face crashing when he was handed proof along with the petition for divorce. "Yeah, so I wasn't sure if you did that sort of thing."

This was why I had come in person—to put eyes on Juke. Had nothing to do with my very slight interest in the bar downstairs owned by my ex-boyfriend.

"Spy on cheaters? Sure I do. All part of the territory when you're a private investigator. I can get pictures and even get access to his bank accounts with the help of an attorney. She got an attorney yet?"

"I don't think so, though I've made her a short list."

"Well, usually an attorney recommends me, but business has been slow lately, so I've got the time." He riffled around on his desk, scattering papers and causing pens to fall onto the floor. "I've got a form you can take. Just a basic agreement for my services and junk. If I can just . . ." A few slurred curse words escaped him.

I watched him struggle to find what he looked for, remembering how happy he had once been and wishing Loralee had survived. Here was evidence that her breast cancer had taken two lives. But Juke still had a chance if he could get his act together and get sober.

"It's fine. You can just email it to me," I said, rising and retrieving a few pieces of paper and one of the pens. Doubt knocked on the door of my sensibilities. Juke might not be able to do much of anything to help Cricket in the shape he was in. "You know, it's okay if you can't do it."

Juke stilled, pressing his large hands on the desk. "I can do it."

"I'm not sure. You seem a little drunk." No one had ever needed to baby a Balthazar anyway.

"Fuck you."

I straightened and started toward the door. "Yeah, that's what I needed to know."

"Shit. No, wait." Juke stood, throwing up his hands. "Stop, Roo. I'm sorry. I . . . I just lost a client today, and I got bills threatening to drown me. I'm only able to keep this place because Dak's a solid guy. I could use this case. I need the money."

His admission slowed my advance toward his door. My family didn't lift a pant leg to show their Achilles. Ever. Secrets were like fleas in my family, and no one bothered to set off a bug bomb. Which is why no one had warned me that Ed Earl was transporting meth in plastic-wrapped frozen feral hog parts.

So Juke admitting to me that he needed the case gave me pause. And he'd used my childhood nickname.

"Okay. I don't even know if Cricket will hire an attorney right now, but I'll take your card." I reached over and grabbed one from the holder on the table near the door. Next to it was a dead plant. The whole place was sad, really.

"I'll do a good job, and I'm not a drunk." Juke sounded like he believed himself. Maybe he did. But I had lived in lockup with a lot of people who lied to themselves. My bullshit meter was on point.

"Well, Cousin, you look drunk. You smell drunk. This place is like a lair for a drunk." Swiping my hand across the cluttered, stale space, I lifted an eyebrow, daring him to tell me differently.

Juke spread his hands. "You're right. I need to get my shit together."

I said nothing, just looked around. The office wasn't big, so the other unseen half of the second story must be another office. A private investigator likely didn't need a ton of room. The carpet looked as if it might have been nice sometime back in the 1980s, the walls were wood paneled, and the computer wasn't exactly a sleek Mac but was probably functional. Juke had once worked in cyberinvestigations and knew his way around a hard drive. A shelf held cameras and other things that could be used in surveillance. Maybe. Thing was, it would be a waste of talent for Juke to just give up and become a total drunk. "It's the end of the day. Why don't we grab a drink? Um, like some coffee or something? We can talk about the case and how you've been."

"Coffee?" Juke's face sagged into a grimace. "I guess I could go for a cup. Or a beer."

I shot him a look.

"A cup of joe it is," he said.

Honestly, I could have gone for a beer myself, and I hardly drank anything but an occasional glass of wine. I had made an exception the night I did the stakeout with Cricket, but only because I couldn't afford the kind of wine she'd probably casually taken from her collection. Hey, I'm an opportunist. "Where's the closest diner?"

"We can go downstairs. Dak always has coffee."

I wasn't prepared for that. "Um, you want me to take you to a *bar* to get sober?"

"Dak makes a helluva cup of coffee." Juke shoved the form he'd finally located at me as he passed by.

I did not want to see Dak. Not on a good day. Definitely not on a day when I wore my least favorite pair of jeans and had a grape-jelly smudge on the cuff of the vintage blouse I had found in Cricket's castoff bin. I'm not sure why she'd tossed it. Probably didn't feel vintage enough for her couture corner. The avocado-green silk was by some designer I had never heard of and hung beautifully, so there was that, but my hair hadn't been washed that morning. Settling on applying a few bobby pins, I had done a twist thing that was likely super sad at present. I pressed my naked lips together. "Um, I—"

But it was too late, because someone who had obviously had—I eyed the top bottle in the wastebasket—too much Wild Turkey was already out the door.

I smoothed my hair, shoved the form for Cricket into my canvas bag, and followed my cousin down the metal steps. At the bottom, Juke pivoted toward the back door.

"Shouldn't we go around?" I asked, not wanting to go through the rear of the bar.

"Nah, Dak don't care." Juke pushed into the freshly painted back door, nearly mowing someone over. "Hey, Shirl."

"Dak said he's not serving you, Juke, so turn back around and get on up to your place," the woman said, pulling something from the fryer and jerking her head toward a guy wearing a cook's cap. Like she might need backup.

"Just coffee. I swear. This is my cousin Ruby. She's in charge of sobering me up." Juke jerked a thumb back at me. I gave a weak smile and wave.

Shirley narrowed her eyes. "Okay. But I'm watching you."

Juke made a face and headed for the swinging metal door. "Bring us two coffees when you gotta minute, Shirl. I'll tip you good."

Shirley looked at me like she expected me to say something. I had nothing. So I just followed my cousin into the bar, praying that Dak wasn't there.

But he was.

Right behind the bar to our left, wearing a soft T-shirt, a bar towel slung over his shoulder, and jeans that clung to his muscled thighs.

Damn it. Why hadn't he lost his hair and gained thirty pounds?

And to rub salt in the wound was the fact that he was still gorgeous. His adorable dimples were doing their thing as he laughed with a group of guys nursing beers at the bar. Two televisions behind him showed baseball games. And the variety of liquor reflected in the mirror gave any upscale bar a run for its money. Dak caught Juke out of the corner of his eye, his gaze narrowing slightly, telling me that my ex had had enough of my cousin.

But then his gaze found me.

He stilled, holding a glass in one hand, a bottle of Captain Morgan in the other.

"Hey-ya, Dak," Juke called, bellying up to the bar.

"No happy hour for you, J-man," Dak said, jerking his eyes back to the task at hand. But I knew him. He wasn't as unaffected as he pretended, and something about that caused a tiny frisson of pleasure to click its heels. Which was dangerous. Because even though I had caused our breakup, my heart still ached for Dak.

"Just coffee." Juke pulled out a stool for me, then took the one beside it. "You remember my baby cousin Ruby? Y'all may have been in school together."

Dak turned away from us, setting the rum on the shelf. "Sure I do."

Somehow I managed to slide onto the stool without losing my composure. It had been almost nine years since he'd left me at the Carters' barn, tears in his eyes. I had broken his heart when I had stayed to party with kids I had no business being around. But that was the year my dad had taken off, my mom had lost her shit, and I had embarked on a death wish, smoking too much pot, drinking too much Crown, and daring anyone to tell me what to do. Even my boyfriend.

Dak had had a future—LSU baseball had been knocking at his door, along with dozens of other top programs in the nation. And I'd had nothing. I had felt like a Balthazar, destined to amount to shit, so I had self-sabotaged. By the end of that year, Dak had taken off for Baton Rouge, and I had dropped out of North Caddo, picking up my first arrest for possession and resisting arrest. My second had come six months later when I had stupidly gone with some guys who broke into cars to steal guns. I had been a dumbass in more than one way.

But Dak hadn't.

He'd done what he'd set out to do and graduated from LSU with a degree in finance before entering the draft and playing for a year in the minors. He'd moved up to the big show but blew out his knee when someone took him out at the plate. The injury had been too much to overcome, so he'd come back home, bought a house on the lake, and opened a bar. Deep down I was so proud of him. No one had the laser focus and work ethic of Dak. He never quit.

Except on me.

But I couldn't hold that against him. I'd done that to myself.

"Coffee for you, too, Ruby?" Dak asked almost too politely.

"Um, sure."

The guys at the bar buzzed over a home run on the screen, and Dak backed up to take a peek. Then he resumed making a fresh pot of coffee as Juke turned to me. "So tell me about this boss of yours. What's the story?"

"Not much to tell. Same song and dance. He's cheating. She found out."

Juke raised his eyebrows and snagged a toothpick from his pocket. Chewing on it, he eyed the liquor behind the bar with a hunger I wished a man would direct toward me. "I'm assuming he ain't got a clue she knows?"

"Pretty much. She and I did a stakeout, and that's where she saw him. At the tennis pro's place," I said, trying not to watch Dak as he smoothly measured grounds and flipped buttons on an industrial coffee maker at the end of the bar. Dak wasn't short, but he was so muscular that he looked stocky. But there wasn't an ounce of fat on him. He'd been the perfect catcher—strong, agile, and smart. He could read the field and anticipate the play, and with his arm, he could throw out even the speediest of runners. I had loved watching him play.

The phone I'd set on the bar jittered like the wake-up call I needed.

Ty Walker.

The future dragging me from the past.

"You going to get that?" Juke asked, looking annoyed that I hadn't already snatched it up.

I clicked the ANSWER button. "Hello."

"Hey, gorgeous, I just got back in town, and some chick at the shop said that you left early. And that just made that long trip seem even longer." Ty sounded like he was in the car.

"Sorry I missed you. I had some errands to run this afternoon." So Ty Walker had flown back into town and had immediately come to see me? I couldn't understand why he would be attracted to me. A preppy guy like him? A rough-around-the-edges girl like me? Didn't add up, but still, I liked the attention he was giving me. Maybe too much.

"I thought we could go for a drink or something."

"Weirdly enough, I'm at a bar now," I quipped before I could think better of it.

"Wow, I like how you run errands. Where ya at? I'll join you, if that's cool." His voice was honey—beautiful, drippy honey that made me feel something I hadn't in a while.

"Actually, I'm in north Shreveport, my old stomping grounds. You probably don't want to drive—"

"You realize this is Shreveport and not Atlanta, right?" he interrupted, laughter in his voice. "I'm pretty sure I can get through this colossal amount of five-o'clock traffic."

Did I want to mix my new world with my old one? Did I want to line the too-pretty Ty up next to the all-American? I eyed Dak again, knowing that most men would come up short next to him. But Ty was a dish himself. And what did it matter? Dak was a memory.

Handing me my coffee.

"Thanks," I said to Dak, who had made my coffee just as I liked it—the color of a good roux. He set it down without a word, turning his back on me, causing my heart to flinch. Suddenly I wanted Ty there. Into the phone I said, "I'd love to see you."

I clicked the phone off and sent Ty the location pin. "A friend might join us for a drink. Please don't mention my boss or her issue."

Juke cupped his coffee in two hands and snorted. "I don't talk. And don't you mean a hot beverage? Because this doesn't look as good as two fingers of Jack."

I tapped the shiny bar top. "Change your thinking and you can change the world."

Juke rolled his eyes. "Changing the world is overrated."

CHAPTER EIGHT

CRICKET

Early Monday evening while I ate tacos with Scott, my potential attorney had called and set up an appointment for the following morning. Scott had looked questioningly at me across the table as I confirmed the appointment that would end our marriage. After I got off the phone with Jackie Morsett, I lied and told him that I had to go in for a mammogram.

He nodded and said, "I'm glad you're taking care of yourself, honey."

Oh, the irony.

After the call, I lost my appetite and nursed my spicy margarita while Scott shoved down his tacos and the remainder of mine. Then he went off to shag Steph or whatever it was he was doing, and I went home and reorganized my pots and pans so I wouldn't open another bottle of sauvignon blanc and leaf through our family albums that I had created in my scrapbooking class, crying over all that was lost to me.

Of course, the next morning, the thought of meeting with my soon-to-be attorney threw me into a mixed state of denial, anxiety, and determination. Overwhelmed, I stayed in my pajamas too long and watched cute and oh-so-together Kelly Ripa chirp too happily and charm visiting celebrities. Which meant I then panicked because I had left myself only forty minutes to rip through my closet for something perfect to wear to begin divorcing one's husband. I had thought to wear something severe and black, even contemplating lopping my beachy waves into an abrupt pageboy that screamed, *Don't screw with me.* But I settled on a Lilly Pulitzer wrap dress that I had bought too long ago but still loved, and a loose ponytail. I felt more me in that getup, if not a little bougie.

Well, sometimes I *was* bougie. What of it?

Turns out my new attorney, Jackie, didn't care because she had enough badassery for both of us.

Jackie wore a navy power suit, ivory blouse, and stacked gold chains against her dark skin. Her hair jiggled in coils that framed her rounded cheeks. The full lips painted boardroom red, big diamond studs in her earlobes, and cute frameless glasses perched on the end of her nose seemed right on her. She was rounded in all the right places, like someone who knew how to make a good pie, but then you peered behind the glasses into her eyes.

Those dark orbs reminded me of the sharks I'd seen when I took Julia Kate to a New Orleans aquarium a few years ago. They had whirled around, coldly assessing me from behind the twelve-inch-thick glass. I'd taken a step back each time one headed my way.

And if it weren't for Jackie's big smile and warm hands when we shook, I might have retreated for the door. She seemed to be the perfect balance of a woman who could gut you or smother you in a hug. Maybe at the same time.

She would do nicely as my attorney.

"Well now, Mrs. Crosby, I hear you're looking for a female to represent you," Jackie said, her voice smooth, confident, everything I wished I were.

"Is that wrong?"

"Hell no."

"Oh, good."

"Sit." She gestured to a pair of fawn-speckled chairs centered on a zebra rug. I sank down on one and tried not to fidget. I had that habit, and my mother had tried to pinch it out of me on the fifth pew of First Presbyterian Church every Sunday. Jackie slid behind her desk, gracefully dropped into her white leather chair, and tented her hands with long fingernails just the shade of her lipstick. "You want coffee, Catherine?"

I had already drunk a gallon. "No, thank you. And I go by Cricket with most everyone."

She lifted an eyebrow. "Okay, then, Cricket. Tell me your story."

How far back should I go? To the day I had first met Scott on the porch of Hallie Henderson's lawn party? He'd dressed in whites as per the invitation (because *so* many people in Shreveport played cricket or croquet or whatever that whole deb party was about), and his tanned skin, straight teeth, and confident manner had me casting glances at him all afternoon as I nursed a Pimm's cup and tried to look cool in my new sundress and sandals that matched the blue bow in my hair (hey, it was the nineties—don't judge). Or maybe I should go back to the night he'd driven me to Dallas, taken me up in that tower restaurant, and hidden a two-carat diamond engagement ring in my cheesecake. Or the way he'd looked at me as I walked with my daddy down the aisle, careful not to wrinkle the satin runner lest I trip on the way back up the blasted thing. Or the day I'd told him I was pregnant with Julia Kate. Or . . .

I felt tears creep into my eyes.

Jackie calmly passed me a tissue. "It's okay."

But it wasn't. Nothing was okay about everything that had happened to me over the past two weeks. But this is what I was left with—a cheating husband, a wrecked marriage, and a life that would never be the same. Mentally, I tried to tug on my big-girl panties, preferably the Spanx that would help me hold it all together, and said, "I found out a little over a week ago. He's doing my daughter's tennis coach. Saw it with my own eyes. Um, not the actual doing, but I know he's a cheater."

Jackie's face went feral in the best of ways. "Okay, then."

"And I hired a private investigator who's going to get the proof, like with pictures and stuff. I hope that's okay, but I sort of failed at getting an incriminating picture myself." My mind flashed back to me hopping out from the side of Stephanie's house and accidently taking a selfie. My white-lipped, wild-eyed face still stared back at me from my phone. For some reason, I couldn't tap the little garbage can and erase the memory of that night. I needed to see and remember that I wasn't helpless . . . even if I hadn't gotten what I had set out to get.

But now I wasn't alone. I had Jackie, a private investigator, and Ruby to back me up.

Jackie lifted a shoulder. "I have some guys I use, but if you have your own and he's licensed, then go with your guy. Louisiana is a no-fault divorce state, but I want indisputable proof. You may think your husband will go along with an easy divorce, but don't be surprised if things turn ugly. Better to have proof of infidelity when it comes to custody issues and dividing assets. So let's talk about a timeline." Jackie moved some papers around on her desk, pulling out a legal pad, which I found very appropriate.

And then after we ironed out what would happen, I paid her a retainer and walked out of her office, resigned but determined.

Until we had proof, I would remain as I was—pretending everything was normal. Hey, I'm a woman. We're good at plastering on smiles and getting through things. It's what we do. Scott could be fairly oblivious, so I felt certain he wouldn't suspect that I knew he was cheating on me. After the private investigator got the goods on Scott, I would start packing his bags and tell him to leave the premises. I needed him out of the house because that was some legal thing. Jackie told me to make him leave. And I knew too well that he had a place to stay. Jackie would file the divorce papers, we'd serve him, and then we'd get a court date. Easy peasy.

But I didn't want to go longer than a week, so I texted Patrick Vitt and told him to get going. I had Venmoed him the initial fee, along with Scott's particulars. I needed that proof. It was my insurance against getting screwed in the divorce and my way of protecting Julia Kate.

Reeling with conviction, I called into Printemps and told Jade that I would be in later that day. Ruby had class on Tuesdays and only worked mornings, so Jade might appreciate an extra body in the store. Besides, it was time for me to leap back into the land of the living and go about my life. Now more than ever, I needed to focus on my daughter, my business, and protecting my assets.

But first I was going to bring my mother lunch because she had a sore throat, and that meant staying in bed, drinking whiskey, and sneaking episodes of *The Real Housewives*, though she would turn it to *Masterpiece Theatre* if she thought anyone was coming over.

Look at me being the good daughter.

After arguing with my mother over the thermostat—veritable sweat-lodge level—I finally made it to Printemps around three thirty that afternoon, after ensuring that my daughter had a ride to soccer and dropping off the cleats she'd left in her bathroom.

Printemps looked as it always had—clean, cheerful, and full of possibilities—and it gave me comfort to walk in the back door to the familiar smell of overwarmed coffee, beeswax, and old wood. As I suspected, Ruby wasn't there and Jade had done some decent business— selling a cupboard, two serving tables, and a ceramic peacock that I had spied in an English antiques catalog. Knew someone would want the peacock. Two crates had arrived that afternoon from our buyer in France, and with nowhere to put them, Ruby had stored them in the attached garage. I needed to construct a better storage facility, perhaps one that was temperature controlled, since many of the antiques that arrived were sensitive to the Louisiana humidity.

Wanting to get the fragile items inside and on the floor, I grabbed a crowbar and went outside to unpack and start cataloging our new inventory.

After logging in a small pie safe that I knew Jenny Martindale would want for her aunt's kitchen remodel, several sculpted bookends, a snuffbox that I was certain was worth more than it had been priced, and a mahogany Hepplewhite mirror that would look good in my own dining room, I found a packet of books. Étienne had written a note.

Procured these from an estate sale in Calais. Thought as an American you might find these amusing. No charge.

Étienne

I dug into the box and pulled out dusty books that bore several decades of use.

"*The Case of the Negligent Nymph?*" I muttered, frowning at the cover featuring a young, nude blonde clinging to a canoe. I selected another titled *Revelations of a Lady Detective*, and then several pulp-fiction detective magazines, which I stacked beside me as I sat cross-legged on the floor of the garage. I pulled out a few more dusty detective books and found a bundle of penny dreadfuls, including a few that looked to be from *The Mysteries of London*. They were in horrible shape, but I still felt a trill of excitement holding old publications that had intrigued Victorian Londoners with stories of adventure on the streets and that were part of what many believed to be the longest-running novel. The other stack within the box held books titled *How to Be a Successful Detective* and *The Sherlock Holmes Handbook*.

"Hmm, whoever owned these books definitely wanted to be Nancy Drew," I said out loud, smiling as I set the volumes on top of one another. Finally, in the box was the last book, and that made my grin bigger. These had definitely been owned by a female, and I envisioned a young French girl reading these American and British crime dreaming of becoming the next Miss Marple or Trixie Belden. I m) had gone through such a phase as a child, imagining clues everywhei and mysteries in every shadow. I had driven my poor cousin Ronda nuts when we had stayed with Auntie Kay one summer, imagining every bottle cap to be a clue and seeing burglars dangling in trees (just Spanish moss and an active imagination).

Ronda grew up to be a mental health counselor. I had no doubt driven her to it.

I studied the book in my hand—*The Gumshoe Gal's Guide to Becoming a Private Eye*.

The cover was 1950s blue, and the woman on the front wore a flared crinoline dress and stood pressed against a cracked door. The "private eye" clutched a small handgun nestled in the pleats of her skirt; in her other hand was a martini glass. Kid you not. She also wore towering stilettos, totally negating being an actual gumshoe. But who knew? Maybe she had gummed her soles to allow her to sneak around. Her hair was short and sassy, her lips vampire red, and her neckline plunging. She looked like a hot gumshoe gal, and I wondered how my own hair might look short and curly, a sort of Marilyn Monroe throwback.

I took the stacked books and put them into a crate. Probably not salable, but they might be useful for display. I tucked the book in my hand under my arm and rose, carrying a box filled with porcelain dogs. My phone buzzed in my back pocket, so I set the box down and checked the message.

Scott.

Going to dinner with Jeff R. at the club. He needs some marriage counseling. Told him I would listen and pray with him. Be home late.

my mouth opening and closing, because I knew
load of horse dung. Ten to one said Scott wasn't
ng . . . except praying he didn't get caught. So
ts like this and I hadn't had a clue. I had sent
things like, So proud of you for helping your friends, or perhaps, Love your heart. See you tonight.

Staring daggers at the phone, I kicked over an old lamp, breaking
it and not even caring because it was ugly, anyway. For good measure, I
stomped the shade three times, growling like a wolverine backed into a
corner. If wolverines could even back into corners. I wasn't sure. I was
from Louisiana and had never actually seen one. But at any rate, I was
super pissed.

"Screw you, screw you, screw you!" I shouted with each additional
stomp because the shade hadn't been completely flattened.

Now it was.

I clicked on the response button and typed, Ok. You're a good friend.

"And a total ass," I added aloud.

After I sent the text, I texted Patrick Vitt and told him to head to
the tennis pro's house of lust this evening if he wanted to get the back
end of his fee sooner than later. I may have scowled when I typed "back
end," thinking about that uncomfortable-looking foxtail. Then I picked
up the box and what was left of my pride, stepped over the destroyed
lamp, and walked back into the store.

Ruby stood behind the register, wearing a blouse I had tossed into
something she called the Bin of Requirement. Had no clue why she
called it that, but the silk looked amazing on her even if there was what
looked to be a stain on the cuff. She took me in, giving a slight lift of
her brows as she did. Next to her was a good-looking younger guy who
looked vaguely familiar.

"What are you doing here? Thought you had class," I asked, setting
the box on the glass counter next to the register.

"I skipped today, and we were on our way to get a drink when I remembered that I had left something I needed here," Ruby said, digging around in her bag, obviously looking for something. I looked at the gumshoe guide in my hand, thinking that chick had nothing on me.

"Oh." I eyed the good-looking guy beside her. He wore expensive trousers, a Peter Millar polo shirt, and suede chukkas that he hadn't bought at Sears. If Sears were still open and all. A pair of sporty sunglasses hung around his tanned neck. Overgrown frat boy, just like Scott. Normally, I would like a guy who looked like this one. Today I didn't.

"Hey, Mrs. Crosby. I'm Ty Walker. I think you know my father. He banks with your husband." The kid reached out a hand; his smile reminded me of a self-satisfied sloth. Not that he looked slow and cuddly, just well aware of his powers of adorability. And smirky.

"Yeah, I think we met once. At the club?" I ignored his hand, and he dropped it, not looking the least insulted. He seemed like the kind of guy who didn't stand on formalities. Question was, What was he doing in my store, looking chummy with my edgy, never-wore-a-hair-bow-in-her-life assistant?

"Yes, ma'am, I think so," Ty said.

Zack Morris from *Saved by the Bell*. That's why he looked familiar. I had watched that as a teenager, and now my own daughter binged it on one of the many streaming services we just had to have.

"I won't be much longer, Ty. You can go on to, uh, where are we going?" Ruby asked Ty.

"Deacon Blues. And I'll wait for you in my car. We can swing back for your car afterward. Nice to see you again, Mrs. Crosby."

"You can call me Cricket." I eyed Ruby, wondering what in the world was going on. Ty Walker was miles from being her type. Not that I truly knew her type, but she had a nose ring, tattoos, and a great disdain for anything Lilly Pulitzer. I know because she had tossed me a look that said, *Club Med just threw up on your dress* when I came in.

After Ty had left and we were alone, Ruby withdrew a sheet of paper from her purse. "I missed my class to go see my cousin who's a private investigator. Here."

She jabbed a wrinkled sheet of paper at me, and I took it. North Star Investigations? What was the deal with her cousins and astronomy?

"This was nice of you," I said.

She gave a lift of her shoulder. "I'm invested now. Juke worked down south for the Mandeville police force as a detective. He's been here for a few years, and he's good at his job. Maybe he can get what you need."

"I sort of already hired a guy."

"Oh, well then." She snatched the paper back and shoved it into her bag. "I'm glad you're . . ." She made a circular motion with her hand.

"Doing something?" I said.

"Yeah. I'm glad you're ready to nail that asshole to the wall." Ruby's eyes widened, and her mouth dropped open. "I'm sorry. I didn't mean to say that."

"Why? You're right. And I met with an attorney today. Her name is Jacqueline Morsett, and I paid her retainer this morning. I've got my hammer, baby."

Ruby chuckled. "Yeah, you do. And I've heard of Jackie. She's good. If I'd had . . . um, if my cousin had used her instead of some idiot, things would be different. She is very good at her job."

I noted her stumble. Hmm. I jabbed my thumb over my shoulder toward the parking lot. "So what's with Ty Walker?"

Her cheeks pinked. "Um, nothing. He came in to get some stuff his dad ordered, and we, um, just struck up a . . . friendship. I guess."

"Oh," I said with a grin, and her flush deepened, which was cute because other than her being irritated at me in the car the night we'd done the stakeout, this was the most human I had seen my little robotic assistant. Adorable. "Well, it's nice to have 'friends.' Especially really handsome ones who drive a BMW. Just be careful with that one, though. He seems a bit—"

"What?" Ruby's expression darkened.

Something in her tone told me to tread carefully. Her hackles were up, and I was intuitive enough to see through the defenses she often mounted. Ruby likely hadn't been raised like me—carefully tended by a mother with expectations, means, and the appropriate shade of bubble-bath-pink nail polish on her fingernails. I had been coddled. She likely wouldn't know coddling if it whopped her in the head. "He's . . . I don't know. He reminds me of Scott, and look where that got me."

"I'm not you."

Touché.

I decided to change the subject. "What did you do with the dress you took last week? The secret project? I'm curious."

Ruby stilled, and for a second or two I felt that she was deciding whether to trust me. I hoped she would. After all, she knew that Scott had asked me to try anal beads. And that my marriage was about to implode spectacularly. Quid pro quo and all that.

"I like to play with remaking dresses. My gran taught me to sew when I was little, and I'm resourceful." She lifted a shoulder in a shrug and stared at the shelf of porcelain eggs I had put out to highlight Easter.

"Sounds interesting. Have you finished the one you're making with the Givenchy?"

"I'm about done." Eyes still on the eggs.

"Can I see it? I mean, I would love to."

"I may wear it to that Gritz thing with Ty. Maybe. He wants me to go." She sounded like she'd rather tend lepers in quarantine than go to a gala. I didn't really blame her.

"Please bring it. I love repurposing things. Maybe you can make me a dress sometime." If I liked it. What did I know? She might Frankenstein something hideous, and then I would feel obliged.

Ruby finally looked at me, sweet vulnerability in her eyes, which sort of disarmed me. Ruby was stoic, distant, covered with so much armor I could only see the whites of her eyes at times, but in her gaze now, I could see that she wanted me to like what she did. "Okay. I'll bring it tomorrow."

Ruby hefted her bag onto her shoulder—such a big bag for a little thing—and slid past me.

Just as the little bells sounded at her departure, my back pocket buzzed.

Patrick Vitt.

I'm on it.

"You better be for what I'm paying you out of my grandmother's rainy-day fund," I said to the screen before tucking the phone back into my pocket.

I spent the next hour closing down the store, putting everything in its place, and texting Julia Kate about why I had brought her backup cleats and not her new cleats. My daughter needed to learn that HER cleats were not MY problem to begin with. But that was my fault, wasn't it? I had always taken care of all the little details, rushing to the school to take her the homework she left on the counter or rushing to the field to bring her a mocha latte before the game. Which had proven a mistake that one game when she barfed up the five-dollar confection on the sidelines.

When I went out to the van to go home, I found it warmed by the sunlight falling through trees beginning to adorn themselves with new green. The beauty of the late afternoon and the thought of an empty house had me steering the opposite way from my gated home. I wove through the oaks, with their knobby roots stretching up from the soil, and old mansions that needed a good scrubbing but were still unable to disguise their refined bones. In one I had danced with Clint Fairchild at a Christmas dance. Another was where I had hunted big plastic eggs filled with chocolates. A bridal shower in that one, a first babysitting job across the street. Azaleas bunched around the old homes with their blooms at the ready, an old neighborhood holding on to what once was, even as gunfire peppered the night around them. A few turns took me to where I had intended to go but hadn't wanted to admit.

Why I wanted to see my husband's truck parked outside her house, I couldn't say. Maybe in some way I liked the hurt. Or more likely, I wanted to believe he was truly praying with that nitwit Jeff Reagan. I shored up whatever compelled me to do what I was doing with the thought that I had to make sure Patrick Vitt, private investigator, was parked outside and being discreet about it, and that Grandmother's pin money/rainy-day fund/mad money, which she had left in a hat-box, stacked ten inches deep around her mother's pearls and diamond brooches, was being used in a worthwhile manner. The hatbox sat empty on a shelf in my closet because the money and jewels were in a safe-deposit box in my maiden name. I had my secrets, too.

I turned onto Stephanie's street, the dimness making the cars parked along it look like cutouts from a movie rather than real vehicles. Dusk and dawn did funny things to reality, made objects look softer or stamped against something in relief. Just different. Which was why I had always liked both times of day.

My heart sighed with relief to see that Scott's pickup truck wasn't in the driveway. I moved my gaze down the street, and about two blocks down, his Tundra sat beneath a magnolia tree. Something hard and heavy collapsed in my stomach.

What did I expect?

I had known his whole praying-with-Jeff thing was a load of bull crap.

Several cars sat along the street, and any one of them could have been Patrick's. I had no clue what he drove, so this was an absolutely worthless endeavor only serving to make me feel even worse than I did about Scott cheating on me. I hadn't stopped my car. Instead I had been creeping down the street as if I were a burglar casing the houses. When a lady walking her dog eyed me suspiciously, I pulled over and pretended to have dropped something on the floorboard. After counting out five seconds, I lifted my head and gave her a little self-deprecating shrug.

"Nothing to see here, lady. I'm not spying on my husband while he's slipping the sausage to Stephanie," I said through my teeth as I smiled at her.

She gave a half wave and tugged her dachshund down the block.

I put the van into drive, and just as I let off the brake pedal, the front door to Stephanie the Tennis Pro's opened.

Scott walked out.

Feeling panicked, I slammed the van into park and prayed he couldn't see me around the Roto-Rooter truck parked a house down from where I sat. My van was a nondescript silver, a dime a dozen in this town, but it didn't matter because he seemed zeroed in on something across the street. He stuck his hands in his pockets and walked briskly to—I moved my head to peer around the plumbing truck, pressing my cheek against the cool glass—a small white car parked across the street. Scott crossed the street and rapped at the window. The window slid down, and I could see the side of a man's face.

Was that my private investigator?

Something twisted in my gut.

Holy crap! We'd been made.

But then I watched, stupefied, as Scott reached into his back pocket and pulled out his wallet.

What in the hell?

It was pretty evident even as the darkness descended what was happening.

My dick of a husband was paying off my . . . well, my own private dick.

Son of a biscuit.

CHAPTER NINE

RUBY

Ty had just dropped me off at my car when Cricket pulled into the parking lot around back. I glanced at my watch as I walked to my hand-me-down car, which I had left on the street earlier. My ten-year-old Honda was a far cry from the sleek new BMW that Ty drove. The only way to warm my seats was to swish my behind around a few times briskly. He had a little button for instant hot buns. Lucky duck. I paused at my slightly dented door as I caught sight of Cricket's face.

Uh-oh.

I had spent the most unusual afternoon at the Bullpen before going for a coffee with Ty at some fancy place with people on computers and confections that I literally didn't know how to pronounce. In fact, if I had said, *Give me a cup of coffee,* the cashier might have been confused.

By that point, I'd had so much caffeine that I probably wouldn't sleep that night. But even if I managed to close my eyes, I would probably be haunted by the two hot guys wrestling around in my head.

As I had sat there with Juke at the Bullpen before Ty arrived, nursing decent coffee (for a bar), I had tried to study my ex without looking like I was watching Dak. I wasn't sure I succeeded, because every now and then our gazes caught before I quickly darted mine to the button on my cuff right next to the jelly stain. Or Juke's jittering leg. My cousin needed a drink. Dak's refusal to even glance his way other than to set a little silver milk pitcher on the bar told me that Juke wasn't going to be served what he craved.

The whole situation had been bizarre to begin with, and then Ty had walked through the door of the bar into my side of town. Correction. My *old* side of town. But I had to give the dude credit for coming north to meet me. He showed up wearing a pair of Brooks Brothers khakis. Or what I assumed to be Brooks Brothers. I wasn't exactly versed in modern preppy. He'd paired them with a tight polo shirt with short sleeves that hung up on his toned biceps, and flashy sunglasses perched on his burnished locks. He looked straight off a yacht.

Juke wasn't as impressed as I was. And my ex–soul mate standing behind the bar looked like he had a bad case of acid indigestion. Or the red ass. Maybe both, but I was certain he didn't like Mr. Million Bucks heading my way. And that made me oddly pleased.

"Hey, gorgeous," Ty said as he slid onto the stool next to me. He peered over the bar to my cousin and flashed his 5,000-watt smile. "Hey, I'm Ty."

Juke made a sound that might have been approving but probably wasn't. More of a choking sound he covered with a cough. "Juke. I'm Roo's cousin."

"Roo?" Ty shot me an amused look.

"Ruby. We always called her Roo. Like that baby mouse on *Winnie the Pooh*."

"That would be a kangaroo, Juke. Thus the 'roo' part. And I don't go by childhood nicknames anymore."

Juke made a sour face. "So sue me."

"Well, I think that nickname is as cute as you are," Ty said, giving me a little wink. He then slapped the bar. "Yo, can I have a Mic ULTRA?"

Dak turned and cocked his head. "We don't have Michelob. But you're welcome to choose any of these on tap. Four-dollar happy hour on tap and well." Then Dak turned back around and slid some empty mugs to the side of the bar before pulling out a few Miller Lites, popping the tops, and hooking up the two guys who were still talking about some pitcher and the nasty slider he'd thrown when he played at UNC.

"Well, this guy is a charmer," Ty joked with a roll of his eyes. He didn't get perturbed like most guys would. I liked that about him. "You two drinking coffee, huh?"

"I wasn't in the mood for a cocktail, and Juke wanted coffee."

Juke made another noise that sounded a lot like "Fuck off."

Ty hooked an eyebrow and called out, "Bud Light is fine."

Dak said nothing. Just grabbed a frosty mug from beneath the bar, slung it beneath the tap, and filled it. He didn't even bother to let the foam settle. Just slapped it down kind of rudely in front of Ty and said, "Start a tab?"

"Nah." Ty pulled out his wallet and tossed a five onto the bar. "I think one here will be enough."

The foam dissolved, leaving it only three-fourths full. I tossed Dak a glare, but he didn't see it because he was too busy being an asshole and keeping his back to us.

"Jeez, tough bar," Ty joked, taking a slug of his drink and smiling like he hadn't just been cheated out of some decent beer. Or what was considered good beer by my family. Bud Light was for special occasions—otherwise it was PBR or Busch.

"Y'all datin' or somethin'?" Juke asked, sipping his coffee and making a face.

"Yeah," Ty said.

"Not really," I said at the same time as Ty.

I may have blushed a little and tried to cover it by taking a big gulp of my coffee. Ty Walker and I were *not* dating. Okay, so maybe this could be considered our first date since we weren't standing in

Printemps discussing carpets or paintings from Scandinavian auction houses. But as first dates go, this one blew. "We're going to Gritz and Glitz together in a few weeks."

"Gritz and what?" Juke asked.

Ty caught my eye, looking extraordinarily pleased at my statement. So I guess I had just agreed to go to the stupid gala with him.

"It's a benefit," I clarified, staring at Dak's broad back even though I didn't want to. My eyes kept wandering toward him, like they had never gotten the memo that I was totally over him. "To raise money for charity and stuff."

"That's a weird name for it." Juke shrugged and trained his eyes on the bottles of whiskey seductively reflecting the bar light. My eager-to-catch-a-new-case cousin had fled, to be replaced by a man who likely needed rehab, if the way he couldn't rip his gaze from the mirrored shelves was any indication.

At that moment I wondered what the hell I was doing there. This was my biggest weakness—trying to fix things like I was the righter of wrongs. I had no business tying on my Supergirl cape and sobering up Juke, helping my boss, or sitting my dumb ass in the bar of the man who still made me twitchy. After all, I had been trying to cut ties with my family, and in the course of a week, I had called on both Griffin and Juke to help me. Really . . . what the hell was wrong with me?

My mission to better myself, look for new opportunities, and afford a down payment on a house far from my family compound was being jeopardized by my stupid inability to keep my nose out of other people's business.

I reached down and patted the large canvas bag I had stitched out of an old sari I had found at Goodwill. The crumpled application was inside, and I had already told Juke what I knew about Cricket and her douche of a husband. It was time to bounce. Only problem was, now Ty Walker sat on a shiny stool, sipping a half-full beer, looking as out of place as a debutante at a dirt bike race.

Juke downed the rest of his coffee. "You know, I'm gonna hit the road. You sobered me up sufficiently. Tell your girl to give me a shout when she's ready."

Well, it wasn't like my cousin was going to be a brilliant conversationalist anyway. "Sure."

The stool made a horrendous shriek of protest when Juke pushed back from the bar. He tossed a ten on the counter and hitched up his jeans, which were saggy, and not in a cool way. "Tell Shirl to keep the change. Maybe she'll be nicer to me next time."

"Okay. Bye, Juke."

Ty leaned back. "Hey, nice to meet you."

Juke jerked his head toward Ty and then laid a heavy hand on my shoulder. "Good to see you, Roo. Thanks for, uh, the coffee."

I knew his gratitude wasn't about the coffee—after all, he'd just paid for it—but I could hear it in his voice. He was barely treading water, and I hadn't exactly tossed him a preserver. But I had at least acknowledged his struggle.

Ty had leaned forward, cupping his beer and staring at the scores scrolling across one of the television sets, giving me privacy. As much privacy as one can give when sitting elbows to ass next to someone at a bar. But at Juke's departure, he turned his full attention on me. "What was that about?"

I wasn't about to blab any information. I didn't really know Ty, and my trust factor was like a 1.5 on a scale of 100. "Nothing. Just some family stuff."

Ty looked like he might press me but seemed to decide that I wasn't the kind of girl who likes to be squeezed. He read me right. Instead he gave me another pretty grin. "So what you been up to since I've been gone?"

"Not much. School, work, and I'm doing a little project for my dress for this shindig you've talked me into," I said, darting my twenty-sixth glance toward Dak, who caught my eye. I jerked my gaze back to handsome Ty. *Stop it, Ruby Lynn.*

"A project?"

"So growing up, I loved to experiment with designing my own clothes. I found this cool dress"—I didn't say that it was a Givenchy because I wasn't sure if I knew how to pronounce it correctly, and Ty seemed like the sort of dude who might know that word—"and I'm pulling off the bodice and joining it to this great satin skirt that goes to just above my ankles. I'm thinking about adding an emerald bow or maybe a mulberry cummerbund at the waist. Oh, and maybe some beading just around the neck. I'm going to consult Cricket on that. I'm not sure how fancy Gritz and Glitz is."

"You're going to *make* your dress?"

He made it sound like I was going to show up in a gunnysack with a piece of hay clutched between my teeth. Maybe some boots rimmed with fresh cow patty.

"I was planning on it." I tried not to sound defensive.

But failed.

Dak appeared and grabbed the half-empty coffee mugs. He glared at Ty, causing my "date" to slide me a what's-with-this-guy look. After Dak set the used mugs aside, he folded his arms and stared at both of us.

I tried to figure out exactly what Dak was doing. But came up with exactly . . . nothing. So I looked back at him, my jaw clenched.

Finally, Dak said, "If she makes something for whatever the hell you're talking about, it will be nicer than anything you've seen before."

I fell off the stool.

Okay, not literally, but I might as well have. I'm pretty sure my mouth gaped open like a goldfish as I watched Dak attempt death by glare at Ty before moving to the other end of the bar as if he'd said nothing more than "It's raining outside."

Had my ex-boyfriend—the man who had taken my virginity and branded my heart for all time before vowing to never speak to me—just come to my defense?

Ty looked even more confused. "I'm assuming you know the bartender? And making the dress is cool. I didn't mean anything by that. It's just that I don't know anyone who does anything like that. All the girls I've dated live for shopping in, like, stores and stuff. It's awesome that you can make your own clothes."

But his words sounded like rocks dropped into a tin can—flat and empty.

I decided to give him the benefit of the doubt. "I know the bartender. We grew up together. And no worries. I'm sure you don't know many people who can do what I do."

Truer words never spoken.

And I may have said them with a little bit of bitchiness and a whole lot of confidence that I normally didn't have but could fake pretty effectively.

"So you want to get out of here?" Ty asked, pulling on his traditional aw-shucks attitude. He reached over and took the hand I had resting on the bar and gave it a squeeze. An apology, no doubt. It sort of worked. He was a nice guy and trying, for heaven's sake.

"Sure."

But as I said that word, I realized that there was part of me that wanted to stay and talk to Dak. To see how his knee was healing. To ask about the house he'd bought on Caddo Lake, the same one my friends had raved about—a three-bedroom bungalow with a wall of windows that overlooked the sunset in the west. To remind him about the catalpa worms. The best fishing spot. To bemoan that the Bait and Burger had closed, ending double-meat Fridays. To watch the way his brown eyes sparked when he laughed, to see that flash of dimple. To regret forever that I had just thrown away what we'd been like the stupid girl I was.

But I wasn't going to do that because I had vowed that I would not be that stupid girl. That's why I had enrolled in college, moved across town, and found a boss like Cricket to mentor me in more than just the difference between an American tea table and a French one. I refused to chase a rabbit down a trail to nowhere. I wanted to be someone worthwhile.

So I left the Bullpen with Ty, stopping by Printemps to drop off Juke's paperwork to Cricket before going to some coffee slash cocktail bar and pretending I was the hip, rebellious girl he seemed to want me to be.

It hadn't been a bad date. We found some commonalities—The White Stripes, Abita Andygator, and an abhorrence of cilantro. He hadn't tried to stick his tongue down my throat and seemed genuinely interested when we talked about horror films and my diverse taste in music. He'd dropped me back at my car at Printemps with a smile and a quick kiss on my cheek. So here I stood, debating on whether to pretend I hadn't seen Cricket looking so tragic.

"Well, hell," I said, relocking my car door and hurrying up the drive and around back where I usually parked. Cricket had already climbed out and was stomping up to the back door.

When she heard the crunch of gravel beneath my half boots, she turned, alarmed. "Oh, hey."

"Hey," I said, rather dumbly. "Why are you back?"

"No reason. I'm fine," she snapped.

"Yeah, you seem like it."

Cricket made a face like she knew she wasn't fine and knew that I knew she wasn't fine but was giving me an out. For a moment we regarded each other like two pups in a dog park. Should we? Shouldn't we?

Finally, Cricket's shoulders sagged. "Okay, so I'm not okay. I'm pissed. And frustrated. And pissed."

I moved closer to her perch on the back stoop. "You deserve to feel really angry and betrayed."

She seemed surprised. Like I was supposed to tell her that she should put on her big-girl britches and stop moping. I could have said that, but sometimes a person didn't need to be the hammer, especially when the nail looked awfully wobbly.

"You're right. I deserve to be furious. And you want to know why I'm so mad?"

I said nothing because I was fairly certain this was a rhetorical question.

"That private eye I hired? The one that was so highly recommended? Well, Scott just moseyed outside the harlot's house to my investigator's car and paid him off!"

I blinked, trying to register her words fully. "Wait. What?"

"I drove down *her* street. Okay, I know that was stupid and I shouldn't have done it. But Scott said that he was going to pray with Jeff Reagan, and I knew he was lying. And, I don't know, I guess I'm a glutton for punishment. I couldn't help myself. But then I told myself that I was just checking to see if Pat Vitt—that's the PI—was there and not distinguishable, you know? And I had only sat there for a minute or two when I saw Scott, plain as day, walking out of *her* house and pulling a bunch of hundred-dollar bills from his wallet. Well, I'm assuming they were hundreds. But he totally paid my guy off!" Cricket had started pacing on the stoop as she told me this tale, her hands punctuating where it was needed. "And I just couldn't go home. So I came back here. And I don't know why."

I reached into my bag and pulled out the form I had taken from my cousin's desk. I held it out to her. "Here. Juke's my cousin, and I can vouch that though he has his flaws, being a greedy douchebag is not one of them. Call him, fill this out, and then get him to nail Scott."

Cricket took the crumpled form. "But what do I do about Scott? Now he knows I'm onto him. He's going to be more careful. It's going to be impossible now."

I nodded. "Maybe so, but maybe not."

Cricket bit her upper lip and stared off into space. "You think I should play this off? Act like I know nothing? Or should I be proactive and start packing his bags?"

"Depends on what he says. Depends on if your dick of a dick told him anything. I think you better call Patrick Whoever and find out what's going on. Then you can see what Scott does or says. Don't show your hand yet."

Of course, all this was easy for me to say. I didn't have a husband slapping the salami to his daughter's coach. And I didn't have a life about to fall apart. I really had no business telling Cricket what to do . . . other than an instinct for how dirty dogs like Scott handled themselves. Guys like him thought they were untouchable. He wouldn't stop doing the tennis pro, and he likely thought Cricket as bothersome as a fly. Hardly anyone took her seriously even though she was a sharp businesswoman. She looked too harmless, too sweet, too darn nice to play unfairly.

Cricket trained her blue eyes on me. "You're good at this."

"Not really. But I ain't bad at it, either."

CHAPTER TEN

CRICKET

After seeing my private investigator take a bribe from my husband, I couldn't seem to calm down. I tried to do some centering thing that a yoga instructor had once shown me, but that was like throwing a teaspoon of water on a grass fire. So instead of trying to channel the flames, I called Patrick Vitt. He didn't answer, of course. So I left a message telling him that I had seen him accepting the bribe and that if he didn't want me to report him for unethical behavior, he would send me my dang payment back and keep his mouth shut. And I also called him a disgraceful human who deserved to be roasted on a spit. Then I felt a little bad, so I added that I would pray for him.

But I would *not*.

After I pressed the END button, I felt better. But that didn't change the fact that time was ticking. I needed to protect myself, my daughter, and my future, so I had to get proof of Scott's adultery before he could better position himself. And Scott would probably do that. He could fight tooth and nail to take everything down to the dust gathered in the corners of the house if I didn't safeguard myself.

I climbed in my van, still struggling to figure out how I had been so betrayed and if perhaps I was getting accustomed to men betraying me. Which was a very cynical position to take, but that's where I was.

Ruby was right—I needed to let Scott make the first move and play it cool when he arrived home. *If* he arrived home. Maybe the whole jig was up and he would just say *Screw it* and stay with Stephanie. But I suspected he wouldn't. Scott played his part in life well—an upstanding businessman who loved his community and church. A man like him wouldn't willingly admit to any wrongdoing . . . even if he knew people suspected he was having an affair.

So I went home and tried to be the woman I had always been. I was standing in the kitchen chopping lettuce for a salad when Scott came in the back door. I gripped the knife tight and said a little prayer that I could hold it together. After all, Scott didn't know that I knew that he'd paid my guy off. And I wasn't sure that Patrick had admitted to my hiring him, though I couldn't see Scott not asking. So I knew my husband probably knew that I had hired an investigator. Which meant there was a lot of knowing and very little owning up going around.

Glancing up as the door opened, I said, "I ran a little late today, so you guys will have to settle for a salad tonight."

Scott set his briefcase on the mudroom bench as Julia Kate came in, earbuds in place, head bopping in time with whatever music likely abused her eardrums. "Oh, sure. I've been cutting down anyway."

"You have seemed interested in dropping weight lately," I said casually, trying not to interject any meaning into my words.

"Exactly," he said, assessing me with a look that could have been anything.

I held his gaze.

A few seconds ticked by before he smiled. "How was your day? Things good at the store?"

Pippa arrived on the scene, dancing merrily around Scott and Julia Kate, the official "welcome home" whirligigging that always brought a smile. Julia Kate dropped to a knee and gave the little dog the attention she demanded.

Just another day in the Crosby household, looking the part of the all-American family.

"Yep. We got a new shipment in. Étienne stuck some fun detective books in with the shipment. Took me back to when I was a girl, and I thought JK might like a few." I glanced at my daughter.

Julia Kate pulled the earbuds from her ears. "Huh?"

I gave her the look my mother had given me my entire life. That hook of eyebrow that had always made me squirm. Of course, Julia Kate never squirmed.

"Oh. Sorry. I meant, ma'am?" Julia Kate dumped her book bag and tennis racket on the bench and headed to the pantry.

"Books," I said, nodding toward the stack I had brought home. "I found some fun vintage detective books today in a shipment. I thought you might like them."

Julia Kate emerged from the pantry with a bag of pretzels, chomping away. She narrowed her eyes at the stack. "Those are, like, old."

"Yeah, but old doesn't mean they aren't good. I loved these sorts of books when I was your age. And why are you eating? I'm making us a grilled chicken salad." I thumped the knife against the cutting board for emphasis.

"Yuck. I'll have some macaroni and cheese instead." She went on chomping on the pretzels.

This was a conversation we'd had many times in our lives—the daily minutiae, the give-and-take, the crumbs on the freshly swept floor. Same routine, different day. But today it bothered me. Not merely the fact that Scott had committed the ultimate betrayal of our little family. But that my daughter had come in, dumped her crap, rejected my healthy dinner, and now expected me to make her something different and unhealthy for her dinner. "Fine by me, but you'll have to fix it yourself. Boxes are in the pantry."

Julia Kate gave me a look. "But you always make it for me. You make it the best."

"You can eat salad or make your own dinner. Your choice," I said, cutting through a juicy tomato that Jade had brought me. Her grandmother grew hothouse tomatoes and knew how much I loved them homegrown. The scent of summer wafted up, like a little promise that things would get better.

But they would be worse before they would be better.

Which is what I found out that night when I slid into bed next to what should have been my snoring husband. I had stayed up, rinsing out the pot Julia Kate had used for mac and cheese, doing laundry I had put off, and watching a series that my friend Shelley had vowed was the best thing she'd seen in years. There had been a Scotsman and lots of sex. Shelley knew what she liked, and I couldn't argue with her on this one.

Pippa followed me back to the bedroom, her little nails clicking on the hardwood. She sank onto her fluffy bed in the corner as I moved toward the king-size bed, slipping off my slides and carefully easing into the sheets my mother had given me for Christmas one year—the spendy ones that were the same price as a used car. They felt like delicious butter, as did the pillowy comforter I had found on clearance at an outlet mall. A truly good find. I settled onto my pillow with a ghost of a sigh, hoping I didn't wake my husband.

But Scott wasn't asleep.

As soon as I had smoothed the hem of my gown, he reached over and curled his arm around my torso in the age-old ask: *Wanna get busy?*

He couldn't be serious. Hadn't he just had sex with Stephanie?

I patted his wrist, giving it what I hoped was an affectionate squeeze that relayed the message *I'm too tired*. But he didn't take it as that. Instead he slid his hand up to cup my breast.

Stilling my body, I tried to keep up with my racing mind. Because I knew he knew I had hired a private investigator. He knew that I knew he was cheating. So why would he . . .

116

But then it hit me. This was the test. This was him dipping a foot into the waters. Scott had moved his knight or pawn or whatever—hey, I didn't play chess—to see what my next move would be.

So what would it be?

I didn't want to have sex with Scott, but I didn't want him to know that I knew what I knew. Or did I? Terrifyingly, everything about my marriage hung in the balance with my cheating husband's hand on my right breast. Did I pretend we were still happy, or did I come clean with what I knew? I didn't know what to do.

Luckily, at that moment, we heard a horrible yakking sound coming from the direction of Pippa's dog bed.

"Oh no." I jerked up and leaped out of bed as Pippa commenced some horrid whompy-whomp sounds.

"Ugh," Scott groaned, flipping over and turning on the lamp.

But it was too late for the light because my left foot had already registered disgusting, warm dog barf beneath it.

"Oh my God!" I shrieked, making gagging noises myself while hopping on my right foot.

"I'll grab a towel," Scott said, climbing from the bed and disappearing into the en suite bathroom.

I lifted my foot, holding it up so I didn't get any on the rug. Of course, Pippa was still seized up in arched vomit mode, copious amounts of whatever she'd eaten hitting the expensive Turkish wool rug I had tracked down through my most contrary of vendors. I held my breath and tried to quell my own reflexive response to my dog emptying her stomach.

"Here." Scott thrust one of my white decorative towels at me.

"Not this one. It's a monogrammed hand towel."

He gave a huge sigh. "Seriously? Cricket, use the damned towel."

"Just . . . just . . . just take her out, please."

Another heavy sigh from my ass of a husband as I hopped on one foot to the bathroom and turned on the bathtub faucet. I could hear

Scott in the bedroom, trying to get Pippa out the door. Julia Kate's voice joined in. I focused on cleaning my foot, and when I emerged from the bathroom, having slathered lotion on my clean foot for good measure, I found Scott back in bed and my monogrammed towel scrunched up over the vomit.

"You didn't clean it up?"

He glanced up from the magazine he'd plopped onto his lap. "I wasn't sure how to clean it. Or what cleaner to use."

I thought about hitting him. I truly did. But then I gathered myself the way my mother had taught me and stalked past him, out the door, and downstairs to where my daughter stood at the back door, no doubt watching over our vomiting Italian greyhound. "Thank you, JK."

"Poor Pippa. I think she ate some of my washcloth or something. I found it chewed up in the bathroom this afternoon, but I didn't think she'd actually eaten it."

I made a grossed-out face and fetched some gentle carpet cleaner from the cabinet beneath the sink. "I guess it's good she vomited it, then."

I went back, ignored Scott, and cleaned up the carpet as best I could. Probably needed to get the rugs cleaned, anyway, but those sorts of tasks were low on my priority list. High was the son of a biscuit—okay, fine, son of a bitch—lying in bed, leafing through a golfing magazine. Silently, I rose and started for the door. I stopped. "Pippa is still sick. Think I'll stay downstairs with her for a while."

Scott lowered his reading glasses. "So I guess you're not interested in what we started?"

"I stepped in dog vomit, Scott. And I just cleaned up the rest of it. You think I'm going to straddle you after that?"

He blinked once. Twice. "I think you didn't need dog vomit as a reason to not straddle me, Cricket." Then he reached over and turned off the light.

His words hurt, but they were true. Maybe they found their mark, because in those words was the shovel that would bury our marriage. He was right—I had stopped wanting to have sex with him. Some of it was because I was changing—I no longer felt sexy or desirable. Some was probably hormonal. Some was Scott sucking at foreplay, at showing me love before we climbed into bed. Those were all decent reasons, but it didn't change the fact that he was right . . . and that it had probably started before he'd had the affair.

Though I was livid at the thought of his deception and devastated by the betrayal that had cut me to my very core, I had ignored an issue that should have been addressed. Our marriage bed had long grown cold, and I hadn't minded it so much. Oh, that didn't excuse what he'd done. I'd left that door open a crack when I ignored the problem and stopped communicating with my husband. Scott had kicked it open and screwed someone else. Not exactly the best response to our failure to address our issue. Not even close to the best way. I wasn't responsible for his bad decision, but I was responsible for mine.

I padded back down the stairs to find Julia Kate locking up. "What do you want me to do with Pippa, Mom?"

"You go on to bed. Leave her with me. I have some thank-you notes to catch up on, and I'll keep an eye on her."

Pippa slunk toward me, head and tail down in canine apology. Julia Kate gave me a hug and made her way upstairs as I switched on the urn lamp and plumped the couch pillow in the hearth room. Pippa sank down onto her haunches with an elaborate sigh.

I looked down at the dog.

She looked up at me.

"Thank you, Pippa." I stroked her head and opened the end-table drawer where I kept my thank-you notes.

$\backsim$

The next morning as I stood in front of the mirror next to Ruby, looking in awe at the dress she'd made for the gala, I felt that weird clicky feeling you sometimes get when you know something big is about to happen. I had only felt that a few times in my life. Of course, you get it on big days—graduation or when someone slips an engagement ring on your finger. But there are other times when you just know that whatever it is that's happening, it's going to change you forever.

That had happened that morning when I'd arrived at Printemps, bleary eyed from a sleepless night on the couch—Pippa had vomited one more time—and heavy because I knew I was about to get my period in a few days, which meant cramps, bloating, and what was possibly a colossal pimple on my chin.

Ruby was rearranging a display up front, and Jade stood behind the checkout desk tapping on her phone. She slid it into her back pocket when she saw me and fastened on a smile. "Morning, Cricket."

I set a mocha latte on the desk. "Here ya go. Just a little thank-you for holding down the fort while I was under the weather last week."

"Thanks. I'm glad you're better." Jade was pretty—curvy with a natural Afro and the most interesting eye shadow. Ruby told me that Jade did online makeup tutorials and that her YouTube station had thousands of subscribers. I could see why—her eyelids were a work of art. Today she seemed to have summoned Picasso.

"Yep. All is well," I lied as I made my way to Ruby, who was clad in red from head to toe. It was a look that was bold and so original that for a moment I stood and stared. Her leggings were shiny, like faux leather. The half boots were suede with a small bow above the stacked heel. The boned bustier topping the ensemble would have made me look twenty pounds heavier, but on Ruby's frame, it looked amazing. Around her neck she'd tied a red silk handkerchief.

I handed Ruby her weird order—chai latte made with soy milk and no sugar—and raised my eyebrows. "Wow, you've really embraced your fashionista. Is that the Christian Lacroix bustier that Maddy Hassell brought in?"

"I paid for it." Ruby took the offering.

"Ruby, did I accuse you of something?"

Her cheeks pinked. "No. Sorry. I tend to be defensive without coffee."

"Well, then, you should drink up." I glanced at my broom-closet office. I had a lot to catch up on, but I felt lollygaggish. Avoidance was a talent of mine. I mean, obviously. "Seriously, you have mad fashion sense. Did you bring the dress you made?"

Ruby positioned a snuff jar at a particular angle and took a slug of her latte. Her cheeks remained pink, and something in her seemed twitchy. I sensed that my response to whatever she'd done with the Givenchy mattered more than she would let on. She finally looked up. "I have it in the kitchen."

"Oh, good. Grab it and let me see. Oh, better yet, put it on."

She looked as if she might argue, but then she lifted a shoulder and slipped into the kitchen. I hurried back to my office and dumped my bag and the detective books Julia Kate had dissed. Maybe I would do a fun display with them. I could use the black velvet dress with the bow just above the kick pleat. Oh, and that adorable hat with the net. I could add an antique magnifying glass, maybe some opera glasses. I lived for a theme.

Ruby appeared in the open doorway, and I gasped.

Yes. I literally gasped, which sort of startled my assistant.

The cream-colored top that had once had sleeves (and a stain) had been cut away to create straps. The bodice curved sweetly just below the rise of Ruby's breasts. Small tucks created a ruche that nipped her waist. The skirt was black satin that flared out in a sporty peplum before hugging her thighs. At the knee, the skirt opened with a fanned kick pleat. The inside of the skirt was lined with raspberry satin and ended right at Ruby's ankle. Around her trim waist she'd fashioned a floppy bow out of the raspberry satin. The effect was glamorous, vintage, and somehow very modern. If she'd been on *Project Runway*, they would have said it was a safe design, but Ruby lived in the real world and knew what suited a woman.

"That's amazing," I said, standing and taking her by the hand. Ruby pulled back and made a face. But I tugged her along nonetheless. "Come on. I want to see it in the three-sided mirror."

Under the lights I had erected for those who wished to try on our vintage offerings, Ruby looked even better. I touched the strap of the gown. "I can't believe this was the Givenchy."

Ruby didn't smile, but I could see the pleasure in her eyes. "I know. I loved the color. The fading made it softer. Like old newspaper, but prettier."

It was at that moment I caught my mother's reflection in the mirror.

Her Roger Vivier heels tapped a determined staccato toward us, like a Valkyrie descending.

"Hello, darling," Marguerite said in her contrived upper-crust southern drawl, her Chanel perfume greeting us before she was even within five feet. She stopped abruptly next to me, her hand raised to no doubt press down one of my errant curls that had escaped to bounce defiantly, but her eyes landed on Ruby. "Oh. Oh, what's this?"

I smiled at Ruby, who looked somewhat alarmed. Marguerite did that. She had never been the sort to make anyone feel at ease. Like a general in the army or something, she made a person feel as if they should straighten up and worry about the lint on their pants. "You've met my assistant, Ruby. She designed this dress for Gritz and Glitz."

My mother stepped closer to Ruby, peering at the fastidious tucks and pristine edges of the gown. "Well, this is . . . quite stunning. It looks straight off a runway, only better because it's not hodgepodgy. Some of those designers these days glue things, for heaven's sake."

Ruby's lips twitched. "This gown is pieced from some unsalvageable vintage dresses Cricket had. The top is from a fifties Givenchy, and the bottom was from a Balenciaga, also from the fifties. The ruffle was in pretty bad shape, so I pulled it off and streamlined it and added the lining, which I bought at a fabric store."

My mother was speechless as she made the finger motion for Ruby to twirl.

Ruby obliged.

"That's incredible. You have such talent, my dear."

"I made another dress. For Cricket or whoever. I'm not sure it will fit your shape, Cricket, but I couldn't stop myself because the skirt was just too pretty to toss. I'll grab it." Ruby sort of hurriedly slunk away toward the back of the store. The tight skirt of the stunning creation she wore only allowed for so much stride.

My mother arched a carefully drawn-on eyebrow. "How surprising."

It was. I'd had no clue that Ruby was so talented. Of course, the younger woman had an eye for style. She always paired pieces creatively or donned sleek ensembles such as the monochromatic one she'd been wearing earlier, but I had had no clue that her skills as a seamstress and, well, designer were so heightened.

Ruby came back with something covered in black garbage bags. "I didn't have a garment bag."

She untied the joined bags and pulled them from the dress.

"Oh," I breathed as a swoosh of the creamy-white Givenchy spilled forth. Ruby lifted the hanger where she had pinned the top of the gown. The bodice was a black-and-cream polka dot that stretched across the neckline, piped in black velvet and secured at the shoulder with black ties. The skirt fell, lusciously, in panels to below the knee, and beneath the creamy fabric was a five-inch black tulle underlay. It was daring, fun, and quite gorgeous.

My mother actually clapped. "Darling girl, that is . . . Well, I haven't seen anything that pretty since my mother paraded around town in just that sort of thing. I cannot believe you took old gowns and refashioned them so divinely. I'm stunned. You know what, I'm calling your aunt, Cricket. She needs to meet this girl."

My mother rarely got excited by anything, but her normally cool blue eyes were flashing and . . . she was smiling! Goodness, my mama was pretty when she looked stirred.

I laughed, and I swore it felt rusty because I couldn't remember the last time I'd had a reason to feel quite so good. "Wait a second. Don't you go trying to ship Ruby off. She's my girl Friday. I need her here."

"Ha, she's more than an assistant," my mother said, with a gleam in her eyes. But then she looked at me, and those eyes narrowed. "Goodness gracious, Cricket, you need to book a day with Jeannie. Sugar, you're looking peaked. A moisturizing facial and"—her eyes lowered—"a manicure would do you wonders. You know that you must take care of your skin at your age. I'm telling you, dear, that when you tip over into your forties, your skin starts getting crepey and losing elasticity. Let me see your neck."

I swatted at her as she drew closer. "Go call Aunt Coraline and stop fussing about me."

"Who's Aunt Coraline?" Ruby asked, hanging the creation she'd unveiled on the side of the mirror.

"My mother's sister who works at *Vogue*. She's someone who might be interested in you." As I said those words, I knew that my aunt would be fascinated by Ruby's talent, but I wasn't certain that Ruby wanted those doors open. Wasn't like I could shove her out into New York or London or Paris on a hunch. My mother and I knew what we liked and appreciated Ruby's talent, but what if my assistant didn't want to do what we were pushing her toward? What if her dream wasn't studying at fashion institutes or working for a designer where the competition was so fierce, a person had to know where their scissors were at all times?

"*Vogue*? Like the magazine?" Ruby asked.

"That is correct." My mother still looked at me way too discerningly. "What are you doing here anyway, Mother?" I asked.

"What do you mean? A mother can't come see her daughter?"

I made a face. "You never come to the store. You don't like dusty antiques. I believe that's what you always say."

My mother lifted a shoulder. She wore her standard uniform for the week—trim trousers tailored to her specifications, a white Talbots button-down, and a cashmere cardigan. In the summer, she eschewed the cardigan for rolled-up sleeves. She wore my grandmother's diamonds in lobes revealed by tucking her tawny, shoulder-length bob behind her ears. Elizabeth Arden red stained her plumped lips. High cheekbones, firmed skin, and ladylike makeup completed her look. Oh, and those Roger Vivier buckled shoes with the two-inch chunky heel. "Fine. So I got a call from your husband. About the investment opportunity. I tell you, Catherine, I do not like family members involving me in their schemes. Or whatever that Walker man is dreaming up."

"*Scott* called you about an investment?"

"I'm not here to tattle. I just wanted you to understand my stance because I told him no. And I didn't want you to be upset with me."

"I'm not upset. I'm a little confused, though. Scott stays away from that sort of thing. He knows a few bankers who got in over their heads on some bad deals. But Donner Walker is one of his old frat buddy's brothers, and I think he got cornered into introducing him around. I didn't think Scott was actively involved in a deal or anything." I also hadn't known my husband had been cheating on me. Did I really know Scott the way I thought I had?

My husband had always been such a man of integrity, taking pride in his reputation, his ability to serve, his standing in the bank. Scott liked to say the only way he was comfortable was if he squeaked when he walked, which I thought weird, but I knew what he meant. He wore an American flag on his lapel, wrote personal notes on monogrammed stationery, and attended every mayor's prayer breakfast. He'd groomed himself to be trustworthy, a man with whom people wanted to do business, a man who didn't screw a tennis coach or ask his mother-in-law to invest in an "opportunity." My husband had changed . . . or maybe he hadn't. Maybe he'd always been exactly what he was, and I had just fit the image I wanted of him into my world. The past two weeks had shown me that I had been wrong about him—he wasn't truthful, steady, or admirable.

"Well, maybe he's not involved per se, but I am not interested in anything that Jack has not approved." Jack was Mother's investment guy who she sometimes slept with, not that I was supposed to know. I had once caught them coming out of a hotel in Bossier, both looking, well, very satisfied and loving toward one another. I had never told her I knew.

I shrugged. "I don't know why Scott even asked you. I'll see what's going on when I talk to him next."

"Don't bother. Now, are you going to try on this dress Ruby made? I myself have settled on wearing the Ralph Lauren this year, but if I were younger and bustier, I might arm wrestle you for that dress." My mother commandeered a small chair and sank into it. Had my mother ever arm wrestled? I couldn't picture her even attempting it.

So, thing was, I didn't really want to cram my PMS-bloated body into that tight dress right now, but Ruby looked at me with something I hadn't seen from her before—hope. "I'm feeling fat today."

"Oh, pish." My mother waved her hands. "You need to switch from wine to vodka. And stop using salad dressing."

"Sure, General." I carefully took down the dress, admiring the waterfall of fabric. Maybe it was too young for me. It would show a lot of skin, and I may have consumed way too many carbs last week in my effort to comfort myself over losing my marriage. God, why couldn't I be one of those tragic figures who refused to eat because they were so bereft? Instead I ate an entire hamburger-with-extra-olives pizza from Johnny's Pizza . . . in one day.

I went to my office because even though it was the place where I had learned of Scott's infidelity, it felt like my safe place. Cute note cards, my Lilly Pulitzer planner, the stack of detective books, the adorable paisley bulletin board, and an original oil abstract in soft blush, navy, and gold hugged me. I could ignore the marks and scars on the white walls because I knew what that felt like. I had them, too.

The dress fit me, for the most part—Ruby had a good eye—but it was tight in the bust and maybe a smidge tight in my waist, but I managed to zip it without busting the zipper. No mirror in the office, but I loved the swish of the skirt and the way it felt against my skin. When I reemerged in the room with the mirror and my mother (two things that always tell the truth), Ruby assessed me with a practiced eye and nodded.

My mother tilted her head. "It works."

Ruby hooked a finger in the back of the dress. "I can let it out so you can breathe."

"Or I can stop eating Rolos out of Julia Kate's Easter basket hidden in the back of my closet," I said, turning to look in the mirror.

They were right—it worked. It worked well, and I wasn't sure that I had ever felt so glamorous, except at maybe my junior prom and my wedding day. The dress played up my assets—my nice boobs, my curvy figure, the sweep of my shoulders (thanks, Gran!), and my trim ankles. Most of Shreveport turned out in understated dresses for any gala, with the exception of Christmas in the Sky, the Shreveport Regional Arts Council fundraiser, which was scintillating and titillating and allowed for some sequins. Otherwise, most events required evening wear to be a tasteful background for Grandmother's pearls or the jewels hidden during the War between the States. Yes, there were southerners who thought the term *Civil War* rather distasteful. Lord help us all if we were ever not tasteful, sold the family silver, or wore white shoes after Labor Day. Our grandmothers would turn over in their overpriced caskets.

But this dress wasn't one of those sedate, ladylike ones. No, this one was not that.

If I were the same ol' Cricket, I wouldn't dare to wear it to Gritz and Glitz.

But I didn't feel like that Cricket anymore.

Still, I turned to my mother. "Mama?"

Marguerite wasn't one for shocking anyone with anything. She drove the speed limit, after all. But she nodded. "It suits you."

Ruby nodded. "It does. I knew it would."

I smiled at myself. "Then you need to tell me how much it costs because this is my dress for Gritz and Glitz."

"Are you joking? I'm not charging you for that dress." Ruby shook her head.

"Yes, you are," Marguerite said, rising and giving Ruby one of those looks I was often the recipient of. Ruby blinked a few times and shot me a panicked look.

I gave the smile I used when Julia Kate had to get shots at the doctor. "She's right. You are charging me."

"But you've given me a job, and we're . . . I don't know, I just don't feel comfortable taking money for this dress."

"But you will. And people are going to ask where I got this dress. They're going to ask where you got your dress. So maybe you need an answer for that. Perhaps this is an opportunity, Ruby. You're taking business classes, and, obviously, you're extremely talented. What does that mean? What do you want?"

Ruby opened her mouth and then closed it, with a sigh. "I don't know."

My mother walked toward Ruby and patted her cheek. "You need to find out, dear girl."

I wanted to ask, *Who are you, lady?* but didn't dare because my mother wasn't the sort to answer existential questions. But she was acting oddly. Why was she acting oddly?

But I didn't have a chance to siphon out why my mother was showing up unannounced and encouraging me to wear sexy dresses.

Marguerite made her goodbyes, which is to say she said, "My best, girls. I'm off to play bridge," and then she left.

I was left with no answers to my questions about my mother. Those would have to wait, anyway. I had much to do that day, starting with figuring out this private investigator situation.

CHAPTER ELEVEN

CRICKET

After my mother left and Ruby slunk off to get work done, I went back to my office, took off the refashioned dress, and pulled on my short-sleeved blouse, too-tight jeans, and comfy slip-on sneakers. After taking off the glamorous gown, I felt positively frumpy. Bluh. But then my eye caught the private investigator's form Ruby had given me the night before. Resolve moved inside of me. Or maybe gas from the PMS. Either way, I picked up the form.

Juke Jefferson.

Sounded like a football player.

I sank into my chair and picked up a pen. After filling in all the information needed, I stared at the instructions. Fax to 318-555-PEYE.

Um, no. I wasn't doing this via phone, fax, or email. This time I was going to lay eyes on the guy who would, God willing and the creek don't rise, get the goods on my jerkface husband.

So I shoved the form into my bag, went to the kitchen to heat up my overpriced coffee that had grown cold while I tried on the dress, and hollered to Ruby that I was going out.

On the way to Juke's office, I called to make sure he was available. Because halfway down the road, I realized that a private investigator might not keep bankers' hours.

A man answered with a muffled, "'Lo?"

"Mr. Jefferson?"

"Speaking." He sounded like I had woken him. I glanced at the van clock. It was 9:52 a.m., for heaven's sake. But maybe he'd spent the night on a stakeout or something. I didn't really know exactly what a private investigator did on a day-to-day basis.

"This is Cricket Crosby, a friend of your cousin Ruby. She recommended your services for collecting some photographic proof. I would like to stop by and visit with you before giving you a retainer."

"Fine by me."

"Perfect. I'm on my way now. I'm assuming you're in the office since you answered the phone?"

"Uh, yeah. But now? I'm not exactly . . . that is to say, can we set up an appointment?"

I sighed internally. The old Cricket would have agreed. This current version of Cricket had to be assertive. Time was of the essence. I mean, technically, Scott could go underground, and I could end up with a whole lot of nothing as my proof of his infidelity. "Actually, if you can't meet with me presently, I will have to move to the next private investigator on my list. I'm running out of time."

"No, don't do that. If you can give me twenty minutes to, uh, finish what I'm working on. I have a report that is, uh, due. Say, ten thirty? That work?" He suddenly sounded more alert, and I thought that I heard a toilet flush.

So at that point I was halfway to his office—maybe ten minutes away. But I could sit outside his business and check my phone messages until the appointed time. I had been putting off PTA and other committee business that I could catch up on easily in the van. "Sure. See you in thirty minutes."

Ten minutes on the dot, Waze told me I had reached my destination.

I rarely had cause to visit the area of the city that sat north of downtown, and I found it busier and more industrial than I remembered. Oil-field-supply companies, used-car lots, and pawnshops shoehorned in between fast-food restaurants, tax-return places, and discount stores. People clustered at bus stops and walked down the busy highway that would take one to Caddo Lake or the small towns that had once flourished under oil booms. This area felt like another world compared to the maintained flower beds, stately trees, and well-designed shopping centers that dominated south of town, but at the same time there was something so matter-of-fact and grounded about the business community embracing the two-story brick building that housed North Star Investigations. Here was no pretense. No baskets of petunias and boxwoods to obscure what went on behind them. What you saw was what you got.

That transparency spoke to the duped woman inside of me.

I pulled into a space in front of a bar that occupied the downstairs of the building and cracked the window, as the last day of March proved to be much warmer than the day before. I killed the engine and picked up my phone to check my messages. Patrick Vitt had called, offering an apology and a refund and relaying that he had not told Scott who hired him. Well, there was that.

After a few minutes, the sun streaked through the gray clouds, warming the van, making me sleepy. My eyes drooped, closing in spite of my phone jittering with responses to texts.

Until someone banged on my window.

"Oh my God!" I screeched, reaching for my center console, where I kept the pepper spray Scott had bought me at a gun show. It was probably in the bottom with the lost ChapSticks and packages of crumpled saltines. Could I reach it in time?

But then as I groped a bottle of forgotten hand sanitizer, it registered who was lurking outside my van door.

Griffin Moon.

"Hey, yo, it's me," he said, pressing his ginormous hands in a somewhat calming manner. "It's Griff. Remember?"

How could I forget? He'd witnessed the single worst night in my life.

Slapping a hand against my chest to calm my galloping heart, I managed, "Jesus, you scared the hell out of me."

I pressed the button to roll down the window, but the van had been shut off too long. Instead I opened the door.

Griffin stepped back, giving me room. "Hey, sorry. I thought you saw me."

He was a hulk of a man, even bigger than I remembered. Standing about six foot three or four, Griff had muscles that bulged, a jaw that could rival granite, and dark eyes that didn't pussyfoot around with being shifty. A very direct man. A man who fit easily into this industrial world of motor oil, fast cash, and liquor.

"I didn't see you," I said, standing and ignoring the way my knees cracked. My night on the couch watching our dog vomit and listlessly roam the living room had caught up with me. "What are you doing here?"

He gestured to the left, and I saw a fenced-in area with razor wire spiraling across the top. In front of the small garage sat a sign that mimicked the one on his tow truck. BLUE MOON TOWING. "That's my place. What are *you* doing here? I sent the car to the shop you wanted."

He thought I was here for him? No, wait, he thought I was here for the convertible.

"You did, and I already have it back in my garage. Um, I have some business here," I said, unable to stop my glance toward the redbrick building to my right.

"The bar doesn't open until one p.m.," he said, one side of his lip quirking up.

"Not the bar." I started to add *moron*, but I wasn't pressing my luck with this tough customer. Griff's sense of humor was somewhere between none and nonexistent.

"So you're here to see Juke?" His question was more than a simple question. I knew that.

I sort of rolled my eyes. "You know why."

"Yeah, I get it," he breathed, propping his arm on the top of my open door. It drew my eye to his bicep and sort of closed me in with an intimacy that was both unnerving and a teeny bit exciting. Which was stupid. Like, way stupid. Because I was a woman about to divorce her husband. A brokenhearted, scorned, PMSing woman who would not look at men or ice cream for at least a year. Okay, I was going to eat ice cream. Who was I kidding?

"Thank you for your assistance that night. I know I was a little, um, bitchy. I'm not usually that way, but it was a bad night."

Griffin's eyes may have softened. Or maybe the cloud passing over the sun played a trick on me. "Seemed like it was, but I'm glad I could help. Usually, I'm not on call at night. But one of my guys didn't show."

I wasn't sure why he told me that. It was an odd thing to say. Was it an apology for his being grumpy? "Well, again, I'm thankful."

At that moment, a ginger cat curled about his boots with a plaintive meow. Griffin reached down, and I nearly closed my eyes because a guy like him might give it a thumping. But Griffin, the tough biker-looking dude wearing work pants that hung perfectly on his hips, a tight polo with his name scrawled across the left of his chest, and a dangerous-looking tattoo that twined up his neck, nuzzled the cat and kissed it right between its green eyes.

I may have melted a little inside. Just a wee bit.

"Zeus," Griffin explained, setting the cat down. "He's a rescue."

If the man would have said, "I'm the principal dancer in Swan Lake," I wouldn't have been more shocked. I tried to recover by pretending to look for my phone in the van. "Well, he's a pretty cat."

Of course, my phone was still in my hand, so then I acted like someone had texted me. Which they had while I was napping. Shawna Kincaid wanted me to call River Cities Jewelers about the donation for the gala.

Griffin started backing up, inching toward his place, which I hadn't even noticed earlier because I had been so intent on finding the right office building. "I'll leave you to it. I was just passing by and noticed you. I try to keep an eye out. We don't have a lot of mischief out here, but every now and then . . ." He left off, allowing me to fill in the blank.

"Oh, well, thanks for checking." And I meant that.

"Later," he said, shoving his hands in his front pockets and turning his back to me. The cat followed him like a puppy.

"Later," I called, checking the time on my phone. It was 10:27 a.m. Close enough to the meeting time, so I climbed the metal stairs up to the office of Juke Jefferson, private investigator. The stairs were a bit rusty, but I felt optimistic. Not because of Griffin, who I was certain still thought me a blonde piece of fluff, but because . . . I wasn't certain. Because last night my husband had caught me trying to catch him cheating. And then he tried to have sex with me like I would want him to even touch me. And then I had to clean up two piles of dog vomit. So why I felt better, I hadn't a clue. But I did.

I knocked on the door, and someone hollered for me to "come on in."

I pushed inside, and my immediate impression of Juke and his office made me wince. Not merely because it was decorated in early-eighties shag carpet and wood paneling or because Juke looked a bit rumpled with a swatch of shaving cream on his chin, but because the overall aura (if one believed in such) was of despair. My hopefulness darted behind reality and hunkered there.

"Hello," I said, saying a prayer that my first impression was dead wrong.

Juke didn't rise but waved toward a chair that had seen better days twenty years ago. "Hey, take a seat."

The closer I got to him, the more he smelled of Barbasol shaving cream and mint toothpaste. I glanced at the lone tweed couch and noted a neatly folded blanket, an empty tumbler, and a television monitor angled toward the sofa. I didn't need a private eye to tell me that Juke had likely been sleeping one off when I phoned.

I sank down a bit too prissily on his chair and crossed my legs in the ladylike manner my mother had insisted upon. "I'm Catherine Crosby, but you can call me Cricket. I'm here about my husband. I need photographic proof that he's screwing my daughter's tennis coach. Only problem is that he now knows that I know, so he might be harder to catch."

Juke arched an inquisitive brow—one that could stand a bit of grooming.

"You see, I hired Patrick Vitt because he was recommended but—"

"He's an asshole," Juke interrupted.

"Yes. He is. But I didn't know that when I hired him. At any rate, he allowed himself to be paid off by my husband while he was sitting outside her house, and—"

"Wait," Juke interrupted again, holding up a hand and leaning forward. "You're telling me that Pat took money from your husband while he was on the job?"

"Yes, and he didn't even try to deny it. I saw it with these two eyes." I jabbed my fingers toward my eyes.

"How'd you do that?" Juke leaned forward, crossing his arms on the cluttered desk. At that moment, I allowed hope to emerge from where it had been hiding. Juke looked pissed, if not still a bit slovenly. With some grooming and maybe less booze, he could clean up nicely. He had pretty eyes and a full head of hair, and his shirt looked clean. Not to mention, he was outraged by a fellow PI's abuse of power. He'd earned a bit more favor with me.

"I was just making sure he was watching the house," I said.

Juke narrowed his eyes at me. "Yeah, okay, I get it."

And I knew he did. I couldn't help torturing myself, and I didn't know why I kept driving by that stupid woman's house. Probably needed to get a therapist on my payroll, too. But in actuality my weird obsession with seeing my husband parked in front of Stephanie's house had proven fortuitous. If I hadn't spied, then I wouldn't have seen the transaction. Patrick probably would have told me that he had nothing and would have strung me along until Scott made the first move and left me.

"So your old man knows you're trying to bust him?"

"Well, not necessarily me. Scott just knows someone is watching him. Because Patrick refused to tell him who had hired him. He just agreed to taking the money and leaving him alone."

Juke snorted. "Honor among thieves."

"Yeah, I guess, but Scott knows it's probably me. Who else would it be? And he didn't confront me last night, but the game is afoot. Trust me."

Juke leaned back in his chair, the squeak making me wince, and tented his hands over his stomach. "Well, that will make it difficult. We're going to have to be smarter than—what's his name again?"

"Scott."

"So tell me about Scott."

I spent the next ten minutes going over everything I could think of that would help Juke—Scott's personality, his friends, his habits, his job—and then I paid the retainer that Patrick Vitt had refunded me through Venmo minutes ago. Which made me wonder just how much my ass of a husband had paid him out on the street. After I finished, I rose and extended my hand.

Finally, Juke stood, and I saw that he, too, was tall like Griffin, but not nearly as muscled. Juke looked like someone had backed over him a few times, and his eyes looked haunted. I wondered about his story but not enough to pursue it. He took my hand. "I'll do my best."

"Thank you. I expect to hear from you in a few days."

"May take a week or so."

"The sooner the better. I have an attorney, and she's proceeding with typing up the petition. She'll file as soon as you get the proof we need. We want to strike first."

He dropped my hand. "Okay, then."

I started for the door.

"We're not all bad, you know," Juke said.

I looked back at him. "What?"

"Men. Not all of us are such dickheads. I'm not one of those guys. I can't be bought."

I gave him a small smile and a half shrug. "I hope not."

CHAPTER TWELVE

RUBY

Ten days later

Gran was turning seventy-five years old on Monday, so I pretty much had to go to the huge birthday bash on the Saturday afternoon of Gritz and Glitz, even if it meant seeing my entire family, including my strung-out mother who was somehow still considered family. My mom pretty much existed on the painkillers and antianxiety meds she got from a pain management clinic. She'd slipped eight years ago on a piece of ice while waitressing at one of the casinos, which netted her a small fortune in a lawsuit and a resulting steady diet of pain pills. We didn't talk much because we didn't have much to say to one another. She had never been a good mother and wasn't likely to change in the future. And lest anyone think I was a shitty daughter, I had tried time and again to connect with her with no result other than frustration that I had put myself out there and she hadn't even bothered to open the door. My mom hadn't even been pissed that my uncle, her former brother-in-law who she had always hated, had used me without my knowing and then got me locked up. In fact, my darling mommy had relayed to Gran that I was an idiot, and hadn't bothered coming to my trial or sending me a single care package, even at Christmas or on my birthday. So let's just say that I was cool with our official position to tolerate each other when we came into contact.

Gran, on the other hand, had been more of a mother to me than a grandmother. I had lived with her for most of my childhood since my parents were constantly splitting and getting booted out of their rental houses. Gran had baked me a graduation cake when I got my GED, sat beside me when I learned to drive, and glared at the prosecution at my trial. She was my greatest supporter and my chief confidante. I wasn't missing her birthday celebration even if Ed Earl would be there.

When I arrived, I tried to wander up to the large congregation of people in the backyard of the farmhouse without anyone noticing me. Gran took great pride in the house on the outskirts of the small town, refusing any sort of junk left in her front yard and instead populating the expanse with daffodils, tulips, and iris, which danced in the afternoon breeze. Of course, this meant that many of my grandfather's old heaps tic-tac-toed the backyard. Half-rusted livestock troughs held newly staked tomatoes, and Gran's greenhouse was missing a panel. My uncle Jimbo, along with Ed Earl, manned the large grill off the patio, while the rest of the males clustered around souped-up pickups parked on the woods' side, drinking beer and bragging about their hunting and fishing skills.

Most of the women in my family, including my gran and her sister, Jean, sat in a circle on the green lawn under the huge live oak. The matriarchs were sipping coffee and laughing like the two old hens they were. The younger women, including my mother, sat to the side drinking beer and wine. I crouched down next to my grandmother and kissed her weathered cheek. "Happy birthday, old yoman."

It was our joke—something I called her because I couldn't say my *w*'s when I was a toddler. My pawpaw always called her "woman" when he referred to her, a habit I picked up, quite adorably.

"Well, sugar, you made it," Gran said with pleasure, turning her faded hazel eyes on me. She wore a sparkly blouse and some polyester pants she'd probably bought in 1984. She looked like home to me. "Welcome home. I know it was hard coming here."

And with those words, my jaunt to Mooringsport had just become worth it. "Hey, I got you something."

I handed her a gift that contained the hand-painted porcelain earrings I had found at Printemps the first day I worked there. They were almost identical to the ones I had lost when I was eight years old and had meddled in my grandmother's jewelry box when I had been forbidden to play with her few good pieces. My grandfather had bought her the earrings in Mexico on an anniversary trip, and she'd been heartbroken when I had lost one in the backyard playing "house."

"You didn't have to get me a present!" she exclaimed, looking pleased anyway.

Aunt Jean set her coffee down. "Go on and get you somethin' to eat, Roo. Jimbo and Ed Earl have cooked enough for Coxey's army."

My mother finally noted me. She wore a too-tight T-shirt with a country and western band emblazoned across the top, ripped jeans, and boots that weren't doing her back any favors. Her hair was dyed black, with a wing of sapphire blue swooping back from her forehead, and she was pretty for a woman in her late forties, though hardship pinched her mouth, and too much sun marred her skin. She arched an eyebrow. "Thought you was too good for us and all."

Conversation sort of fell off, and everyone turned their gazes on me crouched beside Gran. All except the multitude of children throwing the football and skipping rope in the side yard. They continued whooping, grunting, and bickering, as children did when unsupervised.

"It's Gran's birthday," I said.

"Well, you didn't show up on *my* birthday," my mother said, crossing her legs and taking another drink of whatever was in her faux Yeti tumbler. Probably straight-up vodka.

"You noticed, huh? Surprising," I said, turning my focus back on Gran. I wasn't going to indulge my mother, who loved to draw attention to herself. That's why she'd stayed a cocktail waitress when she could have worked at a dozen other jobs. She liked the low-cut blouses, the flirting, and making my daddy jealous. The fights they had made us quite popular in the neighborhood, as they usually brought the sheriff and everyone outside in their robes to watch my mother sobbing and my daddy in cuffs. Good times.

My mother sighed heavily and opened her mouth to say something more, but Gran held up a finger. "It's my birthday, Leta. Let's be nice to each other."

My mother snapped her mouth closed and rolled her eyes.

Gran distracted everyone by lifting my gift, and it seemed to work, because all eyes went to the small package in her hands. My grandmother took her time, sliding the tape loose with her long nails. She carefully folded the flowered paper as if she might use it again and shimmied the box open. "Oh, lookee here. These are just like the ones your pap got me in Cancún!"

"I felt like I owed you these," I said, grateful for my grandmother for so much, though most recently for getting my mother's attention off me. "I found them in the store where I work."

"You didn't owe me a thing, but I love them. I'm wearing them to church tomorrow." Gran carefully put the lid on the box and leaned over to plop a kiss on my cheek. She smelled like coffee and Estée Lauder, and I was sucked back to my childhood in an instant. I closed my eyes briefly and pretended that the water under the bridges I had burned wasn't so raging.

At that moment Ed Earl wandered over. "Hey there, Roo."

I glanced up and gave him a frosty look before looking back at Gran and Aunt Jean. I wasn't talking to him.

"Go on now, Ed Earl," Gran said, shooting him a warning glance. "You got burgers to grill."

"I want to talk to Ruby Lynn. We have some things to say," my uncle insisted, jabbing the spatula in his hand in my direction.

Ed Earl was the meanest of my gran's five kids. She sometimes joked that she'd dropped him on his head more than a few times as a child, and it hadn't made him stupid—it had made him mad, and it had stuck. There had been many a time that Gran had said she was done with him, but the woman couldn't help herself from letting him back into the fold. She loved him in spite of his shortcomings and illegal doings, especially since he'd given her three grandbabies to love. My three male cousins were apples that had not dropped far from the tree, but a grandmother's love was shade enough for rotten fruit.

"Ed, it's my birthday, and I don't want no fuss. Got it?" Gran jabbed a finger at Ed Earl.

"I'm not fussin', Ma. Just need to talk to Roo."

I didn't want to talk to my uncle. There wasn't anything to say. I would never forgive him for taking two years of my life. "I have nothing to say."

Standing, I threw Ed Earl my best "Go straight to hell" look and moved toward the table holding platters of chicken wings, bowls of slaw, potato salad, and fluffy fruit salads made with JELL-O and Cool Whip. I took a plate, even though I wasn't hungry, because it was something to do and would maybe keep my relatives from trying to talk to me.

But no one in my family ever took a hint.

"Hey, Roo," said my uncle Jimbo as he slopped a huge serving of baked beans on his plate. "Madison made these."

"Who's Madison?"

"Mikey's girlfriend. She's real nice. They're having a baby in the fall." Jimbo pointed over toward a girl who stood beside Ed Earl's youngest son. Madison wore shorty shorts, a tank top with something glittery, and too much makeup. She kept glancing over at the side yard, looking nothing like a happy mother-to-be. I tried to angle my head to see who she was looking at but couldn't get a good look.

"Oh. Good for them, then." I didn't want to make small talk. At this point, I wished I hadn't come. I could probably go ahead and slip out. Gran had her gift, I had made an appearance, and I truly needed a little time with my hair in order to look good for the gala later that night. I would wait for Gran to blow out the candles, and then I would skedaddle.

Jimbo took a bite of beans right over the table, dropping one on his oversize Salt Life T-shirt. He smudged it with a napkin, picking off the bean and popping it into his mouth. Jimbo was the only one of Gran's kids who had remained single. He'd had some girlfriends here and there, but they never managed to stick. Eating beans off his shirt might have explained that. He smacked a few times in satisfaction and then leveled me with a stare. "You know, you really should talk to Ed Earl. He needs to say his piece."

"And you need to mind your own business, Jimbo. If he wanted to say his piece, he could have said it to the judge over two years ago when I was being unfairly accused."

"You could have told them where you got the stuff. You didn't."

Yeah, I could have. I had kept my mouth shut during my arrest and trial when I should have squealed like a piggy. Ed Earl and his stupid ring of drug dealers would have gone to prison, and I would have gotten slapped with probation for being a rat. And it's not like I hadn't wanted to send my deserving uncle up the river. I had. But Gran might have gone down, too. Ed Earl and some other lowlifes had been making meth in her old trailer on land she owned. He'd even stored the meth in Gran's outside freezer and given her tainted money, making her an accessory. As much as I wanted to nail my uncle, I couldn't put Gran at risk. So I became the sacrificial lamb, just as my uncle had intended. He knew I wouldn't talk and that I wouldn't get much time for the crime. His selfishness knew no bounds, but according to Juke, he'd gotten enough of a warning from some guys in a cartel that he'd ceased his operations. So at least he'd gotten out of the game.

The result of Ed Earl's betrayal was Gran refusing him any contact with the family until he cleared his shit out and straightened the hell up. Ed Earl was probably still involved in something illegal—that was his nature—but if he was, he was very quiet about it. Gran ran this family. And family was everything.

All the Balthazars knew that.

Even me.

"I don't want to talk about it," I said, smacking a spoonful of potato salad onto my paper plate and walking away. I headed toward the side yard where the kids were zipping around and saw Griffin standing by himself, tapping on his phone. Ah, that's what Madison was looking at.

I went and stood beside him because no one would mess with me when Griff was around.

He looked up. "Oh, you came."

"It's Gran's birthday."

He grunted and shoved his phone in his back pocket. "Yeah, well, it's a command performance. Saw your boss lady a week back. She was seeing Juke."

"Yeah," I said, trying the potato salad. Wasn't bad. Lots of mustard, the way I liked it.

"Not sure she'll get much out of him. Juke's on the bottle. Has been for months."

I eyed Juke, who stood silently, leaning on one of the trucks, beer in his hand. "He told me that he was fine."

Griff glanced at me with what I assumed to be disbelief. Hard to tell with Griff. He wasn't generous with his emotions.

I sighed. "Look, Juke needs a break. Even if he's drinking too much, he wouldn't do it on the job. He was a good cop."

Griff grunted. And that was his answer. But I also found it amusing that he'd brought up Cricket. I had never been super close to Griff, but I was as close to him as anyone. He was an enigma in our family—not only smart but principled and ambitious. He'd never caused any trouble—keeping his nose clean, getting a degree at the local community college in business, all the while working in a garage for tuition money. He was a neat freak who was impossibly handsome and often quiet, and he had a soft heart beneath his sometimes-scary demeanor. And it seemed he might have an interest in bouncy blondes with cheating husbands.

As that amusing thought struck me, I caught sight of Dakota Roberts.

What the hell?

Shit.

"Huh?" Griff asked.

"What?" I said.

"You said 'shit' like something was wrong." Griff cracked his knuckles and gave pregnant Madison, who was watching him like a dieter watches a lonely piece of pie, a dissuasive glare. Hey, I got it. Madison might have been pregnant with my other cousin's kid, but Griffin was a prime piece, if one were going to compare a man to, say, filet mignon.

"Uh, I forgot I had something to do today. Something important. I'm probably going to take off," I said, trying not to sound panicky.

Griffin shrugged. "Cool."

"Tell Gran I had to go. Tell her I love her." I looked over to where my grandmother sat, waving her veined hands, no doubt telling a tall tale. Her scruffy gray hair stuck up, and her new glasses made her eyes look adorably big. My heart swelled even as my gut roiled at the thought of facing Dak's disdain or having to run from whatever Ed Earl wanted with me.

I didn't stick around for Griffin to agree or not. Luckily, I had worn sneakers, and my car keys were in the small crossbody strung across my torso. Free to move about the family compound.

I snuck around the side along the nandinas that sheltered the daylilies that had yet to bud and walked around to the front of the house, only pausing to hurl the football that had bounced my way back to

Cousin Derrick's oldest. I had parked my Honda at the end of the road, angled for an easy getaway. Hey, if I had learned anything from my family, it was how to make a quick departure. Unfortunately, they hadn't taught me the art of not getting caught.

Which proved to be true as footsteps sounded behind me.

I hurried my own pace, hoping I could escape before I had any more awkward encounters. I still had to endure a night of pinched toes and people I didn't know. Could this day be any more torturous?

I got my answer when I reached my car.

Dak had been following me, an odd look on his face.

I didn't want to talk to him any more than I had Ed Earl. My past wasn't just knocking; it was a swarm of Vikings with a battering ram. Sliding into the Honda, I jabbed my key into the ignition and pulled the door closed, locking it for good measure, though I knew Dak wasn't the kind of guy to jerk it open without my permission. I turned the key, and my car did its normal *grrr*ing as the engine attempted to turn over. But didn't. I turned the key again. Click. Again. Click.

Damn it.

I looked at my steering wheel, wishing I had asked Griff to take a look at it last week when I had visited Juke. It had been acting reluctant to start for a few weeks. Perfect timing to die. Story of my life.

Dak stood outside my window and yelled, "Sounds like your alternator!"

I opened the door. "How would you even know?"

His mouth flatlined. "Want me to take a look under the hood?"

"Do you know what you're looking for?" I asked, feeling prickly. Why was this happening? My plan had been simple—show up, give Gran her gift, and get out without any entanglements.

"Not really." Dak looked like he always did—like something I wanted to wrap my arms about, and at the same time something I wanted to erase from my life forever only because he reminded me of every stupid thing I had ever done. "But I can give you a lift back in town. I was on my way out."

"What are you doing here anyway?" I asked.

"I brought Drake out. His truck's in the shop. He's been hanging with Harlan—they have a duck lease. Harlan's taking him back home so . . ."

Drake was Dak's much younger brother—a bonus baby for the Roberts family. I remembered Drake as a plump, silent boy who always peeked out at me from behind corners when I visited Dak's house. I couldn't imagine him as an eighteen-year-old driving a truck, but I guessed that was his age now.

"I don't need a ride," I said, glancing back at Gran's house, wondering if Griff would come look at my car and figure out the issue. Or maybe my cousin would even give me a ride into town. I pulled out my phone and glanced at the time. Three thirty-eight. I had to be polished and ready to go for drinks with Ty at five thirty.

Ed Earl came around the corner of the house, his gaze on me.

"Okay, where's your ride?" I asked Dak.

"Over there," he said, pointing toward a shiny F-250 that looked exactly like what he would drive. Dark gray, no frills, tires big enough to get him unstuck.

"Let's go," I said, walking toward the truck.

Dak followed. I only knew this because I heard the crunch of his shoes on the gravel. I wasn't looking back because Ed Earl might think he had a chance to "say his piece," which I fairly knew would be a grovel about how he'd had no other choice and how if he'd turned himself in, he would have gone away for hard time and his family would have starved. Violins played in my head, and then I dashed them to smithereens with the big hammer of resentment that was always nearby.

"Unlock," I called back rather bossily.

But Dak did as I asked, the locks unclicking so I could scurry up into the passenger's side. As I fastened my seat belt, I peeked through the windshield and saw Ed Earl standing in the drive of Gran's house with his hands on his hips, looking at me with disgust.

Dak climbed in and cranked the truck. "Are you running from Ed Earl?"

"No . . . Okay, yes. I don't want to talk to him."

"Because . . . ?"

"He's responsible for me going to jail?" I said, not unsarcastically.

Dak slid his gaze toward me and then backed out of his spot, which was jammed between my mom's Jaguar (yes, that's how she'd spent her back injury money) and a jeep that looked like every sixteen-year-old boy's wet dream. Which meant it was one of my cousins'.

We bumped down the road skirting the lake. Daffodils clumped at the base of big pine trees, a bunch of schoolgirls nodding at gossip, and the sun played peekaboo with the puffy clouds. The sticky new green paired with the cerulean sky deserved more than my sour mood, but my afternoon hadn't gone the way it had in my head when I had struck out for Gran's right after I got off my shift at Printemps. And to make it worse, now I had to buy a new alternator or starter or battery or maybe even a new car that I couldn't afford. So yeah, screw the beauty around me. I wasn't in the mood for its cheer.

Thankfully, Dak was silent as he wended around sharp turns and stop signs as we entered the small community of Mooringsport. Here was a town that time had escaped. One could be convinced it was 1957 or 2022. Same houses, same junk stores, same vista of the cypress-studded lake. I liked that about the small dot on the map—the way the old town never changed. I'd take comfort where I could.

We sped over the bridge, heading south, and I watched a boat zip along the channel, its frothy wake disrupting the glassy water. I sighed. "Beautiful."

Dak looked over. "Yeah."

And that was pretty much it for conversation for the next five minutes. I took that time to soak up the way he smelled, the nineties country music on the radio, and the stack of little trees that made the cab smell like men's cologne and leather. Dak draped one forearm on the steering wheel while the other propped against the console between us. The man had great hands with strong, blunt fingers and knuckles that had met a few noses. They looked like the kind of hands a woman wanted on her body. I certainly had at one time.

"I like the bar," I said after we'd departed Mooringsport and were zipping along Highway 1 over the speed limit but not so fast that I couldn't appreciate the rolling fields interrupted by stands of woods flowered with dogwood and redbud.

"Thanks. When I left the league, I wasn't quite sure what I wanted to do. Had some offers to coach in the minors and a few bites on broadcasting, but that's not me, you know. I thought about all my strengths, and alcohol was one of them. I mean, I was good at making drinks and indulging in the oil of good conversation. Plus, after being on the road so much, I wanted to come home and stay in one spot." His mouth curved into a self-deprecating smile as he glanced over at me.

I felt that smile down to my toes, but I jerked my gaze away so I didn't reach out and touch his arm. Which was a crazy compulsion I had. "I understand. I think about leaving this place, but the 'out there' is scarier than being in the same city as my mother."

"She's still here?"

"Didn't you see her at the party?"

"I wasn't looking for anyone. Mostly, I'm just looking out for my kid brother." He shot me a look of apology. I got it. My family wasn't the kind that people wanted their daughters to marry or their sons to get mixed up with. He changed the station and then looked back over at me.

"So Juke said you're working for an antique store?"

"Yeah, it's a really nice one right off Line Avenue, and I'm about to graduate with a business administration degree. I'm thinking about continuing with school, but not sure. I might have a new opportunity soon. Or not." My mind flitted to Cricket and her mother's insistence I do something more with my reconstructed haute couture pieces. I wanted to believe that I could parlay my love of creating something new from something old into a career, but I doubted that was possible. Two women cheering for me was a far cry from actually getting other women to buy my pieces. What was the market for something like what I did? And such a venture would require money—I couldn't sell the pieces out of Cricket's store. I would probably have to take it online. And that was a whole new ball game—ads, marketing gimmicks, seeking influencers. I didn't have that kind of money to invest.

My sigh was heavy.

"Oh, surely it's not that bad. You're smart and pretty. Already have those two things going for you, and you seem very intent on overcoming what happened to you."

His words smoothed over me like a balm. I allowed myself to feel his words, and then I got irritated at myself. What did I care what Dak thought of me? We'd broken up long ago and had had nothing to say to each other until now. So why had I allowed that small flame that flickered for him to surge up? Especially when I had the handsome Ty waiting in the wings for me? Ty liked me. Thought I was cool. Didn't have to deliver false praise because he already thought I was worthy. Maybe. At least I tried to convince myself of this.

I knew my weaknesses. And it wasn't the hunk next to me humming to an Alan Jackson song. My past had made me defensive, had dragged me down so that I was embarrassed of who I had been and what I had done. And some of that was okay to own. Spending two years in a correctional facility where I folded laundry and cleaned toilets as the high points of my day, always looking over my shoulder for trouble, trying to keep my head down and merely survive had stamped itself on me. The impossible shame of being a convict cloaked me in despair. Many days I wondered how I could overcome my past. How could I knock off the chip on my shoulder? Brush away the prickling that I wasn't good enough to deserve happiness?

So to his words about overcoming my mistakes, I said nothing. Instead I looked out the window at the ragtag houses passing by, at the occasional flattened opossum on the shoulder of the road, and at the faded white line that boxed the truck within the asphalt. Gone was any spark of agreeableness. That's what shame did to a person.

And Dak knew my shame.

"I know you live on Cross Lake. If you don't want to take me all the way into town, I can call someone." But I didn't know who. Jade was holding down the afternoon shift so Cricket could get her hair done. I had a few friends I could try. And my grandmother was probably eating a piece of her birthday cake.

"Don't mind dropping you off. Bar is covered for the afternoon. Where to?"

"You know where the old El Chico was in Madison Park? I live in a duplex over that way. Querbes' golf course is in my backyard."

"So you have a collection, huh?"

"What?"

"Of golf balls? Probably get a lot in your yard." Dak maneuvered his truck onto I-49, and I thought how surreal it was that I was sitting beside my ex-boyfriend talking about golf balls . . . and that in a few hours I would be going to a gala in a ball gown. How weird had my world gotten?

"You still play? I can pay you for the ride with a bucket of practice balls," I said.

Dak looked over at me. "You don't have to pay me to help you, Ruby."

Again, something in his words both soothed and irritated me. I didn't want to need anyone. That was the point of everything that I had been doing. Relying on my family's regard for me had landed me in prison, relying on friends had always proven disappointing (or maybe I had always chosen the wrong kind of friends), and relying on something good to come my way had always shown me that nothing was as good as I thought it would be. Was I cynical?

Um, you think?

I liked the idea of determining my own direction, so, again, I said nothing, even though his tone was as inviting as worn flannel. I wanted to curl up in it and assure myself that he was right. I was worthy, I could overcome, I could accept help.

For the remainder of the ride, I hummed along with some Reba McEntire song that reminded me of days I didn't want to remember and tried to beat back the way I used to feel when he held me in his arms and hold tight to my intention to remain unaffected by him. I directed him to "take a left" or "hang a right" until we arrived at my modest duplex with the double porch swings and planters of tulips. I rented the space, but I had taken ownership of making it pretty with a spring wreath and a few hanging ferns. The elderly lady next door had contributed some money toward my efforts to spruce up the rental. I liked the results.

"Here I am," I said, gesturing to my place. I did a double take when I saw the bouquet of flowers on the doorstep.

"Looks like you have a delivery," Dak said, turning into the driveway. "I'm guessing they're from your boyfriend."

"I don't have a boyfriend."

He looked at me and lifted a shoulder. I knew he was remembering Ty and judging him. Okay, so Ty dressed in circa-eighties douchebag, but he'd been cool to Dak when he'd acted like an ass. My date that night wasn't necessarily a guy Dak would hang with, but that didn't mean Ty wasn't a good guy.

"Well, thanks again, Dak," I said, dropping my hand and feeling for the crossbody I had dropped onto the floorboard when we'd first left Mooringsport. My actions shifted me closer to Dak, and I felt his hand tug my hair.

I grabbed my bag and looked up.

"It's been good seeing you, Ruby."

He could have said many things—I could see that in his eyes. Maybe something inane, like *Way to finally get your shit together,* or encouraging, like *You're doing good, kiddo,* or perhaps even sentimental, as in *I wish things hadn't ended the way they had.* But Dak wasn't prone to needless words. Never had been. So by telling me it was good to see me, I knew what he meant because I felt the same roller-coaster emotions, that vacillation between regret and acceptance, that small question of what if, that whiff of attraction, of longing, or wanting something that probably could never exist again because we were no longer those stupid kids who believed in white picket fences and staring off into the sunset side by side.

I lifted my body and looked him right in his pretty eyes and said, "Yeah, you too."

My right hand groped for the door handle just as he leaned toward me.

My stomach tightened in expectation because I wanted to feel his mouth against mine. Part of me needed to taste what once was, revel in the desire I had always felt for this man. Part of me knew it would be bad because I could slide right down that slippery slope. But he bypassed my lips, instead brushing a kiss on my cheek. "Be well, Ruby. You deserve happiness."

His words were like the swish of a hand over a fevered brow—desperately wanted but, at the same time, useless to do any good.

So I opened the door and climbed out. When he backed out of my driveway, I didn't look back at him. Instead I took the bouquet of red roses nestled in baby's breath and lifted it to my nose. They smelled of waxy nothingness. The card attached read, "Looking forward to tonight."

I unlocked my door and took the flowers inside.

CHAPTER THIRTEEN

CRICKET

Once upon a time I had loved going to balls. Mardi Gras, cotillion, or deb functions with sparkles, champagne, and the opportunity to judge the band procured for the Baron's Ball against the one they used for the ARTini bash. This was always a fierce discussion topic among my friends for some reason. Oh, along with the flowers. Did they spend enough? Who did them? But at any rate, I had always looked forward to tugging on a fancy dress, painting my toenails blush, and fastening on my grandmother's good jewelry. But after a few years, it was the same people having the same conversations around the same glitzy watering holes. I had begun to dread all social events that involved wearing heels and making small talk, but because of Scott's reputation and because the bank depended on him to hobnob with people who brought him new business, I went for the prescribed two and a half hours and then massaged my feet all the way home, looking forward to pajamas and Netflix.

But for some reason that escaped me, I was looking forward to attending Gritz and Glitz tonight.

Okay, the reason didn't escape me—I loved the way Ruby's dress looked on me, and I relished the opportunity to brag on my assistant's ability to create something bold, original, and, for all the Gen Xers out there, upcycled. I knew that people were going to be intrigued by me wearing something "so not me," the way I knew that Scott wouldn't be able to find his black dress socks and Julia Kate would want money for pizza that night.

So after finding Scott's socks and leaving a check for Johnny's Pizza, I sprayed my extravagant updo with something akin to shellac and stepped into my sexpot dress. I had already put on a pair of delicious black-heeled sandals that tied at the ankle in anticipation of not being able to bend down once I was zipped into the dress. I trailed out of my closet into the bathroom, where Scott was securing his cuff links in the mirror. The man always looked spectacular in a tux, which made me sigh just a little, but I tucked away any tenderness I felt for him when I saw the box with the fox butt plug winking at me from his own open closet.

Okay, fine. It didn't wink, but I could see the corner of the box, and it might as well have been laughing at me.

"Can you zip me?" I asked, clutching my dress to my bosom, because though the man had seen me without clothes a thousand times over, I would be damned if he ever saw my size-DD boobs ever again.

He turned and made a face. "Where did you get that dress?"

"Ruby."

"Your assistant loaned you a dress?"

"No. She custom-made this dress for me. She has her own label. She'll be famous one day." A bit of an exaggeration, but I believed in my heart that Ruby's talent for refashioning couture could take her places. I was determined for her, and besides, having a bit of a project in Ruby kept me from thinking about how my life was unraveling like a bad hemstitch.

Scott tugged the zipper up as I sucked in. "There ya go."

I readjusted my breasts, wiggling snug into the creation, and then turned to my reflection in the full-length mirror on the bathroom door.

I smiled at myself.

Scott was watching me, a glint in his eye. "You look good, Cricket."

Smacking my red lips together and turning my head so I could see how my vintage updo made my neck look more elegant, I said, "I know."

And then I grabbed the black Chanel evening bag my mother had loaned me and strolled out the door, leaving my husband staring at me bemusedly.

Twenty-five minutes later, we were stepping out of the Uber and onto the red carpet of the Municipal Auditorium where Elvis had once titillated young girls and Hank Williams had put the *Louisiana Hayride* on the map. The gorgeous art deco building had been transformed with arches swagged with champagne fabric, and so many twinkle lights a person couldn't hide too many flaws. Thank goodness for Spanx and Botox, right?

"Oh. My. Gawd. Cricket," someone punctuated beside me. I turned to find Susie Simmons's eyes as wide as her husband's nipples. Don't judge me—I noticed how huge they were one day when I took Julia Kate to the club to swim. Let's just say they were disturbingly large, just like his wife's eyes. The rest of her was more forgotten scarecrow from her diet of sparkling water and air, so maybe that's why her eyes were so big in her thin face. As to her husband's large nipples, I'd have to chalk those up to genetics.

I turned to her with my normal society smile. "What?"

"What are you wearing, you daring bitch?" she drawled with a braying laugh. "You look like effing Marilyn Monroe. Oooooh, someone named Scott is getting lucky tonight."

Scott chuckled and curved his arm around my waist. "That's right, Suze. She's all mine."

I may have thrown up a little in my mouth.

Luckily, I saw Ty Walker and Ruby drive by. "Hey, Scott, go on in if you want. I see Ruby, and she doesn't really know many people. I'm going to wait on her."

"Fine by me," he said, dropping the husbandly husband routine and jabbing a ticket at me. "I'll be at the bar."

I took the ticket and turned to wait for Ruby. Luckily, the weather had cooperated, and velvet dusk debuted a few stars and a gentle breeze that allowed for bared shoulders and showing off pedicures. Ty drove a BMW and looked nice in a navy tuxedo. But Ruby, when she emerged from the car, looked like a silent film actress. And I swear to Coco Chanel, everyone standing outside the event stopped talking and turned to stare.

She was an edgy, dramatic, dark Cinderella.

Just magnificent.

"Hey, Ruby," I said, stepping up because for a moment she looked like a baby seal surrounded by hungry polar bears.

"Hey, Cricket," she said, giving me a nervous smile.

"You look amazing," I said as I hugged her, twining an arm around her waist, much as I would if she were my child, and walking her up the stairs. Ty walked behind us, giving me a smile when I glanced back. "Hey, Ty. Nice to see you again."

"You too, Mrs. C. Your dress is crazy nice."

I didn't like being called "Mrs. C.," like I was Mrs. Cunningham and he was the Fonz, not that Ty would even know what *Happy Days* was, but I did like that he noted my dress. "Thank you. It is crazy nice. Ruby made it."

"Yeah? Well, when she told me she made her own clothing, I envisioned the apron I made my mother at summer camp. I didn't realize she was talking art."

I felt Ruby's pleasure at him calling her creation art, and I took huge gratification in everyone studying us as we entered the building. Every woman turned, wineglass in hand, to give us the once-over, and all the men looked pretty dang appreciative, especially the gay ones, like my friend Chris, who drifted over to us and muttered, "My, my, my, I see some ladies who are causing quite a stir. Shall I toss in some vodka and rocks?"

I couldn't think of one single person in my life more naturally charming than Chris, with his soft, draggy vowels and his slightly smart-ass but sincerely warm smile. Not to mention, as the most sought-after interior designer, his taste and judgment on what was "just so" was exactly what Ruby needed to take the next step with her venture.

"Chris," I crowed, kissing his cheek and giving him a pat on the bottom—a total inside joke between us that he loved. It had to do with an older gay client and a night with too many tequila shots when Chris and I were staging a house for a movie. "I know you know Ruby, but do you *really* know Ruby?"

Chris cast his eyes on my sidekick. "Well, well, Ruby child, look at you all dressed up for the ball. And with a dish of candy to boot." Chris ran his practiced eye over Ty, who didn't seem to mind being thusly assessed. I got the feeling Ty liked to be admired by anyone.

Ruby gave Chris a thankful smile. "Thank you, Chris."

"And who made your lovely gowns? Do tell."

I grinned at Ruby. "It's a custom-made line by an up-and-coming designer. We'll have these for sale at Printemps later this spring."

Chris gave an exaggerated mouth drop. "Are you telling me that you're carrying custom couture now? Shut the front door."

I shrugged one shoulder, not exactly certain how to answer that. Ruby and I hadn't really talked about what came next for her. It was obvious to me that something *should* happen, whether I phoned my aunt and begged her to come down and meet Ruby—and visit Marguerite—or whether Ruby wanted to build her own business from the ground floor up. We needed to talk about it, even though I supposed it was *her* decision and I hadn't a role other than as her biggest supporter. "You'll know soon enough."

"Oooh," Chris drawled, eyeing Ruby. "You girls have a secret. I love secrets."

I was about to make a casual comeback when my eye caught sight of my husband's biggest secret—Stephanie the Tennis Pro entering the foyer with a few other similarly fit younger women. She had her hair in a high ponytail, wore a slinky dress covered in sequins, and carried a clutch that I happened to know cost $880 only because I had seen it in the Bergdorf Goodman email I had deleted from my computer a few days ago. How did a tennis pro afford a Christian Louboutin bag on her salary?

I glanced over to where my husband stood with his cronies, sipping scotch and telling middle-aged-white-guy stories. Scott glanced at Stephanie, and I saw him acknowledge her. She, in turn, smiled slyly at him.

"Uh," I said, before realizing that Chris would totally catch it.

He arched a waxed eyebrow.

"Nothing. Just my Spanx riding up into places only my doctor should see."

"Well, that tells me everything I need to know about Scott," Chris said with a laugh. "Shall I fetch you ladies some chardonnay?"

If only he knew what Scott had been up to in recent months.

"Beat you to it," Ty said, handing off a glass of something gold and fizzy. "But I went with champagne because these dames deserve the bubbly."

"Too true," Chris said, finding the perfect opportunity to flirt with a straight guy. Or I assumed Ty Walker was a straight guy. They turned to one another and discussed golfing, which was more boring than timing a centipede crossing the kitchen, which was something I had done weeks ago when I was mourning my marriage. Seemed twenty-six minutes and a few seconds in change was the winning number. And then Pippa had come in and promptly eaten the centipede, which seemed like a very unfair reward for the creature reaching its goal.

Ruby looked amused at Ty being tied up with Chris as she stepped back toward me so we were nearly shoulder to shoulder. Then I watched as she crowd-surfed with her gaze. Her eyes lingered on Stephanie for a moment, as if she knew who the woman was.

"That's her," I whispered under my breath.

She straightened, and her mouth went flat. Then she uttered a really dirty word that made my eyes pop. But I loved it. Loved that she came to my defense. Loved having someone else know about Stephanie. Somehow it made my burden less.

"Yeah, she is, isn't she?" I said, somehow feeling emboldened in my dress.

My mother arrived, along with my father and his wife, so the next thirty minutes were spent trying to defuse the barbs my mother tossed Crystalle's way while helping everyone find their tables, which were not close to each other, thanks be to God. My mother settled into talking with her friend Roberta, and my father and his wife—who I might add did *not* resemble a blueberry, as my mother had suggested in a very passive-aggressive, backhanded-compliment kind of way—were sipping gin and tonics and catching up with their former neighbors. I noted that Ruby was being attended to by her date, so I slipped out of the main room to check if all was ready for the live auction that would occur in two hours' time. We had placed all the auction donations in a holding area off the foyer and had been awaiting a few last-minute items. If they didn't arrive, I would have to ensure that an announcement was made and they were stricken from the booklet I had designed.

We had several pieces of art, a handful of collector's guns, and a baseball signed by Babe Ruth; otherwise, the live auction consisted mostly of trips and experiences. Scott and I had once bid on a hunting trip to Argentina, which he promptly sold for more money to one of his friends. Yes, my husband profited off charity. I hadn't thought that much about it at the time, but now it seemed pretty shoddy and exactly the kind of thing a cheaterpants would do.

My sojourn to the holding room proved useless since my friends Shelley and Donna had everything perfectly placed, a gaggle of pretty high school girls waiting to showcase the items, and cute little paddles with funny pictures of celebrities on them as the bidding tools. I could just hear the auctioneer say *Sold to Lady Gaga!* and how confused some of the older people would be. Already a gentleman had exclaimed within my hearing, "Is that Ingrid Bergman?" when he'd received his paddle upon entry to the gala. I wasn't even going to try to explain Gaga to him.

Still, not my problem. I was the cataloger and creator of the auction booklet. My cochairs would have to worry about explaining who the Fresh Prince of Bel-Air was. And since all the items had arrived, I had no announcements to make later.

I waved farewell to my two friends and slipped out, nearly mowing over a waiter. The foyer had thinned out, with only a cluster of people here and there, including Stephanie, who was laughing as if the world belonged to her.

Or maybe as if my husband did.

I stepped back into the shadows tucked around the corner of the foyer and closed my eyes, pressing myself to the wall. Beside me, a gate had been erected to prevent people from sneaking into areas they shouldn't. But as I stood clinging to the wall like a nervous bungee jumper, I heard someone talking from beyond the gate in the gathered darkness, which was faintly lit by the glowing exit sign.

More specifically, it sounded like Scott saying something about "being worried."

I inched a little closer, trying to peer into the darkness but stay hidden, which was not easy to do with a flared dress and clacky heels.

"I'm telling you, he was watching me," Scott insisted.

My heart started racing.

Another unrecognizable male voice asked something like, "How do you know?"

"He was sitting outside of Steph's house. I watched him out the window for a while. He didn't take any pictures or anything, but I could tell he was watching. I just had a feeling."

I heard a muffled question I didn't quite catch, and Scott said, "My wife? Maybe. The guy wouldn't say. He just told me to pay him five hundred and he'd disappear. Refused to give his name or who he worked for."

Another muffled response.

"I gave it to him. What else could I do?" Scott said, his voice in a whisper yell. "Cricket might suspect something, but I think she won't bother snooping. She's content with her life. She never rocks the boat. So this has to be about the deal. You said it was foolproof. I'm telling you, I'm not going down, not for what I'm getting. I'm out."

The words grew heated, but my mind was too busy hanging up on the words "deal" and "going down." And then it leaped back to my mother's words in the store last week, about how Scott had some kind of opportunity for an investment. A prickling of suspicion rose on my neck.

What exactly was Scott Benoit Crosby up to?

The only other bit I caught before the two slipped back the opposite way was something about "Keep them comin' or you'll regret it" and "Leave that to me." Those words were from whomever Scott was talking to. I saw a vague figure as they slipped around the corner, but I couldn't even begin to guess who it was since he wore a dark tux and had a medium build and conservative-looking haircut . . . just like half the men at the gala.

I pressed a hand against my galloping heart, my mind whirring like the blender I rarely used. Except for margaritas. I was brilliant at margaritas.

Pulling my thoughts from chasing that drunken bunny, I tried to decipher exactly what Scott could be involved in. I already knew he was engaging in an extramarital affair, but this sounded . . . illegal. Or at the very least worrisome. And Scott didn't think I would do anything. *She never rocks the boat.*

He didn't know me.

"He doesn't know me," I said aloud for good measure.

Then I pulled myself from the wall, determined to figure out what kind of risky business my soon-to-be ex-husband was up to. It might come in handy to have leverage, and if he was doing something illegal, I needed to know what that was. Which meant I needed to talk to Juke and impart this information and see if Ruby's sad-sack cousin had managed to get what I needed for my attorney. The private investigator looked like he could use extra money, so I could add on the research into Scott's business dealings and perhaps discover who had just essentially threatened him. That seemed like a smart thing to do. And in the meantime, I could do some snooping around the house. My advantage was that Scott thought I was a nonthreat, so he might have left some evidence of what he was involved in lying around.

I walked down the hall back into the function, saying hello to a few people, and found myself facing Stephanie and her friends.

"Hey, Cricket," she said, giving me her normal cheerful smile.

I flinched. I couldn't stop myself. And then something ugly and dark stirred in my belly. What would she do if I launched myself at her and wrapped my hands around her throat? Because that was the feral inclination that surfaced inside me.

Destroy. The. Threat.

And, oh Lord, now I was thinking in Susie Simmons's punctuated style.

I tamped down the darkness instead and smiled at the usurper of my throne. "Hello."

"I'm Julia Kate's tennis coach," she confirmed as if I couldn't place her, but the slight widening of her eyes told me she sensed danger. Or maybe that was my very active imagination.

"Of course, yes," I said, smiling at her and her young, fit friends. "It's lovely to see you. How are things at the club?"

I wanted to add "skank" to the end of that question, but really, did I blame her? She was a tennis pro, and Scott was a VP of a local bank, heir to stock in a shipping company in Cut Off, and mostly fit and decent looking. Part of me understood. And the other part of me wanted to drop her into a fast-moving river with a stone tied to her ankle.

God, I was bloodthirsty.

"Oh, things are heating up this spring. Everyone seems to want lessons when the weather turns nice."

"I bet," I said, somewhat dismissively. "I need to run. My mother wanted another martini."

"Of course," Stephanie said with her pretty, shiny lips. "It was good to see you."

I didn't respond. Instead I gave a winky little wave and moved away. Inside I was trembling, but on the outside, I was convinced I looked like the normal Cricket—happy, kind, nonthreatening.

"I can't believe she talked to you," Ruby hissed as she fell into step beside me. She must have been looking for me because I doubt she knew anyone at the event other than Ty.

"She has no reason not to. She thinks I don't know. Or she could think I suspect and likes getting her jollies by pretending to be friendly to the cuckolded wife."

"Can women be cuckolded?" Ruby asked, opening the door for me so I could slide inside the main room.

"I don't know, but I know that this woman is tired of not rocking boats. I'm biding my time, Ruby. You know what that means?" I took her arm and pulled her to face me.

Ruby, who looked so beautiful that I couldn't believe she was the same girl who had come into my store that day months ago looking more like a whipped pup than the magnificent peacock she was now, gave me the smile of a coconspirator. Which was better than a shot of whiskey . . . and I needed a shot of something that would chill me out.

"Of course, Cricket. I grew up on biding time and knowing exactly when to make a move. My family has always survived on knowing when to hold cards and knowing how to avoid detection. We only get caught every now and again. I'm a child of misfortune with a side of lawlessness, and I know how to rock a bitch right out of a boat."

She was so fierce, my Ruby. And I truly claimed her as my own. I didn't know what providence had led her to Printemps or when she had stopped being the scurrying mouse seeking to please, but this young warrior was exactly what I needed in my life. "You're goddamned right."

Ruby snorted and I started laughing.

Time to do some rocking . . .

CHAPTER FOURTEEN

RUBY

So this was Glitz and Gritz? Or was it Gritz and Glitz? I kept switching the name up, but that didn't change the fact that the event was terribly bougie with crappy cocktails and a band that played covers of Spandau Ballet and Bruno Mars. I studied the guitarist, who looked as if he were in a trance, strumming out of habit more than any emotion. I guess I would, too, if I had to watch tipsy white women shimmy to Sister Sledge.

"You wanna dance?" Cricket asked me, slurping down her third vodka Sprite with a twist of lime.

"To 'We Are Family'? No, thanks."

Cricket grinned at me, her eyes a little glassy. "You don't know this song."

"Oh, but I do."

"Well, I'm feeling like I should be dancing so I look exactly like what Scott says I am—not a threat." She set her empty glass on a nearby table. "But I am. I most certainly am."

My mouth twitched at that last remark as she sashayed out onto the dance floor. Obviously she knew some of the women dancing, because several of them smiled and opened their little circle. I could hear them complimenting her dress, and something that might have been pride bloomed inside me.

People liked my dresses.

Putting my gown on that afternoon, I'd had reservations. For one thing, I had torn off the oversize bow, electing instead to add a raspberry panel to the bodice that extended up, creating an asymmetrical wave of fabric that stood out from the bodice. I loved the edgier look, as bows weren't really my thing. The alteration had given the dress an eighties vibe that I loved while maintaining the classic silhouette. So far the number of times I had been asked where I had gotten the dress had risen to eight. Of course, I had no true answer, so I changed the subject or vaguely said that I had happened upon it. Cricket had suggested to her friend Chris that the designer would be revealed at her store later this spring. She'd glanced at me as if to silently ask . . . or maybe she was waiting on me to out myself.

I wasn't sure what I wanted to do about this new opportunity, but so far my experiment in tearing apart what was and refashioning into what could be had proven successful.

People liked *both* dresses, and that felt like enough for now.

I turned around to find the table Ty had pointed out to me earlier and nearly knocked the scotch out of Scott Crosby's hand. "Oh, sorry."

Cricket's butthole of a husband smiled at me. "No worries. I'm quicker than I look. Ruby, right?"

We had met too many times for a man like Scott to forget my name or who I was. Cricket had bragged more than once on how Scott prided himself on remembering names and faces because that's what made him successful—building connections in order to drum up business. But perhaps I wasn't worth remembering since I had little money to deposit into his bank. "That's right. I've worked for your wife for three months now."

"That long? Seems like only yesterday she was telling me about you. So are you enjoying the party?"

He asked it like I should be thrilled to listen to bad music and smile at small-minded people. Okay, not all of them were small minded. That was my insecurity talking. I just didn't know anyone here and truly didn't belong with people who chatted about vacationing in Cabo, private chefs, and personal trainers. "It's, uh, interesting."

"I'm sure it is for a girl like you," he said, sipping his drink.

"What does that mean?"

He looked confused. "I meant, you don't usually come to things like this, right?"

"How would you know?"

He looked uncomfortable. Finally. "Look, I meant no offense. Cricket just told me that you . . . uh, forget what I said. That sounded—"

"Elitist?" I filled in for him, liking him less by the second. And that was remarkable, considering I had never actually liked him to begin with.

"I meant no offense." He held up a hand, giving me what I presumed he thought was a charming smile.

"But still you gave it," I said, moving away from him.

I felt no compunction to make nice with Cricket's husband, even if she weren't divorcing him in the future. He meant nothing to me and wasn't anyone worth spending any amount of time with.

Walking toward the table where I had last seen my date, I saw Ty in conversation with a pretty blonde, who might have been a young Cricket. She was touching his shoulder in an overfamiliar way, which pissed me off. Or maybe it was delayed irritation at Scott. At any rate, I glided over and curved my arm around my date's waist, looking up at him with a smile.

"Hey, there you are," Ty said, pulling me to him with a squeeze. He looked relieved to see me.

"Hello," I said to the woman, who had dropped her hand and was now studying me with a mixture of amusement and something I call

Shreveport prissiness. I stuck out my hand and gave her my own faux smile. "I'm Ruby, Ty's date."

"Amelia," she said, taking my hand, giving a small wag, and then dropping it. "I'm one of Ty's friends. We met at Becca Stilton's lake house this past summer during floatillion. We were on Dickie Doyle's sailboat together. We had so much fun on the lake that day."

I supposed that was an invitation to say who I was and how I knew Ty. It was the veritable scratching of the chalk onto the concrete floor. First rule of Female Flirt Club: you sweep the leg . . . or maybe I was mixing up my fight movies. So I went for catching Miss Name Dropper off guard. "That's so weird. I met Ty at a sex club. On land."

Ty choked with laughter as Amelia blinked a few times, her mouth opening and then closing as she tried to discern whether I was joking or not.

"Kidding," I said, laying my hand on his chest. "I met him at the store where I work."

"Oh, you're a salesperson or checkout clerk or something?" Amelia asked, sensing a TKO, because who in his rich mind would date a cashier?

"I'm the 'or something,'" I said, without offering any further explanation.

"Oh," Amelia said, ducking the blow. "Well, I love your dress. It's so unusual."

"Thank you," I said, eyeing her very plain black dress with rhinestone spaghetti straps. Dime a dozen in this room, but Amelia wore it well. The diamonds in her ears were likely real and a few carats each. Her makeup looked professionally done. And if I were a betting woman, I would say that she'd been a Tri Delta at Bama, drove a car her daddy had bought her, and had never worked a day in her life. Except maybe lifeguarding at the club because that was a "hangout" sort of job.

"Well, I see my friend across the room. We were sorority sisters at Bama. I must say hello."

"Tri Delt?" I asked for the hell of it.

"Ohmygosh, yes. Wait, are you one?" She looked puzzled. Out-and-out puzzled.

"Nooo, I was a GDI." I laughed good-naturedly, holding up my hand as if making a pledge. "President for two years."

Amelia did the blinky thing again before shifting her gaze toward Ty. "Well, gotta run. Nice to see you, Ty, and good to meet you, Roni."

Damn, she got that jab in at the last minute.

I turned and looked at Ty as Amelia sauntered over to find her sister. My date looked absolutely delighted with me, and that made me suddenly lighter. He gave me another squeeze and said, "Sex club?"

"Well, I didn't know what a damned floatillion was."

Ty's eyes were dancing. "It's a bunch of people wearing designer sunglasses, drinking White Claws, and tying their boats together in a sort of lake party. There's a poker run, fireworks, and lots of people getting laid. Wanna come with me this summer?"

"That's a loaded question," I punned.

Ty didn't get my pun on getting drunk (or laid, for that matter), but that's okay. He was pretty to look at, thought I was amusing, and was standing beside me, making me feel less cynical and more like a girl wearing a smashing gown at the biggest ball in town. Cinderella never had it so good.

The band struck up "Wonderful Tonight," and he hooked an eyebrow at me.

Dancing to a hokey song with pretty words? Ugh. I needed death metal. But the romance of it all made me nod. He took my hand and led me to the dance floor.

Ty placed my hand on his shoulder and pulled me close. "You do look wonderful tonight."

Inside I may have rolled my eyes a little, but I also felt my heart contract. "I bet you say that to all the girls."

"Only the ones I'm dancing with," he joked, setting his cheek against my forehead, the bristles of his beard rubbing in a more pleasurable way than I remembered. It had been many, many years since I had been held in a man's arms, moving to soft music. Forgotten appreciation for the pressure of his hand on my lower back and the way his thighs brushed against mine summoned a sigh.

He pulled back and looked down at me. "What?"

"Nothing," I whispered, my gaze meeting his. "I had forgotten how much I liked to dance."

And that's when he kissed me.

I hadn't expected it, but it was well done. Ty had plenty of practice, I'd no doubt, and I felt the unfamiliar stirring of desire lift its head from a long winter's nap. His tongue sought entry, and I allowed it because, damn it, it felt so good to be wanted, to be claimed, to be just a girl who had no cares and could kiss a man on the dance floor anytime she wanted. Thankfully, the kiss was thorough, and not a mauling of my senses, so I enjoyed it immensely.

Ty lifted his head and murmured, "You taste like champagne."

My answer was to set my head against his chest and move to the music, enjoying his arms around me. I caught sight of Amelia watching us. I had a flash of sympathy, but nothing too strong. She wanted him.

And I didn't know what I was going to do with him.

A guy like Ty didn't fit with a girl like me. I knew this, and I also knew I was allowing myself to entertain the idea of being with him, which was dangerous. Because he lived in a totally different world, one I would never work in. Oh sure, I would love to have money, but I couldn't see myself hanging out with the Beccas and Amelias of the world. I didn't have sorority letters or a private-school education. I couldn't care less about the style of monogram chosen for an overpriced tote bag. The jewelry, the designer purses, and the gold designer belt buckles—all that worth signaling wasn't something I would ever do. I liked quality things, sure, but I didn't buy things so I could be in a social circle of acceptance.

I couldn't see any of those ladies, Cricket included, helping me dye my hair purple for the Young Mutherf*ckers concert, binge-watching *Zombie Death Wars*, or cruising out to the sandbars of Caddo Lake to drink Jack and Coke with the welders and wildcatters of the ArkLaTex. Those girls' world was a black American Express card. Mine was a black eye.

But Ty holding me in his arms on that dance floor made me feel like I didn't have to worry about what people thought of me.

Hell, why *was* I worried about what these lame-ass people thought about me?

Of course, I still hadn't told Ty or Cricket that I had spent two years in jail.

Ty kissed my temple and whispered, "Wanna get out of here?"

I knew what that meant—I wasn't born yesterday. But I really wanted to get out of there, so I nodded. "Yeah. And do you think we can get something to eat? A Natchitoches meat pie and a mini–crab cake wasn't nearly enough. No wonder half these people are bombed."

Ty chuckled, taking my hand and leading me off the dance floor. "A burger sounds amazing."

So we went to Head Honcho's, a burger dive right off Centenary's campus. It was mostly empty, just a few tables occupied by collegiate types with earbuds in, and we only got one double glance for strolling into a dive in our dressy duds. I didn't want to ruin my dress, so I layered napkins, tucking them into my bodice, as we settled into cheeseburgers, tots, and cherry Cokes. Ty had chosen a booth in the far corner, and for a moment, with all the retro decor, I felt like we were in a fifties movie. Like a reverse characterization of *The Outsiders* with me being Ponyboy.

"So tell me about your family, Ty," I said, realizing that I didn't know too much about him. Maybe I needed to if I was going to go much further.

"Not much to tell. I grew up in Georgia. My mom and dad divorced when I was eight. My mom lives there with her third husband, who is a total asshole, so I don't see her much. I've been ping-ponging between my parents for a while, but I usually stay with Dad. He has an investment company along with some other businesses. We also build housing projects and stuff like that. That's why we moved here. He's gathering some new investors for a real estate deal revolving around a retirement community. We hope to break ground in the fall. It's a pretty big project and should make the investors a tidy profit."

"Why come here?"

Ty shrugged a shoulder. "He had friends here. Grew up down around Alexandria."

"Oh, that makes sense. So are you the attorney for his company?"

"Yeah. I graduated law school two years ago. I thought I would work for the company I interned with, but when Dad ran into his own lawsuit, he talked me into coming to work for him. I'm the guy who works the numbers and pulls permits and so on. Dealing with the government in any capacity is exhausting. Moves at the speed of a sloth."

I snorted. "Sounds fun."

"What about you? You said you have family around here. What's the deal with yours?"

Here was the moment to tell him. To lay out my cards, talk about my mother, my absent father who called so rarely that I often forgot his voice. To talk about how my family could give the Corleones a run for their money. "Most of my family lives in north Shreveport. Remember that bar we went to?"

He popped a tot into his mouth and nodded. "Sure. The dickhead bartender and your, um, colorful cousin?"

"Yep. My cousin Griffin owns a tow truck company right next to the bar. My colorful cousin is a private investigator who leases space above the bar. The rest of the clan lives out near Caddo Lake. My grandmother has a place right outside Mooringsport. So we're a little country."

And a little criminal.

"I like country."

"Oh, not gather-eggs-and-sip-lemonade country," I laughed, teetering on whether to dive in or not. I knew I should give him the lay of the land, but I wasn't ready to have him dump me in a burger joint in the middle of Shreveport.

"Well, good. I can't imagine you barefoot, gathering eggs, and then making me lemonade," he said, giving me a smile.

"Oh, I can do those things, though I would never go into the coop barefooted. I don't like chicken poop between my toes," I quipped, chickening out, poop or no poop. Admitting to someone that you're a convict sort of puts a damper on any situation, unless it's one in which you're required to be a badass with some street cred.

"I could see how that could be a problem," he said, looking hungrily at my tots.

"Do you want some of my tots?" I asked, noting he'd mowed through his.

"Please." He reached over toward my box.

I smacked his hand. "You should never touch a lady's tots without permission."

His eyes widened. "Oh, I don't usually need permission. I know how to read a room."

"So you're saying I'm asking to have my tots touched?" Flirty banter was so much better than serious talk about my family and my precarious future. Yep, let's just do innuendos.

"Oh, I'm not just going to touch your tots. I'm going to devour your tots." He struck fast, swiping two and popping them into his mouth. He made an exaggerated face of ecstasy. "Oh yeah. Your tots are soooo good."

I couldn't help but laugh at the sexy, silly Ty who had been chipping away at my defenses and keeping me enough off-kilter that I found myself tumbling toward him. If things kept going in this direction, I would have to tell him about my time in the clink and about my family that sometimes skirted the law. I couldn't keep hiding who I was. It was as bad as not telling someone you'd been married or that you had herpes or something. If one got to a certain point in a relationship and hadn't come clean, it looked deceitful. And that was something I didn't want to ever be. I wasn't going to blast my past mistakes to the treetops of Shreveport, but neither was I going to treat what I had done . . . or rather hadn't known I had done . . . like a black mark. I tired of carrying shame. My back was bowed from it.

"Take my tots," I said, sliding my box of delicious golden potatoes his way.

"You're a girl who gives it up easy. Nice." He wriggled his eyebrows, his pretty eyes dancing beneath the lurid fluorescent lights.

"I can't believe you said that," I said, balling up my straw wrapper and throwing it at him.

He caught my hand and lifted it to his lips. "I know you're not easy. But that's okay. I like a challenge."

And that did it. My heart sort of tipped over on its side in a good old-fashioned swoon. I realized that I wasn't falling in love with him. Nope, not ready to go there yet. I hardly knew him. But I was falling into serious *like* . . . with a guy I could never imagine in a million years would fit with me. But here he sat. And here I did, too.

He released my hand and went back to polishing off my tots. I finished my burger, wiped my mouth like a lady, and squelched a burp. "You know what's nice after a cheeseburger?"

"Marathon sex to work off the calories?" He slurped his cherry Coke and tried to keep a straight face.

"Okay, you know what's nice after a cheeseburger other than marathon sex?" I amended with a giggle. Lord, I had just giggled. Who was I, even? "Playing blackjack at the casino. I mean, I'm wearing this dress, and you look mighty fine in that tux. We might as well pretend we're high rollers."

"Blackjack, huh?"

"If you're willing to take a gamble . . ."

Ty started clearing up his place. "I think I've already established that."

I smiled like a doofus because I knew he meant me, and something about being wanted by Ty was doing things to me, making me feel like I was worth loving. Normally, I would run from that feeling, but here I was at 11:42 p.m. embracing the hell out of it. "Let's go. I'm feeling lucky tonight."

Three hours later and forty dollars lighter, I slipped into my bed. Alone.

Oh sure, there was that moment as Ty walked me to my door when I could have very easily said *Want another drink?* and let him inside for more than just a glass of vino. But something held me back. I wasn't ready. So I enjoyed my kiss good night on the porch and thanked him for letting me be his date to the gala. Then I let myself inside my apartment alone, ignoring the disappointment in his eyes.

I had just tugged on my oversize, ratty fun-run T-shirt and cotton boxers when there was a knock at the door.

"Seriously?" I muttered, wondering how Ty had not gotten the message that our evening was over. Then I wondered if I had left something in his car. I spied my clutch on the table sitting next to the roses Ty had sent me earlier, so that wasn't it. I looked down at my baggy sleepwear and rubbed my makeup-free face, knowing that I looked ridiculous, if not comfortable.

Amelia would have worn a peignoir, I'm sure. Whatever that was I wasn't quite sure. I had seen it in a book once and wondered, but it sounded like something slinky and sexy.

Because I lived by myself in a part of town where crime sometimes spilled over, I grabbed the baseball bat I kept next to the door and carefully pulled the blinds back to peer out to my front porch.

Cricket?

What in the hell?

I hurriedly unbolted the door and pulled her inside just in case someone was lurking in the bushes, waiting to pounce. Which was a weird thought, but one I had often. Hey, my two years in a women's penitentiary had made me paranoid about being jumped. Cricket yipped in surprise but came with me. I noted she was a little wobbly and that she had thankfully not driven herself. The car pulling away from my curb had an Uber sticker on the windshield.

Gone was the dress I had made Cricket, and in its place she wore a sweatshirt, jeans, and running shoes. And she seemed to be (a) a little drunk, (b) in a state of shock, or (c) both.

"Cricket?" I said, relocking the door.

She turned to me. "Huh?"

"What are you doing here? How did you know where I lived?"

"I'm your employer." She looked around, somewhat dazed. "I like your place. It's very cozy."

I glanced around, taking in my small apartment through her eyes. A couch I had recovered with ticking, bright-orange pillows with daisies, scuffed but clean wood floors, and indigo velvet drapes. My furniture had been obtained from secondhand shops, with one piece from Cricket's store. I had chalk-painted a buffet and had some cheerful daisy plates on display. The overall effect was slightly bohemian with a punch of modern mixed with desperation. I had economically pieced together what I could, but Cricket was correct—it was cozy.

She continued to look shaken, so I steered her toward the kitchen. "Here. Let me get you some water."

"No. I'm fine."

"You're standing in my apartment on the opposite side of town at"—I glanced at the clock on my microwave—"one eighteen a.m. I think you need some water and a place to sit down."

She lowered herself onto a barstool. "Okay."

I fetched a glass and filled it with purified water from a pitcher in the fridge. Setting it in front of Cricket, I pulled a stool around to the other side and sat down. "So what's wrong?"

My boss hadn't been crying; in fact, she still wore mascara. Her lips had been chewed bare, and she looked decidedly paler than she had earlier when she'd been determined, jovial, and intent on making Scott eat his words.

"He stole it all."

I hesitated, trying to decipher what that meant, before giving up and asking, "Who stole what?"

"Scott. He's emptied our savings accounts. He's cashed out our retirement."

"He did what?" My mind reeled with what she was telling me. Her husband wasn't just bopping the tennis pro. He was screwing Cricket, too. In the worst possible way. What an enormous asshole. "How?"

"After overhearing him with whoever that was tonight, I couldn't stop thinking about what Scott was up to. He asked my mama to invest in something and no doubt hit my father up this evening. So after he went to bed, I snuck down to the office. I don't usually look at our accounts—well, not the savings and stuff. I pay all our expenses like the mortgage and health insurance out of our personal account. And I have mine for the business, of course, but Scott manages all the rest of our money. I mean, he's a banker, so I never thought about double-checking him."

"Okay, so how did you discover this?" I asked, walking to the fridge and pulling out some wine I had left over from a few nights ago. I uncorked it and poured two glasses, setting one in front of Cricket. Maybe she needed wine more than water. I knew I did.

"Well, he changed his password on his phone, but he's predictable. Julia Kate's birthday and the dog's name was my third try, and it worked. I found his password list and then got on my laptop and accessed our accounts—all of them. When I saw that he'd cleaned out our savings and retirement, I couldn't deal. So I pulled on what I could find in the laundry room and called an Uber because I'd had a lot to drink, so I couldn't drive. But I couldn't stay there. I thought I might actually kill him. I was so mad I couldn't even see straight. And we have some really sharp knives in our kitchen block. I didn't trust myself not to snap." She picked up the wineglass and tossed back the contents. Slamming it to the counter, she looked at me, tears rimming her lashes. "Ruby, he stole our money."

I didn't know what to say, but I knew exactly how she felt. Because the same sort of thing had been stolen from me—not money, but years of my life. So I was mad as hell for her. "Okay, we're going to figure this thing out. You want to stay here?"

"I can't." She looked down at her hands clasped around her glass. "I can't let him think that I'm any different than I was before. I have to play the part he believes of me. Or none of this will work. But now it's harder. I have to figure out what he did with the money before I file for divorce. I'm afraid he invested it. If he did, I have to make sure I'm on the account or something."

I reached out and clasped my hands around hers, even though I wasn't a touchy-feely sort. "We're going to figure it out."

Cricket looked down at our hands and then back up at me. "You make me believe that we can do it. Thank God I have you, Ruby."

CHAPTER FIFTEEN

CRICKET

"Ouch!" I said, swatting my hand at Ruby as she jabbed another bobby pin into my hair. "That hurts."

"You want this thing to come off?"

I scrunched my face in irritation, squelching the need to rub my poor head. "No, but I also need my scalp to, you know, cover my skull."

Ruby huffed. "Well, if you don't want this to come off, you're going to have to let me secure it properly. Stop whining."

"I'm not whining," I said, as the points of the short, dark wig covering my blondeness swung forward. Ruby had netted my hair flat against my head and might as well have used a staple gun with the amount of jabbing she was doing.

I sat on a stool in the kitchen of Printemps late Monday morning, looking so not myself in a tight Cannibal Corpse T-shirt, a pair of faded jeans shredded at each knee, and clunky black lace-up Doc Martens. But I guess that was the whole point—I wasn't supposed to look like myself.

Ruby had begrudgingly agreed to help me disguise myself because she felt guilty.

Well, she should. She was the one who had recommended her worthless cousin as my private investigator.

Because Juke had proven to be as useless as teats on a boar hog, which was such a disappointment to me because I needed someone to be in my corner, someone who could get some incriminating evidence. But that hadn't happened. Because when I went to his office early that morning, I had found him drunk. Off. His. Ass.

Which had put a damper on the determination I had set jauntily on my head that morning as I breezed out the door to ensure that by the end of this week, Scott would be out of the house.

After I had come back from Ruby's early Sunday morning, I had washed my face, pulled on jammies, and slid in bed beside a snoring Scott. I hadn't even tried to strangle him. So that was a good thing. For him.

That morning I had risen early, snuck into his office, and snapped pictures of his schedule for the week, sending them to my phone. I erased any evidence of my snooping the night before, even zapping the history on his phone just in case he decided to go crazy and check. I would absolutely have to be more careful now that he knew someone was watching him. Then I went to the kitchen and made blueberry waffles, bacon, and a fresh pot of Scott's favorite Blue Mountain Jamaican blend. I even turned Alexa to eighties soft rock and sang along like I was the happiest bluebird in the bush.

Scott had come in, looking bleary eyed from a hangover, but seemed thrilled that I had made him breakfast. He didn't know that I was holding the oars in that nonrocking boat and that he was very lucky that he wasn't dead. I mean, I had actually contemplated who would play me in the Lifetime movie *When Cricket Cracked: A Shreveport Murder*. Would Reese Witherspoon be available? So . . . yeah, he was lucky he was eating waffles and not the end of whatever pistol I could figure out how to use from his gun safe.

Then I had spent the day at my mama's house helping her clean out her greenhouse. I picked up dinner and chocolate cupcakes with bunnies that I felt sure Julia Kate would like. I even managed to kiss Scott good night and not throw up. I closed my eyes on Sunday night knowing that my husband couldn't possibly suspect me of suspecting him.

Boom.

Mission accomplished.

When I awoke on Monday morning, I was a determined woman.

So I had called Ruby and told her that I was going to run a few errands before I came in that morning. I dropped Julia Kate at school, which was back in session, thank goodness, and went to Lowder's to get cinnamon rolls for my private eye. He seemed like a man who needed a little care, and since this conversation was important, buttering him up with delicious pastry seemed a good bet. I was hopeful Juke had gotten the incriminating photos and evidence of my husband's infidelity because then he could do the extra snooping to see exactly what kind of deal Scott was involved in and where he might have placed our life's savings. If it was something illegal or unscrupulous, that might be the leverage I needed to get the money he'd taken back into our accounts . . . before I filed divorce papers. Unless he'd invested it in some stupid opportunity. But I couldn't see him doing that. He was cautious with money.

Ol' Scott was about to get his fat butt rocked right out of the boat . . . and then I was going to pull the cord and motor away, leaving him in the middle of shark-infested waters.

So after I procured the pastries, I pointed my minivan north.

I had decided not to alert my PI as to my intentions. I figured if Juke wasn't in his office, no big deal. I could make an appointment and go back. But something inside me—one of those intuitive hunches— urged me to drop by.

No cars or trucks were parked at the bar, but there was an older van parked beneath the metal staircase leading up to North

Star Investigations. I climbed the stairs, balancing the bakery box, and knocked exactly ten times, trying not to be aggravated that I was constantly being stonewalled in my progress. As I knocked, I thought I caught a whiff of whiskey through the crack beneath the door but wasn't certain. By the time I had turned around to leave, I was irritated. Juke had wasted two weeks of my life with no proof of adultery.

Then the door ripped open.

"What? Goddamn it!"

I turned, set my free hand on my hip, and glared at the bare-chested man standing in the threshold of the office.

"You're drunk," I managed to growl between my clenched teeth.

"No shit," Juke said, looking me over. "Do I even know you?"

"Do you even know me?" I repeated his words, my voice rising as I advanced toward him. "Are you serious? I'm your client, you idiot!"

He stepped back only because I shoved him, entering the office, frowning at the mess. Juke closed the door and rubbed his head, making his hair stick up like porcupine quills. "You are? Which one?"

"I'm Cricket. Ruby's boss."

"Oh yeah." He squinted at me, staggering a little as he journeyed to the desk, which held three Chinese-takeout cartons, a half-empty bottle of Wild Turkey, and a stack of folders that had almost slid off the desk. The place smelled like sweat, booze, and kung pao chicken.

"What are you doing, Mr. Jefferson?" I looked around at the couch that he'd been sleeping on, the sweatshirt crumpled on the floor, and the overflowing trash can. "This place is a disaster, and so are you. You're drunk at nine in the morning, for heaven's sake. You don't need clients. You need rehab. I'd like my money back, please."

"Hold on, hold on," he said, pressing the air and half falling into his chair. The resounding squeak was like brakes being applied on the conversation.

I stood and waited, still clutching the cinnamon rolls. I would be danged if he would get the still-warm pastries. Over my dead body . . . which no one would probably find in this pigsty for months.

Finally, after he'd sat looking confused for long enough, I said, "Do you have the pictures of my husband?"

Juke reached behind him, snagged the T-shirt on the back of the chair, and shrugged it on. "Sorry about that. Um, your husband is the banker, right?"

"Oh, for heaven's sake," I said, turning toward the door.

"No, no. Wait. I have something."

I stopped. "What?"

"He's a busy guy, your husband. Been meeting with all sorts of high-in-the-instep people. Don't worry—I've been watching him for you."

I turned back toward him. "But do you have pictures of him with Stephanie, the woman he's screwing?"

"Not yet."

"Not yet?" I parroted, using the sarcasm I kept for special occasions. "Thing is, I needed those yesterday. I have a meeting with my attorney to go over my financials, which at the present moment is very little. I need proof of his infidelity so I don't have to wait six months, which means I need leverage, Mr. Jefferson. I came here this morning hoping you'd done your job, but it seems you haven't. And I had more work for you, work that with your background in law enforcement might have intrigued you. I think my husband isn't just cheating on me. He's involved in something bigger."

Juke was drunk, but he wasn't stupid. His ears might as well have twitched. "What do you mean bigger?"

"You know, no. I'm not going over this with you. I'm terminating your services. You can keep the deposit. I'm done with waiting on someone to help me. I can see that I will have to help myself. Good day, Mr. Jefferson."

He tried to stand too quickly. Throwing his hands onto the desk to steady himself, he called out at me as I opened the door, letting blessed fresh air inside. "Wait. Don't go."

"Sorry. These are business hours. You should be sober and working. Not sleeping one off. Done, Mr. Jefferson." I shut the door and angrily stomped down the metal steps toward my van. This time no Griffin Moon stood near my door. No one seemed to be in the area, and normally, I would have felt in some sort of danger in an area like this, but I didn't. Mostly because I was fuming. If someone had tried to jerk my Louis Vuitton from my arm, I would have ripped his head off and used it for a kickball.

I nearly dropped the bakery box on the last step. "Stupid son of a—"

"Hey!" Juke called down. "Don't fire me."

"Too late." I jammed the box under my arm, stomped to my van, climbed inside, and cranked it. I said a lot of bad words under my breath while I did it, too. I enjoyed saying every single one because they were justified. I jerked the van into reverse and, with my tires squealing, backed out of the parking lot. Shifting into drive, I left an exasperated and barefoot Juke standing in the parking lot. In the rearview mirror, he threw up his arms and then dropped them.

I pulled my eyes away from my fired private investigator and trained them on the road ahead.

What was I going to do now?

"Screw it," I said, digging a cinnamon roll from the box and biting into it. I had vowed to resist them, but Juke's idiocy had me stress eating. "Mother of God, these are amazing."

I chewed and told myself I would only have half of the pastry, knowing I was a liar. I would eat the whole dang thing. But that didn't fix my current problem.

Hiring a third investigator seemed ridiculous. I mean, jeez, how did a gal get a good dick in this town? And that thought made me laugh.

But it wasn't the good kind of laugh. It was the "I'm so tired of bull crap, but that's still sorta funny" laugh. Yep, I was at the end of my rope, and it wasn't even five hours into the workweek. Time to turn this over to my attorney. Should have done that in the first place.

When I got to Printemps, I dropped the remaining cinnamon rolls with Jade and Ruby and retreated to my office. Plunking down into my swivel chair, I kicked my feet up on my desk. I never do that. It was a novelty. But sometimes a woman needs to feel in charge of something even if it's merely her desk. My action knocked the small stack of books to the floor, and one fell open.

"Dang it," I muttered, leaning forward to pick it up.

It was the 1950s detective book, and the page was open to "Chapter Nine: The Art of Surveillance."

Thirty minutes later I had an idea that was nuts but also sort of exciting. As an only child, I had watched a lot of syndicated television shows growing up. My mother had tried like heck to get me overinvolved in ballet, piano, violin, and watercolors, but I had balked around middle school. Thankfully, my father had finally told Marguerite to leave me the hell alone. They'd been in the process of marriage counseling, so she'd shifted her focus to that, letting me quit swim team and getting the deposit back from ballet camp. I sat on the couch and watched *I Dream of Jeannie*, *Full House*, and tons of other shows, including my favorite kind—detective shows. Maybe growing up in the nineties—a time of grunge and angst—but watching all those seventies and eighties shows had injected me with just enough zaniness and optimism that I was fairly certain my idea would work. No one was more motivated than a soon-to-be single mother with little savings.

Ruby was sitting in the kitchen on her lunch break, eating a cinnamon roll and riffling through a list of mechanics. Or that's what it looked to be as I snuck a peek over her shoulder.

"Car trouble?" I asked her.

She jumped. "Oh, I didn't know you were there."

See? I was good at detective stuff. As long as there were no little fluffballs nipping my ankles or fancy cameras to work. "Wait. Doesn't your cousin own a garage?"

"Yeah, one of them does. But if you're talking about Griff, that's a towing service."

I slapped the detective book on the kitchen table. "I need your help."

"What's this?" she asked, gazing at the cover with the blonde wearing a cocktail dress and heels beneath her trench coat.

"The answer to my problems," I said, tapping the cover for extra emphasis.

"A book?"

"Not just a book, but a book about how to be a private investigator. Like on your own," I said, crossing my arms and giving her a confident smile.

"Oh no. That's a bad idea," Ruby said, sucking at the cinnamon roll or whatever was in her teeth. Which was sort of gross, but not grosser than gummy flour stuck in one's teeth. "You need to let an expert do this."

"Have you ever watched *Remington Steele*?"

She wrinkled her adorable little nose. "Is that, like, a new streaming series or something?"

I rolled my eyes. "No, it was an eighties show starring Pierce Brosnan. I was a little young for it, but since I was an only child who refused to go to ballet camp, I watched reruns of it one summer. But I digress. The premise of the show was that this woman inherited a detective agency, but no one would hire her because she was a woman—"

"You're joking," she interrupted.

"I know. It was the eighties. But anyway, she assumed this identity of Remington Steele, because the name sounded tough and all, but then this sexy guy—Pierce Brosnan—who is like a former thief becomes 'Remington Steele,' and they solve cases together and fall in love. It was a really good show. Oh, so was *Moonlighting*. That one had Cybill Shepherd and Bruce Willis. I really loved that one."

I stopped talking and tilted my head, waiting for her to connect the dots. Finally, Ruby made a little noise that told me she was having trouble understanding what I wanted to do. "Um, so . . . you want to open your own—"

"No." I waved a hand. How could she not see what was so obvious to me? "Of course not. I just want to Remington Steele these pictures. And maybe in the process figure out how to stop my stain of a husband from stealing every dime we've saved together and then marrying Two Serve Sally."

"By . . . ?"

"*We're* going to get the goods on Scott and give them to Juke, and because he now owes me one, he'll present them to my attorney like he took the pictures. So they're legit. And will stand up in court." I smiled like a cat with a goldfish under its paw. Because I was brilliant. I should have thought of this in the first place.

"Cricket, that's crazy. You can't do that. Call another PI."

"I'm running out of time, and when I went to see your cousin this morning, he was drunk. And he has bupkis on Scott."

Ruby ripped off the top of her notepad and crumpled the paper. "You're joking. He said—"

"But that's what I'm saying. We can't depend on these men anymore. And I don't have time to fill out more paperwork and go through this a third time. I can get the pictures. I'm certain. All I have to do is maybe disguise myself a little. You know, a hat and sunglasses. Maybe I can borrow your car? Then Juke can pass my photos off as his photos. Simple."

Ruby's phone buzzed on the table. I saw the caller. It said *Griff*. She ignored it and looked up at me. "I don't know, Cricket, this sounds risky. What if Scott or Stephanie catches you? You're not exactly easy to overlook."

"What do you mean by that?"

She gestured to me. "You're pretty, blonde, and curvy. You're exactly the kind of woman men look at. Women, too."

Well, that compliment made me feel better, even though it shouldn't have because for this specific instance I needed to be not pretty, blonde, or curvy. "I can wear a disguise. Don't they have temporary hair color? Oh, a wig! I can wear one of those. That will totally work. I snapped a picture of Scott's calendar. He has a lunch today at Rendezvous in Bossier with someone. And what banker drives all the way almost to Haughton to eat? I'll tell you—the kind who doesn't want to be seen by people he knows because he's with his sidepiece. I think some"—I tapped the open chapter that I had bookmarked—"surveillance is in order. All I have to do is get a table close enough to get a few shots of them together."

"And not get recognized by your *husband*." Ruby looked down at the book. Her phone rang again.

"Answer your phone. I'm going to the beauty-supply store to get a wig." I grabbed my purse before she could protest. She reluctantly answered her phone as I slipped out the door. Thirty minutes later, I was talking to an experienced saleslady who had sold me on how great I would look in a short, sassy brown wig—it would be just the thing for the role-playing I was doing to spice up my marriage.

As if.

I purchased all the things that went with a wig, along with some burgundy lipstick and fake eyelashes that she swore were easy to put on, feeling a little guilty about lying to her. She seemed so excited for me. When I got back into the van, I called Ruby and asked her if she knew what I should wear to look not so suburban mom–like. She said she would cover it, so I went back to Printemps, sent Jade home so I wouldn't have to answer questions about disguising myself as Maddie Holt, the alter ego I had carved from my two favorite fictional investigators from the eighties, and prepared myself for my biggest role—the woman who nails her cheating husband.

So presently I was trying really hard not to complain as Ruby jabbed a dozen more bobby pins into my scalp. Because she was helping me do this. She'd even gotten me a lunch date as my cover.

"There," Ruby said, combing her fingers through my sassy bobbed wig, tugging on it slightly to make sure it stayed in place. "You look pretty damned good as a brunette, hottie."

A shadow fell over the back door.

"Oh, he's here." Ruby eyed me as she backed toward the kitchen door of Printemps, flipping the lock and opening the door.

Griffin Moon stepped inside, ducking down so he didn't brush his head against the doorframe. "Fine. I'm here. Here's your keys."

He didn't sound happy about it, no matter what Ruby said.

Griffin was my "date" for the luncheon. I had argued that I could go to the restaurant alone and pretend to take some selfies, capturing Scott and who I hoped would be Stephanie in the background. I would take a book. Lots of people dined alone, reading a book. But Ruby said that it would draw more attention to me. People noticed when someone was alone, but they never thought twice about a couple. Couples were normal. So while she was on the phone with Griff, who was bringing her car to the store because he had already had it fixed for her—something Ruby was peeved about—she'd told him that he was going to be my date. Like an order, from what I understood.

Hadn't gone over well with the big guy, but according to Ruby, he didn't have to like it. He just had to do it. And Griffin had agreed to accompany me as my cover.

My "date" set the keys on the counter and looked at me before glancing away. Then he looked at me again.

He hadn't recognized me.

Good sign.

"Thanks for going with me, Mr. Moon. At least you get a free meal out of it," I said, moving to brush the shaggy bangs of my wig back and finding nothing to brush. Ruby had put the false eyelashes on me, and I kept thinking the thick butterflies batting at my eyes were my bangs.

"I can buy my own meals."

Well, whatcha gonna say to that?

"Don't be a grump. You owe me," Ruby said, picking up the lipstick and dabbing at my lips with it. "There."

"Owe you for what? I bought you a new alternator. And I towed y'all that night. I think I've paid whatever I owed you back tenfold—"

"I paid you for the tow," I interrupted.

"Griff," Ruby huffed, studying my eyes. She grabbed her makeup palette and swiped a bit more shimmery something beneath the arch of my brow. "Zip it. If you want to be an asshole your whole life, fine. But do it tomorrow. Or in three hours. For now, you're going to be a good guy and look out for Cricket."

"All for a harebrained scheme. You two are—"

Ruby shot him a look that should have sent him staggering backward and sinking to the floor in a death spiral. Instead Griffin just closed his mouth.

From what I could see from beneath the curtains glued to my eyelids, Griffin wore clean jeans, a pressed button-down shirt, and buffed boots; his hair looked damp, and his scruffy beard was neatly trimmed. Probably his date-night or church clothes, which made me feel sort of special, though I probably shouldn't have. Wasn't like I was the least bit interested in Griffin Moon. For all intents and purposes, I was still married and thus faithful to my cheating husband.

"It's not a big deal," I said, waving Ruby away from her last-minute fussing. The clock on the wall said it was half past noon, which meant in order to make Scott's meeting at the bar and grill outside Bossier City, we needed to get going. "Just taking a few discreet pictures. That's it."

Griffin grunted, which I took as acceptance.

"We need to leave." I stood and tugged the shirt down because it had a tendency to ride up. The thing clung to me like a kid in the deep end of a pool, and my girls were prominently on display, which wasn't wholly desirable considering I was trying to be incognito.

Griffin noted my rack in the clingy shirt. I shot him a warning glare, and he jerked his gaze up to my face. His cheeks may have even pinked a little, bless him. And look, I won't say that I didn't get a little trill of pleasure at this good-looking grump of a man noticing that I looked decent in a tight shirt and jeans. I did. But I didn't need to be ogled. I was on a mission.

"Maybe I better grab a jacket," I said, looking down at my chest.

Ruby looked me over. "Yeah, in that getup you might get too many looks."

Griffin opened the door as I grabbed my sweater. "You're not putting on that mawmaw sweater with that, are you?"

"Good point," Ruby said, jogging out of the kitchen and coming right back with her olive-green bomber jacket. "Try this."

The jacket fit snugly but covered all my bits. I ignored the comment about the mawmaw sweater—I liked that sweater—and pulled my wallet out of my purse, slid my credit card into my back pocket, and picked up my just-charged phone. I hadn't even checked my reflection, but I was certain that I looked enough like someone else that a distracted Scott wouldn't notice me. I shoved my biggest framed sunglasses on and turned to Griffin. "Well, do I look like Maddie Holt?"

He stared at me for a good two minutes. "Who's Maddie Holt?"

"She's your date, big boy." I turned to Ruby and said, "Wish me luck."

"Good luck, crazy lady," Ruby said, holding out her fist while trying to suppress a smile.

I bumped it and then slid past Griffin into the sunlight. A blip of doubt gave me a mental stumble. Maybe this was stupid. I had no business disguising myself and trying to get proof of Scott's adultery.

But what recourse did I have? I had hired two professionals who had failed to get what I needed. An appointment with Jacqueline in two days meant I needed to have the proof—she had the papers ready for me to sign, and the filing would declare adultery. So I needed Juke to present my photos to my attorney. He owed me that much. This would work. It had to.

Griffin gestured to Ruby's car. "We better take Ruby's car. Unless you want to take the tow truck?"

"Ruby said to take hers. I'll fill her tank as a thank-you."

He nodded and then did something that would have normally knocked my socks off if I were wearing any—he opened the car door for me like a gentleman. Like a date. Like he thought I was worthy of such a gesture.

I slid inside Ruby's sun-warmed car and buckled up. The interior smelled like Bath & Body Works had made a baby with french fries, and that was something I could get behind. A hula girl danced on the dash of the older car. Griffin climbed in, and I literally had to shift to the right to give him room. His shoulder brushed mine, which was somewhat reassuring rather than invasive. Nerves had grabbed hold of my stomach, making me jittery. "Thank you for coming with me."

Griffin didn't respond. He just started the engine, a ghost of a smile hovering near his lips.

CHAPTER SIXTEEN

CRICKET

Rendezvous was packed for a Monday, which was quite fortunate for an amateur private investigator and her reluctant beard.

Griffin held the door for me as I walked into the crowded foyer of the bar and grill. I immediately moved to the dining-room doorway to see if I saw Scott. Took me only seconds to spot his thinning crown and the green striped shirt I had bought him at T.J. Maxx. It was a designer shirt he thought I had bought at his favorite overpriced men's shop. For some reason, I took pleasure in knowing that. He was sitting alone near a window in the back of the restaurant. I made my way to the hostess stand, Griffin trailing behind me. A harried-looking, pretty hostess looked up in expectation. "A table for two. Near the window in the back, please."

"That will be about a thirty-minute wait," she said, picking up four sticky menus and passing them to a waitress escorting a few older gentlemen to the dining room.

"What about the bar?" Griffin asked, leaning over my shoulder.

"Oh hey, Griff," she said, flipping her blonde hair over her shoulder and looking at me with interest. "Um, yeah, the bar is first come, first served."

Griffin smiled at her, a very intimate, sexy smile that made me frown. Hey, he was *my* date. A fake one, but this chippie didn't know that. I nudged him and gave him "the look." His lips turned down, but he got the message.

"Thanks, Bethany. We'll wait at the bar until a table in that area is open."

Bethany looked at me again. "If you want first available, I can seat you in, like, five minutes."

"Nope, what the little lady wants, she gets," he said, looking down at me like he would bend the knee and kiss my foot. Then like a flashbulb, an image of Griffin kissing his way up my leg popped into my thoughts, making me feel weird. Oh my God, I had to stop doing things like that. I didn't even like the man.

"Okay, whatever. You going to the Honky Tonk on Wednesday? It's ladies' night," she trilled with a really bright smile that said, *I'll do you in the bathroom if you show up.*

Or that could have been my imagination.

"Nah, I got something going on that night. Have fun for me," he said, giving her a wink. "And when you have a table, holler."

He took my elbow and steered me toward the bar with the scattered stools. There was only one spot with two stools open. I slid onto one and hissed, "I can't see Scott from here."

"Relax," he said, drawing up the other stool and lifting a finger to the bartender. "Your guy's date hasn't arrived, so you have time. Have a beer and chill out. You're making me nervous, and I don't get nervous."

"I'm not nervous."

He smacked his hand on the bar, and I nearly jumped out of my skin. "Yeah, I see that."

I huffed. "Whatever. This is my first time, you know."

"Oh, I know," he said, turning his attention to the bartender who had arrived in front of us. "Two Great Raft Commotions and a glass for the lady."

"I don't drink beer," I said, sounding exactly how I didn't want to sound—prissy.

Griffin shrugged. "What do you want, then? I'm betting a glass of chardonnay or a pinot grigio."

I truly did want a glass of pinot grigio, but I wouldn't give him the satisfaction. So instead I said, "Actually, I do drink beer. So that's fine."

Looking nervously at the opening to the foyer and into the dining room beyond, I tried to figure out how to handle this. In my mind, I would be seated very near Scott and Stephanie. I could pretend to take a picture of Griffin or maybe a selfie. Perhaps the woman I was playing would like to take selfies, maybe put those silly ear filters on her pictures. But then I remembered I was wearing a T-shirt with some god-awful band that Ruby loved on it. No filters for my persona. This Maddie Holt character would straight up post an unfiltered selfie. Maybe even flipping off the camera.

The bartender set the cold cans in front of us, placing a glass beside mine. He popped the top of each and looked at Griffin. "Start a tab?"

"Nah," Griffin said, tossing a credit card onto the bar. "We're waiting on a table."

I watched my pretend date take a draw on the beer, the foam on the top sticking to his beard. He really didn't have a beard. Just some groomed scruff that was likely supposed to make him look more dangerous. Like a clean jaw might make him less of a man. I didn't like beards. They were scratchy, and sometimes guys got food caught in them. Who wanted to make out with a guy who had crumbs in his beard? But that foam caught on the hair above Griffin's lip? I could lick that off. You know, if I were into Griffin.

Which I was not.

I still loved my husband.

But that was a lie. I didn't. The hurt was still there, but that was more about my pride and the memories we'd made together in a gold-tinged time where we had laughed, made love, and cooked breakfast together while dancing to George Michael. That's what I felt—grief for what was. Given the chance, I would not take Scott back. Maybe not even if he hadn't cheated on me, which shocked me. But for some reason, I felt like someone else.

And not because I was wearing a wig and Doc Martens.

But because in the last few weeks, I had changed, and I liked this new me.

"How am I going to know when Scott's date gets here?" I asked, ignoring the glass and drinking out of the can. My mother would have died if she'd seen me sitting at a bar, looking the way I did, drinking beer out of a can.

"Give it a minute and then go to the restroom." Griffin took another sip. I watched his strong throat as he swallowed.

"Oh, good idea."

"You like the beer?" he asked, nodding toward the can in my hand.

"Sure." I didn't love beer, but I didn't hate it. I usually only drank beer when I was already drunk or eating crawfish.

He smiled knowingly.

"What?" I asked.

"You don't like beer. You're drinking it only because you want to prove something to yourself. Or me." He cupped his beer in his hands, studying the can.

"Oh yeah, Mr. Know-it-all? For your information, I do like beer." To prove it, I took a swig, wiping the residual from my mouth with the back of my hand. Hey, there were no napkins. The beer had a slight bitter aftertaste, and I tried not to make a face, but I could tell that Griffin had noticed. "Okay, I'm going to the bathroom. Save my stool."

"From who?"

"I don't know. Bethany, maybe?" I flirted, sotto voce. I stood and lightly ran my fingers through the soft hair at his nape, scratching my nails against his skin. "Ladies' night, Griff."

I sauntered off, telling myself that I was playing a part but knowing that I had enjoyed my little femme fatale flirting. Which was stupid because it was obvious to me that Griffin Moon had been around the block a time or twenty. For heaven's sake, he knew the pretty blonde hostess from nights at bars. The big, handsome man drew the eye of every woman under the age of ninety. Which, come to think of it, made him a bad choice as my fake date. Ruby had screwed up on that one. I should have taken the UPS guy with his potbelly and no butt. No one would have looked twice at him, bless his heart.

The restroom was located in the middle of the far wall, putting Scott to my left. No one sat with him, and for a moment, my heart leaped with relief. But then I remembered that I needed to catch him with Stephanie. I needed the photos. I scooted by a table with a few guys wearing zip-up overalls and stained ball caps. They looked like they were straight in from working a job that gave them brown necks and dirty trucks.

One said, "Hey there, sugar. We gotta extra chair."

I looked at him like he'd lost his damned mind before I realized I wasn't tight-assed Cricket with her Lilly Pulitzer and day planner. I was Maddie of the revealing shirt and sassy, short hair. So I said in a register two tones lower, "I got my own chair. But thanks."

And I kept moving, watching Scott out of the corner of my eye. His attention was on his cell phone, which he was typing on. Just as I reached the restroom door, another man in tan trousers and a blue sport coat arrived. Scott rose with a smile, extending his hand and slapping the guy on the back as he pulled out the adjacent chair.

Poop balls.

No Stephanie.

This was an actual business meeting, which meant for the third, or maybe fourth, time, I had struck out. No proof. Empty hands. Stupid Cricket.

I pushed into the bathroom because to change my mind might have invited something more from the oil-field guy and his friends. The bathroom was empty, thank God. So I went to the sink and stood, looking at myself in the mirror.

Except it wasn't me.

I touched the hair framing my face, liking the darkness. Maybe my hair would be close to this color if I stopped coloring it golden honey. It looked good against my skin and made my blue eyes stand out. Of course, that could have been the colossal lashes framing my eyes. The sparkly shadow helped with deepening the sky blue. Or maybe they looked brighter because of the tears pooling in my lower lashes.

I bit my lip and channeled my emotions somewhere besides my utter failure. Again. I now had as much confidence as a fiftysomething dude with erectile dysfunction . . . and an empty bottle of Viagra. Just dead in the water on this whole venture.

"Damn it," I said to my reflection before washing my hands and jerking out a chunk of paper towels. I exited the bathroom, glancing once again at Scott, who was pulling papers from the leather portfolio I had engraved with his initials for Father's Day a few years back. He hadn't even tossed one glance my way.

I skirted the flirty good ol' boys and made my way back to the bar, where Griffin nursed his beer.

"We can go now," I said, sinking onto the barstool with a sigh.

"Why? I thought you wanted a table near the windows?" Griffin looked over at me, his dark eyes searching and seemingly finding what he was looking for. "Oh. She's not with him."

"No. Just a regular meeting and a huge waste of time. I'm sorry Ruby got you involved in this. It's pretty obvious that I'm going to get hosed in this whole thing. It's the way the world works. You think that the good guys could win every now and then, but the dickheads just keep—"

"Whoa, did you just say *dickhead?*" His mouth twitched.

"You know what? I can cuss. I can. I do it all the time. I say horrible things, but this is not the time to convince you that . . . that I'm not lame." And dang it if the tears didn't come back. And my stupid lip trembled.

"Hey," Griffin said, reaching out and rubbing my back. "It's going to be okay."

I should have felt comforted, but his sympathy only made me feel worse. The tears that threatened slipped past their barrier. I dashed them away with a furious brush of my hand and picked up my lukewarm beer and took too big of a gulp. Fire shot up my nose. And that fire was beer.

Griffin dropped his hand and grabbed a fistful of napkins as I gasped and started coughing. Beer dripped from my nose, and I made quite a spectacle of myself, pushing away from the bar, drawing everyone's attention as I tried to expel the invader from my sinuses. So much for being covert. Turns out Maddie Holt wasn't good at stealth. No, she liked everyone looking at her, with her big boobs and beer shooting out of her nose.

"Oh God," I said, mopping at my face between intermittent coughs.

Griffin watched me, looking like he wanted to pat me on the back again but was perhaps afraid of my bodily fluids. I blew my nose rather loudly and then held up my hand in apology to everyone who was watching me try not to die.

Griffin held the stool as I slipped back on it. The bartender set a glass of water in front of me and went back to pouring drinks.

"Sorry."

Griffin handed me another napkin. "Your eyelash is on your cheek."

"Dang it," I said, feeling my face. Sure enough. I pulled the other one off, too, wincing as I might have removed a few of my own real lashes. "I really suck at this."

"No, you don't. But you should probably just forgo beer."

"Yeah," I said, pushing the half-full can away.

"Look, if he's screwing around, he'll mess up eventually. They all do."

They. Not we. There was some comfort in his words. Griffin Moon, for all his dourness, wasn't like Scott. "But I need the proof now. I have a meeting with my attorney on Wednesday, and I can't keep pretending that I'm happy with Scott sleeping next to me. I want him out. I want to move on, progress, be . . . I don't know . . . competent at something other than making cupcakes for the PTA and selling old furniture."

"I'm pretty sure you're competent at a lot of things."

I pulled out my phone and accessed the picture I had taken of Scott's schedule. "Maybe I can prove it tomorrow. Tonight he has a grant meeting, so I doubt he'll go see Stephanie for a roll in the hay, but tomorrow he has a meeting at some place called the Channel Marker. I don't know where that is, but maybe—"

"Wait." Griffin held up a hand. "The Channel Marker?"

"Yeah."

"That's out on Caddo Lake. And a local dive. Why would he be meeting someone there?"

"I don't know, but he's up to something else besides cheating on me. I know that. I overheard him talking to some guy about a deal. And Scott was worried about 'going down' for something. Maybe I won't need proof of his cheating if I can get proof of something else. I just need some leverage. He's cleaned out our savings and retirement. I want that back before I file for divorce." I really shouldn't have been telling a stranger my business, but Griffin was already involved. He knew my husband was cheating, and he'd escorted my alter ego to this bar and grill. Too late for involving him. He might as well know what a douchebag my husband was.

Griffin's expression darkened, his fist on the bar clenched. "Okay. Tomorrow. We'll try again. Come to my office at the yard. I'll go with you up to the Channel Marker. Wear the same thing. You look nothing like yourself in that getup."

I patted my wig. "Do I look bad?"

Now why in all of creation had I asked that? Like some insecure schoolgirl. But danged if it wasn't the first thing that came to mind. Deep down inside under my "You don't like him" vow was the dumb girl who wanted to be attractive to Griffin. Ugh. I hated her.

He looked at me, taking in the whole look. Then he shrugged a shoulder. "I like it when you're fussed up. That shirt and boots aren't you. But I dig the short, dark hair."

"Oh. Well, thanks. I think." I looked down at the napkins in my hand. "I can go alone. I'm not afraid to."

"Have you ever been to the Channel Marker?" he asked.

"Obviously I haven't."

"I'm coming with you. No arguments."

"Okay, fine. I'll take your help." I was resigned to the fact that I had another date with Griffin tomorrow. No, not date. Just a person helping another person. "I've sort of lost my appetite. You want to get—"

Griffin flagged down the bartender. "Bring us the loaded cheese fries and a club sandwich to share."

"I guess that means we're eating?" I said with a sigh, wanting to get out before Scott had a chance to see us. Besides, he'd ordered for me without even asking what I wanted. I never ate cheese fries. Those were for teenaged girls or, well, guys like Griffin. They were, like, a bajillion calories. I would just stick to my half of the club, removing the bacon, of course.

But fifteen minutes later, with gooey cheese, sour cream, and bacon covering the enormous plate of carbaliciousness, I changed my mind. Cheese fries were sort of genius, and my lunch date wasn't bad, either. I even ate my half of the sandwich with the bacon. Life was short. And I could add another twenty minutes to my workout.

And bonus—when we left Rendezvous, Scott was still chatting up his business-lunch date. He'd never even laid eyes on me or Griffin.

On our way back to Printemps, Griffin and I talked about music, arguing over our favorite country music legends and then which barbecue place in Memphis was our favorite. By the time we pulled into my parking lot, I realized that for the first time in many, many weeks, I had enjoyed myself, forgetting about my problems as we debated the merits of dry versus wet ribs. Ruby's cousin had a knack for conversation once he pulled the stick from his butt.

As Griffin shifted Ruby's car into park, I said as much. "You know, outside of total failure at catching Scott and almost dying from choking, this was kind of fun. I mean, cheese fries are amazing. Who knew?"

"Um, everyone."

I smiled. "Yeah, I guess I lean toward a salad and Perrier."

Griffin snorted. Then he turned off the engine. "Look, I know you took Juke off your case, but I think you need to tell him what Scott did with your savings and tell him about your suspicions that he may be involved in something sketchy. Juke used to work for the sheriff's office and knows how to investigate all kinds of things from drug rings to white-collar crime. He still has contacts. Snapping a few pictures of your husband with another woman is one thing. Trying to nail him on something else could be harder . . . and dangerous."

"Well, I had planned on asking Juke to do that. But this morning when I went to discuss things with him, I found him drunk. Or so hungover that he still seemed drunk. The man needs rehab, not more work."

Griffin banged his hand on the steering wheel. "Damn it. I had hoped . . . Look, let me talk to him. He lost his wife a few years ago and then his career. You're right. He needs help, and the family can't ignore that any longer. Still, let him help you for the next day or two."

I hadn't known that Juke had lost his wife. Ruby had never said much about Juke at all. Then again, Ruby was fairly quiet about her past life. But I felt bad for Juke, losing so much in his life and trying to fill it up with the wrong things. I knew loss. I knew redirecting and trying to undo and redo everything. "Okay."

Griffin nodded. "Thank you. Everyone needs a second chance. There are some in life who let it pass them by. Others pick it up and don't look back. Like Ruby."

I paused at those words because I didn't know what he meant. Second chance for Ruby? When had she lost her first chance? I started to ask but instead held my tongue. "Well, guess I better go back to work. Thanks again for helping me out. I know I'm not your favorite person, so it was really—"

"Who told you that?" he interrupted.

"I'm not stupid. I know that you didn't like me on sight. That you thought I was frivolous and silly. Some rich lady from south Shreveport with her first-world problems."

Griffin made a face. "You presumed a lot."

I smiled. "It's okay because there is more to me than what you see. See ya tomorrow, Griff."

Climbing out before he could answer, I hurried toward the back stoop.

"Hey," he called out, showing me Ruby's keys in his hand. "Can you catch?"

I nodded, knowing that I wasn't going to catch the dang keys. I was always picked second to last in gym class. Sarah Roberts was always last. Mostly because she had one leg shorter than the other.

Griffin launched the keys with an underhanded lob. And miracle of miracles, I caught those bad boys. My smile told that story, and Griffin sort of chuckled. "Okay, Maddie. See ya tomorrow. And don't forget, only my friends call me Griff."

I blinked.

He pointed at me. "Which means you call me Griff."

I went into my store feeling pretty decent for someone who had failed so badly.

CHAPTER SEVENTEEN

RUBY

When I pulled into my driveway, I found Ed Earl sitting in the front porch swing. And for a moment he reminded me of a steaming pile of horseshit on the pristine lawn of an English estate.

Very offensive to the senses.

It had been a long day requiring three pep talks with Cricket and a lot of haggling over the price of a set of Wedgwood with a plump older woman who thought she deserved half off because one dang cup had been set on the nearby 50-percent-off table. Capping off my Monday was a missed assignment that caused my homework grade to drop to an 87 percent and a conversation with Griff over Juke that made me uneasy. My family had tried to talk Juke into rehab several times, only to have him bounce back, but it was obvious that my cousin was struggling and needed some intervention.

So to find Ed Earl waiting on me wasn't like a nail in the coffin of my day. It was a damned wrecking ball plowing through what was left of my decent mood. Which was not much at all.

I parked and climbed out, slamming my car door extra hard. "You can just get yourself up and take yourself home. We've got nothing to say, Ed Earl."

"Aw, come off it, Roo. I'm tired of chasing you." He stood, the swing slapping his large calves. Ed Earl was a tall drink of water and mean as a cottonmouth—a lethal combination in a criminal. A daunting one in a cousin.

"Who told you where I lived? Because I'm going to kill them," I said, coming around the front and climbing the steps. I had no intention of letting Ed Earl in . . . or of talking to him beyond getting him off my porch and out of my life.

My gaze snagged upon a bud vase sitting beside the welcome mat. A cluster of yellow carnations. I swallowed hard, waylaid by the simpleness, totally off-kilter from the significance of such a flower on my front doorstep.

Why does everyone want roses all the time? They're so overdone and overpriced. I like the bright ones, the ones with ruffles, the ones that announce they're happy to the world.

I can get you those, babe. Say the word and your world can be daisies and yellow carnations.

Word.

"That was there when I got here," Ed Earl said, nodding his giant bowling-ball head toward the tiny vase.

I reached down and lifted it. No note. But it didn't need a note.

Digging my house key from my bag, I thrust it into the dead bolt, twisting and pushing so I could get inside quick and shut the door in Ed Earl's stupid face.

But he had steel-toe boots and the reflexes of a cheetah or some other fast, vicious creature and prevented my evasive tactic.

"What's with you, Ed? You can't take a hint?" I turned on him, my own version of a dangerous creature. I wanted to punch him until he screamed, until he felt every bit of the fear, loss, and hopelessness I had felt every night I had lain on that shitty cot, one eye open for Raya D., the meanest bitch in Long Pines Correctional, who had taken a disliking to me when I wouldn't give her my stupid Valentine's cookie. I wanted to extract the hate I had carried, rolling it on itself, into a seething ball. Then I would shove it so far down his throat, he'd turn purple. But the thing was, I couldn't find that hate. Maybe it was gone. Maybe I couldn't locate it because I had allowed what Ed Earl had done to me to happen. I had played my part and not been strong enough to push him to the ground and put my foot on his throat when I'd had the chance.

His jaw clenched. "But we do have something to say. Or I do anyways."

I glared as he refused to budge, blocking my path into the safety of my home. Beyond his shoulder I saw a neighbor heading my way, her yippy dog zigzagging on the leash. "Fine. Come inside. I don't need the whole neighborhood knowing my business."

He moved out of my way, and we both went inside my apartment. Ed Earl made it feel two sizes too small. I didn't ask him to sit down because I didn't want the memory of him on my sofa.

"You wanna Coke or something?" I asked, only because I noted that Cricket was quick to offer refreshments and write thank-you notes for everyone. She was also big on "hostess gifts," telling customers, "Wouldn't this make the most precious little happy?" I had honestly never thought about taking a "happy" to a friend's house. Booze? Yeah. But a scented candle? Eh.

"Nah, I'm good." He stood with his hands in his pockets, looking around. "This is a real nice place, Roo."

"Please don't call me that. It's Ruby."

"Yeah, okay, Ruby." He stared at my curtains while I set the yellow carnations on the counter next to the overblown roses Ty had sent me. A dozen and a half for no reason at all. The carnations looked defiant against the show-off cousin. But they looked like me. I liked them.

"So?" I turned and set my fists on my hips.

Ed Earl sighed. "You already know I'm sorry about what happened between us. I never would have asked you to take my shit to the shelter if I had known Jerry Jefferies was a damned rat. I never would have involved you."

"But you did."

"Yeah, I did. No takin' that back now. And you did my time. You gave up a lot to do that, and I owe you. Sorry ain't good enough. I realize that now." He reached into his back pocket.

My first inclination was to run because Ed Earl always packed, and five years back he'd shot out his brother's windshield over a stupid poker game. But then I realized Ed Earl wasn't going to shoot me. He wasn't drunk or pissed. Not to mention I was still trying to wrap my head around his words. *He owed me.* Excuses I had expected. But the sincerity of his last remark had thrown up a temporary barrier to my irritation. "What do you mean?"

He withdrew an envelope, walked over, and set it beside the carnations. "There. I don't know how else to make it right. So maybe this will help. But I want you to know something, little coz."

I swallow hard, looking at that envelope, then back at my cousin.

"I changed. I know you don't believe me. But when all that happened, I had no intention of changing my ways." He chuffed and shook his head, looking disappointed in himself. "Hell, even after you going down for all that, refusing to squeal, being loyal when you had no cause to be, I was unmoved, Roo. For all intents and purposes, you should have served me up to the DA on a platter. But you didn't. You just took it. And yeah, there was some crap that went down with Martine Perez over turf and everything. They threw a Molotov through Mama's window. You probably didn't know 'cause Mama's just like you—she keeps it close to the vest. I found her that next morning with the family Bible, and she'd cut my name out. Didn't even bother with a marker. Just cut it out like it was never there, and then she told me that I wasn't her son no more. That was . . . that was somethin'. She ain't never done nothin' like that before."

I pressed my hands against the counter because I had never heard Ed Earl issue any regret. He didn't wound like the rest of the world. Wasn't in his nature. "I didn't know."

"Nah, she wouldn't have told you. You know her. But I went away after that. Went out west to see your dad."

"*My* dad?"

"Yeah, ol' sonofabitch is out in Wyoming. Left the bikers and is working on a ranch."

"I haven't spoken to him in many years." My father had had a breakdown of sorts. He'd walked away from us all. Not much reason other than he said he couldn't stay. Maybe he'd had enough of being a Balthazar and wanted to knock about without a name. Once when I was small, he'd told me that he had tramp in him. That he was a rolling stone. Didn't matter why to me, only that he'd left and I hadn't been enough to keep him here.

"He's different. All the anger just seeped out of him. He reads all the time, takes the peyote sometimes, but that's it. Don't even drink no more. Being with him just did something to me. Sort of like a movie or something. I could see my life, and it was no good." Ed Earl kicked the heel of his boot with the toe of his other one, his gaze on my rug. Finally, he looked up at me. "I didn't know how to change myself, Roo. I knew only one way in life. Bobby said I could just stay out there. Said the guy he worked for was always looking for a strong back. But my boys're here, you know? And the example I had set for them had to be changed. I owed them that. I had to undo some things before I could find any kind of peace or new life. Sometimes you gotta fix what's behind you so you can look in front of you. So I came back. I got right with Jesus. I got right with Mama. And I told the Perezes I was out."

He walked back over to the envelope and tapped it with a thick finger. "I don't know if this will do. I tried to figure what each year was worth to you. You don't have to forgive me, but you have to take this. I can't live with myself if you don't. So even though you're mad as a wet cat and have every right to hold on to what irks you, you have to take this."

I didn't have words because I hadn't expected something so raw from Ed Earl, so I stood, still unable to give him what he wanted.

Ed Earl seemed to be waiting on me, maybe to open the envelope. Maybe to say something. To take his apology, to absolve his burden.

Finally, he said, "You'll take it, right? Give me your word that you'll keep it."

"I don't—"

"I know you don't. You didn't ask for it. It's freely given. It's the least I could do. Just give me this small way to make it up to you, Roo. Say you'll keep it."

"Fine."

He lifted his ball cap and gave me a nod. Then I watched as he crossed the room and opened the door. His eyes met mine, and I saw the regret before he softly smiled and took his leave.

My feet wouldn't move for a few seconds, and I could do nothing but stare at the door. Then the envelope. Then the yellow carnations. I felt violated, my soul hanging out on a line, flapping in the winds of the past that had just blown in. My first inclination was to lock the front door, so I did. Then I put a kettle of water on the burner, needing the comfort of chamomile tea even though I had yet to have dinner. For the first time in my life, I wished for the companionship of a pet, something warm to curl beside me. I don't know why I was grasping for something to give me solace. Nothing bad had happened. But those flowers and that envelope just sat there, not necessarily wanted but messing with my mind.

I poured my tea and then went over to the envelope, lifting it, studying the smudge of something—maybe ketchup from his fries that day or a streak of mud from his day doing whatever he did now. I think Gran had said it was something in the oil field.

Flipping it over, I broke the seal, nicking my finger in the process. A thin line of blood appeared, but I charged on, pulling out what I knew would be inside.

A check.

For eighty thousand dollars.

Forty thousand bucks for each year I spent locked up.

A small smear of blood brushed against the side of the check. Blood money. Oh, the irony of my O negative blood on this particular check. I breathed out a bemused sigh that sounded quite lonely in a space that I was normally very content within.

I didn't want Ed Earl's money, but I had agreed to keep it. Maybe I would think about that tomorrow or next week. I slid the check back into the envelope, stuck it in my bill stack, and took my cup of tea to the couch, my sight line giving me the ability to contemplate the carnations. Which was dangerous.

I didn't want to think about the implications of yellow flowers, either.

Beside me in a bag were a few castoffs Cricket had given me to play with. A 1959 Christian Dior was the first victim. The two-toned champagne satin dress had a fitted corset bodice with a scoop neck and three-quarter sleeves. The hourglass silhouette had a small, nipped waist with a thin tie. The skirt had pleating that made for a pleasing shape. The bottom layer of the dress was stained with rust and water marks, likely a mishap in a trunk packed away in an attic or basement. Keeping the pristine bodice was a no-brainer, and I liked the idea of cutting off the skirt, leaving a sort of peplum of the original skirting. If I could score some decent black velvet, I could sew it into a column and make this party dress into a ball gown.

I wasn't sold on that yet.

My next pull was a riot of color—an orange-and-black silk dress with a corset and two black spaghetti straps. The waist was tiny with a large, fluffy bow that affixed to the side. The skirt was a column that went to the ankle. The back of the dress was ripped, the bow dangling, and the fabric pilled in a few areas. The skirt was essentially free of nubby snags, so I could salvage that and use it in some way. I grabbed a sketchbook I had bought at a craft store, feeling like a fraud because what did I really know about designing dresses? Well, other than that necessity was the mother of invention, which encompassed having to make one's own clothes because you didn't have a pot to piss in. In that, I was an expert. So I started sketching a few ideas using the black-and-orange floral silk. Could I add in another color to soften the Halloween vibe? Or maybe I wanted to embrace the bold colors? Occasionally, when I contemplated a particular element, my gaze landed on those carnations.

I groped for my tea, and finding it cold, I went back to noodling with a potential redesign of the black and orange. Jack-o'-lanterns. Basketballs. Tigers. Maybe a white-and-black tiger print to balance? Or would that look too hodgepodge? If I could refashion the bodice in some manner, I could use tuxedo pants. Or . . .

The doorbell interrupted my contemplation.

For someone who could count on one hand the number of visitors I had received in the time I'd lived in my duplex, I was certain I had now surpassed the record.

I struggled to get up, shoving aside the throw I had pulled onto my lap to cushion the sketchbook, and went to the door. Looking outside, I resigned myself to deal with those dang yellow flowers.

"Don't you have beer to pour?" I asked.

Dak allowed a smile to touch his lips. "I have employees who know how to pour beer. Besides, Monday's slow."

"Which makes me wonder why you're standing here when you've got all that spare time to *not* pour beer."

He shrugged. "I wish I knew."

Me and him both.

I swung the door open in an unstated invitation, and the boy I had once loved who had grown into a man I barely knew stepped inside my world. I closed the door behind him. "I'm having tea. You want some?"

"I actually brought some of Aunt Linda's chicken salad." He offered me a brown paper bag.

"So you show up unannounced with chicken salad? And you sent me carnations?" I didn't have time to beat around bushes. Dakota wasn't one for pussyfooting, either. He was always deliberate, never unsure, a trait that had served him well in life. He had never been one for ulterior motives or grand gestures. Not that carnations and chicken salad were grand. Quite the opposite, which suited me. And he knew that.

Yeah, thing was, Dak knew me.

"You always liked both."

"I did." And maybe I still do. So I took the bag because Aunt Linda's chicken salad was a thing of beauty. She used Blue Plate mayonnaise, which was Louisiana's answer to Duke's. And in my opinion, a better answer. Linda chopped the celery fine and added toasted pecans from her prolific tree out back. She bought the chickens from a place out on Sentell Road—farm to table before it was a thing. And the combination of those things at her fingertips became a palate-stirring comfort food that was like southern gospel on the lips.

I took the bag to the kitchen and pulled out a plate, some club crackers, and the lemonade I had fresh squeezed yesterday. My gran always had club crackers and lemonade for visitors, which hadn't seemed so weird until I truly thought about it. But old habits die hard even in a new generation, so I was set up for that chicken salad.

Dak had made himself at home on my couch. I placed the plate holding his offering on the coffee table atop some photography magazines and beside the bluebirds clustered on a branch that my gran had made when she took ceramics at the Mooringsport Baptist Church. We both tucked into the chicken salad in companionable silence, Dak sipping in appreciation at the homemade lemonade and me scarfing down half the chicken salad without so much as a how-do-ya-do.

"My stars and chickens, that's some good stuff. How is she not rolling in the dough selling this? It's the crack of chicken salads," I said, leaning back on the couch, careful not to touch Dak as he polished off his half.

It was odd. For so many years we hadn't spoken, and here we sat like two who'd never been apart. So unsettling, but at the same time, not as uncomfortable as it should have been.

He nodded. "You would think. But she says she only likes cooking for those she loves. Guess the rest of the world is SOL."

I glanced over at the yellow carnations, and he caught me. I looked back at him with a question in my eyes.

Dak lifted one shoulder. "I just . . . Well, those others were the wrong flowers. That's all."

I made a moue with my lips, studying his discomfort. "What are you doing, Dak?"

He rubbed a hand over his eyes, for a moment looking quite tortured. "I don't know, babe. I mean, sorry. Ruby."

I sat like a statue, unsure how to proceed.

He dropped his hand and looked at me. "I don't know."

I counted off ten seconds of silence. "Okay." And then I sighed, "Okay."

And I didn't know what I meant by that, but I couldn't sit there and examine something neither one of us understood. We were getting nowhere. So I picked up the television remote. "The Cubs are playing. Wanna watch?"

"Nah. Water and bridges are things I sometimes don't like to contemplate." He clinked the ice in the glass, and I almost rose to fetch him more lemonade. But then I remembered that his hands weren't broken. He cocked his head. "I think *American Idol* is on."

"Done," I said, clicking on the TV and finding the right channel. Dak settled back, crossing his feet shod in running shoes. He wore Adidas joggers and a short-sleeve T-shirt with some 5K ad on it. He sported a fresh cut and a tan from fishing. He looked good sitting next to me, and it didn't escape my notice that I had invited Dak inside while I had sent Ty away. Of course, inviting Ty in pretty much acknowledged I would be having sex with him. But Dak was there for something he didn't know he wanted. I understood that perfectly because that's where I was, too.

So I sat beside my ex-love watching people yodel, bomb, and dazzle with their vocal abilities, deliciously full on chicken salad, with a check for $80,000 sitting not ten feet away.

CHAPTER EIGHTEEN

CRICKET

The Channel Marker wasn't exactly seedy. But it was a close second. And so I was pretty relieved to have grumpy Griffin Moon with his scowl and big clomping boots entering the joint behind me.

I glanced around for the perfect spot to spy on my husband.

The long, scarred bar with its fish netting and rusty barstools would have me too out in the open. Clusters of low tables, the kind men gathered around with cigarettes hanging from their lips to play card games, scattered the majority of the room. Maps of Caddo Lake interspersed with neon beer signs seemed the standard decoration for lakeside drinking. Behind the bar was a sign selling bait and a half wall covered with corks, hooks, and pocketknives. The place smelled of stale beer, cigarettes, and some faint funk that reminded me of a fraternity house.

"I'll grab some beers. You may want to go to the restroom and . . ." He gestured at me, drawing his fingers up and down. My hands flew to my wig.

Thirty minutes earlier, Griffin had met me at his tow yard. Out in front of the freshly painted office with the blue-moon logo on the large plate glass sat a shiny Harley. Griffin came outside, waving farewell at someone behind the counter, and silently handed me a helmet.

"You're joking, right?" I asked.

He made a face. "No. I thought we'd take the bike. The tow truck seems too conspicuous, and my regular truck is back at my place. It's a nice day."

"People die on these things, and besides, that helmet will mess up my wig." I had on the same outfit as yesterday. The shirt with the rock band that seemed to enjoy death a lot, the ripped-up jeans, and the dark lipstick. Ruby had brought me a tattoo that would come off with baby oil to go on my wrist. It was a heart with a sword through it. She'd also brought me a denim shirt, which I put over the T-shirt since my boobs hadn't magically shrunk overnight. I had wounds from the bobby pins Ruby had jabbed into my hair to keep the wig on.

"You won't die. And I bet you the first round that you'll like it," Griffin said, holding out the helmet and waggling it. "Come on. Live like you mean it."

I ignored his helmet and folded my arms across my chest, mad that he somehow knew what to use against me. Daring me to be bold. Tempting me with letting go of my mundane life that had led to my husband plowing the tennis pro. Standing up on a desk and dead poeting me into seizing the day. "Stop that."

"Stop what?"

I inhaled and exhaled deeply. "Daring me."

Griffin smiled something very devilish and unlike him. I felt it in parts that didn't need to be feeling a dang thing. "Is it working?"

I grabbed the helmet and tugged it on. "I guess I get the bitch seat since I don't know how to drive a motorcycle."

This amused him. He actually laughed, muttering "bitch seat" under his breath, and set about cranking up the scary-looking bike. He motioned me to him, and this is where I realized that I was about to straddle him and wrap my arms around his waist. I would be pressing my breasts to his back and getting real intimate with Griffin Moon, and that thought made my tummy tremble.

But once I was on the surprisingly comfortable seat, Griffin showing me where to place my feet, I didn't mind holding on to him because the takeoff scared the hell out of me. I became a spider monkey clinging to his back. No room for Jesus on this bike ride.

Never having ridden a motorcycle before, I couldn't have imagined the way the fear bloomed into euphoria once he took us onto the highway heading north. Colors spun by me, a whirring of shapes, as my stomach settled and I relaxed the fists knotted in his shirt, flattening my hands against his muscled stomach. The wind tore at me, but I loved the way Griffin zipped in and out, hugging the curves as the remnants of city washed to greener pastures and tall pines. Eventually the rolling pastures met the lake. And then Griffin pulled into a gravel lot with a sad-looking square building painted light gray that held down a corner. The infamous Channel Marker.

Griffin parked next to a utility truck and shut off the motorcycle. He ripped off his helmet and shook his dark locks. I caught the odor of something fresh and manly and almost leaned closer to him for a good whiff. But luckily, I caught myself. The last thing I wanted to do was get caught huffing Griffin like some lunatic.

So when we entered the bar and he turned to me and indicated that my wig was askew, I hurried to the his/her bathroom, which, upon entry, I discovered should have firmly been a "his" bathroom. Cedar walls held a condom dispensary and a paper towel holder that was empty, and the concrete floor was caked with stuff I really didn't want to think about. On the sink stood a roll of brown paper towels with a bar of soap beside it. The mirror, speckled with age, proved that my wig was indeed crooked. I did my best to tidy it and then pulled out the gloss I had shoved in my front pocket, reapplying it. I wished I had cause to wear sunglasses, because I had elected to go without the fake eyelashes this go-around. Still, I didn't think Scott would recognize me as his wife.

When I emerged from the toilet, I found Griffin in the back, two bottles of Bud Light on the table in front of him. A couple of men sat near an aged jukebox scanning the *Thrifty Nickel* for boats. I could hear the rumble of their debate over which one would be the best for frogging. A single older gentleman in denim overalls with a bandana sticking out of his back pocket sat alone, a bottle of Coke in front of him. They all turned and watched me as I made my way toward Griffin. Tinny country music played over the large corner-mounted speakers.

I slid onto a stool, one that put my back to the door. A Heineken mirror on the wall opposite the door was angled enough for me to observe who entered and exited. "Thanks for the beer."

The corner of his lip quirked. "Hope you enjoy it."

I set my cell phone on the table, prepared to use it if needed. Scott *could* bring Stephanie here. Maybe. But probably not. I was pretty shocked that *I* was sitting in a bar where someone could also buy bait and a pocketknife.

"You look nervous. Take a few sips to take the edge off. I'll go find some music. What do you like?"

"Norah Jones."

"I'm pretty sure that's not going to be there. So how about Tanya Tucker or Tammy Wynette?"

I shrugged and did as he suggested, taking a few swigs, telling myself to relax as I stole glances at my Apple Watch. It was almost appointment time, and Scott was never late. Part of his standard MO. Always be on time.

Griffin moseyed back and had just sat down when the door opened. I tensed, and he picked up his bottle, clicking it against mine, and mouthed, "Relax."

Easy for him to do.

My gaze strayed to that mirror, and I could see Scott, dressed in trousers and a button-down, no tie, entering the bar with another man wearing a suit. They surveyed the room, so I jerked my gaze to the tabletop, keeping my head down so I didn't draw their attention. The door closed behind them, and the bartender called, "Howdy."

They made their way to the table with the older guy in overalls. Surprising.

A round of greetings took place and an introduction. Standard business protocol. Finally, I caught a good look at the older gentleman in the suit. It was Donner Walker, Ty's father.

Something zinged inside me.

Was this who Scott had been talking to at the gala?

Griffin leaned toward me. "The guy they're meeting is Skeet Brookings. He's an oil guy, but not just oil and gas. He owns half of Caddo Parish. His pockets are as deep as time."

Now that wasn't surprising. I knew that name mostly because Mr. Brookings banked with Caddo Bank, and Scott had mentioned him a time or two. This was a big fish.

The sound of Brooks & Dunn covered the men's conversation, and I felt a flash of annoyance that Griffin had possibly drowned out the sounds of whatever they were talking about with country music. My mind raced with what I knew about Donner Walker. I remembered something about a potential retirement community or some type of development, but maybe it was more like an investment company that bought and sold real estate? I couldn't remember because I rarely paid attention to that stuff. Chances were good that it had been the arrogant Donner Walker that night. But what were they up to? Just because they were meeting with this Skeet fellow didn't mean what they were doing was illegal. But the clandestine conversation at the gala had seemed odd. My gut said something was fishy . . . and that it had nothing to do with the bait this bar sold.

Obviously Scott believed in this venture because I was assuming he'd put all our money into the investment opportunity. No way would Scott venture our future on something with risky returns. So I needed to figure out exactly what was going on. But in order to do that, I needed to not alert Scott that I was concerned about our money and manage to do some deeper digging into our financials.

"I can't hear what they're saying," I whispered to Griffin.

He smiled. "It's okay. I know Skeet well. Let's let them conclude business, and then we'll pay Skeet a visit."

Good plan. Then I would know exactly what Donner had dragged my husband into. "Maybe we can get Juke to do some background investigation on Donner Walker."

"Who?"

"The guy in the suit. I'm almost certain that's who I overheard Scott having a conversation with at Gritz and Glitz. He was talking about going down for something. But the guy, Donner, said he had to stay the course. It sounded sketchy." I couldn't believe I was blabbing this to Griffin, but the thing was, I trusted him. Wasn't like he didn't already know that Scott was a turd.

"What's Gritz and Glitz?"

"A gala thing. That doesn't matter. I just suspect there is more to what Scott is doing than screwing me over." A flash in the mirror caught my eye, and I saw Scott rise from his stool. He looked to be heading over to—"Shit."

Griffin noted the movement behind me and dragged my stool toward him. Then he did something that stunned me. He leaned over and started nuzzling my neck. Like totally kissing it, his arm curving round me to bring me closer. My mind registered that he was protecting me from being busted, but my body liked it a little too much. For one thing, he was good at kissing necks. For another, his hands were on my body in such an intimate way that I felt the heat deep in my belly unfurl and do a little tap dance toward the basement, a place that had not felt such stirrings in quite a while.

"Shh," Griffin warned, midsmooch, as I tried to relax. I felt him glance up. "Help ya?"

"You don't happen to have change for a hundred, do you? The bartender's short." Scott sounded normal. Polite. The same as he always did.

"Nah, dude. Sorry," Griffin said, sounding put out about having his make-out session interrupted.

"You got your hands full. I'll leave you to it," Scott said, sounding amused.

And it might have been spiteful of me, but I didn't care. I cupped Griffin's jaw and pulled his mouth to mine.

And Griffin wasn't born yesterday. I mean, obviously. So he took what was offered, angling his head and tucking right into my lips like I was dessert. And though I knew I was going to lie to myself about this whole situation, convincing myself that we were merely two people acting into each other so my ass of a husband didn't discover I was wearing a wig and spying on him, I let myself enjoy the heck out of that kiss. Griffin tasted hot, yeasty, and about as dangerous as that box of cinnamon rolls I had dipped into the previous day. I wanted to keep going, wanted to open my mouth, slide onto his lap, and straddle him. But that was wrong. Very wrong. Because like it or not, I *was* married. And I wasn't a douchebag like my soon-to-be ex-husband.

So I broke the kiss and whispered, "Is he gone?"

Griffin nodded, and I swear, that man tried to look unaffected, but I could tell that our little lit match had left some smoke behind. Which meant satisfaction curled up inside me like a fat ol' tom.

I mean, I knew *I* would be thinking about the scruff of his jaw, the way he smelled, and the way my body had craved more for many days. Griffin might as well have something to think about, too.

Risking a glance in the mirror, I saw Scott return and the old fella dig out a twenty from his ratty billfold, obviously covering his own beverage. The three men went back to their discussion as I sipped my beer to disguise the sudden jittery feeling that had nothing to do with the fear of getting caught by Scott and everything to do with my little break in sanity.

"So let's try to look normal," Griffin said, taking a sip of his beer. "So have you ever been fishing?"

"Fishing?"

"Like on a lake. Hook. Pole. Fishing."

"Um, once when I was at summer camp. I didn't really like killing the worms. Because then you used their poor dead carcasses to catch fish that you then also killed. It was a chain of killing."

Griffin's mouth twitched. "So you're opposed to killing things for food."

"No. I eat meat and fish."

"Oh, so you're opposed to the killing of the food but not the eating of the food." He nodded, his face in mock thought. "Isn't that a bit hypocritical?"

"Well, when you put it that way," I said, rolling my eyes because I now understood that Griffin enjoyed getting under my skin. And I would really enjoy him getting under my jeans. Which was wrong. But maybe I could admit to myself that somewhere deep inside, under the vows I had taken and the morality code I had believed in, I was attracted to Griffin. And I would like to do dirty things to him.

But I wasn't going to.

Not until this thing with Scott was finished. And probably not even then.

We made some small talk and drank our beers until Scott and Donner rose and shook Skeet Brookings's hand. The men all took their leave, Skeet, carrying a handful of brochures, jetting off before the other two. Five minutes after they'd all pulled out of the parking lot, Griffin and I climbed back on the motorcycle. Ten minutes later we pulled up in front of a modest brick house set against the choppy gray waters of Caddo Lake. Cypress dressed in Spanish moss clustered in the shallows, and an old pier stretched into the embrace of the lake, a single johnboat rocking against the weathered wood. A shiny orange tractor sat to the side of the house, a grown man's toy for playing in the dirt. The grounds were clean, the flower beds freshly planted, and the view amazing. Like taking a deep breath just looking at it.

Skeet sat on the front porch amid five hummingbird feeders. Oddly enough, he didn't look surprised to see us.

"Come on up and get some iced tea. Martha just made some, and it's getting hotter than two rats making whoopee in a wool sock," Skeet said, petting an old dog that rose up and gave a long stretch before settling back down at his feet.

For one thing: it wasn't *that* hot. For another, this man didn't seem like someone who had much money. But I knew that looks were deceiving. And last, that dog looked to be on its last leg, bless it.

"How are ya, Skeet?" Griffin said, hanging his helmet on the handlebars and setting the one I was holding on the seat of the Harley. "Been a minute."

"A-yup," he said, eyeing me with interest. "You been catching any lately?"

"Haven't been in a few weeks. Busy."

Skeet raised his bushy eyebrows. "I remember the hustle."

Griffin stepped back as I climbed the steps. "Uh, this is Mad—"

"Catherine Ann Crosby," I said, electing to not lie to this man. Something seemed very wrong in that, even though I appreciated Griffin's attempt to keep my identity a secret. "You just met with my husband and Donner Walker at the Channel Marker."

"I figured that's why you were here. Saw you both there." He tapped the brochures, giving a smile that showed nice dental work. The teeth always told the tale. Skeet Brookings had a mouthful of crowns and veneers. "I ain't so much a fool that I can't spot what those two were up to. But I'm polite-like, so I took the meeting. Been doing banking with your husband and his daddy before him for years."

I sank into a rocking chair just as a woman came out, wearing an honest-to-God frilled apron and carrying a tray with iced tea and shortbread cookies.

"Well, now, it's so nice to have company. I saw y'all comin' up the road and put out some cookies I just baked. Lord knows Peter doesn't need all of them. His cardiologist would appreciate y'all helping him out by taking some." She set the tray on the small wooden table between the rockers and brushed her hands. "I'm Martha Brookings, Peter's wife of nearly sixty years. Can you believe that? Sixty years. Can't get rid of me now, you old coot. I know your secrets."

Skeet slapped her behind. "Don't matter. I keep you for your cookin', woman."

Martha looked pleased about that. "I hope y'all will excuse me. I got a roast in the oven, so I'll just leave you to your business."

She disappeared, and Griffin immediately dug into the iced tea and cookies.

I looked Mr. Brookings in the eye. "You're right. What my husband and Donner are up to is exactly why I'm here, Mr. Brookings."

"Skeet, please."

"So, Skeet, my husband is either having a midlife crisis, he's fallen into a pile so deep he can't get out, or he's just a total butthole, pardon my language. And honestly, it could be all three. That being said, since he and I will be severing our relationship soon and I'm trying to protect myself and my daughter, I'm hoping you will help me out. I'm asking for your discretion, please. If you can't give me that, I've probably already said too much. But Griffin trusts you."

"For good reason. I'm what they call 'good people,' Mrs. Crosby. Spent my whole life trying to choose right over wrong. Jesus is my Lord and Savior, and I regard him as my ultimate authority."

I assumed that meant he wasn't going to go squealing to Scott about this little visit. "That's admirable, Skeet. So what exactly are Scott and Donner up to?"

The older man rubbed his face and took a long drink. "Well, I've been around for many a moon, Mrs. Catherine, and I'm fair to middlin' sure that the Donner fella is trying to pull the wool over people's eyes."

He passed me the brochure with smiling older people and then one with the logo of a tree with *Peachtree City Securities of Georgia* across the front. I glanced through both, trying to absorb exactly what Walker wanted from Skeet. "So he wants you to invest in a retirement center."

"Nope. He wants me to buy promissory notes, giving him money to buy mortgage notes, underwrite loans, and buy and sell real estate at a profit, which he in turn will share with investors. He says there's a return of at least twelve percent and it's very low risk. The note matures in three to five years. This is what he prefers to invest in—retirement centers and so forth. He's even recruiting a company to build one here."

"So it's legit?" I asked, studying the claims on the brochure.

"It looks legit, but to an old guy like me who gets poached all the time for 'investment opportunities,' I'm doubtful. He's been in business for what looks to be eight or nine years, and now he's shown up here in Louisiana looking to offer this opportunity. I would say recruiting new investors is paramount to Walker. Looks like a—"

"Ponzi scheme," Griffin said, brushing cookie crumbs from his beard.

"No way," I said, trying to wrap my mind around Scott actually willingly participating in something like that. We'd seen a few friends get tangled up in such get-rich-quick schemes, and Scott would never take our money and invest in something that would fold in on itself and give Donner Walker a cell in federal prison next to some Bernie Madoff–type who had fleeced tons of people out of their life's savings. But as bad a husband as Scott had turned out to be, I couldn't see him cheating his friends and family. And putting our money into it? "He wouldn't sink our money into something shady. He's a banker, and a smart one."

Skeet shrugged and scratched his belly. "He may not have invested. These guys need trusted people in communities to vouch for them, to send them prospective investors. They usually pay a commission. Maybe even cut them into the profits. Maybe your husband is collecting finder's fees for feeding plump suckers to this Walker fellow."

"But he cleared out our accounts. Our retirement, too. I just don't think . . . None of this makes sense." I stared out at the iris blooming beneath the oak trees. At the squirrels frolicking just beyond them. At my life turned upside down.

There were some givens in this whole situation. One, Scott wouldn't invest in something shady. I was certain about that. And two, I was sure he'd probably vouched for Donner Walker, the big brother of his fraternity roommate, whose family Scott had always been dazzled by. The Walker family owned a plantation in Natchitoches and had been populating the banks of the Cane River for many generations. One uncle had been governor, a cousin a senator, and another a crony of Edwin Edwards. But ol' Donner had married a Georgia girl and taken his talent of being a rich white dude to Atlanta. Donner had sought Scott out a few years back, and I remembered my husband talking about how successful the man's company was and how Donner had wanted to bring some economic stimulation to the local economy. And third, I knew Scott was cheating on me. Last, he had taken our savings and retirement and put it somewhere.

So what did all that add up to?

Something really unsettling swirled in my stomach, and for a moment I thought I might toss my cookies in a nearby shrub.

"You okay?" Griffin asked, abandoning the shortbread and iced tea. The old dog even looked concerned. "You look ill."

"Actually, I'm not okay." I swallowed hard and looked back at the brochure in my hand. "I can't see Scott investing in this. Not if he knows it's a scheme . . . which means he has other plans for the money he took from our accounts. He's a banker, so he can move money around easily. He's hiding it from me. He's planning something."

And then it hit me. Something I had seen when I had first riffled through his office those many weeks ago. That bank he'd gone to when we'd vacationed over Christmas. A brochure for Grand Cayman National Bank and Trust had fallen out of a folder. When I was at the spa, Scott had said he had a banking friend who worked there and he was going to visit him. But he'd lied. I knew where he'd put our savings, our retirement, and probably all the kickback money Donner Walker was paying him to steer fat cats his way.

"Oh my Lord," I said, clutching my stomach, listing a bit in the rocking chair. The puzzle pieces lined up. The emptying of accounts. The Cayman bank. The passport in his desk drawer. The weight loss. The new girlfriend. Click. Click. Click.

Griffin and Skeet looked at each other as if they were afraid I might pass out. But I wasn't passing out. Because the anger that flooded my body gave me the strength to stand, to fist my hands beside me, and to growl. "He's going to leave the country."

"Huh?" Griffin asked.

"Scott is taking his girlfriend and our money, and he's leaving the country. I'm going to fucking kill him."

CHAPTER NINETEEN

RUBY

We sat in Dak's bar trying to grapple with what Cricket had discovered that afternoon. It wasn't easy to catch hold of. Maybe because if Scott was colluding with Donner Walker to bilk people out of millions of dollars, Ty had to know what was going on. Which meant that the guy who'd romanced me for the past month was worse than a douche. He was a slimy, no-good pilferer of innocent people's bank accounts.

How depressing.

"I don't know what to do with this information. How can I get the money back? It's probably now in a foreign bank," Cricket said for the third time, jarring me out of how this whole hinky business was affecting my dating life. My poor boss now knew that not only was her husband cheating on her, but he was cheating his friends and customers.

How *very* depressing.

"We're going to figure out what to do, Cricket. Juke said he'd be down in a minute. He'll have some ideas or maybe know someone we can contact who can investigate what Donner Walker and Scott are up to." I slid the glass of wine that the waitress, Shirley, had set on the table toward Cricket. I knew that alcohol didn't solve problems, but Cricket had been vacillating between flushed pink with rage and white with horror. In this case, the wine would probably help.

Griffin had excused himself to go to his office to check on things. He'd left his bike outside, and I had marveled that Cricket had climbed on that death trap with him. I had a hard time reconciling the woman straddling a hog behind my cousin with my prissy boss who always sat with her knees together. I kept trying to picture them roaring up North Market, rattling across the Caddo Lake bridge, drinking longnecks at the Channel Marker, but that image escaped me.

Dak stood behind the bar, casting glances my way occasionally. There was something about a handsome guy behind a bar, towel flung over his shoulder, biceps singing a siren song, that made a girl look thrice.

"You've looked at him, like, ten times," Cricket said, taking a gulp of chardonnay. "You have something going on?"

"No. I mean, we're friends. We used to . . ." I stopped because I couldn't really answer the question because I didn't know what we were. He'd come over and watched *American Idol* with me before saying good night and disappearing into the darkness of my driveway. And then we had texted a few times throughout the day about who we thought would get voted off that night. This was something we used to do when we were dating in high school. Both of us had loved watching the talent show and choosing our favorites, then calling in votes and actively campaigning our friend groups to get more votes. And we had made crazy bets. Like if someone got voted off who one of us swore wouldn't, there was a penalty of buying a Coke or wearing an awkward shirt to school. We'd had a lot of fun with our affectionate rivalry for those years we'd been together. Silly children.

But what was Dak to me now?

I was afraid to examine it too greatly. My heart had always been on the table when it came to Dakota Roberts, and I wasn't sure I could stand having it sliced and diced again, even though deep, deep, deep down I longed for him. But I wasn't ready to do anything more than have a cautious friendship, if even that.

Still, I couldn't ignore that it had been easy to suggest that Griffin and Cricket meet me at the Bullpen after I closed Printemps, which I did early, at Cricket's direction. Honestly, Tuesday was a super slow day anyway. We'd only had a few looky-loos who purchased nominal items and one sale of a bed from the online offerings. Both Cricket and I had been distracted and needed to attend to posting new items and prepping for the Junior League's Spring Fling shopping event, where we would house a booth. That was a month away, but time was flying.

On the way to the bar, I had put in a call to Juke, telling myself that was the real reason I had chosen Dak's bar as our meeting place— for ease. Cricket needed Juke's help with this new potential criminal element, and to my relief, my cousin actually sounded sober and inter-ested. He said he was out working and should be back at the close of the day. He said he would join us at the bar and that I should tell Dak to make fresh coffee. Good sign.

Cricket set the wineglass on the table. "You used to what? Did you date the bartender?"

"Well, actually, he's the owner of this bar, but yeah, we dated when I was in high school. After my dad left and my mom started having some issues, well, lots of issues, we broke up. Dak was going to LSU on a baseball scholarship, and I still had a year left in high school. Just made sense."

"Oh, your father left?"

Here we go. Perfect opportunity to come clean. It was beyond time to clue Cricket into who she was dealing with. We had formed a sort of friendship, and I was afraid of jeopardizing that—and of losing my job—but I didn't want to hide my past any longer. "Yeah, my dad was sort of at the end of his rope. Not necessarily a breakdown but close enough. My family has a bit of a reputation in North Caddo Parish. You probably wouldn't know them, but most out here do. The Balthazars are fringe people."

"Fringe people?"

I cleared my throat. "Like on the fringe of being a crime family. I mean, not like cartel or anything. We just have a certain reputation. Or used to. My uncles and cousins sometimes ran afoul of the law, but we've mostly straightened up. And my dad, he just, well, I guess he just needed to be away from the temptation. So he left when I was a junior in high school. It sort of set me off a little. I may have picked up some bad family habits."

Cricket leaned forward, her manicured nails brushing against her wineglass. "Like getting in trouble?"

"Yeah, I raised a little hell in high school, ended up dropping out after I skipped so many classes that I was failing most of them. I smoked a lot of weed, sold some to kids at the school. Got picked up for being an accessory to stealing cars." I couldn't keep the shame from my voice. The girl I once was had faded away, but she'd been there. She'd been angry, reckless, and very much a Balthazar.

"Oh. Well, it's obvious you've found yourself. Look at you, in school with a job and a future waiting for you to grab. I saw the new dresses, by the way. They are fantastic, Ruby."

I swallowed hard at her words. "Yeah, thanks. I *have* changed. But I need to tell you something. It's hard for me to say, and I hope it won't change things between us. It could. I know the risk, but I think I need to say it. Should have told you long ago."

The clink of glasses and the hum of a college spring football game being telecast above the bar weren't loud enough. I didn't want to shout my admission to Cricket and have everyone in the bar hear it. Of course, there were only about twenty people occupying tables and stools at the bar. "Um, so . . . I served time."

Cricket blinked rapidly and leaned even closer to me. "Wait. Like you actually went to jail?"

I closed my eyes because it sounded so horrible coming from the mouth of someone I respected, someone who would never have allowed herself to be used in such a way. "Um, yeah. It's a long story, but it ended with me at Long Pines Correctional doing almost two years."

My boss sat back, her eyes shifting from left to right and back again as she grappled with what I had just revealed. She cleared her throat and looked off. I waited, feeling like someone had their hands around my throat. I shouldn't have told her. She'd never asked. The application hadn't asked about felonies, only prior work experience and references. But I should have disclosed it. My parole officer had told me to be truthful on job applications, and I always had until this one. Because I had wanted to work in the store with the beeswax and vintage dresses.

Finally, after several seconds that felt like hours, Cricket leaned forward. "That must have been horrible, Ruby. I can't imagine."

This time it was I who had to take a moment to comprehend that she was . . . offering me sympathy for having to endure prison? I sucked in a deep breath and blinked away sudden tears. "You're not going to fire me?"

"No. Why would I fire you? You're one of the best employees I've ever had, and you're, well, Ruby, you're my friend. I *know* the real you. Or I think I do. I mean, let's face it, I could possibly be a bad judge of character." She gave a self-deprecating laugh that put me immediately at ease. "Why did you have to serve time? Did you kill someone?"

I laughed at that. "No. And if I had, it would have been more than twenty-two months of incarceration. No, I unknowingly transported meth for my uncle. He hid it in frozen wild game that he 'donated' to the Hunters for the Hungry nonprofit. He had a whole distribution thing going that was actually pretty clever. I certainly had no idea he was dealing meth. Like a moron, I dropped it by the place where they kept all the meat. When the police busted me, I didn't squeal. I couldn't. Ed Earl had been using my grandmother's land and her bank accounts to hide the product and the money. I couldn't risk getting my gran involved, and Ed Earl would have gone away for a long time. So I refused to talk, and because I had priors, I had to do the time."

"Oh my God," Cricket breathed, pressing her hand to her mouth. "That's crazy."

"I know. It was . . . well, something I'm not willing to ever repeat. And because I got railroaded by a member of my family, I knew how you felt when you found out your husband was cheating and thought you were too stupid to figure it out. I was angry for you because I had been there. Well, in a way."

Cricket reached over and put her hand over mine. "I'm so sorry, Ruby. Life has dealt you an unfair hand, but I'm going to help you find a better dealer. I mean, not a dealer, but you know what I mean. I'm going to help you get your business started. Because your deconstructed dresses fashioned into—" She stopped, her eyes growing big.

"What?" I asked.

"It's an analogy, Ruby. You've taken the good parts and made them into something better. It's like a theme for both of our lives. Well, at least yours. You're re-creating your life, Ruby, and it's worthwhile." Tears glittered in her eyes and she smiled. "Oh, oh . . . What do you think about calling your clothing line *Deconstructed*?"

I turned my hand over in hers and gave it a squeeze, my heart suddenly lighter. That burden I carried had been lifted, and Cricket had taken it and tossed it over her shoulder as if it were nothing more than some spilled salt. "You know, I think Deconstructed is a perfect name. Even though the ripped-up parts are used to reconstruct the new thing."

Cricket withdrew her hand, took a sip of wine, and narrowed her eyes. "True, but without the deconstructing, you have no history. It's the deconstruction that matters. Without understanding who you are and accepting all the good and bad parts of your past, you don't know the things worth keeping, and you can't get rid of the things that need to be tossed. You can't remake yourself."

Her words sank inside me, causing me to cast yet another glance at Dak. "That's true. Maybe I focused way too much on the stains and rips rather than seeing how the rest of me could become something better. I can't change my past. I can't hide it under a big, ugly sweater, either."

"No. Neither of us can. I guess we all find out in life that a little deconstructing—a bit of pulling away, examination, trimming, and refitting—helps us discover what will hold up. And if we're lucky, we get a chance to become something even better." Cricket nodded as she affirmed these things to herself. Her color was back to normal. Distracting her with the sins of my past had at least taken her mind off the sins of the present.

"This whole analogy thing is pretty good, Cricket. Oh, and I meant to tell you another thing—Ed Earl came to see me last night and gave me a check for eighty thousand dollars." I couldn't believe I was blabbing about the money, too. It was like once I had opened the closet door to my real self, I had tap-danced out in a shimmy dress. "I'm thinking it would be great seed money for my new side business. Maybe get a website and some advertising? Or something."

"Eighty thousand? That's a great apology," Cricket said, her lips finally curving into a smile. "How about we do a soft launch of your line at the Spring Fling? That could be perfect. Do you think a month is enough time? I know someone who can do the website. We have only four dresses, though. I would think you'd need a few more. But you can also do custom. Yes, ready-to-wear and custom pieces . . . hmm."

Juke entered the bar through the kitchen as Cricket mulled over a plan for my business, tossing Shirley a wave as he beelined for our table. "Hey, Juke is here. We'll talk dresses later."

Cricket lost her smile as she drained the wineglass and set it down.

"Hiya, ladies," Juke said, turning and catching Dak's eye. "Coffee if you don't mind, Dak."

"Well, you look positively normal, Juke," I said, noting that his shirt was clean and his jaw was freshly shaven.

My cousin waved my compliment away as he hooked an empty chair with his foot and dragged it over to our table. "Yeah, okay, I get it. I know I've been acting a fool. But Griffin threatened to beat me into oblivion, so I decided I like my mug enough to keep it pretty."

I snorted.

He looked slightly hurt.

"Well, I'm very glad you've decided to stop spending your days dead drunk," Cricket said as Shirley set a cup of black coffee in front of Juke and then disappeared without a single word. "I'm giving you a second chance, thanks to Griffin. You owe your cousin a great deal. He seems to care more about you than you care about yourself."

Cricket's admonishment was delivered a bit high-handedly.

Juke, however, looked nonplussed. "Well, Mrs. Crosby, the anniversary of my wife's death always does that to me. Makes me want to numb myself so I can't feel. Not healthy, but I usually get past it. What can I say? You caught me on a bad month."

His words were almost too honest. Made me twitchy to hear him say such a thing so easily. Shouldn't it be hard to admit that kind of hurt? I had my fair share of dings growing up the way I did, but I could never be so matter-of-fact about my own shortcomings. Maybe that was my problem. I played everything too close because I didn't want people to know I was human. That I hurt. That I cried. That I had weaknesses. And I had just spilled the greatest shame of my life to Cricket, and she hadn't rejected me. In fact, she'd extended me grace and comfort.

Cricket's face reflected an apology to my cousin. "Uh, I guess it must be hard. I'm sorry for your loss."

"Thanks. But you're right. I'm glad to have family that cares enough to pull my head out of my ass."

Those words seemed to slide inside me like a quarter into a slot, swirling down, dropping into the till of my soul. In my quest to rinse the stink of prison off me, I had set my family aside as if they had no value. Juke had tried to self-medicate, isolating himself from his life, and I had tried to wall off a part of who I was. Like those dresses I made from the marred fabric of a past life, I needed to accept my own history. I needed to value the people who cared about me. Even Ed Earl had shown he cared enough to make amends, and his penance might allow me to pursue the dream of designing my own line of reconstructed clothing. So though I still harbored resentment toward him, I couldn't overlook that he had given me a real opportunity to take a chance on myself. My family, for all its flaws, cared enough to hold each other accountable, to make amends, to lend a hand when called upon. They were a piece I needed to incorporate into the redesign of my life. I couldn't throw them away.

Juke pulled out a legal-size envelope and spread several photos on the table. "I believe these are what you've been waiting on."

The photos were of Scott and Stephanie. One had even been taken at the gala and featured the two of them in the corner looking chummy. The others were intimate—twined arms, locked lips, time-stamped. One was at the country club, if the golf carts were any indication. One was on a porch stoop with what looked to be Stephanie's house in the background.

Cricket picked each one up and studied the photos.

"How did you get this one?" she asked, pointing to the photo taken at the gala.

"I know a guy at the *Daily*. They were there taking photos, and I asked if he would let me look through them. It was just a hunch. I found them in the background and blew it up. The cheapskate made me buy the photo from him, but it was worth the twenty bucks, mostly because you attended this function as husband and wife, and here he is all intimate-like with his mistress."

"But they're just talking." Cricket set them down. "I'm meeting with my attorney tomorrow. I'll take these to her and see what she thinks. It might be enough, especially since it seems like there were several people who already knew about the affair."

Juke looked pleased. "I told you I would get them."

"Yes, you did. And now I have a little more work for you. I need some research done on a particular man. Let me show you these brochures and explain what we suspect. I'm hoping you have some suggestions on who I should call and how I might be able to use this information as leverage." Cricket began pulling the information Skeet had given her from her bag, and since I already knew the scoop, I excused myself and walked toward the bar where Dak was washing some glasses.

"Hey," I said, leaning against the counter, "you wanna make a bet on who gets voted off tonight? I'm wagering on the crooner. He's lame."

Dak chuffed. "No way. That twangy country chick is about to board a plane back to Georgia."

"Nah, she's good."

"If you like annoying blondes who act like they just left the farm. I saw that girl's Insta. She knows what's up. All that wide-eyedness is an act." Dak set the clean glasses on a drying mat.

"Stalker," I teased.

He looked up, a twinkle in his eye. "I may need to go to Georgia to console her."

I gave him a flat look.

"Hey," he said, flicking the towel from over his shoulder into his hands so he could dry the glasses, "Jeremy just got here, so I'm about to go home to feed Glory. Wanna ride and see my place?"

"Who's Glory?"

"She's the prettiest yellow Lab you've ever seen. Smart as a tack."

That made me smile. "You're mixing your idioms. Don't you mean sharp as a tack?"

"That too."

I knew I really shouldn't go with him—if I did, he would know that I wasn't unaffected by him. But he already knew that. Dak was smart as a tack himself. Thing was, I wanted to go. I wanted to see if his house looked like the one he and I had always talked about. Rustic with big windows that showed the lake from every room, a stone fireplace, and heart pine floors. Maybe double swings on the porch and window boxes full of bright blooms.

He lifted a shoulder. "Wanna see?"

I knew in that moment that he wanted me to go because he wanted me to see all that he'd done. The bar was his public persona—slightly brash and down-home—but his home was who he truly was. Dak wasn't the sort to invite someone in capriciously. So this was big for him.

I looked back at Cricket. Then at the opening door, through which walked my big, good-looking cousin, his eyes zipping straight to Cricket. "Yeah. I would love to see your place."

"Cool."

So after I texted Cricket that I was heading out, I climbed into Dak's truck yet again, and in ten minutes we were skirting the lake, the waters peeking through the newly green trees at me. We hugged the northern part of the lake, small communities of clumped single ranch houses clinging to the edges of larger gated homes on the water. When we got to a huge turn, Dak pulled down an almost-hidden gravel road that dipped down toward the water. Thick bushes were side bumpers for his truck, and when we broke from them, before us was a tree-dotted span of lawn and a brown cedar home with window boxes and a red door.

"Oh, it's so pretty, Dak," I said, my eyes feasting on the hideaway house with the snapdragons and pansies ta-daing in front of the wide windows and stacked-stone columns.

"Wait till you see the back," he said, pulling into a sort of porte cochere that connected a smaller part of the house to the larger area. We climbed out and entered the bigger part of the house, which was an open expanse of kitchen and hearth room with a huge fireplace. The entire back wall had banks of windows that showcased the waters of Cross Lake. A huge yellow Lab came bounding from a back room, barking and leaping in delight at the sight of her owner. She immediately reared up and set her paws on my chest, her dark nose snuffling against my shirt.

"Down, Glory," Dak commanded, and the dog reluctantly dropped down and sat, her tongue lolling out, her brown eyes ecstatic. Had to say, nothing greeted you at the door like a dog.

I gave her a pat on the head for her compliance and begrudging use of good manners. "Hi, Glory."

Her tail whipped out a merengue on the stone floor.

I stood and looked around at the large kitchen with the cypress cabinets, white marble, and soft-beige paint, then on to the living area with the leather couches and the Santa Fe–style rug under the beautiful long pine table. Random landscapes and the faux deer-hide rug told me that Dak had used a decorator, and that decorator was good. The overall rustic vibe still had polish. But the pièce de résistance was the lake itself, hauntingly pretty with the cypress close to the shore and the smooth waters stretching out toward the bridge. "Wow, Dak, this is amazing. I know you love it."

If beaming were truly a thing, Dak was good at it. "I do. After so many years on the road and living in a tiny apartment, I have something that gives me comfort. Not to mention, I bought a boat, and there's a nice boathouse to keep all my rods and gear. Come on. Let's let Glory out, and I'll show you the pier and boathouse."

We spent the next half hour throwing the tennis ball for Glory and admiring the gentle lake lapping at the shore. The boathouse, holding the flashy red bass rig, sported the swing Dak and I had always talked about sitting in to watch the sun set each day. My ex had really done well for himself, and I was happy that he had a place that brought him such peace.

Finally, we climbed back into his truck, and Dak started the engine, glancing back with a scowl as Glory's head popped up at the window, smudging the pane.

"You've done what you said you were going to do, Dak. You played in the league, and now that you're retired, you've built a nice life."

He glanced at his house and then over at me. "It's what I thought I wanted. I mean, I love my house and the bar, but, you know . . ."

"What?"

"It's just missing something."

He shifted the truck into reverse and backed out, not saying anything more.

Of course, I knew what he was talking about—he was missing someone to share all this with. I knew that empty spot myself, but I hadn't been in a hurry to fill it. Just trying to move myself forward in a life I had tanked. Dak had done what he said he would do. But I had sidestepped so often that I was virtually sideways. Things were looking up for me. I had a good job. I had a friend in Cricket. I had $80,000 sitting in my bill stack.

Was I ready to take a chance on love again?

That, I wasn't certain about.

CHAPTER TWENTY

CRICKET

I had left the bar with a plan. Or sort of a plan. I would let Juke do an investigation on Donner Walker's company, and I would go home and spend one more night pretending to be the dedicated wife of the Caddo Bank executive vice president and the respected mother of Julia Kate Crosby. The next day, I would turn the photographic evidence over to my attorney, who had already filed the divorce papers. I still wasn't sure what to do if Juke learned that Scott was involved in a scheme. And I wasn't sure how to get back the money Scott had hidden. Maybe I could blackmail him or something? Say I was going to go to the Feds with the information. But I wasn't even sure who the Feds were. That was just what people always said in the movies. And though I had disguised myself as some biker chick and straddled Griffin—no, not Griffin, the motorcycle—I wasn't cut out for blackmailing someone. Lord, this whole thing felt like something out of a John Grisham novel.

Was the man who had rubbed my feet when I was pregnant really planning on leaving me and our daughter for a life with a tennis pro? All this time I had been trying to protect myself and Julia Kate while Scott was feathering a nest that had no room for even his own baby bird. I couldn't reconcile *this* Scott with the man who had always prized his stellar reputation. In fact, next week, Scott was supposed to receive the University Club's Man of the Year Award at a luncheon. Integrity, honor, and service—the hallmarks of the award—didn't describe a man who did what Scott was doing.

I was baffled. No, I was angry. I wanted Scott to pay.

I pulled into my garage and noted my mother's car in the circle. Sure enough, Marguerite sat at the kitchen island. I stepped inside, having changed from my rocker duds but still sporting the tattoo that I needed to remove with baby oil. My mother's gaze zipped to the heart and sword like an eagle spotting a struggling field mouse. Suddenly I was a teenager again, trying to hide the evidence.

"Catherine Anne, what have you done to yourself? Have you taken leave of your senses? A tattoo? Do you want everyone in town thinking you're trash?" Her voice rose an octave with every query.

"Well, first, having a tattoo doesn't make you 'trash.' That's a bit elitist, judgmental, and some other offensive thing I can't think of right now. Besides, on some people tattoos are sexy." My mind went immediately to Griffin and my inordinate interest in what other tattoos he might have on his body and the specific locations of imagined tattoos. Which was crazycakes.

"Piddle. Tattoos are for sailors and women of—"

"Watch it," I interrupted, setting my big purse on the marble. "You are reverting to your roots."

She looked at me, puzzled. "What does that mean?"

"Well, I'm just saying that your sassy open-mindedness from last week was appreciated. No, it was desirable. You actually seemed human, Marguerite. Please return to the previous version of yourself." I made my request light because that's how I got mileage out of my mother.

Marguerite made a face. "Just because I have a certain way of believing doesn't make me a monster. I don't like tattoos. Simple as that."

"You don't have to *like* tattoos. You just have to not cast aspersions on people who have them." I walked to the cabinet and fetched a large glass, filled it with ice, and poured a sweet tea. Calories be damned. Sweet tea was the balm to the soul to southerners. And probably northerners, too. Everyone who appreciated the good things in life. "Plus, this was just a fun one Ruby and I were playing around with. It comes off with baby oil."

My mother tilted her head. "Okay. Fine. I will try to quash my inner critic of others."

I threw out my arms and spread my legs, pretending as if the earth were quaking, looking around in panic.

"Oh, cut it out," my mother drawled, picking up her martini glass and taking a sip. "A leopard can change its spots. I'm trying to be hip. And woke. And all that other stuff young people are asking old birds like us to be. I even listen to NPR."

I stopped my silly pantomiming, trying not to laugh. She could obviously see this and shot me a look. "Yeah, you're so woke, I bet you don't sleep."

She rolled her eyes. "Well, it's hard sometimes when you were taught that being ladylike was desirable in a woman. I wore a girdle and slip for thirty years . . . to bed with your father."

"Well, that explains Crystalle." I tossed her a smile. "I know. You're trying, Mama. And I'm proud of you. And look, you can even make your own martini. I thought you didn't know how."

She rolled her eyes again. "I've been making martinis since I was fifteen. Made them for your grandfather and all his old cronies. Now, how's your Ruby? She progressing on her little fashion venture? Color me interested."

"Really? Like in an investment?"

"Well, I'm damned sure not going to invest in whatever your husband is after me about. He called again today. It's getting uncomfortable, sugar. Does the man not understand no means no?"

"Look. Don't worry. He's about to—"

"Mom!" the shout came from the back of the house.

"In the kitchen," I called back, turning to the sink and applying some dish soap to the tattoo. No way Julia Kate would miss it.

"Oh my God. You forgot to sign the permission slip!" Julia Kate came stomping into the kitchen waving her phone. Her ponytail was lopsided, and a sleep line ran across one cheek.

"What permission slip?"

"Exactly," she said, waving the phone again. "And now I can't be in Kaitlyn's group. It filled up. I mean, what is even wrong with you? You're always gone, and you never forget this kind of stuff. I can't believe that I have to be in stupid Geoffrey Mourad's group. He picks his nose."

My mother looked at me. I wasn't sure if she was waiting for me to correct my daughter for yelling at me or if she, too, was wondering why I was not on the ball. God, if they only knew what I knew.

I pulled a paper towel from the holder and wiped my hands. Tattoo was staying for the time being. I watched Julia Kate's eyes drop to the somewhat faded tat.

"First, don't enter a room ranting at me. I'm your mother and deserve a modicum of respect. Second, I don't know what you're talking about, so slow down and walk me through it."

"Wait. Why do you have a tattoo?" Julia Kate asked, sliding onto the stool next to my mother and setting the paper she'd been waving on the countertop.

I arched my brow.

She accepted her fate. "I'm sorry for yelling at you, Mama. Now, why do you have a tat on your arm? And of something so *weird*?"

Accepting her apology with a nod, I said, "Ruby and I were just playing around. She's designing dresses—a really fun, gorgeous line of dresses—and we were goofing off." I was amazed at how easily the lie slipped off my tongue. Wasn't like I could tell her that I was spying on her cheating, no-good father. And that thought made my heart hurt.

I looked at my gangly, awkward Julia Kate with her colorful banded braces and just-budding womanhood and felt such sorrow. Poor child.

Poor entitled, spoiled little girl who would soon learn the hard truths of the world. How could I save her from the hurt and shame? How could I fix this? I hadn't a clue how to protect a girl whose world would turn upside down any more than I knew how to straighten out my own wrecked world. I only knew that I had to protect Julia Kate as much as I could while also letting the truth rise above the shame of having a father who did, well, what Scott was doing. My first inclination was always to cover up and present the best version of everything. But there was no best version of a man cheating on his family and possibly helping to hoodwink his community of friends and business associates into something that could force them to lose their life's savings.

"Weird," Julia Kate said, but with a little smile that told me she thought I was funny. "I like Ruby. She's cool."

"Oh, so *her* tats are cool, but my temporary one is weird."

Julia Kate smiled cheekily. "Pretty much."

My mother sipped her martini, her eyes twinkling, which was very uncharacteristic of her. But the woman *was* pretty nuts about Julia Kate. "Your hair needs a trim, Julia. Why don't you let me call Brad? He could give you some lowlights and give you a becoming cut. You're going to be a beauty, my darling, but you must learn to wash your face and try to look as if you didn't emerge from a cave. Let me see your nails. Oh, and we should have Therese measure her for a proper brassiere."

Julia Kate looked at my mother as if she'd just seen her for the first time.

I laughed. "Welcome to my world."

"Um, no thanks, G-ma." My daughter scrabbled away from my mother, rising and rushing toward her backpack, which she had dumped on the catchall cubby at the kitchen door. "Will you sign the slip now?"

I made a "Stop it" face at my mother, who merely sniffed in offense. The woman would have Julia Kate waxed, corseted, and lipsticked with a bow atop her head if she had her way.

I dutifully grabbed a pen, perusing the form, which was for a field trip to a working farm to learn about sustainability and modern farming. Huh. Guess it wasn't a bad field trip. Julia Kate probably needed to learn about waste if the number of water bottles on her bedside table was an indication.

"They're going to let us feed the baby cows with a bottle," Julia Kate said, leaning over as I scrawled my name on the blank line. I had a twinge of something as I wondered if I should remain "Crosby" or go back to my maiden name.

"Calf, not a baby cow."

"Oh yeah. And they have donkeys and goats, too." Julia Kate whipped out her phone and started showing me pictures of adorable farm animals. "This one is named Rosebud. She wears a little hat and everything. But only at Easter. They don't force the animals to be pets or anything."

"Well, I'm sure the donkey liked her hat. I mean, it's a cute hat." I tried to smile even though inside I still felt twisted by all that had happened. It kept banging around inside my head—Scott Crosby was a cheat, a liar, a criminal.

Julia Kate pocketed her phone into her jeans. "Oh, I forgot. This creeper guy handed me this envelope for Dad."

She hurried over to her open backpack and pulled out a clasped envelope. My mother sipped and watched, like a well-moisturized vulture awaiting a kill. Or awaiting another opening to suggest a makeover for my daughter.

An alarm flag had raised inside me over Julia Kate's words. *Creeper.* "What do you mean? Some guy handed this to you? Where?"

Julia Kate nodded, looking adorably young. "When I was walking up the drive. I thought he was, like, a yard worker or something. He just said, 'Hey, give this to your daddy' and hurried away toward a black car. But he was scary looking."

Scott's name was scrawled across the sealed envelope, which felt like an evil omen. Every fiber of my being wanted to rip open that envelope, but I refrained and set it on the counter. "I'm sure he was just what you thought. Dad had some work done on the pool, and it might have been one of their guys leaving us the bill. But I'm glad you were aware of your surroundings. It's good to be careful and trust your instincts."

"Yeah," Julia Kate said absentmindedly, fetching her phone after a series of dings. She picked up the permission slip, kissed my mother's cheek, and strolled out, her thumbs moving furiously on her iPhone.

"She's going to run into a wall," my mother said, finishing the last of her drink.

I cast another glance at the ominous envelope. "Those phones are their world."

"So sad." My mother slid from the stool and repositioned it back perfectly. "Well, I must go. I need to water the plants on the back patio before the sun sets. Let me know when I can take a meeting with Ruby."

"You're really interested in helping her?"

"Yes. I am. I have money and I have time."

Another thing flipped upside down in my life, but this was a good thing. Just shocking that my mother—the woman who took to her bed when I got a second ear piercing in college—wanted to support Ruby with her tattoos (maybe my mother thought she was a sailor?) and her nose ring. But I had to admit that once Ruby allowed her guard to lower, she was easy to love. My mother wasn't unaffected by underdogs. Neither was I. Maybe because I now felt like one. "Well, I know Ruby would appreciate both. I agree with you—she's talented and worthwhile."

My mother, who called everything "tacky" when I was a teen, proceeded to mosey out my door like the most avant-garde of women.

Yeah, my world was definitely lopsided.

I tidied up the kitchen, my gaze straying to the envelope I had set aside for Scott. Something was odd about it, and finally, after wiping the fridge handles with Clorox for a second time, I went to my bag, pulled out my vintage detective book, and looked in the glossary for how to open correspondence without being detected. And there it was—the tried-and-true steam method. This book was brilliant.

So I set the teakettle on the burner and poured a glass of wine. I glanced at the clock, hoping that Scott needed a quickie with Stephanie and would be home late. Pippa barked at the back door to be let inside, so I let her in, and as she slunk past me into the kitchen, I caught a whiff of her.

"Oh God, Pip, what did you roll in?" I asked, gagging a little as I flung the door back open and herded the shamed Italian greyhound back out onto the covered back porch. "Julia!"

I wasn't about to bathe the dog when I hadn't been the one to leave her out unattended all afternoon.

"What?" my daughter yelled.

"Come take care of Pippa!" I countered.

Pippa sat on my jute rug between my outdoor patio furniture, reeking. I did a scan of our backyard, looking for what offensive dead thing my dumb canine had rolled in. Didn't see anything large and moldering on first glance. Julia Kate showed up at the door right as the teakettle chortled its readiness.

"Oh my God, what's that smell?" Julia Kate asked, her face screwed into one of disgust.

"Your puppy. She's going to need a bath. And she's your responsibility."

"Unh-uh, I'm not bathing her." Julia Kate backed away.

I lasered her with my best no-nonsense mom glare. "Yeah. You are. Use the dog shampoo in the guest bath. Or you can find the dead animal she rolled in and bury it. Your choice."

Julia Kate looked at Pippa and frowned. "Fine."

I left my daughter to wrangle the bath-hating pup toward the guest wing and the shower with the handheld nozzle while I went on a hunt for dead things. Took me five minutes to find the dead baby bird that had served as eau de parfum for Pippa. I used a shovel and buried it deep under my camellia bush. With a sigh, I hurried back to the house and an angry teakettle. I washed my hands and picked up the envelope, trying to ascertain the best way to loosen the glue from the flap so I could open it. I checked the book, but obviously the author thought I should be able to figure this out on my own.

I held the envelope over the stream of steam, and in that moment, I realized that the envelope wasn't special. I had a whole stack in my craft closet. The writing was in black Sharpie. All I had to do was get Ruby to write Scott's name across the front. Or I could do it left-handed.

I switched the burner off and ripped into the envelope.

At first, I thought I had copies of the photos Juke had managed to get of Scott with Stephanie, because these, too, were taken at a distance.

But these weren't of Scott.

These were of my daughter.

Julia Kate laughing at the outdoor picnic table at school. Julia Kate sipping a caramel macchiato at the Starbucks. Julia Kate swinging her tennis racket. Julia Kate in her pajamas on the back patio tossing a ball for Pippa.

My blood went cold; my knees collapsed.

I clung to the countertop like a mountain climber hanging on for dear life. Bitter acid rose in my throat as my mind scrabbled with what these photos meant.

They were a warning. For Scott. Donner Walker, or whoever was in bed with him, was using my baby to send a message. I allowed myself to sink to the floor, still somehow clasping the envelope in one hand, my stomach lurching at what I had just innocently—no, brazenly—stumbled into.

Oh my God, I had been treating this whole thing like a game.

These photos said differently. This was no longer about a mere divorce. No, Scott had mixed himself up with someone who needed him to understand what was at risk. Donner Walker was no mild-mannered businessman perpetrating a scam. He was a shark who needed my husband to keep his mouth closed and his illegal scheme afoot.

And here I was playing detective like some idiot who thought she had the skills to bring Scott to heel.

I managed to rise from the floor, though my legs were still shaking. I hurriedly shoved the photos into the envelope and picked up my wineglass, gulping it like it was Gatorade and not a really nice pinot grigio.

"Mom! Can you bring towels?" Julia Kate shouted from the closed door of the guest bathroom.

"Sure!" I croaked, tucking the envelope under my arm and hurrying to twist the lock on the side kitchen door and the back door before retreating to the laundry room with its comforting smell of fabric softener. I shoved the envelope under a stack of clean towels and grabbed some from those awaiting washing to use on Pippa. I hurried back, tossed them inside to where Julia was laughing at the dog trying to eat the soap bubbles, and picked up my cell phone.

I didn't text. I called.

Ruby answered on the third ring. "Hey."

"I need help."

"You got it."

And that's the exact moment I knew Ruby wasn't just my new friend. She was the person I had needed in my life more than I ever knew.

CHAPTER
TWENTY-ONE

RUBY

I hadn't planned on seeing Ty Walker that evening. I had spent a weird late afternoon with Dak, touring his house and meeting his dog. Somehow it felt significant, but I wasn't ready to attach anything to what exactly that significance was.

Truth was, Dak scared me.

And then there was Ty—a perfectly nice guy who made me feel wanted, pretty, and all the things I thought I needed in life. A perfectly nice guy who could possibly be the dirtiest scoundrel this side of the Mississippi. And I have to say, there is a lot of land on this side of the Mississippi River.

But I wasn't sure if Ty knew what his father was up to, though it was hard to believe he wouldn't know. And I wasn't even certain that I wanted to date him anyway. Yeah, that night at the gala I had sort of fallen into a serious crush, but Dak had played with my emotions, smudging up my plan to find a guy who could make me a better person.

So when Ty called and suggested we meet up for drinks, I stupidly said yes even though I wasn't totally enthusiastic. In hindsight, I had probably agreed because I wanted to check myself on how I felt about Dak, and the best way to see if those heartstrings had indeed been plucked was to sit on a stool in a fancy restaurant, swilling expensive wine with a rich pretty boy.

Obvs.

"So how was your day?" Ty asked, looking earnest in his soft cotton button-down and dress slacks. The shirt fit him like someone had sewn it right on to him and was unbuttoned at the neck to show that sexy dip between the collarbone. His jaw was smooth and suitably manly, and he smelled like a pullout sample from *Town & Country* magazine. Total-package kind of guy . . . but what was beneath all that fancy ribbon?

"It was good. I closed early and met Cricket at a bar. I didn't drink, though, so I'm not sloshed or anything. Cricket's been going through a rough patch lately." Ah, there I went, doing a bit of testing of a different body of water.

"Oh? Like how?"

He was interested. Hmm. "Just her marriage and stuff. Her husband is a bit of a dick."

"Scott?" Ty lifted a finger at the bartender, ordering another bourbon. "I think he's a nice guy. He's, you know, like every other guy my dad's age—still trying to keep the juice up—but he's all right. They having marriage trouble, huh?"

I needed to be careful here. "Yeah, I guess. Cricket's kind of private. She seems to think he's up to something."

Ty's gaze shifted away from me, and perhaps there was a little tightening of his jaw? Interesting. "Like cheating on her? Or . . . something else?"

I shrugged. "Nah, I don't think she thinks he's cheating. I think she just feels like their marriage needs work, but he's been really distracted lately, so I think she may be concerned. I'm just her sounding board on ways to jazz things up."

He looked relieved. Maybe. "Like in the bedroom? That's crossing the line, isn't it?"

"Oh, because I'm her employee? Yeah. I suppose. But we're friends."

"Well, that's good. Scott's been a friend of my dad's for a while. Scott was my uncle Sam's best friend back in the day. He's been helpful to my dad, just introducing him to friends and stuff. I would hate to think Cricket is, you know, thinking he's a bad guy."

"Well, I've never been impressed by him. Glad you like him, though."

Ty shrugged. "He's cool. I guess. And it's good you get along well with your boss."

"Yeah, Cricket is really helping me put together a plan for my business. And no worries, I can't really help anyone in the bedroom, so we don't go there." I gave him a self-deprecating laugh with the intention of steering him away from talk about Cricket having suspicions. I had done the litmus test, and it felt very evident to me that talk of the Crosbys made him nervous. Which seemed to point to him knowing exactly what his old man was up to. Which made him suddenly not attractive at all.

But if Cricket could lie beside Scott every night, pretending to be a loving wife, then surely I could pretend to like Ty enough to glean any information that might help Cricket nail not only her asshole of a husband but also the chief douchebag and his mini-me son who was sitting in this spendy bar no doubt buying me overpriced drinks on someone's hard-earned retirement. Maybe. My gut was good at telling me exactly who people were.

Ty smiled at me in a flirty way. "I bet you do all right in the bedroom."

And, ick.

"So how was your day?" I decided to change the subject.

"Same ol'. Just filing paperwork and dealing with all the red tape that comes with buying and developing property. It's super fun," he drawled with a roll of his eyes.

"Where are y'all buying property? I thought your dad works in investments or something."

"He does. But we have several companies under the umbrella. I run the legal and some of the development side of things, like the land stuff. Dad runs the investments. It's complicated, and I don't want to bore you with the monotonous details."

"'Cause I'm not smart enough?" I couldn't help myself.

"No," he said, looking at me with an incredulous laugh. "Because it's very uninteresting."

Probably not to the SEC. But I didn't say that, of course. So I said nothing.

Ty looked worried. "You know I know you're smart. And you're very talented. I can tell your dresses will do well. Look at how everyone couldn't keep their eyes off you at the gala. I thought I was going to have to fight a few guys who were looking as if they might like to take that pretty dress off you."

"You're pouring it on a little thick," I said, letting him off the hook.

"Maybe you're worth pouring it on. You want another drink?" he asked, nodding toward the half inch of wine left in my goblet.

"Nah, I have an early class, and then I'm closing tomorrow afternoon. Busy day."

Ty leaned in closer, stroking my shoulder bared by the tank I had paired with some super-distressed jeans and heeled zip booties. "Wanna come see the house I just bought in Trace? There's a hot tub overlooking the seventh hole."

"I don't have a suit."

Ty brushed my jaw with his lips and whispered, "You won't need a suit."

If I hadn't known what I knew about him and his dad, and if I hadn't just toured Dak's hot tub–less cabin on Cross Lake, I might have been tempted to slip naked into Ty's therapeutic waters, but as pretty as the package was, the box could hold dog shit. And honestly, I wasn't sure if I wanted to unwrap him and find out. At this point, I had soured on a guy who was even related to a douche who could do something like his father was doing. "Sounds heavenly, but I have a quiz tomorrow. I have to study."

"Oh, come on. You can study at my place." He gave me another sexy smile that should have worked. It damned sure would have on that sorority hussy who nearly mounted his leg at the gala. Couldn't remember her name, but I remembered the way she'd looked like she wanted to rip out my throat and then put her monogram on his towels.

"I'm pretty sure my notes won't survive a hot tub," I said, with teasing in my voice.

"Come on, beautiful. I've been dreaming of all the ways I'm going to make you scream my name." He looked dead serious about that.

"Wow. You're very confident, aren't you?" I said, picking up the glass and gulping the last of my wine. He was kind of creeping me out, the way he had when we first met. But I knew how to handle douchey guys. Growing up with all male cousins meant I knew how to fight dirty if it came down to it.

Ty smiled. "Nothing wrong with being confident."

"Touché." I pushed back the stool. "But I must have priorities, and school trumps hot-tubbing and screaming names."

"Not if I do it right."

That made me laugh. "You *are* confident."

"Don't you like that in a man?" he teased.

"Only when he can actually deliver the goods. So I might regret spending the next few hours with my books instead of finding out what kind of delivery guy you are, but I'll take that chance."

"You're killing me, you know," he said, tossing a twenty on the counter and stepping back so I could slide past him.

"Yes, I know," I said with a smile, enjoying the repartee even as I knew this was likely our last date. My gran used to say, "Always leave them wanting more," and I'd never really embraced that idea. But it seemed apropos for this situation. I liked the tiny bit of power I held over this particular guy. Maybe because I didn't seem to hold that same power over Dak. With him, it was flip-flopped, and he seemed to be able to pull some strings that made me dance despite my best intentions. But I didn't want to think about my messed-up feelings for Dak. I did indeed have a test tomorrow. And a check for eighty grand staring at me from my bill stack. And a ringing phone. We stepped out into the sticky night, and I pulled my cell phone from my crossbody.

"Hello," I said, motioning to Ty that I had to take the call. He held up a hand and started in the opposite direction from where my car was parked.

I really shouldn't have allowed him to think I was still into him. But then again, it could come in handy if I needed him to help Cricket. I was hedging my bets.

"I need help," Cricket said into my ear.

"You got it," I said, meaning that. I held my hand over the microphone and called to Ty. "Bye. Thanks!"

"Wait. Are you busy?" Cricket asked.

"Not really. I just finished having drinks with Ty Walker."

"You're still seeing him? You know—"

"I know. But I wanted to keep an eye on him." I climbed into the car and started the engine. "What's up? What do you need help with?"

"I don't know if I need help. All I know is that I can't do any of this anymore."

"Any of what?"

"Trying to outsmart Scott. I can't do it. I'm pulling the plug and going to the police. I'm not going to worry about the money."

Only really rich people could say things like that. Probably because Cricket had more money in more places than she could count. That's how the wealthy were. People like me, not so much. We robbed Peter, paid Paul, and hid from Louie. "So you're letting Scott win?"

"You don't understand—it's no longer a game. Julia Kate came home today with an envelope for her father, and it changed everything."

I pulled out of the lot and wondered if I needed to go to Cricket's house. I had never been there, which seemed weird, considering we were clandestine partners in righting the wrongs that a certain male had perpetrated against a happy blonde who owned an antique store. But my business calculus test was important, and surely this was something I could handle tomorrow morning. "So what are we dealing with?"

"Well, of course, I opened the envelope, because I'm investigating him, you know. So at first, I thought I would steam it open. You know I have that detective book, and learning how to open letters and stuff without getting caught was actually in there. But then as soon as the steam started going—"

I sighed because this was how Cricket told stories. Took her forever. She wasn't one for getting to the point quickly.

"I realized that it was so stupid to try and open it without him knowing. It was a plain clasped envelope, and all I had to—"

Turning the radio down, I hooked a left to my street as Cricket prattled about envelopes and me writing Scott's name. But when she got to the actual contents, I felt my heart drop. "Wait, there were pictures of Julia Kate? Like a warning or something?"

"Yes, they were pictures from her everyday life taken in the last few days. And I think it has to be directed to Scott. This Donner guy is bad news. He wears fancy suits and donates money to charity, but I think Scott is in over his head, and so am I. I can't worry about the money right now. I have my own accounts, the store, and a lawyer who will help me sort through a mess if Scott gets in trouble for whatever the hell he's involved in. I have to just stop fooling around with disguises and playing at being a PI. We gotta tell someone what Donner and Scott are up to."

"But you'll be letting him get away with it. What if he takes off with the tennis slut before the authorities can do anything about it?"

"I read somewhere you weren't supposed to call women 'sluts' anymore." Cricket sounded like she was reading a guide on how to navigate the social-justice Olympics.

"Cricket, she stole your husband and potentially your entire IRA—you can call her whatever the fuck you want to. There's no justification for what she's done. Yeah, Scott's a shit, but she doesn't get automatic absolution because she doesn't have testicles."

"Ruby."

"What? I'm serious. Slut shaming is the least of your worries."

Silence on the end of the line.

I continued, getting warmed up, my mind tripping over itself to figure out how we could right wrongs and make that scumbag pay. "Okay, I have to think. You can't let him win, Cricket. I understand what you're saying. That it feels, um, hotter in the henhouse, but we're going to make him give you that money back. Don't do anything yet. Let me do some research. What time is your appointment with the attorney tomorrow?"

"Two in the afternoon."

"I have a test in the morning. Jade is working until two tomorrow, so if it's okay, I won't go in until after we figure things out. Let's meet at Juke's office at noon. I'm going to ask Griff to come, too."

"Why?"

"Because he's tough and he's smart. And I think he has the hots for you."

"What? No. Griffin doesn't even like me." She sounded shocked and maybe something else . . . pleased?

"Yeah, he does."

"But I'm married."

"For now."

Cricket sighed. "Okay, whatever. All I'm saying is I'm not sure about this, Ruby. I'm not as strong as you are. I've been fooling myself thinking I can be some badass who makes her husband pay."

"Bull-to-the-shit. You're strong. Stronger than you think. And you've got me. Together, we're going to figure this out. I promise."

I wasn't sure my words were true. But I wanted to believe them. I longed for a world in which the dickheads got theirs and those of us who had treaded water for so long, just looking for a place to rest, a hard piece of ground to build something, could win. So if I lied, it wasn't because I didn't want to believe my words. Women like Cricket, women like me, we deserved to come out ahead sometimes.

"I don't see how, but I will meet you at Juke's office. I'll pick up lunch for all of us. Maybe Cush's or Fairfield. I'll text you for your order."

Of course she would. One thing I knew about Cricket—every occasion deserved sustenance.

"Don't worry, Cricket. We got this."

If I put it out into the universe, the gods of justice would hear it. *Please, gods of justice, hear me and make this work.*

CHAPTER TWENTY-TWO

CRICKET

My palms were sweating. I had always thought that was just a saying, but my hands were legitimately wet, and I could feel perspiration beading on my upper lip. Oh, and I was certain that at any moment, I would vomit on the table.

A few days ago when we had come up with this plan, it had sounded easy peasy, lemon squeezy.

But that was a few days ago, on the day I had nearly bailed (and probably should have bailed) on this whole being-an-amateur-private-eye thing. Now I knew how Nancy Drew felt. Or those meddling kids in the souped-up van with the dog. I was so nervous that I couldn't even remember the name of the cartoon. But they stuck their noses where they shouldn't have, and so had I. Meddling kids. Meddling Cricket.

I pressed my hands against the folder in front of me. And looked back at where Griffin was nursing a beer. He winked at me, which gave me a small bump of confidence, but not nearly enough to stop the pit stains that were no doubt marring my silk blouse.

After I had discovered the threat in the pictures of Julia Kate, I'd had a near breakdown that involved three-fourths of a bottle of pinot grigio and a failed science experiment. The last one was because Julia Kate had forgotten that she had to turn in a project that involved household products being combined for chemical reactions . . . which she had to film. The night ended with me half-drunk and Julia Kate in tears because I had refused to call an Uber to take us to Kroger to get more baking soda. At this point, I accepted the fact that I had allowed my child to fail. In the grand scheme of life, a zero in physical science wasn't the end of the world.

Not to mention, Scott hadn't come home. He hadn't answered my texts, and his Find My Phone app had long been turned off, so I went to bed alone and woke to a message that he'd stayed over at a friend's house because he'd drunk too much. Join the crowd. No mention of who the friend was, and since I had a foggy headache from the wine and intended to file for divorce anyway, I didn't worry about responding with much more than Okay.

Julia Kate accepted that her dad had worked late and slept on a friend's couch. She was much more interested in how she was going to navigate not having the science experiment done correctly and in how that would affect her grade and in how she wasn't going to get into Princeton or Yale. I hated to burst her bubble and tell her that was a far-fetched possibility even if we had gotten the baking soda, so I just let her rant.

I dropped my daughter off, went through CC's Coffee House for a double-shot espresso, and then dropped by the store to make sure it hadn't burned down and that Judy Barr had gotten the French armoire she'd been hounding me about via text. Twelve texts was excessive. Like I could do anything about a dock strike. The morning was busy for a Wednesday, and Jade was in a good mood. Me? My stomach felt sour and my mind floaty, and my entire life teetered on the edge. But I soldiered on, pretending to be interested in the history of Wedgwood for some older gentleman who seemed *very* intent on giving me a lesson. Finally, I left the store at eleven a.m., picking up lunch and heading north to Juke's office.

When I arrived, I had every intention of throwing in the towel on my little PI side hustle.

But the three Balthazar family members who awaited me had a different plan.

"Ah, lunch," Griffin said, taking the bag from me as I turned and shut the door. "I'm starving."

"You're always starving," Ruby said from her place on the couch. In true Ruby fashion, she wore an electric-blue miniskirt, lace leggings, and a vest that had been given the *Annie Hall* treatment with an eighties executive-woman vibe. No, maybe it was more Melanie Griffith in *Working Girl*. Either way, Ruby looked cutting edge, making me feel like chopped liver in my capri leggings with the oversize linen shift.

"True," Griffin said, digging out the full-size roast beef po'boy labeled with his name. The rest of us had turkey club sandwiches. I passed around the iced tea and made myself comfortable on the other end of the couch, which didn't look quite as suspect as it had weeks ago. The normally delicious sandwich tasted like ash in my mouth. I wrapped it up and saved it for later while the rest of the crew demolished my offering.

After a few minutes, Juke wiped the mayo from the corners of his mouth and said, "We have a problem."

"I already knew that," I said.

"No. A bigger problem, because my contact who has a contact at the SEC told him your boy Donner has been under investigation for a while. Word in their office is that the lead investigator is ready to make the arrest. Any day now."

"Fine," I said, with a shrug of my shoulders. "I read about divorce, and if Scott goes to jail, I don't even have to prove adultery. Federal prison speeds things up."

"But what about your money?" Ruby made an impatient face.

"It's just money. I'll be okay. I mean, yeah, I'm mad that he essentially stole our retirement and savings, but maybe going down for helping Donner swindle people will clear up his priorities. I'm honestly relieved to hear they might be closing in on Donner, because those pictures of my daughter were the smelling salts I needed to wake me up to the seriousness of this matter."

Juke looked at Ruby, who looked at Griff.

For a moment, none of them spoke.

Then Griffin balled his lunch bag up and sent it for three points into the empty trash can. "You're right. Your daughter is important. And money is money. Not like it's the end all be all of life. But what if you can get your hands on that offshore account?"

I thought about that. "Well, yeah. I would at least want my share."

Ruby nodded. "For Julia Kate. College is expensive."

"And once the SEC is involved, the assets will be frozen if Scott was taking kickbacks or sharing in the profits. If he mingled the money, even the stuff that is legally yours and untainted could be hung up," Juke added.

I thought about that. "But isn't the money safer offshore, then?"

"Yeah. But the account isn't in your name, so you can't access it. But I have a plan that might work." Juke leaned back, his eyes clear, his stubble a thing of the past. He looked much healthier and very interested in making my sleazy husband pay. Which I sort of liked about him. About all of them. They'd been scheming while I had been panicking. My heart did a pitty-pat of pleasure.

The gleam in his eye sparked something in me. "You really have a plan to get the money back?"

"Unless you don't want to."

"It's not that I don't want the money. I'm not stupid. Scott has cheated on me and cheated on his clients. He will pay for his crimes against his clients, but I guess what you're saying is that if I don't try to get the money back, if I don't demand some justice for me and my daughter, he wins against me."

Griffin kicked his chair back on two legs. They may have actually groaned. "I don't want him to win, sunshine."

"So how do I do this?" I asked, setting my lunch bag at my feet.

"A sting!" Ruby said, her lips curving and a sparkle in her eyes.

I frowned. "A sting? That's the grand plan?"

Juke held up a hand. "So here's how we think you can do it. When you go to your attorney today, you need to ask for some paperwork. If you have the pictures of him with Stephanie, you can expedite the divorce, just as you learned. You don't have to play your cards about knowing about the Donner Walker deal or the SEC investigation. In fact, you don't want your husband to know you have an inkling about his involvement. You'll show him the photos that I took. Then you'll tell him he's busted. Maybe cry a little. Take the conversation emotional so you make him feel bad. Then you'll give him some papers to sign. One is a waiver of service. Basically, it says he agrees to not be served the divorce papers, and you'll file that in court. But we also want to see if your attorney can come up with some other forms and things he has to sign. And in the middle of the papers, we'll slide in an amendment request for the bank account, adding you as an administrator on the offshore account."

"Wait . . . why would he sign that?" I asked.

"He won't know. We'll slip it in," Ruby said.

"No." I shook my head. "No way Scott signs anything without reading. He's a banker, and he always makes a huge deal about reading what he signs. He once even read the Apple agreement on his phone. Only lunatics do that. Besides, it won't hold up in court. He'll say I tricked him."

The three looked at each other again. I had put a pin in their plan.

"But what if we make him nervous so he's not interested in reading?" Griffin asked.

"How?" I countered.

He paused, lifting his chocolate eyes to the ceiling in thought. "Do you still have the other photos? The ones of Julia Kate?"

I nodded. I had stuck them in the file with all my paperwork for Jackie.

"Has he seen them yet?"

I shook my head. "I haven't seen him. He spent the night on a 'friend's' couch."

Ruby looked furious. Like an electric-blue harpy ready to peck Scott to death.

"Good," Griffin continued with a nod. "So you're going to ask for the divorce, shed the tears, lay on a guilt trip. He may balk at the papers. True. But you insist that he owes you that much after having an affair. And then you do a little 'Oh, and by the way, Julia Kate gave me this envelope this morning' and slide that envelope over to him. We're going to guess he's going to be nosy enough to open it. Or you may have to prompt him in some way. Then I'm going to come in and sit down close by. Just watch him. Nothing unnerves someone like a big guy like me staring them down. Once he sees the pictures and I'm really giving him the eye, he's going to start sweating. He'll think the scumbag sent me."

"That doesn't mean he'll sign the papers," I said.

"No. But you can start pressuring him to sign them," Juke said, wiping his mouth again and leaning forward to tent his hands. "You know him, and you know what to say to get him to sign the waiver. Maybe we can throw some other things in there. Some accounting of property. Maybe a bogus acknowledgment of insurance, stuff like that. Just filler. We'll make it almost like a closing on a house. You get tired of signing all that junk, so you go on autopilot. And he'll be wanting to get out of there because Griff's making him sweat. It could work."

"And you don't have to have it done in a court? Seems like you would need—"

"A notary?" Juke asked.

"Guess who's a notary?" Ruby said, glancing over at Griff.

Griffin grinned at me. "I'll bring my stamp. And once it's over, he'll realize that I'm not some heavy hired by Donner; I'm the notary witnessing the signing. Dak can probably be the witness."

I sat there for a few seconds wondering if this was the craziest idea I'd ever heard or if it might actually work. Could be both. Probably both. But what did I have to lose? If Scott discovered that I was trying to sneak—

"Wait! I need to access his offshore account. I'll need the numbers and stuff."

Juke nodded. "Yeah, so everything hinges on you being able to get the account number and password."

"If I can get that, can't I forge his signature anyway? Just move the money?"

Juke nodded. "Well, you could, but you'd be breaking the law. This way, you do it legal. Or at least legal for the bank. And once Scott and Donner get arrested and await trial, he might actually be glad you have access. Unless he really is a heartless bastard who cares nothing for his own daughter. I'm betting you may have married a weak man, Cricket, but you didn't marry a monster. Once you're on the account, you're on the account."

"I want nothing to do with any money given to him by Donner," I said, more to myself than to the others in the room. And that was true. I was deeply angry at Scott for his betrayal, and I could justify taking all the money the way he did. But I wasn't that person. I didn't want to be that person. I wanted what was mine, to protect me and my daughter, because that was honest money and belonged to me.

"Fine." Juke shrugged and spun in his chair.

Ruby reached over and set her hand on my arm. "But only if you want to do this. If it isn't what you want, no big deal. Like you said, you'll be okay. But if you want what's yours, you may have to take it."

I set my free hand atop hers and gave it a squeeze. "I need to think about it. I need to think about how Scott might react. He's careful in his business dealings, but if he were rattled, he might give in and sign the papers. Maybe."

"It's a risk," Juke said.

"Even more of a risk is ignoring those photos. Those scare me. I have a child who a goon is threatening. I can't ignore that to chase money."

"Don't ignore it," Juke said, narrowing his eyes. "This Donner guy has built a house of cards, and the wind is blowing. He's panicking. This is likely a control tactic designed to coerce Scott into doing what he wants. But the reason doesn't matter. I'll tail Julia Kate. Follow her home. Keep her safe until this is over. Most of my work can be done in the car. I owe you that much for my earlier failure."

"You think those photos are bluster?" I asked, glancing over to Griffin. His eyes looked resolute. Maybe even a bit soft? At any rate, he gave me a look that stilled me.

"Juke will keep her safe," Ruby said.

They all stared at me, waiting for me to decide. Part of me wanted to walk out and go straight to the police station with the information I had. But what would they do? How long would it take to start an investigation? The police force had shrunk. Word was, law enforcement was overworked and understaffed. The other part of me wondered what the ballsy girl detective in my book would do. She would steam open letters, sneak around alleys, and carry one of those tiny guns she could fit in a garter belt beneath her flouncy cocktail dress. Of course, that was an old book with old ways. A silly fancy of mine that I had dreamed up to help me cope. To help me feel like I was doing something.

Should I take the risk? Could I trick Scott? He was already rattled. Maybe . . . just maybe . . .

"Okay. Let's try it. I want to one-up him just for spite," I said, clapping my hands together.

Everyone looked pleased. Of course, it was easy for them to formulate a plan and not worry so much if it didn't work. They had nothing to lose. They didn't have children. Well, that I knew of. I had a lot to lose. But even with those thoughts, I found a blooming warmth inside me at the thought that these three—what had Ruby called her family? Oh yeah. That these fringe people cared enough to come up with a crazy plan to help me.

And so I left the private investigator's office and journeyed to my attorney's office, where I begged Jackie to produce the waiver of service and was pleasantly pleased that she was willing to make a call to see if she might speed the proceedings along more quickly. Then I went home and started looking for the information about the offshore account. First, I looked in the closet, noting that the foxtail sex toy was gone. Good riddance. And then I scoured Scott's desk. Finally, I backtracked into the folders we kept from our travels and found the brochure for the bank he'd visited. In the small folder, I found generic information, but I also found a deposit slip, and faintly imprinted on that deposit slip were the outlines of numbers. I could see all of them, except I wasn't certain if one was an eight or a three. I scratched onto my notepad the website address and the possible account number and went to the computer. Only took five minutes and I was into Scott's account. He really was stupid about passwords. Thank goodness he was stupid about passwords. Of course, I nearly failed when the site asked for a PIN. But a quick look back at the bank's folder and I found that scratched on the bottom.

He had several million dollars in the account.

What an ass.

I took pictures of the accounts, noting that Scott's was the only name on them, and then I erased my search history and started typing up documents that listed our assets, our insurance policies, and our IRAs and the retirement accounts he'd already raided. I even made up a statement that said something about electing to not undergo marriage counseling. Altogether, I amassed a nice stack. Not exactly mortgage signing, but enough to annoy my soon-to-be ex-husband.

Which led me to where I now sat in Dak's bar, waiting on Scott.

For the past few days, I had sweated Donner being arrested, but thankfully, Dak's contact inferred that it would be next week at the soonest. Ducks in a row and all that. Scott hadn't been staying at the house, telling me that he was helping a friend through a rough patch. Juke had assured me that the friend who needed helping was Stephanie, and that the rough patch was likely adulterous sex. But I quibble. I told Scott it was fine, and that I was so proud that he was helping a friend who was trying to quit drinking or whatever, and that I was super busy with Spring Fling so I would have been poor company anyhow. We both knew that we were avoiding each other, but that was fine for a few days.

This morning I had sent him this text:

I know things aren't good between us. I think we need to talk. Meet me at the Bullpen at 12:30 p.m. Let's stop avoiding the problem.

To which he responded:

Okay. Yeah. We need to talk. And what's the Bullpen?

I typed back the location. He sent a question emoji. I ignored it.

So at this point I wasn't certain he'd come, but then again, I knew Scott. He probably thought he'd be doing damage control, and if he were going to scoot out of the country, leaving me and his daughter, he would at least want to profess to himself and anyone else he valued that he had been straight with me. Or maybe not. Did I really know him anymore?

So I fiddled with the straw paper, glancing back at Dak, who polished his bar like it was a Rolls-Royce. Ruby was at Printemps, awaiting my call. Juke was upstairs, hopefully not drinking.

Looking down at my watch, I noted that Scott was five minutes late. He was never late.

Maybe he wasn't coming.

I picked up my phone and checked my email, allowing myself to get distracted by an anniversary sale at Nordstrom. A few more minutes ticked by. Still no Scott.

My phone buzzed.

Scott.

On my way. Got tied up.

"I bet you did," I muttered.

"Huh?" Griffin asked behind me.

"Nothing. He's on his way." I resumed ironing out my straw paper and then making it into an accordion.

Five minutes later, Scott entered the bar. He wore his normal banker clothes—khakis, a light-colored button-down, and loafers—totally a fish out of water among the jeans and occasional tank top. I clenched my trembling hands and then pressed them against the folder in front of me. I noted that Scott saw me and hurried right over.

"Hey," he said, pulling up a stool, "sorry I'm late. Had a meeting run over."

"That's okay. I understand." And hadn't that been what I had always said to him, now that I thought of it? I had always made life easier for Scott, picking up his dry cleaning, buying the coffee creamer he liked over the one I liked, ironing his shirts, and cutting the crusts off his sandwiches. I smoothed his way through life.

He eyed my iced tea. "So what's with this place, way out here?"

"It's beneath my private investigator's office, so it was easy."

His blue eyes flashed, and I could see right then and there that he knew but was going to play dumb. "Private investigator? For what?"

"You."

"Me?" Again with the feigning.

"Yeah. You're sleeping with Julia Kate's tennis instructor, and I want a divorce."

CHAPTER TWENTY-THREE

CRICKET

For months I had wanted to shout those words at Scott—*I want a divorce!*

But now they seemed so anticlimactic. Maybe it was because I'd had a lot of time to come to grips with the dissolution of our marriage. Or maybe because the grief and anger seemed farther away now. Or maybe my "give a damn" was busted and I wasn't interested in fixing it.

Scott, however, played his part at hearing the uttering of those fated words. His eyebrows shot up, and he looked momentarily like a carp caught behind glass, all wide eyed and gulping. "What? A divorce?"

I lifted a nonchalant shoulder. "I know you think I'm a dumb blonde. But I'm not."

"I don't think you're dumb, and you're wrong. I . . . I . . . I really need a drink." He held up a hand to, I'm assuming, Dak. I had sat facing the proliferation of neon beer signs and baseball memorabilia tripping over themselves along the wall so that Scott would be forced to look at the room behind me, specifically at where Griffin sat just over my right shoulder. We had decided he would sit far away enough so that he didn't attract immediate attention when Scott first arrived.

"What can I get cha?" Dak called.

"A Mic ULTRA."

"No go on that. Bud Light work? Or we have the Great Raft beers?"

"Reasonably Corrupt will do." Scott folded his hands and looked at me in a way that told me I was about to be gaslighted. Or dressed down like a silly child.

"How appropriate," I uttered under my breath.

He gave me a flat look. Dak appeared at my elbow with a can of the local beer and a clean glass. Setting it down, he gave me a look that made me feel a little calmer. "Anything else? Cricket?"

"No, I'm good." A total lie, but what was a little white lie at this table?

If Scott had his part to play, I had mine. I needed to summon the hurt and anger knocking around somewhere in my heart so that I looked like the distraught, betrayed wife. "Look, let's not even try to do this whole 'Who, me?' thing, Scott. We're too old to play games. I know you've been cheating. You know I know you've been cheating. You even paid off my first investigator. So let's just move to the 'What now?' portion of this meeting."

Scott poured his beer, frowning at the foam. He took a sip and sighed. "I'm sorry, babe."

Those words did what they should have done—they hit their mark. Suddenly my bravado caved. Maybe the hurt and anger weren't so hard to find after all. Moisture gathered in my eyes as I stared at the three little hairs he'd missed shaving that morning. At the silver frost at his temple. At those familiar hands cupping the glass. At the gold band he still wore on that left hand, the band I had placed there reciting vows in front of the church. I fumbled for the folder with the photographic evidence, opening it, looking down at him holding Stephanie in his arms, so I could bat away the sadness and regain my composure.

His gaze zipped to the photos, and I saw the apology in his eyes, which flung another arrow at my heart. I had no doubt that Scott was sorry for hurting me. Somewhere under his horribleness was the man who had loved me once.

Surely.

"I have an attorney and have already filed for divorce," I said, sliding the pictures so he could see that there were at least five of him and Stephanie in compromising situations.

"Who's your attorney?"

"Jacqueline Morsett."

"I don't know her."

"Would I use someone you knew? No. I need someone who hasn't played golf with you, Scott." I tapped the photos and lifted my eyebrows. "Besides, this is really all I need."

"Cricket, we don't have to—"

"Yeah, we do. There's a reason why you did this to us. It's a horrible thing to do to our family, Scott, but our marriage hasn't been what it should have been for a long time. I'm not accepting blame. This affair is on you, but I accept that maybe you felt unloved. I know because I have felt much the same, like something has been missing for a while. So maybe we were on our way to being over anyway. It's just, there are better ways to end a marriage than screwing someone else, you know?" A tear or two may have fallen.

He looked chagrined. "I know. I am very ashamed of myself."

"But not enough to stop. You're at her house all the time. Again, I'm not stupid." But I felt that way at that moment. Like a very stupid woman who had been so focused on small things that didn't matter—what font to use on name tags at Open House, what to put in Julia Kate's Easter basket, if I should have Botox—when I should have seen that Scott and I were pulling away, a gulf ever-widening between us.

"Stephanie and I fell in love," he said, looking into his beer. He couldn't quite meet my eyes after he said that, could he?

I sighed, another arrow thumping into my heart. "So I guess that is all that needs to be said. No sense in pretending we're even going to try to fix anything. It's done. I haven't told Julia Kate anything yet. I think it would be better coming from us both, so we need to choose a time soon to sit down with her. She's at a difficult age, so she's going to need lots of support. Maybe a therapist, too. At any rate, we are both going to have to be around to give her constant presence and ensure she feels loved."

Ah. And there was the flicker. He wasn't planning on being around. No, Scott was taking his size-2 ball lobber and heading to the crystal waters of the Caribbean. He'd made this mess and was going to leave me to clean it up while he relaxed in the sunshine. Just like my cat growing up. Jingles had loved to knock everything off the countertops and saunter away like a total ass.

I broke those arrows off and hurled them to the ground. Not so sad anymore.

"Sure," he said.

"So I want to do this amicably. We can split everything we've built during our marriage, including the house Printemps occupies—I'll pay you half the market value. Anything we came into the marriage with, we take. Like the lake house is my family's place. That sort of thing. I want to be fair. I won't allow the anger I feel for you to override my integrity. I expect the same of you."

"Well, I need to get an attorney and let him advise me—"

I held up a finger. "That's fine. But I would prefer that you make up for your indiscretion by helping me pursue an expedient divorce. Because you committed adultery, we don't have to wait the standard six months, and though I know you stepped out on me, I also know that you would never treat me unfairly or leave your daughter without means." Those words didn't roll so easily off my tongue. Because that's exactly what the bastard had planned to do.

"Of course not," he said as he glanced away.

Slapping him across the face and screaming *Liar* would probably not be the best thing to do, considering I wanted him to sign the papers, but I swear I almost did it. Because he was a crappy, crappy person.

Instead I opened the folder with all the paperwork, my stomach dancing a jitterbug. But I felt very determined to try to proceed with our plan. I wasn't money hungry, but I *was* irritated at Scott. Okay, more than irritated. I was incensed that he was going to steal from me and our daughter. That he was so selfish that he would leave me, skip town, and shower our resources on Stephanie like we meant nothing to him. So this was about winning. About rocking his damned boat. "I have some papers here for you to sign. Jackie filed the divorce papers, and these are your copies on top. The first document to sign is a waiver of service, which says that I gave you a copy of the divorce petition. Beneath it are a few others regarding our communal property and stuff like that."

Scott pressed his hands in the air, eyeing my stack of papers. "Okay, yes, I will do what I can to make this easy for us both, but I don't feel comfortable signing all those documents today. I'm going to need some time to read through them. To get an attorney."

I closed the folder, anger creeping up inside. "Okay, then. If that's how you want to play it. If you want a fight, we can do that. Jackie seems like a real tiger. I made sure of that before I signed for her representation."

"Wait, I didn't say that I want to fight the divorce. I'm just saying give me a little time."

Scott hated a social scene, even at a place like the Bullpen. "Fine. Whatever."

"Come on, Cricket."

"What?" I said angrily, raising my voice, brushing tears away. "What can I say? All those years, Scott. Things were off but not irreparable. We could have worked it out, but you didn't give us the chance. And a tennis coach? Really, Scott? She's, like, fifteen years younger than you. You did what my dad did to my mom, and you know how much therapy it took to get me over that. I am just now on decent terms with my father."

"I'm sorry, Cricket," he said, and he actually sounded like he meant it. "I didn't intend for it to happen. I promise you."

I crossed my arms and turned my head, brushing at the tears. I felt Griffin change tables behind me. He had just moved closer, the way we had planned. Scott jerked his gaze toward that area, and tension flashed across his face. A niggle of worry in those blue eyes gave me a trill of accomplishment. It was working.

Now I just had to get him off-balance so I could urge him to sign the documents.

"Oh," I said, snapping my fingers and then digging into my bag, "I meant to give this to you this morning but forgot. Julia Kate said some guy gave this to her and asked her to give it to you."

He set down the beer he'd just sipped, glanced again at Griffin, and then took the envelope. "Wait, where did some guy approach Julia Kate?"

"She said he just came up to her when she was walking home from a friend's house. Probably one of the pool guys or something. But since that's your project, I thought I would hand it over to you."

He looked at the envelope, his brow furrowing. "Sure. Thanks."

"So obviously we need a plan for you to move out."

"Yeah." His eyes stayed on the envelope, and I could tell it worried him. As it damned well should have. But he made no move to pick it up and look at the contents.

"I'm going to grab a Sweet'N Low. Be right back." I slid off the stool and walked to the bar where Dak visited with a few customers. I waited for him to finish a conversation about the Saints' potential quarterback and then asked for a packet. I wanted Scott to have enough time to open the envelope, because it looked like he wasn't going to do it with me sitting across from him. As I passed Griffin, who wore motorcycle boots and a shirt that showcased his bulk and tats, I cast a quick look. He gave me a slight nod.

All was well.

I sat back on the stool, ripped open the pink packet, and stirred it into my already-sweet tea. Scott had definitely opened the envelope, and it had hit him where he needed to be hit. His hands seemed unsteady as he grabbed his beer and downed it.

"I need to go. We can talk more tonight," he said.

"So you're coming home?"

"I think I should. For Julia Kate." *Bingo. You should come home for her. Because your creepy business partner is threatening to harm your innocent, beautiful child who has nothing to do with any of this crap you brought on to us.*

"Okay, but before you go, I need you to sign the waiver. The rest are things dealing with insurances, the house mortgage, and oh, this one here lists our cars and how much remains on each loan. It's all just stuff that indicates what property we own together." I shifted through some of the papers. "Oh, and this one, this one is a statement saying that we elect to not do counseling. This one is for bringing in an advocate for Julia Kate specifically. Nothing legally binding, of course. Here's a pen."

I heard the scuff of the chair behind me, and Scott's eyes jerked to Griffin. "There's a guy. He's at a table behind you. I think I've seen him before."

"Who?" I said loudly, acting like I would turn my head.

"No, stop." Scott patted the table, looking rattled. "Give me the pen."

I shoved the pen toward him. He picked it up, tugged at his collar, and signed the top document, which was the waiver. I flipped to the next sheet.

He glanced again at Griffin and signed it.

"And here," I said, flipping to the next. He signed. I flipped again. He signed. Finally, I got to the bank form.

We had agreed that I would tap my right foot twice on the stool leg when I reached the bank form. I clicked my sandal against the steel. Behind me I felt Griffin standing up.

Scott jerked his gaze to Griffin and sucked in a deep breath. "I really gotta go, Cricket."

"Just three more," I said, tapping the collection of forms.

"Fine," he said, scribbling his name and date on the bank form. Then he quickly completed the last two.

Oh. My. God.

He signed it.

I truly couldn't believe that he'd scribbled his name across so many forms without reading them. Totally atypical of my paranoid husband, who might leave a receipt on the table, but who'd read every contract we'd ever signed. I almost wanted to jump up and scream *Sucker!* but I managed a sedate "Thank you, Scott. I really want this to be easy, and I can see that you do, too."

Griffin appeared to my right, giving me a bit of a start. "Ready?"

Scott looked up at him with alarm. "Uh, can I help you?"

"I'm just the notary," Griffin said, pulling out his stamp and pressing the seal onto the top page. He plucked the pen out of Scott's hand and scrawled his own name boldly beneath the seal.

"The notary?" Scott said, slightly stupefied and perhaps a bit sheepish. "Oh . . . you were . . . watching the signing. I thought—"

"She'd hired me to kick your ass?" Griffin asked with a predatory smile. Goodness, the man looked extremely dangerous. And hungry. Like he could carve out Scott's liver without a second thought. Griffin looked at me, amused. "I can kick his ass if you want me to. I know a great place to dump a body. Lots of gators."

Scott looked at me like he believed Griffin. I shrugged and smiled. "You know, Griff, it was a toss-up, but I think we can let him live to see another day."

"It's your party, sunshine," Griffin said, continuing with his stamping and signing.

Scott looked vastly uncomfortable. I understood. A month ago I'd felt pretty uncomfortable around Griffin, too. And this whole bar scene was way different from anything Scott frequented in town. Country club it wasn't. But I found I liked the way I felt here, and the people who occupied this space were the real deal. They were just what I needed in my life.

My husband looked across at me as if he were seeing me for the first time. I knew I didn't look all that different, but I felt different. Like the skin I'd been wearing had sloughed off to reveal a softer, more supple Cricket. I had done a peel on myself, getting rid of the tired, worn outer layer and bringing forth someone who could truly see herself. This new Cricket was more than a wife and mother. More than a committee chair. More than an agreeable daughter. Just more than.

And it felt good.

Really, really good.

So I smiled at Scott.

The man looked positively perplexed. I guess that made sense. A minute ago I had cried over him. At present I felt almost relieved that I no longer had to wash his underwear or go to a mind-numbing social event just so he could "work" the room. With the stroke of a pen, he'd submitted to our divorce. Now it was a matter of going before a judge and dissolving what was left between us.

It was over.

And I had gotten the money, too. So yeah, I smiled.

Griffin shoved the papers into the folder and handed them to me. "No charge."

"You sure?" I asked.

He looked over at Scott, a disdainful, almost hateful look. Then he did something crazy. Something spiteful. Something that seemed to highlight that Scott was an absolute idiot, at least to Griffin.

Griffin kissed me.

His lips were hard, and the kiss looked overfamiliar, like he kissed me all the time. Then my biker hero straightened and said, "See ya later, sunshine."

Scott's mouth sagged open, and if we had not just ended our years of loving and laughing together, I would have burst into hysterical laughter. His face was that horrified. But I didn't. Instead I found that cool lady detective in the stilettos and jaunty hat and said, "You bet, handsome."

"What in the ever-loving hell?" Scott asked, sputtering and flushing.

"What?" I asked, picking up the folders and sliding the one with the pictures of our daughter in it over to him.

"That man . . . Are you *cheating* on me?" He vibrated with sudden outrage, which I found vastly amusing.

"Of course not," I said as I stood and gave him my best withering Scarlett-O'Hara-wearing-the-sin-red-dress glare. "*I* am not an asshole."

And then I walked out.

CHAPTER TWENTY-FOUR

Ruby

Dusting was such a belittling task. Because the next day dust would reappear like a bad blind date ignoring your polite rejection and doing what it wanted anyway. But I dusted the antiques regardless because it was my job. Besides, shiny things sold better.

I skirted around a large dining room table set for twelve with rose-strewn porcelain that any grandmother would be proud to serve a slice of tenderloin upon and fluffed the napkins showcasing lovely Japanese napkin rings. In the center of the table was a wooden box of plated silver, monogrammed and forgotten by some granddaughter who would rather have a new Louis Vuitton than the family silver. Cricket found this a travesty. I found it practical. Silver was a bitch kitty to clean.

I put the dustcloth away and signaled to Jade that I was going to work on my deconstructed haute couture. Cricket had agreed to my using half the kitchen as a small studio. It was tight quarters, but I could fit my sewing machine and a dressmaker dummy. Plus, the coffee maker was right there. As long as the store wasn't busy, I could work on the small line we would debut at Spring Fling in a few weeks. After the debut, Cricket would work on a studio for me upstairs.

Time was of the essence, and I had deposited Ed Earl's check and used a nice chunk of change to hire a Russian designer on Fiverr to create a logo. Finally, after grappling over styles back and forth yesterday, the designer had created a flared dress on a dressmaker's dummy with a measuring tape swirling around it bearing the name. The image was clean edged and done entirely in Wedgwood blue, and my font for "Deconstructed" was an old-fashioned script with an elaborate scrolled *D*. Normally, not my vibe, but it screamed vintage and southern at the same time, so I thought it had a better shot at reeling in the women who might buy my creations.

"Here you are, darling," I said to my dressmaker's dummy, using a fake Russian accent. I was currently giving shape to a white jacket with art deco black braiding that created an hourglass illusion at the waist, making it striking, modern, and not so dated.

I had run across this Carven suit jacket on Instagram from a Houston thrift shop. Someone there knew good craftsmanship if not couture, which was something I myself knew little about, and I had purchased it inexpensively because the braid trim had come detached, and the white jacket was patinaed into a cream. The "Esperanto" suit jacket was a masterpiece, even with the ruined braid. But I planned to fix the braid in some way. Pairing that with black custom-fit pants would create a feminine power suit that meant business but was chic at the same time. Perfect for the mini collection.

I almost felt like a real designer.

Glancing at my watch, I went to the coffeepot and poured another cup, though I didn't need another afternoon caffeine jolt. Waiting on Cricket to call was hard.

So I texted Griffin. He ignored me.

I texted Dak. He texted back. Everything cool.

Well, that told me exactly nothing.

I sat down and started removing some of the braid. In order to refashion and not steal the intellectual property of whoever had designed the jacket at Carven, I needed to take the best elements of the design so that the piece retained the essence but was used in another creative way. I pulled out my sketch pad and started doodling, getting lost in the various ways I could use the horsehair trim. Which is why I suppose I didn't hear Jade calling me.

"Ruby!" Jade burst into the kitchen.

I jumped a foot off the chair, and my drawing pad tumbled to the linoleum floor. "Oh my God, J!"

"Sorry. Your uncle's on the phone. He said your grandmother is being taken by ambulance to the hospital."

My heart plunged down around where my pad had fallen. "What? What happened?"

I flipped my phone over, realizing I had gotten so wrapped up in sketching and distracting myself from Cricket's sting operation that I hadn't looked at it in fifteen minutes. There were ten texts and two missed calls.

"I don't know. He didn't say," Jade said.

I lurched from the chair, scooping up my phone. "You good to cover the store?"

"Of course. I can stay. Go." Jade disappeared as I went out the back door, all thoughts of Cricket, Dak, and how to dump Ty fleeing from my mind. Gran was sick. Gran could be dying.

Please don't let her die.

I unlocked my car, climbing in and dialing Ed Earl.

"'Lo?" he said, sounding like he was driving.

"What's wrong with Gran?" I demanded.

"Not sure. I'm on my way, following the ambulance. She just sorta collapsed and said she felt funny. She'd gone to the dentist and had a tooth pulled, so at first, I thought it was that. She said she hadn't been eatin' much. But then she looked weird, like part of her face was drooping."

"That's a stroke," I barked, squealing tires as I left the parking lot. "Which hospital?"

"I don't know. I think WK Bossier. That's the closest."

I hung up on him. Then I turned toward downtown, jetting out in front of a Land Cruiser, which honked at me. Like I cared. My grandmother, the only person who was an anchor in my life, could be dying.

"Please don't die," I murmured as I stepped on the gas. "I promise to do better, God. I know I'm a bad person and do bad things, but please, please don't let this happen. I need her."

And as I said those words to my empty car, I knew they were true. I needed her. I needed my family. I had let what Ed Earl did to me separate me from my past, from the place where I had learned to be stubborn, to be resourceful, to make do, and to make the best of my circumstances. Those were the lessons I had learned at my grandmother's knee, and though I had unhealed wounds, staying away from the people I thought were bad for me had not allowed my sores to scab over and go away. Instead of moving forward, I'd carried my burden like a prisoner lugging around his chain, and I'd hurt no one more than myself.

"I'm so stupid. I will do better," I said as I merged onto the interstate that spanned the Red River, uniting the two sides of the metro area. Perhaps even an analogy to my life. Bridges and all that stuff.

By the time I got to the hospital, I felt desperate with panic. I hurried toward the sliding doors and slammed into the triage desk. The nurse eeped in alarm, rolling back in her chair.

"Hey, I'm looking for Eunice Balthazar. She came by ambulance," I barked at the poor woman.

"Ruby," someone called behind me.

I turned to find Ed Earl and Jimbo sitting in the waiting area, muddy boots marring the carpet, jeans covered in motor oil, plaid shirtsleeves cut off at the shoulders. They looked like they always did—a bit slovenly, country as a turnip, and ready to kick ass if needed. Other people in the waiting room eyed them with trepidation, except for three or four who were on their phones and probably wouldn't notice if Elvis himself entered the building.

"How is she?" I asked, moving toward them.

"Don't know yet. Some sissy-looking doctor came out and said they were running tests and had given her some kind of shot that was supposed to help," Jimbo said.

"We're going to have to wait," Ed Earl said, giving his brother a look that said *Move down*. Jimbo did, but I knew I couldn't sit. I had too much nervous energy. I shook my head and went and slumped against the wall, pulling out my cell phone and googling "stroke." So much information, but website after website said that time was of the essence. Thank God that Ed Earl lived with Gran. If she had been alone . . .

And really, when had I ever uttered the words *Thank God* in relation to *Ed Earl*?

Maybe never.

But in this case, I was grateful for him.

We waited thirty minutes, during which time Ed Earl stomped down the hall and bought two packages of white-powdered doughnuts and two Cokes. He brought me a bottled water without asking, like he knew a Coke would be unwelcome. Like I was the kind of girl who always drank bottled water. I used to be the girl who would have had the root beer and a Snickers.

In my mind I heard my thrifty gran complaining about fools buying water when it was free from the faucet. My lips twitched. Goodness, she'd taught me so many things in life, some amusing, some so valuable. I hoped that she was okay. Please.

My phone vibrated. Cricket.

I wanted to take the call, but that would require stepping outside. I wasn't going to miss the doctor giving us an update. So I quickly texted my situation. In true Cricket fashion, suddenly her situation wasn't important and mine was. She wanted to come to the hospital. I told her no. And then I went back to sit next to Jimbo and Ed Earl to await word on Gran.

Thirty excruciating minutes later, a thin, balding man in scrubs came out and said, "Is there a Ruby Balthazar here?"

I had legally changed my name, of course, but Gran had refused to accept my new one. I stood. "Right here."

Behind me I could hear Jimbo complaining that they were her sons and why did she call for Ruby, but I didn't have time to explain that sometimes a woman needs another woman. Or that I would make Gran less nervous than they would. The doctor motioned me back through the double doors.

"I'm Dr. Angelo, and I've been taking care of your mother—"

"Grandmother," I clarified for no real reason. What did it matter?

"Yes, well, we think Mrs. Balthazar has had a TIA, a transient ischemic stroke. What that means is that there was a brief time where blood didn't flow into the central nervous system. Most of her initial symptoms—the numbness, the slurred speech—have abated, but we still need to run a few tests to rule out some things like dehydration and a bladder infection. Both of those last things can cause the same sort of symptoms, so we're running a blood panel and a urinalysis."

I had just spent the last half hour reading about the various kinds of strokes. This was the best to have because it was considered a ministroke and usually didn't cause long-term effects. "Is she feeling okay?"

"Most of her symptoms seem to have abated," he said, gesturing toward a long row of curtained bays. "You can go and see her. She's in number six. Once we have the results of her panels, we will determine if we need some follow-up diagnostics. We will probably do a CT. And then perhaps an MRI if we need more information."

"Thank you," I said, nodding at a nurse who hurried by carrying an IV bag.

I pulled back the curtain for Bay 6 and found my grandmother wearing a floral tunic and green leggings. On her feet were the slippers I had bought her a few years ago. Kitty-cat whiskers jutted out to each side. She looked pale in the bright overhead light, a yellow cast to her age-dotted skin. Never had she seemed old to me, but at that moment she sure as hell looked fragile. "Gran."

"Sugar, you gotta get me out of here. I'm making gumbo for Johnny's birthday tomorrow. I have two fryers in the pot that need to be deboned."

I almost laughed. Almost. Because this was the woman I knew and loved. No time to take care of herself, too busy managing everyone else's lives. "I think that can wait. We need to make sure you're okay before you go home."

"I asked for you because I thought you would understand that there ain't a dang thing wrong with me. Just a little episode. I've had them before, and they're no big deal, but the whole family is coming over tomorrow. I gotta make some soda bread and still need to bake a sheet cake."

"Totally understandable, but if you were having a stroke or could still be having a stroke, that might interfere with your ability to ice Johnny's birthday cake. If you are in the clear, after they do the tests, then I will go home with you and make that buttercream frosting everyone loves and help you debone the chicken. Deal?"

She waved her hand in a disgusted manner. "Tell them to get Ed Earl. He likes cake. He'll help me fly this coop."

"Oh, come on, Gran, even Ed Earl is going to make you get checked out. Cake or no cake. But I can call Jimbo back."

"No, Jimbo is an idiot," she said with a roll of her eyes. "But I guess he's *my* idiot. Fine. I'll do whatever tests they want. But you have to come help me with the cooking. I'm getting old and arthritic, and my kitchen has missed you."

A flash of guilt struck me, as she intended it to. It had been some time since I had sat with her at the kitchen table, sipped coffee, and spent time listening to old stories or clipping coupons from the Sunday paper. I hadn't been to any family dinners or get-togethers, barring her birthday celebration a few weeks back. Now, looking at her so small in that hospital bed, scared of what she might learn, brashly demanding she was fine, I knew that as much as I had to let go of my anger toward Ed Earl, I also had to hold tight to what truly mattered.

My family was irritating, half-wild, backward assed, and sometimes, yeah, criminal, but they'd never stopped wanting me there with them. In keeping myself away because of Ed Earl's betrayal, I hadn't just hurt Gran and the rest of the clan; I had hurt myself. Because I had denied myself two years of feeling something, even if it was anger. And what did I have to show for those lost years in terms of relationships? I had been alone, determined to tear away every piece of my past. But Cricket had reminded me days ago—there were pieces of myself I needed to keep, and my family was one of those things. Pretending them away wasn't going to make me a better person.

"Can I get you something while we wait on the results? Are you hungry?" I asked my grandmother.

"Well, I could pick at somethin'. Maybe some of those little powdered doughnuts they sell in those machines. Or a honey bun." My grandmother lifted a cup of ice water and sipped. "Oh, and bring me a Dr Pepper. You know I hate water."

Over my dead body. She'd just about died. Okay, not died, but if they were indeed TIAs, then they had happened for a reason. They were warning signs, and Gran was going to need to pay better attention to her health. "I'll see what I can find."

I slipped out of the bay and headed back toward the waiting area. As I passed the nurses' desk, I said, "I'll be right back."

I entered the waiting area and was surprised to find Cricket, Griffin, and Juke—all the players in our "Blue Moon Sting," as Cricket had called it. The woman did, indeed, love a theme. "Hey, what are y'all doing here?"

"We came to check on you . . . and your grandmother. How is she?" Cricket asked.

I felt a bit stunned that she had come all the way here on a day that was, well, important. Griff and Juke weren't as surprising—Gran was their relative, after all. "They're running tests but don't seem to think she's in danger at present. I was about to get her a snack."

Ed Earl moved toward us, Jimbo lagging behind. His eyes moved over Cricket, who looked a bit messy but in a sexy way. Over the last few weeks, Cricket seemed to have abandoned the priss for the sass. She looked good mussed up. My uncle looked intrigued by my boss. "I can get Mama something to eat. And who's this?"

Cricket gave him the look one might give a cockroach that had crawled onto a counter. "Who are you?"

He tried out a charming smile, which looked like he had a stomachache. "I'm Ed Earl, darling. And who might you be?"

"Oh," Cricket said, turning away from him and training her gaze on me.

Damn. She had that society direct-cut thing down.

Ed Earl looked confused, which almost made me laugh. I glanced back at him. "Gran said she wanted a honey bun. You can get that, but it's probably her last one for a while. The TIAs she had are like a warning buzzer going off. Gran needs to start paying better attention to what she eats and doing more walking."

Ed Earl lifted his eyebrows, and I knew he knew what the whole family knew—we were about to battle the woman who cooked with bacon grease and kept jelly beans next to her recliner. But he did as I asked, his sidekick Jimbo following him down the squeaky-clean hall toward the room that had vending machines.

"Well, I'm glad she's going to be okay," Cricket said.

"As far as we know," I amended, glancing down to where Ed Earl and Jimbo had disappeared. "So? How did everything go?"

Juke smiled. "Well, she got the signature. It may not stand up in a court of law, but the bank in the Caymans won't know that. She should be able to recover her part, at least. May have to go down there to do it. Not sure."

"Look, I did not lie to Scott; I just didn't tell him what the paper was. If he didn't read them before he signed, that's his mistake and his problem." Cricket crossed her arms and looked a little perturbed at Juke. Juke looked a bit like he faced a prostate exam. Griff just looked like he always did. Like he might grind someone's bones to make his bread.

"Yeah. Right," Juke said, withdrawing his phone. "So I think we can make that appointment with the investigators from the SEC and Justice Department. You can give them the information they need to arrest Donner and Scott, and maybe that will do a lot to help you in regard to the divorce and the recovery of the untainted money. I did some poking around. Even if they freeze your joint accounts, you can petition a judge to release your lawfully gained funds. Might be a hill to climb, but you might be able to get at it."

Cricket lifted a shoulder. "I don't care as much about the money as I do winning against Scott. He doesn't think I'm smart or motivated enough to best him. I want him to know that he's wrong."

Juke motioned at his phone and stepped away, leaving me with Cricket and Griff. I glanced down at where Ed Earl stood against the hospital wall, holding a honey bun and chatting with someone on the phone. "You didn't have to come."

Cricket wrapped an arm around me and gave me a squeeze. "Ruby, you're my friend. I wanted to be here."

"But you have so much going on and—"

She shook her head. "I know you think you're an island, Ruby, but you're not. We all need someone. Look how much you've been there for me. Do you know what that means to me? You roping your cousins into helping me, into conducting a sting to nail my husband? That was pretty cool. And generous. And slightly bloodthirsty, but I like that about you."

That made me chuckle. "Well, we know how to choose our weapons."

Griff snorted.

Cricket grinned and then watched as Juke approached, pocketing his phone and looking like he had juicy info. "Okay. Jim Arnold is the contact. He wants you to come in to meet him as soon as you're able. I get the sense that they're ready to move."

Cricket looked surprised. "Like when?"

"Can you go by tomorrow?" Juke asked.

Cricket pulled a planner out of her purse. "Let me check my calendar. Well, um, I have to go to Julia Kate's school for an awards service at nine thirty a.m. Then I'm supposed to have lunch with Mother and then meet Whitney Peacock about the Spring Fling. She wants me to—" Cricket snapped her mouth closed and made a face.

"What?" I asked.

"I have to go to the academic award thing, but then I can put off the other things. This is important."

Juke nodded. "Good. I'll tell him you'll come by after lunch."

We all stood there, somewhat satisfied, still a little awkward because how do you end a sting? Juke probably knew, but the rest of us were amateurs.

So we all went to the cafeteria and got coffee and a slice of pie while Ed Earl and Jimbo went to see Gran. We were a motley bunch, but I took comfort in my family and Cricket being there with me. My grandmother seemed to be feeling better, and Jimbo bumbled in to let us know that the urinalysis was clear and she was being released. Oh, and he also polished off my pie. Jimbo probably needed to heed the doctor's warning himself since he looked as if he could deliver a full-term infant at any given moment.

So I told Cricket that I was taking the afternoon off to help Gran get settled. To which she said, "Of course you are."

Then I walked with them to the parking lot to say goodbye. Juke climbed into his old truck, throwing me a salute. He seemed pleased with himself, and I was happy that he'd found some purpose and seemed to be doing much better. I would keep an eye on him. And then I sort of let my mouth hang open as Griff handed Cricket a bike helmet.

"You came with Griff? On the bike?"

Cricket grinned. "Heck yeah. I love riding a motorcycle. I mean, I could never get one for myself while my daughter is so young. Can't take that risk, especially since she's about to lose her daddy. And probably not while my mother is still living. She would die if I rode a hog, or whatever you call them. But Griffin is a very good driver. I trust him."

My cousin's chest may have puffed out a bit.

"This is so weird," I said.

Cricket made a face. Then she smiled cheekily. "Well, it turns out I like weird. I hired you, didn't I?"

I should have been insulted, but I knew Cricket didn't mean it offensively. She meant it the way my cousins had meant it when they teased me about wearing makeup, crying when my Tamagotchi pet died, and writing "Mrs. Dakota Roberts" all over my notebooks. She meant it with love.

"You did." I laughed as she slung her leg over the seat of the Harley and wrapped her arms around my cousin's waist.

Griffin looked as pleased as Juke did. As pleased as I felt. Even if I was still worried about Gran and how I was going to get her to stop eating Pop-Tarts every morning.

They drove off, and I turned to go back inside the hospital. And just when the doors slid open, I heard someone behind me say, "That country chick went home. You owe me a Coke."

Dak.

"I believe I was the one who said she was going home. Don't you have to go console her or something?" I asked, turning around and setting my hand on my hip.

"You really want me to?" he asked, looking mighty good in his jeans and Van Halen T-shirt. Okay, it wasn't Rob Zombie, but it would do. And this question was more than something light and playful. This was more than a silly bet over *American Idol*. He was asking me what I wanted. If I was going to stake a claim. If I wanted to pick up what he was laying down.

"No. I was hoping you might come help me ice Johnny's birthday cake at Gran's house. I mean, if you have someone to pour your beer for the next few hours, that is. We can pick up Southern Classic and daiquiris."

Dak smiled. "I have a guy who pours a mean beer. And who passes up Southern Classic fried chicken, anyway?"

"Someone who doesn't have good sense," I said, gesturing toward the open doors.

"You never struck me as someone who didn't have that."

Dak smiled.

And I smiled back.

CHAPTER TWENTY-FIVE

Cricket

Eleven days later

"Ruby, let's go!" I called from the front of the store, trying to keep my anxiety level manageable. Today was the day I would witness Scott's comeuppance. God willing and the creek don't rise.

Jade was standing behind the counter, eyeing me wearing the Carven jacket that Ruby had refashioned into something quite lovely. "Ruby made that?"

I nodded. "She's about to launch a line of clothing."

"Mm," Jade said, twirling her finger for me to spin. I obliged. "That looks good. I'd wear it."

And that was high praise from Jade. She wasn't one to ooh and aah over anything. I looked down at the jacket and pants. Ruby had mimicked the original design minus some damaged ribbon and had added a large black panel at the waist, hiding the original damage to the fabric. She'd streamlined the sleeves and added the same black band at the cuff. The cigarette pants she'd paired with it were emerald raw satin and should have looked absurd. Truly. But they didn't. I had swept my hair up into a twist and pulled on my grandmother's somewhat offensively large emerald earrings. I'd found a clutch at an estate sale that looked perfect with it. The open-toed black Tory Burch wedges were the finishing touch. I looked ready to take on the world. Or at least my soon-to-be ex-husband.

Ruby appeared, wearing the top half of a Bellville Sassoon floral gown she'd fashioned into a blouse with a short blue skirt. The floral champagne-colored top had been stripped of beaded embellishment to make it less dressy. Ruby wore flats and several delicate chains around her neck. I could tell that she'd leveled down her look because she wasn't certain what to expect at the annual "Person of the Year" luncheon. For many years it had been "Man of the Year," but societal pressures had led them to change it a few years back, though they had yet to award it to a woman.

"You look very non-Ruby-like," I said, giving her a smile.

"What?" She looked down at her outfit. "Is it too genteel?"

I laughed. "Genteel? Well, it is a bit, but I like it."

"I have palazzo pants for this top when we debut it at Spring Fling. So it's a bit more, you know, me, but I thought that might draw too much attention and be a bit too dressy for a luncheon. The mayor is going to be there."

Yeah, he was. The University Club's annual event was a celebrated luncheon, and my husband had literally danced when he heard that he was being awarded Person of the Year status for his work helping the Renesting Project. In fact, he'd written his acceptance speech the day after he got the call. He'd literally strolled around the house, punching the air with absolute glee when he'd learned he'd been selected as the recipient.

His accolade was a big coup for the bank and all that. Of course, Richard Morrison, the CEO of Caddo Bank and Loan, had no clue that his golden boy had been making fraudulent, shaky loans to be invested in a Ponzi scheme, or that my "Person of the Year" husband was about to skip town with his girlfriend to dodge the blowback. Let's just say that Scott had been "renesting" himself.

So it was awfully small of me to encourage the SEC investigators and the Department of Justice guys to arrest Scott at the luncheon. But when Jim Arnold, the friend of a friend of Juke's, had asked me if I knew Scott's whereabouts because they were preparing to arrest Donner and him in the coming week, I told him I wasn't sure where Scott was. Which was the truth. I figured he could be at Stephanie's, but I had stopped driving by, so I wasn't absolutely sure. Scott had sent me a few texts about the divorce. He had an attorney and wanted copies of all the papers he'd signed that day. He had also very nicely asked if I would hold off announcing our divorce until after the University Club's luncheon and if I would meet him there and sit with him to present a better picture for Caddo Bank and Loan. His other guests would be Donner and Ty Walker. So it was two birds, one stone, in a very public birdbath.

The investigators thought this was amusing—that I wanted my husband to face utter humiliation in front of people who meant something to him. Which at first made me feel small. The University Club shouldn't have to pay for my own pleasure in seeing my husband in cuffs. They really did some wonderful things in our community, even if they'd shortsightedly honored my cheating husband. But truth was, the University Club had been deceived, too.

The old Cricket would have been mortified to have her husband arrested at such a luncheon.

The new Cricket made sure she wore whore-red lipstick with her big-ass emerald earrings. I was positively bloodthirsty.

"Ready?" I asked Ruby, who was my date. I had asked Scott for an extra ticket. I figured that Ruby had earned her ringside seat for the defeat of the man who'd allowed himself to be pulled down by greed and lust.

"Yep. Let's roll. See ya later, Jade. Don't forget, someone is coming for those iced-tea glasses. I put all twelve in a box in the back," Ruby said as she followed me.

Jade shooed us out, and we headed through the kitchen to the newly waxed Spider. The top was up because, duh, my hair wouldn't survive the wind. But this car now felt more me than it ever had. I trailed my hand across the shiny smoothness of the hood as I stepped to the driver's side, saying hello to my grandmother—the woman who had given me the car, the business, and the gumption to do what I did. My mother had lent me her cold, calculating detachment, but my grandmother had sewn inside me her passion, her rebellion, her thumbing of the nose at convention. I had let that part of me lie dormant for far too long, but I had rediscovered it through this process.

Obviously, since I was heading to watch my husband being arrested.

"Thank you," I whispered as I opened the door and slid inside.

Ten minutes later we pulled into the newly refurbished University Club right off Fairfield Avenue. The club was housed in an old mansion similar to Printemps, with loads of screened porches, curlicue woodwork, and personality. The Old South feel remained intact, and perhaps that was the intent. Cars streamed down the street, announcing the event. I pulled into the circular drive, and a twentysomething guy hurried to me with a smile. I handed over the keys and waited on Ruby to come round.

"Thanks," I said to the young man, who took the keys and gave me a numbered ticket.

"Ready?" Ruby asked, releasing a breath, looking a little nervous, a tad like she had the night of the gala. I had been born into this world, thanks to my mother, so it bordered on boring for me. But Ruby seemed to find it intimidating, and I could understand that. When you hadn't grown up knowing that Lindy Williams ate her boogers and Sheridan Hyde had done the nasty with disgusting George Kuntz on the country-club tennis court, you got a little twitchy around the cliquish women inside.

"Yeah. I'm totally ready. After this, I can breathe. I'll have to do damage control with Julia Kate, but I will be able to breathe. To move. To focus on my future. On your future." I looked over at her, trying to show her that I wasn't nervous. But I was.

Because even though all those words were true, this was the end. I was closing a chapter. No, closing a book and tucking it away forever. So I was feeling full of too many feelings to name, so I didn't try. I just shoved them all into the closet of my psyche and pasted on a smile. Hey, I was a master of pretense at this point.

We entered the club, and after a quick trip to the bathroom to take deep breaths and regather myself, I emerged with fresh lipstick and determination. Ruby looked antsy, so I winked at her as I sauntered up to a few of my friends, who immediately congratulated me on Scott's award. I smiled, nodded, and changed the subject to Amy Barnwell's new haircut, shifting the conversation to what these women really liked to talk about—themselves. Of course, they had much to say about my jacket, which was exactly what *I* wanted to talk about.

I introduced Ruby around as a designer of a new clothing line that would debut at Spring Fling. I hinted that she had interest from an NYC designer and that Printemps would be carrying her designs exclusively in the area. Oh, and a few boutiques in Dallas would, too. I lied about the last one, but that was only because I hadn't yet called my sorority sister Ellen Benoit, who had a hoity-toity boutique and who I knew would love to feature Deconstructed in her very successful shop. If she didn't, I could let a few incriminating pictures from spring break at Cash's in Florida leak. Second place in the wet-T-shirt contest was nothing to sniff at.

Lord, I had become a blackmailer.

No, I was a boat rocker.

Ruby kept shifting glances at me like I had popped a few mushrooms or something in the bathroom. I winked at her again, and then we walked to the dining hall where the luncheon would be held. The dark wood of the room stood as the perfect backdrop for white hydrangeas and fluffy greenery. Faux candles flickered on the tables along with trailing ivy and scattered vases of white roses. People clumped together in conversation as waiters in white jackets circulated hors d'oeuvres and glasses of wine punch. I stifled a yawn because it looked affected and because I hadn't really slept the previous night.

Scott spotted me and pulled away from the men he was no doubt telling dirty jokes to. "Hey, you made it."

"I told you I would," I said, trying not to look like I could pick up a chantilly-patterned butter knife and stab him.

He looked past me at Ruby. "And you brought your assistant."

"Yes. She's been quite handy, and I thought she deserved some dry chicken and seeing the presentation of a worthless award." I studied my manicure, rubbing the lotion I had used in the bathroom into my cuticles. I was being mean. But I didn't care.

"Come on, Cricket," Scott said, looking perturbed. He looked nice in his best suit and the tie I had bought him from some fancy London men's shop he coveted. I should have known he was an utter ass a long time ago.

"What? I'm here. I never said I would play nice."

He frowned. "Then leave."

"Nope," I said, eyeing the table with his name on it, picking out where I should sit. "When *I* make promises, I keep them."

He narrowed his eyes, looking irritated. "That's your problem, Cricket. You're too busy being virtuous to be any sort of fun. That's why our marriage is over."

My hand curled because I thought I might punch him.

Ruby pressed a hand on my forearm and looked at Scott. "Wait, that's why? Because she told me you were . . ." She held up her pinky finger and wiggled it. "I mean, Cricket, I didn't realize that it was your *virtue* that busted your marriage up."

That made me laugh. "Yeah. Being virtuous is a drag. But having a small penis is even draggier. Or maybe the *not being draggy* is the problem. Congrats on your award, Scott. Hope it brings you comfort in the coming months."

My ass of a husband smiled. "I'll be very comfortable in the coming months. You might even say I will be positively warm and sunny."

Yeah, I didn't feel so bad asking for this butthole to be arrested at the luncheon now. The University Club would just have to suck it on this one. I turned on my wedge and stalked to the table, trying to look powerful and not pissed. I probably looked pissed, but what of it? I didn't care anymore what these people thought.

Ruby grabbed two wineglasses and made her way to where I had plopped down at the head table reserved for Scott. She poured the wine of one glass into the other and handed it to me. Then she turned and snagged a glass for herself.

"I have to drive back," I said, taking the extra-full glass regardless and taking a swig.

"I can drive," Ruby said, setting her glass down.

"Last time you drove the Spider, it cost me five hundred and seventy dollars."

She made a face. "I have two words that are the reason I hit that pothole."

I remembered those two words, which made me look over at Scott. And wouldn't you know it, homegirl Stephanie was standing beside him chatting. Why was she even here? But, of course, I knew. They were in love. He wanted her to see him get this big civic award. Boy, was she going to get a surprise. So I wasn't even mad. In fact, I was glad she was there. I wanted her to see him in cuffs and realize her little Caribbean dream was toast.

Shortly after I had finished my entire glass of wine, which made me feel way more relaxed, if not slightly tipsy, Ed Yardley strolled to the podium and asked everyone to have a seat so that lunch could be served. People moved like cows to hay, moseying toward empty tables, sitting, and passing the bread basket.

I glanced at my watch, wondering what time Jim Arnold and his law enforcement team would arrive. Hopefully after dessert. I wasn't truly hungry, but I hated to see good food go to waste. The University Club was known for decent dry chicken.

Donner and Ty showed up, the latter a little cool toward Ruby. She'd told me that she'd told him she wasn't interested in going out any longer. She wasn't sure how involved he was in his father's scheme, but she figured he had to know something of it, which meant she couldn't even pretend to like him any longer. Donner's wife, Marjorie, who rarely attended anything and who was rumored to be ill, had come with him for some reason. She looked gaunt and drawn, eating only her salad, wearing a severe black dress, and uttering only one sentence: "Pass the salt."

The conversation around the table mostly consisted of Donner and Scott talking about their golf game, the shape of the greens at East Ridge, and the price of gasoline. I said very little, answering any question directed toward me in a basic way. Beneath my calm exterior, my gut churned and my heart pumped hard, as if I were about to run a race.

Finally, coffee was poured, and dessert, a lovely chocolate chiffon, was served. Then the ceremony began. Same ol' ceremony as the year before, but this time Scott gave the acceptance speech, which was a very nice speech, mostly because I had helped him with much of it months ago, when I was still in the dark and still in love with my husband. Now those words about family and community clinked like a rusted can on a deserted street. When Scott thanked me for my love and support, people clapped and looked my way. I tried to smile. I truly did. But it was like smiling through a Pap smear. I just kept my feet in those metaphorical stirrups and plastered on my game face, sagging in relief once the attention shifted away from me.

At the end of the speech, Ed stood up and gave Scott a cheap plaque. Ruby leaned over. "How much longer do you think we'll have to suffer through this?"

And she got her answer before I could say, *I don't know.*

In the back of the room, there was a fluttering. I saw the head of the club, a jackass who always gave me trouble when I was planning something at the University Club, hurry toward the door, where two men stood in dark suits. Behind them were uniforms. Not quite a SWAT team, but they had guns and were dressed in black. A low murmur began in the room as people craned their heads to see what the fuss was about. Beneath the table, Ruby grabbed my hand.

I was shaking.

Not sure why. Excitement? Dread? Relief? Shame?

No clue. But I trembled like Pippa in a thunderstorm.

"Hey, wait—you can't do this right now! We're in the middle of something!" the club manager shouted as the two men proceeded into the room, followed by a small contingency of law enforcement. I kept my eyes away from Donner's gaze. Scott still stood at the podium holding his plaque and looking concerned. He glanced over at Donner, who had his phone out and was rapidly tapping.

Jim Arnold didn't slow down on his sojourn toward our table. He called behind him to the distraught manager, "We have a warrant. And we don't care that you're in the middle of something."

"What's going on?" Ty asked his father while watching the parade of black heading our way. He seemed to understand that it revolved around his dad.

"Marjorie, dear, Ty will see you home. I fear this is about me. Unmerited, of course, but I've always had a target on my back. Everything will be okay," Donner said, patting his wife's hand. Marjorie looked like a little lost sheep, and I felt really awful that he'd brought her to this event. Talk about bad timing.

"What do you mean, Don?" Marjorie asked, looking at Ty. "What is happening?"

Donner stood and buttoned his suit jacket just as Jim arrived with the warrant. "Mr. Arnold, I see we were destined to meet again. Could you have not picked a better time?"

Jim raised his eyebrows. "We waited until you had coffee."

The officers were moving toward Scott, who looked panicked. He had tucked his award under his arm and had started moving away from the advance. He threw out a hand and said, "I have nothing to do with this. This is all on Donner. He's the guy you want."

Donner's eyes flashed with hard anger as he glanced at Scott. I could almost see his thoughts. *Never should have trusted this fool.*

Honestly, it looked like something out of a comedy—my husband squealing like a pig and Donner turning and presenting his hands to be cuffed as calmly as I had ever seen him. Marjorie had started crying, and Ty was already on the phone, likely calling another attorney. Ruby and I sat there sipping our wine, our version of eating popcorn as the arrest went down.

"Scott Crosby," the man with Jim Arnold said, "you're under arrest for conspiracy to commit fraud, aiding and abetting, and wire and mail fraud. You have the right to remain silent. You have the right—"

"I didn't do anything wrong!" Scott shouted, still backing away. "All I did was introduce him to some of my friends. That's it. This is on him. He's the one—"

"Shut up, Scott," Ty called, pressing his hand against the microphone of his phone. "Don't say another word."

The organizers of the luncheon were wide eyed, whipping their heads back and forth, mouths open. Everyone else in the room was absolutely aghast and titillated at the scene unfolding. Ed stood nearby, his hand still outstretched as if to shake Scott's.

My husband had moved around toward me, like if he just sat down at the table, nothing bad would happen.

"Mr. Crosby," the other agent said, following him, "you need to stop, turn around, and let me cuff you. Don't make this hard on yourself and add charges."

"But I didn't do anything," he said, nearly tripping as he backed away. He turned toward me, his eyes panicked. "Cricket, tell them."

He was actually asking me to help him? "Tell them what? That you stole our savings and our retirement and put it in an offshore account with the tainted money that Donner gave you to feed him clients? Tell them you're sleeping with our daughter's tennis pro and plan to flee the country? Or tell them that you're the . . . person of the year? Which would it be?"

Scott stopped, his face utterly shocked. If I could have taken a mental picture and framed it for all eternity, it would be that expression. The comeuppance. The moment he realized that I knew everything. That I wasn't stupid. That I had rocked the motherfucking boat. "What?"

The SEC investigator caught up with him, taking him by the shoulder. One of the law enforcement officers jerked his left arm back and cuffed it. Scott's mouth fell open, and I could see the wheels spinning. "Did you do this? Did you set this up? Because of Stephanie?"

I took a sip of wine and lifted a shoulder, not answering.

"You bitch!" he screamed, lurching toward me. Thankfully, he'd been cuffed, and there were several officers there to pull him back.

I had never been called a bitch before. Because I wasn't. I was always the person who smoothed things over, who sent thoughtful gifts, and who remembered Scott's mother's birthday. Being a bitch was so far away from who I was that I truthfully had never, ever been called one. So one might think I would have been insulted and embarrassed at my husband of twenty-one years calling me a bitch in a roomful of our friends and colleagues, but I wasn't. Instead I laughed. "From you that's a compliment."

Ruby let a chuckle escape as she squeezed my hand beneath the table.

"A compliment? You stupid bitch. You have no clue what you've done! I hold the cards, and I'm not going down for this. You'll regret this. You'll wish you had never said anything to anyone. You'll wish—" They were leading him away, and everyone in the room looked on as if they were watching a play. The place was silent. Not even the clink of silverware could be heard as Donner and Scott were led from the room in cuffs.

But Scott's last words made me angry. I stopped smiling and stood, drawing the attention of everyone in the room. They ping-ponged their heads like they were at Wimbledon instead of a normally boring luncheon. "I won't wish anything, Scott Crosby. Except that I never married you! Besides, I'll be in Grand Cayman sipping margaritas while you defend your actions to the courts and all the people you helped to steal money from."

He stilled when I said "Grand Cayman." He jerked away from the officer and came toward me. They grabbed him again and pulled him along. "What did you say? What do you know about Grand Cayman?"

I looked my husband straight in the eye. "That's right. You signed the papers that gave me access that day at the bar. The SEC and Justice Department know all about the offshore accounts. I made sure they did."

I'd never seen my husband go crazy, but at that moment he did. He looked like a wild animal trying to escape the ropes. And to make it even better, Stephanie rose, her face tragic. "You promised me, Scott! I told you we should have left last week, but you *had* to receive this award."

Scott struggled against the agents. "It's going to be okay. I promise. I love you, baby."

Stephanie banged both hands onto the table. "You're an idiot. This is over. It's way over."

"Nooo, don't do this," Scott called back as they pushed him through the door. "I love you. I did it all for you."

Stephanie grabbed her purse and ran to the other side of the ballroom as if *she* had a Yorkie biting her ankles this time. Tears streaked her angry, betrayed face.

It was horrible.

It was wonderful.

It was justice.

I tossed down my napkin as the double doors swooshed closed. "Ready, Ruby?"

She nodded and stood beside me, taking my hand, which was a good thing because I was shaking with rage and a bevy of emotions I still couldn't name. I was certain my legs wouldn't hold me on my walk to the double doors my husband had just disappeared through, but I managed to make it as the room's noise level went from hushed incredulity to out-and-out roaring with exclamation. I had no doubt someone had recorded it and the University Club annual celebration luncheon had just become the hottest ticket of the year.

For a moment, Ruby and I stood and watched them load Donner and Scott into unmarked cars and then pull away as if what they'd done was routine. Maybe it was.

"Are you okay?" Ruby asked.

"I think so." I moved toward the outer door and out into the warmth of the late-spring day. The sunlight was blinding, and it was as if the valet knew I would need my car ASAP. He brought it around immediately, and I collapsed into the passenger's seat, leaning my head back and closing my eyes. I felt Ruby slide into the driver's side.

"You good?" she asked again.

"I am. Stop asking and don't hit any potholes." I pulled my sunglasses from my clutch and strapped myself inside my grandmother's sports car. I withdrew a twenty-dollar bill because I knew how cheap most of those people inside truly were and waved it at the valet as Ruby pulled away.

The kid yelled, "Thanks!"

Ruby pulled out to the right, inching down Fairfield with its shady oak canopy and fading azaleas. A man walked his Jack Russell. Another delivered mail. Another block found three children playing soccer in the front yard. All normal, everyday things going on as if my husband hadn't just been arrested in front of two hundred people and I hadn't just yelled at him as they'd dragged him away. Weird.

After a few minutes, Ruby asked, "Where do you want to go?" We were getting close to the turn for Printemps.

"Can you take me to my mother?" I hadn't even realized I wanted to go there. I had thought to gather my Blue Moon Sting posse, but at that moment, I couldn't do a beer and the Bullpen. I just wanted my mother, even though she would be appalled and might actually lecture me for showing my butt in front of all of Shreveport. Still, the need for your mother—even one who could be a pain in the butt like mine—was something that never went away.

"Sure. Where is she?"

"Good question." I withdrew my phone, which had blown up in the last minute or so. I ignored my cousin and several of my PTA friends, who had sent inquisitory "You okay?" sorts of texts. And sure enough, someone had tagged me in a video. The whole world was about to see Scott get arrested. I hoped they'd gotten a good angle on me. Some angles gave me a double chin.

But then it struck me.

Julia Kate.

I hadn't really thought about my daughter watching the video. It would be all over social media. I had been so wrapped up in gleeful retribution that I hadn't stopped to consider how this would wound Julia Kate. How had I not thought about this? *Shit*.

I dialed my mother's phone.

"Cricket! What in the world is going on?" my mother asked.

"So you know?"

"I do, and I'm incensed. I cannot believe that man. Where are you? Should I come get you?"

"No. Ruby is bringing me to your house. Mom, can you go get JK? Like ASAP. You're closer to her school. I'll call the office and tell them you're coming. I pray she hasn't seen this. She'll be devastated."

"She's going to be devastated anyway. I'll get her. You come here." She hung up.

Twenty minutes later, my mother was handing me a martini and a tissue as the tears streamed down my cheeks. She wrapped an arm about my waist, nudged her yipping dogs with her Roger Vivier chunky heel, and told Ruby to pour herself a drink. Julia Kate sat like a zombie on the sofa, tears leaking from her eyes.

My mother led me to the sofa, where she wrapped an arm around each of us. Then I cried until I was a limp dishrag while Marguerite stroked my back, telling me how brave I had been. When I finally blew my nose and sat up, my mother said, "I think we girls need a little trip this summer. What do you think? Maybe somewhere tropical. Julia Kate?"

"Can I skip summer camp?" my daughter asked in a small voice.

"Yeah," I rasped, feeling guilty as hell that I had not put her first in all this. What kind of mother was I? A terrible one. One too focused on hurting Scott to see the damage I had wrought. My heart clenched, and I looked at my mother, needing her to give me the strength I seemed to have lost.

She seemed to know what I needed because she gave me a game smile, chucked me under the chin, and said, "Life is like a box of chocolates. You never know when you'll have to toss them and go to the Four Seasons."

"Well, it does change in the blink of an eye," I said, unable to stop my lips from twitching.

"Life is like riding a bicycle. You have to keep pedaling," Ruby quipped from the chair across from us.

"Life is a highway. I wanna ride it all night long," I continued.

"Y'all are weird," Julia Kate said.

We all smiled a little, and I knew at that moment, everything would, indeed, be okay.

EPILOGUE

RUBY

A month later

"If you need someone to help you, I am happy to volunteer. I could always take a private investigator class. Since I'm nearly divorced, I have lots of time now," Cricket said to Juke as she sipped her beer out of a bottle at the table where she'd tricked Scott into signing the bank form.

I suspected that she didn't really love beer. But Griffin always ordered her one as some sort of challenge. This one was a dark beer, so every time she took a sip, she made a face.

"I'm not sure I'm ready to take on a partner. Besides, aren't you two busy with the whole dress-line-launch thing and all?" Juke said, looking far healthier than he had in a while. He'd started going to AA and working out. Jimbo told me he had even talked Juke into doing some dating sites. The thought of those two swiping right was disturbing, but I didn't have to worry about it, did I?

With that thought, I darted a glance at the bar, where Dak was chatting up his regulars—three dudes who loved to talk baseball. We had gone on a few official dates, slipping into our past like old friends. Which we were. Both of us were taking things slow. Well, as slow as one could take it when there was all this pent-up passion that had been strapped down for too many years. Not stripping him naked every time I was with him was quite a chore. I had even sat on my hands once. Wish I were kidding. Things were good, though.

And I had started showing up more for family dinners. Gran was grumbling about going to Weight Watchers, but Cricket had been happy because she was something called a "lifetime member," and she got some points or something for signing Gran up. She even went to the first meeting with my grandmother. So far, Gran had lost weight and had started some new medication. I still wasn't on even ground with Ed Earl, but I wasn't ignoring him any longer.

Cricket made a face. "I am a pro multitasker. Ask any PTA member. I can run a store, launch a clothing line, and take pictures of dirtbags at the same time. I mean, I sorta already did it."

Griffin, who had just come back over to the table from shooting pool in the back, shot her a look. "You shouldn't do anything dangerous."

"I'm not," she said, sort of bristly. "And you know what, Griff? I don't like this beer. Life is too short for me to waste calories on something I don't like. Any chance we can talk Dak into getting Michelob Ultra? Or maybe some seltzer-water things. I like those, and they're only three points."

"Three points for what?" he asked, drawing a chair over and sitting on it backward.

"Weight Watchers," Cricket said, tossing her hair over her shoulder. She had a nice tan from her trip to Grand Cayman. Turned out it had been for naught because the Department of Justice had already frozen Scott's accounts, but Cricket's attorney had said that since her money was hers and untainted, she had a good shot of getting it back into her possession. She, her mother, and her daughter had spent a week there at the conclusion of school and had just returned, tanned and relaxed. Well, at least Cricket was. Her mother wasn't really the kind to relax, I didn't think. Julia Kate was going to therapy, and according to Cricket, they were both working through the mistakes she herself had made. Of course, that meant Cricket was overcompensating for the debacle at the luncheon by indulging Julia Kate. She knew she was doing it and had vowed to stop, but I understood, even if I knew it would probably come back to haunt her.

But what did I know? I didn't plan on having kids or anything needier than a dog.

Cricket's husband was too busy avoiding jail time to worry about the money at present. Word from Cricket was that he had also petitioned to get the untainted money unfrozen. He was out on bond and had taken a plea bargain to keep himself out of jail. He was a big squealing pig and was living at the Holiday Inn Express. Someone told Cricket that Stephanie had already lobbed her tennis ball onto the court of a recently divorced judge.

"You don't need to lose weight," Griff scoffed, eyeing her with something that made my heart sorta squeeze. My cousin had it bad for Cricket, which amused me to no end. My boss and silent partner in Deconstructed had been true to her word—no hanky-panky until she was officially divorced—but I knew she nurtured a small flame for my big hunky cousin. They met here at the Bullpen once a week with our Blue Moon Sting posse, as Cricket still called us. And I think they texted some. But I respected Cricket. She had a daughter and a reputation to uphold.

"Men always say that, but I refuse to buy new pants. I have to mind my pennies now that I'm a single working mother," Cricket said, jerking her head toward the bar. Griffin obediently rose and went to find something else for Cricket to drink, mumbling about liking tight pants.

"You should take Cricket up on her offer, Juke," I said, sipping a crisp pinot grigio that Dak had ordered in just for me. "She's great with binoculars."

Cricket rolled her eyes. "Both ends looked the same. And I am good at being a detective. I have a manual that tells me all kinds of stuff. I can open envelopes for you."

Juke looked a little panicked, cupping his coffee and staring into the dark liquid within.

"You know she's just teasing you, Juke," I said.

"Oh, good," he responded.

"I'm not sure I am. I think I could be helpful. You know, on a big case. I might take the course," Cricket said as Griffin approached, handing her off a glass of what was likely the same thing I had. Dak followed him, carrying a bottled water.

"Well, I would like to propose a toast," I said, lifting my glass. "To new friends, to old friends, and to catching cheaterpants and seeing them punished."

"Hear! Hear!" Juke said, lifting his coffee mug.

Dak bumped his water bottle against my glass, a smile hovering on his delicious lips. I slipped one hand under my thigh just as a reminder.

Griffin clinked his beer to Cricket's glass and then to mine.

Finally, Cricket looked at me and smiled. "To both of us. For being courageous. For tearing away the old. For making something new."

We clinked our glasses as everyone said, "Cheers!"

ACKNOWLEDGMENTS

First, I would like to thank my agent, Michelle Grajkowski, who signed me on the premise of this book. It took my writing twenty books before Cricket finally got her spotlight. Thanks for believing in me and making me feel like I'm a fantastic writer on the days I doubt. Most people don't know that agents don't just hustle the books; they hustle the author's fragile ego. Your red-and-white pom-poms are appreciated. Go, Badgers!

Next, thanks to Greg Lott, president of Progressive Bank, who helped me with the particulars of Ponzi schemes and money laundering. Scott Crosby couldn't come close to holding a candle to you. You're a true man of honor. I'm so happy to call you friend.

A hearty thanks to Brian Ong, who answered questions about off-shore accounts and how the investigation would proceed. Any mistakes are mine. I probably made some. But they weren't yours. Thanks for giving me your time.

I'm ever so grateful to Jamie Beck, who read the early manuscript and offered advice. I'm so glad to call such a fine writer my good friend.

Love my FFTH deadline pals. I can never, ever thank you all enough for your support, friendship, kicks in the pants, hand-holding, advice, cheering, and everything else you all give me every day. Friendship weathers hard times, mistakes, and failings. I'm so glad that we hold each other up and find our friendship worthwhile. I truly love you, Sonali Dev, Barbara O'Neal, Priscilla Oliveras, Tracy Brogan, Falguni Kothari, Virginia Kantra, Sally Kilpatrick, and Jamie Beck. You chicks are my glue.

Without *mis amigas* Phylis Caskey, Jennifer Moorhead, and (occasionally) the talented Ashley Elston (who refuses to make a goal sheet), life would be pretty cloudy. You bring the sunshine. Thank you for the brainstorming, the walks, and the unfailing support.

As always, I am grateful to my publishing team. My acquiring editor, Alison Dasho, is clever, humorous, and makes the cutest children. She also intuitively knows what my books need. She has my back, always trusting me to make good decisions with the story line. Her faith is cherished, and I have been so honored to work with her time and again on stories with teeth and heart. My sincere appreciation to Selina McLemore, who fiercely makes suggestions for the better and always protects the heart of the story. She gets me. I'm always super appreciative of my copyediting and proofreading team. It's a hard job. And they do it with care and conviction. Another high five to my crackerjack marketing team and the author-care team at Amazon. You guys and gals are great at what you do.

I am thankful to have good friends and family. Not to get maudlin, but what's all this worth without people to share my victories and my defeats? Shout to Tuscany Krewe, the Wine Posse, Long Lake Mamas, MHS Besties, Bayou Book Bitches, Your Book Escape Authors, Tuesday Lunch Bunch, FUMC circle, my Zumba ladies, and all the other friend groups who love me, support me, and make life worth living.

And finally, thank you to my husband, who has finally come around to this author thing; my dogs, who sit beside me and let me write (except when the sanitation trucks come); and my mom and dad, who come to my book signings no matter what. I would thank my children, but let's be honest: they aren't really helping me get these books done. LOL. Okay, fine, thanks to Jake and Gabe for giving me fodder and occasionally helping me out by telling me what is not said anymore.

And last but not least, thank *you* for buying this book and reading this story. The story is not truly complete unless it is read. I hope you enjoyed Cricket and Ruby. They were a hoot to write!

Cheers,
Liz

ABOUT THE AUTHOR

Photo © 2017 Courtney Hartness

Liz Talley is the *USA Today* bestselling author of *Adulting, The Wedding War, Room to Breathe,* and *Come Home to Me,* as well as the Morning Glory series, the Home in Magnolia Bend series, and many more novels, novellas, and short fiction. A finalist for the Romance Writers of America's prestigious Golden Heart and RITA Awards, Liz has found a home writing heartwarming contemporary romance and women's fiction. Her stories are set in the South, where the tea is sweet, the summers are hot, and the porches are wide. Liz lives in North Louisiana with her childhood sweetheart, two handsome children, two dogs, and a naughty kitty. To learn more about the author and her upcoming novels, readers can visit www.liztalleybooks.com.